Innocence
Androids Never Think

Archie Gerard.

By
Archie Gerard

www.aztix.com

Innocence and Ice

Androids Never Think Twice
(revised and retitled edition)
by Archie Gerard
Published by AZTIX
ISBN: 978-1-908551-01-6 digital eBook mobi format
ISBN: 978-1-908551-02-3 digital eBook epub format
ISBN: 978-1-908551-03-0 print paperback format

First published as
'Zoe Hope' by D G Bayliss in 2011
ISBN: 978-1-908551-00-9
For contact, enquiries, orders or to find out about the
author contact the publisher, AZTIX
www.aztix.com

Dedication

For Christine, with love.

Acknowledgments

My appreciation goes to my daughter Dana for her example and advice as a writer, to my son, Archie for his thought-provoking arguments and for ideas that led to the book's front cover illustration, to librarians for their patience, steadfastness and for cancelling my fines, to my brother-in-law Allan for a vivid account that provided the basis for one of the scenes and to Christine for proof reading and editorial input.

On a more spiritual note, I am grateful to St Paul of Tarsus for his letters of guidance written in the first century AD and to St Jude Thaddeus (patron saint of hopeless cases).

My gratitude goes out to the many writers, artists and musicians, who have inspired me or have given me cause to think more deeply. Not least, I would like to thank the many people out there who actually make the things that we use and who apply their creativity in a practical way—the engineers, the designers, the inventors, the programmers, the manufacturers. Without their endeavours there wouldn't have been a basis for this book

Images:
The cover image uses derivate work from a number of sources:
Clkr.com for London skyline.
inky2010 openclipart.org for tree vector graphic
Soundtrack
My thanks to Alison Bruce for the idea of building a soundtrack for a novel, and for her generosity with her time and advice. I wish her well with her new contract with Constable. See The Soundtrack

Archie Gerard, 2015.

Table of Contents

Prologue – Two Weeks Earlier

A bluebottle that had once buzzed and buffeted against the plate glass window in a futile, uncomprehending, frenzy, lay there, motionless on the ledge. It looked intact, it might have been resting, but it was merely a shell, a dried exoskeleton that could no longer move or breathe or direct its fate. In time the cardboard box stacked against the shop window would be moved and the bluebottle would fall to the floor where it would be crushed, ground into fragments of dust, and be blown and dispersed and returned to the earth.

"Next," called Ludd, with undisguised impatience. A thirteen-year old boy, as if in fear of losing his fingers, placed a mobile on the counter and snatched back his hand.

Ludd, too big for an office chair, too soured and ungainly to put on a show of being nice, lifted and squinted at the mobile's hi-res display.

"It's not talking to my vizars." The boy glowered and touched the control strip on the frame holding the spectacles' iridescent lenses. "See! No picture!" he said, removing the frames completely and turning them so that Ludd could see the inner surface of the screens and the status bar legs. "That's them up at 100%."

"So?" glowered Ludd. He surveyed them with nostril-twitching distaste. "You get the vizars here?"

"No, but they're fresh. Work on all my mates' mobiles. It's not them. This one's fracked ... totally."

Ludd looked hatefully beyond the boy along the lengthening queue. They were the enemy, an opposing army, countless, relentless, a never ending onslaught of consumers with their petty needs, always wanting, always taking, depleting, sapping, his meagre reserves of goodwill.

"So ... Can I have a refund?" said the boy.

"Nope," said Ludd.

Customers queued at Wise Buy long before the shop opened, moping, shuffling, silent, a funeral procession at the grave of obsolete electronics. The virts coped better than most, but then they weren't really there. Their bodies were just place-holders, glassy-eyed zombies left to the drudge of daily life, eyes focused on the inside of their vizars or minds implanted and connected to a virt-world existence where they could cruise or shop or log in at work. Across the days and the years, customers, virts and reals, traversed the lino's dirt-ingrained tack, sidled past brown, dog-eared boxes and gaudy star-burst labels that shouted CRAZY, SLASHED and ROCK BOTTOM. No one noticed, no one cared.

Ludd's eyes itched and stung from staring at the boy, a Minotaur, a powerful ox of a man. He snorted his contempt.

Further along the counter, his sidekick, Vince, was more upbeat. Troll-like, hair black and spiky, he smiled and bobbed and rolled his eyes. A lady in a floral dress was telling her sad tale: her domestoid had a fault, poor coordination, and had self-diagnosed the source of the problem. She held out the board, but Vince's eyes were focused on her.

"What do you think?" she said.

"Huh?" said Vince, glancing at the board in her hand.

"The board, yeah. It's jiggered." His eyes feasted, drinking her in.

"I know. That's why I brought it in ... Well?"

"Huh?"

"Do you have a replacement?"

"Could be a problem. Tough getting parts. What is it? A Sealy Helpmate ..."

"A Versitus mark 2," she said.

Vince looked across to Ludd, who was moodily scanning his screen.

"Hey, Ludd, a synch board for a Versitus mark 2. What are the chances?"

Ludd continued to study his screen, an imperceptible tilting of his head the only response.

"Yeah, like I say. Not much chance ... hens' teeth," breathed Vince.

"There must be some way to repair it," she said, brow furrowing. She reached round for her handbag and picked up the board. "It seems such a waste to abandon a perfectly adequate domestoid for the sake of one small component."

"I know, but they no longer make 'em. They want you to buy you a new one. A bummer isn't it!" Vince shook his head and attempted a look of profound misgiving. "But, yeah!" he said, a twinkle in his eyes. "For a lovely lady like you, I'll do an extra check. Just in case. Sometimes the stock register's not right. Got the board there?"

She forced an appreciative smile. Vince jumped down, slotted the board into his back pocket and swaggered through to the back shop. There, amidst cluttered workbenches and racks of equipment, a technician was working on an arm clamped in a vice.

"With you in a minute!" he gasped. "Seized up." He put down the torque wrench and squirted lithium lube on the joint. Straightening, he nudged his thick spectacles up and peered across.

"So," he said, wiping his hands on his overalls, "what you got?"

"Blonde," said Vince rubbing his hands. "Should see her. Could be an ex-model. I'd rate her eight ... maybe nine."

"Chick?" said Shug.

"Naw ... real class. Sophisticated, smart."

"So, what you doing her for?"

"Versitus mark 2, synch board."

"A Versitus ... You're kidding!"

"Don't give me that! You've got one. Got its left arm last month."

"Yeah, but it's jammed behind that big shipment of Helpmates. The container's stacked to the roof. Can't get anything out. What was the big sour puss thinking?"

"Got a fat wad to take 'em, didn't he. We're greenies now. He's our jolly green giant."

The technician snorted and trudged out, steel door slamming behind.

Vince propped himself up on a bench, picked up an electromechanical jaw, and made the teeth chop together like a ventriloquist's dummy.

'Hello ... where am I?' the jaws clacked. 'My goodness! Where's the rest of my body? Is this all there is? Oh deary ... deary ... dear. Is that all I can do? Talk! Wait, maybe I can eat.' Vince reached the jaws over to some dangling cables and made them bite. As the jaws snapped at the cable, he made growling and gnashing sounds.

Shug, sweating, arrived back, the naked droid, pink and rubbery, strapped onto a tote trolley. The droid was fire-damaged, one side burnt, the side of the face melted revealing charred mechanism inside.

"Should do," said Shug. "Main housing's never been opened."

"Get a move on, will you?" moaned Vince. "Customer priority."

Shug grappled with the droid, got it in a bear hug, staggered, then, like a wrestler trying for a submission, slung it down on the bench. Breathless from the exertion, steel-toed boots clumping on concrete, he fetched a hot scalpel. Smoke drifted under the canopy of light, acrid fumes caused him to cough and wince. Prising back a slab of rubber, he levered back an access plate and, with grease-stained fingers, wiggled the board out of its fixings.

"Here!" he said, waving it in the air. Vince, dropped the jaws to the floor and, bumping down from the bench, wandered nonchalantly over and snatched the board from Shug's hand.

"Ta," Vince said, squinting at it and giving it a cursory wipe with a rag. "Should do."

"Not going to test it?" said Shug as Vince moved in the direction of the door. "Might've shorted in the fire."

"Nah ... it'll work. Anyhow, if it doesn't, she'll bring it back." Vince grinned knowingly at Shug.

"And you're not going to complain about that," said Shug.

"Too right! Return of the luscious lady," Vince leered.

Moving across to a desk, he tore a bag from a dispenser. It was security printed with a criss-cross pattern of 'CYBERSENTORI' and 'VOID IF BROKEN' in 3D hologram lettering. Vince was about to pop the replacement board into the bag when he paused to check that Shug wasn't looking. With a curl of his lip, he took the faulty board out of his pocket and swapped it for the one Shug had salvaged. He wasn't depending on chance. He hummed a happy little tune whilst the 'security-sealer' went about its hissing and beeping, then, with the genuine replacement half-hanging out of his back pocket, he strode back to the fray.

The woman looked up as Vince jigged over and her eyes lit up at the glistening Cybersentori package he placed on the counter.

"How's that!" he said. "Exact same," he boasted taking the one from his back pocket and placing it next to it. "Perfect."

"Fantastic!" said the woman, relief on her face.

"Yup! You're in luck. Wasn't easy ... Searched high and low. Now, let's see," he said, hopping onto his seat and tapping the screen. "If you get this installed by a Cybersentori technician, you get a full year's guarantee. Installed by anyone else and the guarantee's void."

"Yes! I understand," said the woman, peering at the part, glancing up briefly at Vince in a brief moment of mutual understanding. People who stooped to using Wise Buy didn't shell out for Cybersentori technicians.

"I think, let's see. Yeah, list price is 800," said Vince as he summoned up the parts number on the screen. The woman winced. "Yeah, 795 in fact ... before VAT." He looked at the distress in her face. She hadn't abandoned her middle-class cocoon and ventured into the fag end of the city in order to pay the full whack. No, the degradation of queuing out in the street, the abject shuffling across the lino and the ignominy of Vince's stares, merited a hefty discount. He raised his eyebrows, trying to elicit a response, a bit of grovelling perhaps, a bit of cajoling, or, from the fiery types, a flare up, a spot of argy-bargy and some wide-eyed indignation. No, she was settling for pained silence.

"But we're not Cybersentori," Vince said, encouraging, sympathetic, throwing her a bone of hope then tainting it with a grubby low-life wink. He watched and waited, letting the silence become unwieldy, awkward, pressurizing her to respond. She just smiled, polite but with a soupçon of revulsion. Vince looked her straight in the eyes and considered. Quality, real class, top-dollar this one.

"What's your limit?" he quizzed, knowing the discomfort the question would cause. She wasn't used to talking money, haggling—too demeaning. She frowned. "I really don't know ... It's nearly ten years old. I wouldn't want to spend too much."

"So you want me to get the price down for you?" he suggested quietly, eyes half-closed, as if she were seeking a personal favour.

"Yes, I'd appreciate that." She stroked back her hair and tried to find something to fix her eye on. She depended on him, and yet she loathed him.

Now for the part he liked best: the degrading, principle-compromising turmoil of the Wise Buy Computing experience. He drew himself up as if settling down to work.

"Okay, let's see what I can do," he said, tapping with one finger at the screen. He shook his head. "Not good ... not good ... not good. You see we shouldn't give a discount on our last remaining spare," he said, picking up the board, squinting at the serial number, placing it back on the counter, careful, as if realizing its worth.

"We try to keep stock for card holders, people who've registered, contract customers. We promise them priority. If we run stock down to zero, how'd we honour our contracts? You got a contract?"

"No, I'm afraid I haven't," she said.

"Registered?"

"No, I'm afraid I'm not registered either."

"Mmm ..." he said. "Tell you what, you register and we'll get you a good price. Okay?"

Tight lipped, she gave her name, address and contact details.

"Just one last thing—vidcam number?" asked Vince.

"Actually, I'd rather not give that out. Is it absolutely necessary?"

"Fraid so," said Vince.

"Can I ask why?" she asked.

"Got an asterisk beside it," said Vince.

"Yes, but I mean, for what reason?"

"It's on the form, he said, spinning the screen round and pointing.

"See, asterisk. That means it's essential."

"Exactly why is it essential?" She pursed her lips, the look in her eyes hardening.

Near the brink, thought Vince, hackles rising, on the verge of storming out.

"It'll be for the service verification department—every now and then they'll take a peek to see you're not abusing the droid. Tell you what. Let's see what happens if we miss that one out." He smiled broadly, admiring the burst of assertiveness, pleased to see her fight back.

"Want junk mail?" he asked.

"No thanks," she said, voice clipped.

Right, now let's see what we can do for you. "He turned the screen away and made a show of selecting some options.

"Can't get it down much, not without the vidcam number."

"What's it at?"

"About 680 ... before VAT."

"And if you have the vidcam number ..."

"Takes it down to 245. Big difference. See, that's you properly registered." He cocked his head to one side and sucked in his lips. "Your choice lady." Mischievous, he watched as she wrestled with the predicament. Changing her vidcam number would be easy enough, it was updating all her contacts that would cause the real hassle.

"Oh, very well!" she snapped, and she spelled out the number.

"So ... with you registered," said Vince, lolling back, "that makes it 245 plus VAT. Add the registration fee ... another 159 plus VAT ... that comes to ..." he tapped at the keys, "a total of 404 plus VAT."

"What! You said 245," she spluttered.

"Did I? Oh, yeah, forgot to mention the fee. Can undo the registration if you want." He gave her a moment or two to come to her decision.

"I think I'll ..."

"Wait! Just noticed," he said, head bobbing up. "There's a special from Valueconnect. They're pushing Junkall. You take their full junk mail, spam and telephone sales package and they'll price slash. That's a 50% reduction. Takes it right down to 202. That's a real special, new registrants only."

"I'm not stooping to that," she said, the ice-blue sharp in her eye.

"Sure?"

"Absolutely!" she said.

"Okay. I'll see if there's anything else." Vince slouched in front of the screen, prodding it intermittently, observing her sleekly out of the side of his eye.

"Tell you what," he said, "seeing as we'd like you to become a valued customer, forget Valueconnect. We'll do it ourselves. Wise Buy will price match. A mere 202—no catches."

"Why didn't you do that in the first place?" The scorn was palpable.

"Can't price match unless we've got a price to match, can we? Stands to reason. Wouldn't make sense."

"Oh, get on with it!" she blurted. "Just be sure. No catches."

"No catches," he said, chirpy, teeth white and wide. "So that's 202? "

"Yup ... 202 ... 202, plus VAT makes 245." He darted a look.

"You said 'no catches'!" Her voice had a guillotine edge.

"That's not a catch. That's tax. Nothing to do with us, lady. We can't ignore the authorities. It's 245."

"And that's it?"

"Yup, 245. You won't get better than that."

"Just slip your holocard in the reader. Great, now before you verify, do you want to add the annual registration fee in with that or do you want to set up a standing order?" He watched as she froze, brittle and angular. He could see the whites of her eyes and the hollow clench of her jaw.

"Oh no you don't!" she snarled. Vince braced himself and waited, willing her on. Come on lady—let it go! She was teetering, balanced on the razor edge of some unplanned, unmannered and, totally reprehensible action. Lash out, Vince urged. Scream an obscenity—yell some abuse! Live! Let all that scorn and loathing explode into the world.

She was fighting the ultimate war, the battle within. Inhibitions and manners struggling to contain a pressurized cauldron of emotion. She inhaled and closed her eyes.

"I'm not doing this," she breathed. "It's not worth it." Withdrawing her holocard, she reached for the unsealed board that had been left lying to one side. Vince fast, like a terrier on a rat, snatched it away.

"Hey!" His eyes became deadly serious, dark. "I'm doing my best here!"

"Are you?" she said, seeing something in him. "Your best to do what?"

"We had a misunderstanding, that's all. The registration thing, that was for silver and gold. You get extended guarantees, priority evenings, tech support. Brilliant. I'd really recommend that. But basic is free! Honest! No charge. Zip! Okay ... Sorted. Ready to go."

"No, I don't think so, just give me back my board." There was a tremor in her voice, but a steadiness to her eye. "I'm leaving. Give it to me now."

"Why? It's jiggered. Come on—you want this," he said, pushing the sealed bag towards her. "Get your droid back. Clean the house. Put your feet up. That's what you want."

"Don't tell me what I want! My board. Now!" She slammed her hand hard on the counter. Vince jumped, then looked offended.

"That's crazy. What use is an old board," he said. "What's the point? For a couple of hundred, in fact let's make it a hundred, you're sorted. Done!" Something lurked in his voice, panic, desperation.

"You don't want me to have my board back, do you? What the hell are you playing at?"

"Fifty?" he said, picking up the shiny Cybersentori bag and waggling it before her. She stared right through it, unflinching and silent. People were grumbling in the queue. Someone called: 'get a move on' and 'give her the damned board'. Eventually, reluctantly, Vince handed it over.

"Lady, you want the kit, you pay the price."

"Really?" She looked at the shimmering bag, peered at the board through the plastic. "Well, I don't want it." She shoved it hard causing it to slide across the counter.

Vince slapped his hand down on top of it. "Yeah, well, if you change your mind, call back. Always here." Vince watched her walk out. When she was gone, he flipped the dud board in the air, caught it, then dropped it in the bin. He turned to Ludd. "See that ... didn't want the board. It's me they're after. Animal magnetism. Can't help it."

Ludd inhaled into the back of his throat, as if to speak, but, instead gave a slow, desultory, bat of his eyelids and turned away. The boy he had been dealing with was gone, sent off with a reconditioned mobile, and the aftercare advice: not to come back. His next client stepped up, a business man with dark, vizar-like shades, a tight mouth and black gloves. He passed Ludd a sealed envelope. Ludd ripped it open taking care to keep it beneath the counter. Having checked and stored its contents, he turned and picked up a box that had been set aside, placed it on the counter and watched as the man lowered it into the briefcase. Ludd's expert eye noted that everything about the man was unmarked and unbranded, the white shirt, the plain silver tie, the charcoal grey suit without fleck, without stripe.

Ludd grunted 'Next!' No response. He bellowed something undecipherable and the virt next in line lurched, unplugged and returned to the world.

Chapter 1 Friday

Hannah was looking confident and precise—LoveFlux and Bostyle had eliminated all negative expression. Today she was glad of it, glad of the privacy. She could smile after a fashion, muted, understated, non-committal tightenings of her mouth that could look amenable or menacing depending on her mood. The major negatives had been disabled. Fear, anger, even sorrow, were all hidden, securely locked inside her mind. In business, as in poker, emotion was a liability.

Like a carefully contrived advertisement, she sat at her desk, face set, fixed, like a model, the only visible flaw the grains of sand sticking to the gloss of her shoes. Her movements, though small-scale, were significant—the tensing of her temples, the death-watch tap of her nails.

The canvas above her billowed then lapsed, but she took no notice. The awning remained closed, the coffee break had come and gone; she'd been too preoccupied to do the usual—loosen her heels, sit out on the veranda.

From the tilt of her head, she was surveying a data sweep, a glazed curtain of information that hung across the span of her desk. Graphs flitted and grew and morphed into pie-charts and summations, faces mouthed, silent, with scrolling subtitles beneath, video-linked conferences like miniature puppet shows, played scenes from around the world. Her finger scrolled a data patch. She was scanning that morning's data digest, the second element in her routine, at least that's what anyone logging in would see. Her concentration, however, was on the tone in her earpiece, the urgent, demanding no-one's-answering bleat. The glass slab that was her desk was also a screen, one that afforded a modicum of privacy. She sneaked momentary glances, fought the urge to stare down.

"Pick up—pick up!" she hissed, her voice edgy, a vestigial grimace pushing through the frozen nerves. The ring in her earpiece was incessant, like a pulse, a tortured heartbeat. She went over and over the predicament, hoping, questioning, cursing. Come on, Andy! Where the hell was he? Calling him wasn't actually part of the programme. It was a risk, a possible implication, but she needed, above all, to put her mind at ease, know that everything was okay. She thought she'd just check, check on the van, no need to phone Andy. Looking up the tracking code, she found it was running late, significantly over schedule. Not in itself a major problem, Andy was there anyway. He'd just have to wait. Linking to the satellite view, she watched the delivery van, watched the target destination, watched the snarl up of traffic. Roadworks—typical.

And then she thought she'd better tell him—just in case. He might do something stupid, think it's not coming, pop out to the shops, miss it altogether. No—he couldn't—that didn't bear thinking about! A quick call, just to confirm the review was still on. No answer! How can that be? She hung up after letting it ring for several minutes. In the bathroom perhaps? She tried again. No answer. Perhaps he had his music up too loud. She let it ring for another 5 minutes. Nothing! Where the hell was he?

She'd woken up in cold sweats over this. What if he fell ill? What if the driver got lost ... or what if he delivered it to the wrong address? What if the van hit something and the police got called in?

When she'd set this thing up it had seemed clean, fool proof, a done deal. But, during the weeks of waiting, possibilities, like invasive weeds, began to infest her mind.

Andy ... Andy ... Andy. She'd never worked with him before. She'd done some profiling, found out that he wasn't mainstream, and, yes, that he was less than 100% reliable ... but that was just a matter of management. A good manager understands the limitations of her staff, knows how to support, motivate, bring out the best in them. In any case, she'd little choice. He matched the task specs—no one else came anywhere near. The shortcomings were there, but these had been taken into account. The whole thing was razor-wired in, so completely contained that there was nothing to fail. Delivery, pick up, zero contact in between. She'd even coached him, one-to-one consultations, ensured no possible doubt ... no possible doubt! She stifled a bitter laugh and threw her head back. How could this be happening! Was it too much to ask that a delivery be made and that there be someone there to receive it.

She became aware of movement, a shadow on the canvas, someone outside. She tensed, leaned forwards in the chair, her eyes locked on data sweep pretending to be absorbed in the figures. Whoever it was had pulled back the awning, was hovering, but Hannah's gaze was fixed on a chart, apparently engrossed in the corporate world. Translucent displays had the advantage that you could see virtual or real as suited your needs.

The figure passed on, took the hint, and she resumed her vigil, eyes flicking back to the desktop. A patch of red flashing text said 'DIALLING'. That was all, no redirect, no video, no override, no message. He'd disabled everything except pick up and talk. Why? Her eyes flicked to the middle of the desktop to where, out of desperation, she'd called up Andy's profile. Standard Techdomestic shot: head and shoulders, front profile, suit, company tie, name badge. She'd barely glanced at it before, but, now that she was doubting him, she began to see little indications, like his tie being loose and a little to one side, and his jacket lower on one shoulder, and the tufts of hair that had refused to conform, and his eyes—distracted, dreamy, unable to stay focused for the millisecond blink of the camera. What on earth had she been thinking!

Another figure pulled back the awning, came right in, bouncy, nails painted, feet sinking into the sand. Hannah didn't look up.

"Coffee?" chirped the humanoid robot, sun-kissed, rigged out in T-shirt and denim shorts.

"Piss off," hissed Hannah. She glanced down at the tracker and muttered 'Damned droid'!

The park was tranquil, squirrels in the trees, dog scavenging with its head in a bin. One squirrel, dainty, feather-like, made little arching leaps across the grass, stopping to listen and look, before continuing its spasmodic bounds. Of this, the dog was unaware. It was snorting and rustling, the sound of its endeavours amplified by the bin's metal sides. Intermittently, there would be a pause, a snuffling interlude whilst it gnawed or licked a morsel of food.

On a nearby bench, a man, outstretched, dishevelled, was engrossed in a book. Footsteps sounded, distant but closing. An office worker was heading their way, purposeful and brisk, trying to compensate for office chair sloth and lunch time indulgence. As the steps grew nearer, the squirrel on the grass took to the trees, but the dog seemed not to notice. The snuffling and rustling continued. The pickings were poor. No half-eaten pizza, no fries, no discarded burgers. Having hung its lanky frame over the rim long enough, it licked its jaws and gave a final nostril-clearing snort. Head coming out, it rested its paws on the rounded edge and, ears perked, head cocked, checked the status of the world. Footsteps. Locking on to the approaching figure, it paused for deliberation, sped to the centre of the path and, with a playful shake, firmly planted its legs.

Overweight, moving briskly, the man bustled along. As he came nearer, he registered that something was blocking his path, a skinny mutt, a stray from the back alleys. The animal was directly in front of him, and it looked aggressive. He didn't know much about dogs. Maybe it was playful ... or could that be it preparing to attack? Whatever, it would have to get out of his way. He walked straight towards it, but, at the last minute, chickened out, took a sideways step and tried to skirt past the dog. Nimble, it bounded back and again blocked his way. Eyes intent, ears perked up, it looked ready for action—the question in the man's mind was what kind of action? The man tried ducking left, the dog was quick to head him off. Thwarted, the beleaguered worker stopped and looked around.

"Hey, you there!" he called to the man on the bench. "Your dog won't let me past."

The man read to the end of the sentence, put in the bookmark, and laid the book carefully down at his side. He tilted up the brim of his battered felt hat and looked over.

"I beg your pardon. Were you addressing me?" he said, his voice rich and resonating.

"Well, yes, huh ... Sorry! It's just you're dog's blocking my path," said the man, a little off guard.

"I'm Cornelius Brown," said the man. "And you are?"

"John, John Harken ... Look, I just want to get to a meeting. So if you could call your dog ..."

"You are mistaken in your assumption, Sir. The dog doesn't belong to me. I do know him, however. In fact, I tend to think of him as an associate, a fellow traveller on the great road of life." Cornelius tilted his head back and half-closed his eyes as if considering that road.

"Look. I just want to get past. That's all ... without being attacked by this ... this ..."

"Dog. Canis lupus familiaris. Yes, a persistent and intelligent example of the species, but quite friendly. I've never known him to attack."

The man began walking forward but stopped two feet from the dog.

"Look, it won't shift. Surely there's some way of getting past?"

Cornelius considered for a moment before advising. "You could try to understand him ... see the situation from his point of view."

The stranger looked unconvinced and rubbed a sweaty palm over his brow. He looked at the old man and the dog, back and forwards, considering his options. Finally, he made a sudden dart, sidestepping the dog, passing, half sprinting, his mouth gasping in air. A few yards along, the dog, effortlessly, playfully, bounded past and took up a stance directly in his path. The man stopped dead, gasped an expletive, then paused to regain his breath. He looked back at the old man who had returned to reading his book.

"Hey! You ... Okay, tell me about the dog's point of view."

Cornelius keeping his head tilted towards the book, raised an eye brow and gave a censorious look.

"Sorry! Mister ... uh Cornelius, I'm just a bit frazzled. Would you please tell me about this dog's point of view?

Unhurried, weary at being interrupted again, Cornelius placed the marker and laid the book down.

"Unlike humans, dogs don't acquire territory by investing in real estate, or inheriting, and they don't feel the need to prove their ownership with documentation and title deeds. No, their system is far more efficient: they claim territory by marking it with their scent and by guarding it. He may have marked the territory as his domain and see you as a trespasser."

"It's a public park, dammit!" said the man, frustration turning to aggression. Cornelius raised his eyebrows, looked disappointed then picked up the book.

"Sorry ... I'm just ..." said the man. "Right, so he thinks it's his territory."

"Very well," said Cornelius, closing the cover of the book. "If you were another dog, you could show subservience by hanging your tail between your legs, allowing him to sniff you, keeping your head low and pointed away, perhaps rolling onto your back and exposing your underside."

"What the ...!" exploded the man. "I am not doing that!"

Cornelius looked disapproving, fingered the bookmark and became silent.

"Sorry. Right, but I'm not a dog."

"You could try to make friends. Pat him perhaps ..."

The man looked at the dog, then, with a God-help-us roll of his eyes, held out a hand. "Here doggy, doggy. Nice doggy, doggy." the dog eyed him, tense, not moving a muscle. "It's not working."

"Or make an offering, something to eat ..."

"Eat ..." said the man, considering the idea. He snapped open his briefcase and pulled out a packet of low-cal sandwiches. "Want something to eat, doggy?" He held out the sandwiches, tentative, crouching low, trying not to get too near. The dog looked at the package, sniffed, considered, then took it gingerly in his mouth. Having walked a short distance away, it laid the package down and sniffed at it again. If not satisfied, it was at least distracted.

"Right, well," said the man snapping shut his case, "someone ought to have that animal under control." He hurried away, nimble on his too-small feet, mentally logging that exercise was a dangerous thing. The dog waited till he'd gone out of sight, then, carefully, took the packet over to Cornelius.

"My word!" said Cornelius. "You shouldn't really ... but thank you, thank you my friend. We'll share them, shall we?" The dog nuzzled his hand, then, returning to the path, looked into the distance, not after the man, but in the opposite direction.

"My thoughts exactly," said Cornelius. "Doesn't look like he's coming today." The dog, nose high, sniffed, sensing the air.

Chapter 2 Friday

The telephone rang, a sonorous bell, clear, urgent, echoing around the apartment. Chill, mid-morning light filtered through the shuttered blinds. The ambiance was decadent, the urgent energy from without at odds with the shadowy languor within.

Andy didn't see the ceiling, although, lying flat on the bed, he was staring right at it. He was thinking about important things: the sky, the space above, Earth. This blue-green sphere, this rock, this planet, whirring around in neat little cycles, a clockwork toy, a play thing, spinning away in the great emptiness of space. Stuck to the surface, little figures, jumping about during the day, lying still at night, each one running along its own life-to-death trail.

He saw himself as one of them, a tiny biological phenomena, lying there, flat on its back, going round and round, everything flashing past, the sun, the moon, the months, the years. Zip, zip, zip, day after day, night after night—no hand brake, no stops, no exit. A fair ground existence all the days of his life. Even when he was dead, his decaying body and his crumbling bones would keep on spinning, circling forever, careering along the spiral of time.

He closed his eyes and inhaled moist city air. The phone rang and rang, a car swished past below on the street.

Andy had doubts about a lot of things. He should really check it out, but how? There was so much of it; all the barriers and interruptions of life lay between himself and the raw truth.

He closed his eyes and scratched his chest. Ring, ring, ring— the constant refrain from the hall. The blind rattled, a breeze flurried through the half open the window. Andy puzzled and considered in a meandering, leisurely manner. It was his boot sequence, his start up, checking the parameters of his existence before moving on to perform basic functions.

He stretched and rolled over, the sheet wrapping itself round his naked body. Nothing for it. He'd just have to do what he'd done for the past 25 years—go along with this existence malarkey, get up, do it, see how it turns out.

Right, time to get up!

Nothing—not a movement. Message from brain to body, management proposal: how about making a move. Fancy a nice fry up? And the bladder's complaining down here. We're going to have to move eventually. Come on guys, guys, we really need to make a move. He lay for several more minutes in hunger and discomfort. That happened a lot: his body refusing, point-blank refusing to do what it was told. The thing was, people blamed him for lying in. What could he do?

Ring, ring, ring.

A fly was buzzing against the blind trying to escape. He looked around. Mid-morning he guessed, getting on a bit, about 11 judging by the light. Ruffling his fingers through his hair, he rolled his eyes in a semi-stupor and, turning his head, directed his attention towards the ringing emanating from the hall.

That, thought Andy, is a phone. He pronounced the word slowly, as if he'd never heard it before, spelling out the sounds: F ... O ... N. FFFFFF ... OOOOO ... NNNN. Sounded like the name of an animal, a gazelle or something. FFFF ... OOO ... NNNNN. Africa, open savannah. A rocky ridge, a wide sweep of sparse country below. Look! A herd of phone, grazing, ears flicking away flies. One was calling out, its repetitive bringgg,

bringgg drifting over the shimmering, dust laden air. A warning call. Danger. Predator alert.

"Darn!" Andy's body jolted upright as his brain crunched into gear. It began force-feeding him data: where he was, who he was, what a phone was and why it was ringing. He stared eyes wide, heart thumping hard in his chest.

In the shadow of the canopy, the ringing stopped. The red flashing text on Hannah's desk turned to green and said 'CONNECTED'. In her earpiece she heard a click followed by a tremulous inhalation.

"Yeah, hi! Techdomestic here." Andy coughed to clear his throat.

"Andy!" she said, voice urgent and low. "Where have you been? I've been trying to contact you!" Her smile was tight, her voice edgy. She paused, shifted in her chair and, glancing at the vidcam which was currently relaying her image, lifted her chin and brushed back a strand of hair. This must appear normal, business, just another day's work. "Everything okay?" she beamed.

"Hannah—hi! Just popped out of the office. At the bathroom. What can I do for you?"

"Really?" She clenched her teeth and forced a smile.

"Yeah. Sorry 'bout that," said Andy, sensing danger. "Lucky I didn't miss your call."

Hannah's eyes darted down to the desktop. The delivery was ten minutes away. Not long now. The word CONNECTED continued to flash across the screen; no video of Andy. She narrowed her eyes. What was he up to? What was he hiding? Had he diverted the call? Was he actually at the flat?

"Andy," she said with forced patience, "your cam's out. No picture."

Andy knew that. He was on the hall phone in his y-fronts.

"Andy, did you hear me? No picture."

"Yeah, you were saying."

She did a quick scan to make sure no one was on the horizon. "Andy, get your bloody act together! Andy!—Andy! Are you there?" Her voice had risen to a constrained shout.

"Yeah, yeah—I'm here. You know, I can see you. Clear as crystal," he lied.

"You have it switched on?"

"Yeah ... yeah, of course. Power status on. Maybe it's at your end. Sometimes ..."

"Andy, I've been on the phone six times this morning. This end's fine."

"Okay ... Just as well you called. Looks like a link is down. I'll have this baby up and running in a coupla ..."

"Andy!" cut in Hannah, voice low, acidity leeching through. "We are Techdomestic—domestic technology advisers. We are talking about a video phone, Andy, a goddam, pull-it-out-of-the-box-and-plug-it-in videophone!" The silence that followed was as meaningful as the outburst itself.

"Okay ... okay, hang on a sec." Andy covered the mouthpiece of the handset with the palm of his hand and glanced at the clock-display on the base unit. After 11—wasn't even borderline. He'd been on call for two and a half hours.

Plunking the handset on the counter, he sprinted through to the bedroom. A few seconds of rummaging, a tie, but with a broken clip. No white shirt. No standard-issue trousers. He bolted back through to the kitchen and the washing basket.

As he entered, Hannah's voice sounded small and tinny, like a mosquito buzzing the room. He was tempted to hang up, squeeze cancel, but Hannah was not one to ignore.

"Working on it. Lead's faulty. Looks like ... one of the pins ... yeah, one of the pins is bent. Look Hannah, does it really matter? I mean, you know what I look like."

"Of course it matters!" she retorted, having gone too far to back down. "What kind of impression does it give?

"Hey—you know. Shit happens!"

"Does it, Andy? If I was a client right now, I'd be thinking—what kind of technology 'expert' can't get his phone to work? I'd be thinking that a seven year old kid can take a video phone out of the box and have it working in two minutes. I'd be thinking—Andy, are you listening?"

"Yeah, sure! Fire away." Careful, so as not to clunk the phone when he laid it back down, Andy untangled a shirt from the overflowing basket pulled it over his head then wedged the phone to his ear as he did up the top buttons.

"Andy! Andy! You better be listening!"

"Huh! Yeah ... of course."

"I'm drawing a line here," she said, and then she stopped. It was a prolonged stop, an ominous stop. "Andy," she continued, icy and flat, "If you can't get me video within ten seconds, I'm taking you off Home Office." Another pause gave her threat a chance to sink in. Andy grimaced.

"You'll have technical support here," she needled, "and your video will work."

"No, Hannah. Wait ..."

"Ten ... nine ..." Andy ran through to the office, put the phone down, fumbled with the tie! The clip refused to snap into position. As he leaped onto the seat it fell like a limp fish onto the desk. Damn! Something to hold it in place— anything! He grabbed the nearest object, lined up the tie, pressed it against his chest, smiled into the lens.

"Got it ..." he said, hitting the desk's vidphone button with his knuckle and simultaneously flicking the connection to the other phone off with his thumb. "Fault in the ..."

"Andy, you really cut it fine, don't you?" He could see her imperious stare scrutinizing him. "Andy! What's with the tablet?"

"Mmm," he said. "Tablet?"

"Yes, Andy—Tablet! The slab of electronics currently stuck to your chest!"

"Oh, yeah ... yeah! Glad you pointed that out. Nearly forgot. It's a ... it's to ... to show you the report I'm doing."

She looked as if she'd been slapped, hit. She blinked for a moment. When people said he was crazy she'd taken it as the usual office exaggeration, code for a little bit off-beat.

"Am I missing something here, Andy?" she simmered. "You haven't taken delivery of the goods ... " she inhaled, lips tightening. "So, how on earth can you have started the report!"

"Geez! Give me a chance will you! It's ... it's just the headings. I thought you might want to take a look at the—like ... the layout ... before I fill it out."

She snorted impatience. "We send reports, Andy—through the network, we've done that for decades. We don't wave them around in front of cameras!" Hannah paused. There was something not right. Could he be trying to convey something via the tablet, something that couldn't be sent through the network. He knew what was at stake. It could be a work around. She lowered her voice. "Better show me then," she said. "But, in future, use the right channels."

"Show you ..." mumbled Andy. "Yeah. Problem is I've—I've clean forgotten where the file is and ..."

Hannah closed her eyes and took a long, tremulous breath. What was she doing? This was a standard data-update, confirm-delivery-status call. Thirty seconds tops. Instead she'd been on at him for seven minutes and, in the process, was being relentlessly sucked into his nonsensical world. She had to distance herself, keep it formal, take control. She adjusted her posture, regained her resolve.

"Forget the tablet. Before we move on, in case that little video problem should crop up again, Andy," she said, "I'll get

Marge to give you a call when you start duty—at 8. That is your official start time, isn't it?"

"Yeah—8.30 actually. Great idea!" Andy's jaw tightened. It was a really crap idea, but he couldn't say that, not straight to her face. He paused for a second, he had an idea. "Tell you what, Hannah ... I generally get started earlier, look through news feeds, keep up to speed. Why don't I phone Marge when I get up, instead of her phoning me? That way any glitches can be sorted out before I'm on call rather than after." He managed to sound positive, enthusiastic, but would she fall for it.

"Good idea!" she said. Andy felt like punching the air, but managed to limit his delight to a flicker of a smile. Hannah was watching him with the look of a cat playing with a mouse, she was letting him think he'd escaped, that he'd gotten free. She was watching him run around in front of her, calm, aloof, enjoying the moment. She smiled, and he could see her lips widen and her teeth, even and perfect, meet in a congenial smile. "So, I'll get Marge to phone you at, say—7," she beamed, pretending not to have understood. Andy tried hard to look unfazed, denying her the satisfaction of his despair. He looked her straight in the eye, serious, nodding, saying 'yeah' and 'sure' just as often as he could, but inwardly cursing what had brought him to this. There was no point in fighting back, not now—she had the strategic advantage of being fully dressed.

"Anyway," she said, "I was calling about the fridge."

"Huh?" said Andy.

"The fridge!" she said with a hint of panic. "You must remember the fridge!"

"Oh, yeah ... yeah ... the fridge," said Andy, "of course I remember the fridge." He was shifting the tablet, moving it sideways, staring down, adjusting its position. The tie was slipping.

"Andy! Pay attention!"

He looked up, forcing a serious expression, eyes wavering, staring blankly at her, unfocused, inane. She stared hard at him wanting more, but realizing this was probably as good as it got. Move on, she reminded herself, don't let yourself be sucked in.

"The reason I called—I had a spare moment so I thought I'd check the delivery. It's running late ... you know that of course. Anyhow, I've been tracking the courier service. They're ..." she studied the tracking window on the screen, "due at your place in less than two minutes. You remember the protocol, don't you. Don't let them unpack. It's a standard fridge and you'll be doing a standard report. I want it done properly. Keep to the pre-release regulations. No hints to anyone, no sneak previews, not to family, mates, colleagues, girlfriends. No networking, no calls of any kind. I've guaranteed the manufacturer complete confidentiality. You do understand?" She gave him a meaningful look, a reminding look, because what she'd said was only the official part, the part she could actually say over the phone. "Oh, and remember, I'm going to be busy, so, if you've any problems, sit on them. Pick up's Monday at ten. You can contact me Tuesday. Okay? Got that Andy? Tuesday." She could see that distracted look on his face, the eyes not engaging, the confused expression on his lips.

"Andy! Are you listening? You know how important this is!"

"Yeah—Sure ... sure ..." said Andy, lifting the tablet a little higher. "Fridge coming. Confidential. Monday uplift. Report Tuesday—you're not contactable until then." At that moment an electronic buzzer sounded in the hall.

"That'll be the delivery," she said. "Andy, don't you dare hang up. I'll hold—I might not be available over the weekend, but at least I'll know the delivery got through."

He was in his Y-fronts! He gazed in disbelief at the camera.

"Andy! What are you doing? Don't just sit there. Answer the door!"

"Hey!" he said. "Picture's breaking up. Faulty again—Must be the lead into the camera." As he spoke, he reached forward, as if to make an adjustment, and hit the power switch on the vidphone. He stood up, the shirt loose over his legs.

"Dammit! What was it with her?" he yelled, his hands clutching his air. "Paranoid! Totally paranoid"

The doorbell buzzed again. He closed his eyes for a second. It buzzed a third time. "OKAY—OKAY!" he yelled at the intercom in the hall. "Just hang on, will you?"

The pummelling machine was nearly finished. The two year simulated wear cycle had taken under four weeks. Diana waited, tapping the console with her fine, efficient fingers. Nine minutes to go.

Reactive seating was nothing new, in fact it hardly counted as technology. Nevertheless, Techdomestic had a buyers' guide and reactive seating was in it.

She raised her eyes to the ceiling. Nine minutes can seem like an eternity when you're witnessing a set of bum-shaped weights bumping down on to a sagging settee. As if that weren't bad enough, there was the mind-numbing litany of names: Mom, Gerty, Dad, Suzy. The testing machine spouted them in turn and the seating's hydraulics adjusted in under a second. Angles, heights, cushion pressure, seating depth, tilting, plumping, shunting back and forth, setting the profile in time for the next bottom to bounce down.

"Having fun?" It was Philip, ever-watching, ever-enquiring Philip.

"Not really," she responded. "Just down for the results. Should be finished in a minute."

"Why don't you get on with something. I'll bring them up, join you for a coffee?"

"Thanks, but there's a rush on. The ratings go out this afternoon."

"Of course." He flexed his shoulders. "Don't you think it's rather amusing," he said, raising an eyebrow, condescending smile on his lips, "that all the data from all the trials and all the tests, all the opinions and all the ratings—all of it, a whole month's worth—never manages to come together until the very last minute. It's the same every month. Everyone knows the deadline at least one month ahead, sometimes as much as a year ahead, but it's always, always, down to the very last minute." He took a pencil from his lab coat pocket—he always wore a lab coat on the testing floor—and tapped it against his teeth, bemused and smug at the deficiencies in human nature.

"That's just how it is, Philip," said Diana, not bothering to agree. She didn't look at him, kept her eyes fixed on the countdown timer. Three minutes, she thought—Come on!

"But isn't that the thing? I mean—no matter what needs done, people still make it fit. Set the hours, the weeks and people do it, don't they. I mean if someone had switched the calendar, if today were one day earlier, it would still get done. All finished a day earlier."

"Whatever you think," she said. Two minutes! She adjusted the lapel of her suit and selected an option on her slate.

"But what do you think?" he said, pushing. "You must have a view on it."

"All I know is we're busy—we do what we can in the time that we have."

"But," said Philip, closing in on her, a flop of golden hair diagonal across his forehead. He looked down at the screen. "Don't you think we should have plenty of time? Look at how much we spend each year on new systems, more automation, faster processors, increased storage capacity, integrated devices. Shouldn't we be seeing the benefits?"

He looked at her, tapped the pencil on the edge of the screen.

"Philip, I only work here. Maybe you should take that up with management." Twenty seconds, ten, five ... The pneumatic arms hoisted the weighted hind-quarters up to the ceiling. The display flashed 'WEAR CYCLE COMPLETE'. She hit the 'Analyse' option. A laser scanner zigzagged its way over the upholstery detecting sagging, misalignment, variation in surface texture. She reset the laser, called out 'Dad', and got the laser to do a second scan. She repeated it for the three other positions, switched off the laser, stroked the surface of the fabric and ticked a box. She threw some swatches of unworn fabric across high-wear points and hit another button. A bank of cameras photographed the cushions at three different angles. She tapped expertly on the control panel then closed the system down.

"So," said Philip, "what are you doing after work?"

"I'm seeing a dentist, Philip."

"Good idea—must make an appointment myself. But, what are you doing this evening?"

"It's not a dental appointment. It's social, I'll be out all evening."

Philip always needed a reason. She'd made it sound much more than it was. The dentist was Gavin, her brother; he was flying in this morning, combining a Dental Association conference with a family reunion. She would pick him up from the venue then drive him over to their parents.

Sidestepping Philip, she made for the door. Philip, undaunted, called: "Well if you ever ..."

But she waved, preferring not to hear, and called "Sorry, big hurry." It felt cruel, heartless, but it was the only way.

Approaching her access point, a memo, like a pink caterpillar on steroids, was crawling back and forth across her screen. It read: 'Diana—IMMEDIATE—Hannah'.

Chapter 3 Friday

"Andy Naismith?" said the courier driver, face big and oval, nose fleshy, raw, as if it had been thoroughly scrubbed. He gazed at Andy with sad watery eyes.

"Yeah, that's me," said Andy, scratching his stomach under his shirt.

"Got a fridge for you," said the driver jerking his head at the double-parked van.

"Yeah. Been expecting it," said Andy, bleary, thumbs hooked into his jeans. The driver looked down at his logger and began to stab at the touch pad. Andy hung on the pavement, energy depleted by the rushing around.

Why'd she have to phone? It wasn't like it was on the schedule to phone. Didn't trust him—that was obvious. Everything programmed to death, controlled, life made to fit in a box. Coffee break 9.05 to 9.15, email check 9.16 to 10.27, Andy harass 11.30 to 11.46. Wasn't like that when she signed him up. Charm offensive. Have another glass of wine—go on—relax—no need to rush back. 'You'll enjoy this project'. Yeah, well he was sick of it already and it wasn't out of the box. Forget it, forget her. He rubbed his arms and looked up at the sky. It was one of those nondescript days. Cool, grey, might rain, might not.

"If you'd just put your thumb here. That's fine. Now look straight into the scanner, right eye then left." The courier took back the logger and glanced at the screen. "Finger 92. Retina 87. Combined 99.9. Okay. Now where do you want it?"

"Top floor, 113H" said Andy, with a nod of his head. "Lift's on the left." Deliveries were a regular occurrence. As a Techdomestic consultant, one of his functions was to 'appraise technology for the consumer market', or, to be more realistic, muck about with whilst his line manager harangued him for a report.

The driver finished tap-tapping at the logger.

"Right! Kev! We're doing G1-vertical, 4th floor!," he shouted. His assistant had the appearance of an angular youth but, beneath the green overalls, his abdomen was unnaturally boxy and flat. Without hesitation, Kev made his way to the back of the van.

"Good is he?" said Andy

"Don't speak about it!" said the driver. "Felham Porter, mark 3. Does the job, but as dumb as the box he came in."

"D'you let him navigate?" said Andy, ignoring Hannah's instruction not to get involved.

"Not much. If it's real quiet, and we're not in a hurry, maybe. Hopeless when it's busy. Sticks to every damned regulation. Won't overrule auto or go a fraction over the speed limit. You know, last week," he shook his head, face red and pained, "I let him take control—I was having a nap. Got there, a block of flats, no spaces to park. So what's he do? He just keeps on going. D'you know where we pulled over? A bleedin' mile away. As if we were going to cart a washing machine half way across the city." He looked at Andy, watery eyes imploring.

Andy drew his lips tight. The delivery was out of the back of the van, sitting on the pavement, broad daylight. Anyone could come along, bump into it, knock it over. If they hadn't started talking, the courier would've had it inside.

"Won't double park, won't go a hair's breadth over the speed limit," continued the driver. "Won't pull onto a roundabout if there's anything else on the horizon. Some of those roundabouts, if you aren't pushy you'll sit there till sunday morning—Can't read the situation. What do you expect? He's a robot. There was one day ..."

"Will he be okay lifting the fridge?" said Andy, trying to get back on track.

"Oh, sure—the hydraulics can lift anything, but you have to guide them. Silly stuff, anything at all puts him off—a chair, a bit of paper, stairs, awkward corners, that kind of thing. In the depot, where everything's sitting on palettes and there's big open spaces—great. Just give him the codes and away he goes. The managers don't know a thing, they think it's the same out on the job. When you're out in the real world you find ..."

"Yeah, know what it's like. Anyhow, I'm right at the top," said Andy, turning, moving towards the door.

The driver was not to be deterred. "You've got to hear this one! Have you seen any Gillian 800s? We've got one in the office. Realistic or what? There was this new guy, Doug—he'd only started a couple of days—he actually asked her—it—out on a date. No kidding! 'When d'you finish work?' he says. She tells him she won't be finished for another five years." The driver's fleshy features flushed even redder as he creased in folds of delight; his shoulders hunched as he launched into a wheezing, shivering chuckle. "No kidding. That's what she says—in five years—five bleedin' years. She's on a five year lease, you see. Works 24/7. Never stops. Poor guy! Everyone's taking the piss. Taking her out to a service station for an oil change? Better check the tread on her heels. That kind of stuff. Boy, he sure gets some stick. "

"Hah!" said Andy, half-hearted. "Yeah. Like you say, you can hardly blame him—darned realistic. Look, it'll be kinda tight in the lift. I'll take the stairs. Andy had broken another of Hannah's rules—leaving the fridge unattended. It was the only way to get it inside. He loped up the four flights, left the door open and went in and lifted some stuff off the hall floor. Two minutes later, the droid lurched in, and, with machine-slow precision, lowered the box down.

"Right then," said the courier. "A bit unusual this one. Looks like it opens from the ..."

"No, leave it," blurted Andy moving between him and the box. "No problem—get it later."

The driver shrugged. "Suit yourself. You got the other one ready?"

"Other one?"

"Yeah—your other fridge."

"Why?" said Andy, squinting.

"The old fridge. You won't want two fridges, will you? Recycling regulations cover everything these days. Manufacturers recycle one unit for every one they sell, otherwise they get fined."

"Actually, I'll just hang on to the old one."

"You want two fridges?"

"Yeah. Why not!"

The driver fixed him with a watery, red-eyed gaze then looked imploringly over at the droid. It was staring straight at the side of the box. He pursed his lips.

"Okay. Means a little more datawork. You have to verify you've got two fridges—lets the manufacturer off the hook. Can't recycle, not if the customer's still got the goods. Right. Where are we?" He looked down at the logger. "So who's the manufacturer?" Andy looked blank. "The manufacturer of your new fridge? Didn't matter before but then this isn't a straight swap." He peered past Andy. "Didn't see a name on the box."

Andy paused and watched the driver tapping the logger. He had to figure this one out. He could lie, just tell the driver the name of a fridge manufacturer—wouldn't work. Would need model no, serial code etc. Even if it he managed to blag it, the manufacturer would be informed that a certain Andy Naismith took delivery of one of their fridges, an Andy Naismith with no delivery schedule, an Andy Naismith who'd not made any payments. Someone would investigate—Kaboom! Splat! Shit straight at the fan.

"And what happens," asked Andy, "if you take my old fridge?"

"A lot easier," said the driver. "One fridge delivered, one returned. It cancels out. Tick a box on the logger and everyone's happy."

"But where does it go to?"

"Centralized collection depot. All the stuff goes to the same place, gets stacked by manufacturer. It's up to them to recycle."

"I see," said Andy. "Problem is there's stuff in it."

"I thought that," said the driver with a knowing smile. "Look son, you're better to get it over with. Hate emptying fridges myself. We'll pull out the old one, stick in the new one. Get it sorted and done."

Andy looked down as the van pulled away. In the back, heading for recycling, was a perfectly good fridge, his fridge. Actually, not quite his fridge—he'd still some payments to make. Darn! He slapped the wall. In the hall stood a big anonymous box. His usual impulsiveness, rip it open, sod the packaging, hadn't kicked in. He'd lost something he really needed, a basic, down-to-earth piece of equipment and, in return, had acquired a hi-tech liability. He stared hatefully at the box—Whose idea was it to call it a 'fridge'?

The kitchen was a tip: defrosting food heaped on the table, the contents of his washing basket strewn across the floor. Ten minutes ago he was gazing out into the Universe, spiralling through time, contemplating the meaning of existence. Look at him now? Mess—hassle—work. Reality was a pain. The phone through in the office burst into life. He gave a hollow laugh at the phone's bright, hopeful, ring.

"Yeah—like I'm going to answer!" he muttered. He felt like going through there grabbing it and smashing it off the desk but decided it was safer not to go near. He switched on the kettle and waited for it to boil. The phone continued to ring. Definitely Hannah.

Maybe he should answer; maybe he should tell her what she could do with her 'fridge'. Tell her, tell her right now, while he was all fired up. He wasn't a walkover, she ought to know that. He sprinkled coffee into a mug and went for some milk but there was just the empty space. No fridge. He scanned the food laden work surface and spotted the milk at the end near the washing machine beside a half pack of sausages.

The phone ... it was driving him crazy. He lifted the coffee, took a slug and closed his eyes. Resonating inside his head, like his skull was hollow, waves bouncing, reverberating, freaking him out.

He took strength from the coffee and called out: 'Frack it, honey!' He felt satisfaction in knowing that he too could be 'unavailable'. Thank God he'd ditched voicemail. Used to have it, but it just filled up with junk: 'Andy, your report's overdue', 'Andy, could you log in for the group session', 'Andy, we need your comments on some systematics'. 'Andy—Andy—Andy.'

He had to get sorted, ditch this mess and breathe. Padding into the hall, he stopped at the big walk-in closet, his storage system for washed clothes. Lifting a head-torch from the back of the door, he snapped on the head band and angled the lens. The beam shone a yellow oval of light on the mountain of casual wear. In the dim glow he made out a sweat shirt at the back. Well, that was something! Could've taken five minutes to find that. He clambered in, untangled it and threw it behind him into the hall. He scanned the jumbled surface layer then delved deeper. The circle of light was fading, the batteries were flat. He could never remember to get spares; that had been Alice's thing. The cells were down to twenty seconds, each day a little less. The whole clothes finding thing had turned into a kind of speed training exercise. When battery life wasn't a limit, he'd spent as much as ten minutes rooting around for the stuff he liked, stuff that matched, stuff appropriate for the weather. Now it was a race to get the basics. Socks, the only criteria was he had to find two. Jeans, he had some newish pairs but they were down in the depths; the regulars in the top strata had been through countless wash cycles, and, after a year and a half, had a sun-bleached flotsam look. Somewhere amongst it, a pair of candy pink knickers. Alice. That was all that remained, an echo, a glitch in the space-time continuum.

He slung the torch back on the hook. Coffee in one hand, the fruits of his foraging in the other, he padded through to the shower and spun the chrome dial. Showers were therapy, the power to remove sweat, the power to dissolve your troubles away.

When he came out, the phone was still going, coming at him through the mist like a maritime distress signal.

He walked into the hall. "What exactly did she mean by 'unavailable'? He'd kind of assumed that if she was unavailable, she wouldn't be phoning him every frigging minute of the day. That followed, didn't it? Or did it? Just because she was too busy to receive phone calls, didn't mean she was too busy to make them. He stopped dead as he experienced a tentative flicker of understanding. There was something in that, a kind of mystical truth. If she was constantly phoning him, then he would never be able to phone her back; hence she was unavailable. And when she phoned him, she did all the talking; she was still unavailable. That was actually quite smart, subtle—but smart. The phone didn't matter, it was just part of the game. He grinned widely and draped the towel over the back of his neck.

Through in the front room, he pulled on the sweatshirt. It was large, pale blue with white lettering—'27th Annual Nordic Fish Disease Symposium'. A freebie from a conference where he helped set up some gear. Not bad. Warm. Better than one of his mid-teen skinnies. The front room could be chilly, the big bay windows let in the draught. He liked to keep it uncluttered, minimal, like an inner sanctum. Ancient brown leather couch, stripped wooden floor, abstract art, large, graphic and unframed hanging on the expansive white walls. Over at the window, an early Fender, gig-worn and cherished, propped up against a Marshall speaker-amp stack. That was it. No knick-knacks, no gadgets, no clutter. Just the stuff that mattered. He swung the door shut with his foot. The phone? It wouldn't stand a chance.

With the mug of coffee settled on the window ledge, he picked up the guitar and flicked the amp power switch with his bare toe. A satisfying thud, deep, muffled like a horse kicking the side of its box, pulsed through the speaker grills. The beast was awake. A low hum indicated latent power. Andy plucked at each string lightly and they sang out. He twisted the machine heads and they yowled into tune. He clicked up the amp a few notches. Ready. The pick between his lips, the guitar lead flicked out behind him, he reached out, selected a track on a player taped to the top of the amp then took up a stance in the middle of the room.

A studio recording began to play, some shuffles, clicks, a bit of muttering, then a voice counting '1-2-3'. A base guitar kicked in, deep reverberating, almost tuneless, but galloping, growing in volume, unstoppable, like a heavy locomotive thundering through the night. The drummer erupted onto the scene, a pummelling roll, like thunder on the horizon, rumbled and vibrated before falling into line with the base, pushing the beat on, embellishing it, the base and the drums hurtling onwards at speed. Volume increasing, tension mounting, unbelievably they stopped dead, leaving a silence, a vacuum that couldn't possible exist.

Andy stood there, legs apart, eyes closed, limbering up for his turn. The lead singer let out a long yell, an animal cry, that rose, echoing high, ethereal, seemingly limitless, as if it might reach the heavens and the stars, but, having soared without care or fear of consequence, it began to fall, fall, fall, like a plunging angel swooping headlong down upon a dark tainted earth. As the lung-wrenching yell ended, the base guitar and the drummer whammed back into action, hurtling with the heavy headlong beat of before, but the vocalist's yell had left a huge chasm, a primeval longing, a call that resonated through the void to the very beginning of time, a call that reached out, searching, demanding, a call that, tumbling through the aeons, descended on a flat in London and fell upon the soul of a lone guitarist within.

Andy lifted his right arm. The guitar yowled and screamed and bucked like an animal fighting to break free. His grasp tightened, sounds searing, white hot, flashed and cut, slicing back and forth with speed and incisiveness across the base line. Treble notes rose, echoing the vocalist's yell, soaring, unfettered, far beyond the heavens, defying nature, clashing, ringing out like swords in a battle, cutting and searing the endless abyss. Andy squeezed the effects peddle and the last slash of sound echoed and howled and faded into the endless dark of the night.

It was the vocalist's turn. Andy, with a quick flick, cut the volume and began a tight urgent, rhythm complementing the bass and the drum beat, a pulsating harmony to the vocalist's insistent refrain.

Power intro over, Andy could lean back and relax into the pulsing rhythm of the song, could strut a little, swing the guitar around, see the adulation of thousands, acknowledge the acclaim. But, amidst the vying clamour of base and drums and vocals, a different sound registered. It was not part of the avalanche of music, it was not from the crowd, somewhere ... somewhere behind him ... somewhere backstage.

"Excuse me!" called a voice, distant, strained, leeching through from another existence. "If you don't mind."

Andy stopped churning his guitar, opened his eyes, glanced behind. Someone was there.

He strode over to the amp and cut the power. In the silence that followed he felt naked, exposed as if standing in the middle of a vast empty plain. He swung round, guitar low on his hip.

It was a young woman wearing a mauve T-shirt and a stern, reprimanding expression.

"Sorry to interrupt," she said, though no sorrow was tangible in her voice. "I know I've just kind of barged right into your front-living-room, rock festival type thing. I don't normally do that. I respect people's privacy. I knock, I wait to be asked. This might be unfamiliar territory for you, but it's something known as manners, consideration for others."

"Hi, I'm Andy. You are ...?" Andy threw her a tentative smile.

"A very annoyed person," she said, refusing to be drawn into civility.

Andy unhooked the strap of his guitar and leaned it against the window, partly to dissociate himself from it and partly to indicate he'd no intention of continuing.

"Sorry," he said, "I guess it was, y'know—kinda loud."

"Loud!" she said. "Loud!—It was a lot more than 'Loud'. I'm sorry," she said, the muscles in her jaw flexing, her body resolute against the ease of the apology, "but 'loud' doesn't begin to describe it."

"Okay, okay—it was way too loud ... but ... hey," Andy shrugged, his hands turned out in a pleading gesture, "normally everyone's out around now. Usually it's safe to let loose."

"Safe! What if everyone isn't out? Are they meant to clear out, migrate or something? We'll I'm afraid I wasn't out, okay ... I was in. Sometimes people do that—you know—try to live in their homes. I've been up most of the night unpacking, I was thinking of catching up on some lost sleep. I had this crazy idea I could do that, not realising, of course, that my ceiling was about to implode." She flicked back a strand of black hair, the movement more martial arts than female primping. Andy's smile fell on barren ground. "And there's someone else," she homed in. "An elderly man. I passed him on the stairs. I'm sure you must make his life a misery."

"That's Stan. He doesn't mind ..."

"Really? Big rock fan is he? Strange! I didn't notice his Hell Raiser T-shirt; must've forgotten his studded leathers." She put her hands on her hips and gave him a pitying smile. "Have you ever considered that he might just be too frightened to speak out?"

"Actually," said Andy, "he's deaf—98% deaf. I use sign language to ..."

She held her position, her hands still on her hips, her expression still that of one in command, but her eyes had changed, they were wavering, her steel-hard stare was slipping away.

"Whatever!" she said, making do with a dark scowl. "You can't just assume everyone in the western hemisphere is out."

"No, I suppose you're right. Look," said Andy, "I'll keep it down and I'll check next time—make sure you're not in."

She inhaled, considered this. Aware her hard-line stance was embarrassingly at odds with his response, she unfolded her arms and stuffed her hands in her pockets.

"I don't think it's too much to ask to live in your own home without being acoustically assaulted." She made to go and put her hand on the door.

"It won't happen again," vowed Andy. "You have my word."

She looked at him warily, suspicious at the ease of his apology. But there was no sneer, no calculating look, just genuine sincerity. She made her way through to the hall. "Well ... bye!" he said, seeing her to the door. "Nice meeting you."

She was quiet now. All the fire and resolve had fizzled out, extinguished by the promise of cooperation and a few easy 'sorrys'. She felt like she was slinking away, it was almost as if she was the one who'd been in the wrong. Trying to reignite her sense of injustice, she descended the stairs and searched an unfamiliar bunch of keys.

"Hang on," Andy called after her. "Got something for you—consider it a peace offering." Jumping down the steps, he caught her as she pushed open the door, a bulging poly bag held out in his hand. Wary, but curious, she looked at the contents. "A peace offering," he said.

"Frozen pizza and oven-ready chips?"

"Yeah. You okay with that? You can always swap them for something else."

"Swap them?" she said. She scrutinized him for a second, trying to figure him out.

"Yeah, I've got other stuff upstairs—you might want to swap."

She put her hand to her forehead, shielding her eyes. She'd been brought up to be polite, well-mannered, but nothing quite covered this. "No thanks", she said softly as she swung the door shut.

A ghostly sun failed to push through the grey mist of the city, restless avenues and streets thronged to the drumbeat of commerce.

Andy's route was familiar yet, due to the passage of years, strangely vivid, almost surreal. He was hurrying, not his usual meandering self, tennis shoes nimble on the uneven slabs. Sidestepping a huddle of refuse bins at the end of an alley, he emerged into an open residential street. An elongated park, a long damp strip lined with railings separated the buildings on either side of the street. The grass seemed forlorn, littered with leaves from mature trees, sycamore and lime, naked giants, queueing, awaiting the return of spring. He leapt over the railings, the grass slimy underfoot, leapt back onto the tarmac on the other side, cut down an alley and came out onto a noisy thoroughfare where vehicles queued and where the shops weren't shops, but were design-studios and boutiques.

He slowed at a glass frontage, stopped. A beauty salon. They were running a shimmer dye video on their big data sweep window. The 'Siren' look was being tossed around by a haughty, posturing brunette. Hair voluminous, alive, one pendulous, greenish-blue strand bobbed and glistened, an exclamation mark of light in front of her fiery orange eyes. The rest of her black mane undulated and twisted, an ever changing tangle of greens and blue, glowing neon tendrils that writhed over her shoulders and around her swan-elegant neck. The camera viewpoint pulled back. She was outside a nightclub, black leotard, black high-heel boots, black gloves. A living, walking silhouette. Her hair was everything, her hair and her pout and the glowing contacts in her eyes. She strutted through the door and through the crowd which parted like the red sea as she flounced her way onto the floor. The music, lacklustre, faded and stopped. Then the track changed, changed for her, for she was the one. With an exaggerated toss of her head, she stood tall, valiant. Then, perfectly synchronized, she swayed to the beat, effortless, her locks like waves, an undulating cascade of light. The dance floor began to move, move to her beat, and eyes, like moths, were relentlessly drawn to her flame.

Andy squinted dubiously as the ad petered out and accolades scrolled over the screen. Fine for the dance floor, but what about the rest of the time. At the movies—that's going to be distracting—need a balaclava or something. In bed—a blindfold. He hunched as a truck rushed to make it through a green light.

Shuffling sideways to a less distracting section of window, he gazed in at clients outstretched on white, padded recliners. He scanned the salon. Three clinicians, none of them Daisy. Maybe it was her day off, maybe she didn't work here anymore, maybe she sold the business. A heap of stuff could have changed.

One customer was unattended. Could be hers. She might be through the back. He'd give it a minute, watch, try not to look like a stalker. He faltered, maybe give it a miss, head back to the apartment—No, dammit! Stick with it. Get this thing sorted.

As he stepped inside, a clinician, the youngest in the salon, left off from rearranging a display and tried to make eye contact. He looked past her, searching.

"Good morning!" she said. "Welcome. I'm Robyn. Do you have an appointment?"

"Hi, uh—no. Just ... like ... dropped by. Daisy about?"

"I'm afraid she's on her break," she smiled. "We do our best to accommodate, but, if you want a particular clinician, it's best to book ahead. I'll check to see when Daisy is free and who is available next."

"No, it's ..." begun Andy, but he was too late. She'd shut her eyes. When her lids reopened, it was in slow-motion, the eyes glassy and dead. She wasn't hearing or seeing him or the salon any more, she was somewhere else, perhaps wandering through a forest of giant numbers, or swooping over an ocean dotted with sailing boats, each one a diary entry or—she could be anywhere, doing anything on the Dataworld menu. Andy's eyes looked at the emotionless face. He could have slapped her, but she wouldn't have cared. Barely eighteen. Young, smart, implanted up.

Her body twitched and, as if a switch had been thrown. She was back, eyes vibrant, findings at the ready.

"Monica will be available in a little over 10 minutes"

"Ah—no," Andy countered. "It's gotta be Daisy. Is she around?" He jammed his hands down into his pocket; he felt like an accomplice. Every request, every complication, meant a trip into Dataworld-3D. She was still sharp when she came out. No fading. Couldn't have been on it more than a couple of weeks.

"I'm afraid she's booked solid today. Daisy usually is. I'll just check which day she's available ..." Another smile, another blink, another foray into non-existence. Andy felt bitter in his stomach. He felt like shaking her, yelling at her to use the frigging touchscreen, to rip the garbage out of her skull. He sighed and closed his eyes. No point. If she didn't heed the stats, why the hell would she listen to him. Same as always, they all think they're immune. Give it two months and the real world will have become an inconvenience, she'll get reluctant to return. Then the inevitable: excuses, finding reasons to stay on, overtime, migrating, moving into virtwork. Tubed-up veggie within a couple of years.

"Tomorrow afternoon, 3.30," she piped up, breaking into his dark thoughts.

"Huh!" He looked into her eyes. Keen, bright—not too late.

"Sorry. That's the earliest. What were you wanting?"

"Not much. Just—what do you call it—that thing where you get advice. Colour, skin ... stuff like that"

"A style consultation?"

"That's it! Look—she knows me. Five minutes would do."

"Well ... I'll ask. She might be able to squeeze you in."

She looked back to see if Daisy had finished her break. Andy didn't want to look as she twisted round, but his eyes were drawn just the same. There it was on the back of her neck, this year's logo, the little translucent window in the bone behind her ear. Clean first fit. No upgrade scars, no backstreet botches. Still under control, monitoring her virt-real balance, working out at the gym.

"Your name?" she asked, breaking him out of his despondency.

"Em—Jim ... Jim Weir," he said, scowling, his bottom lip protruding as if he was still thinking it over. The girl, ready to blink, paused before adding his name to the scheduler.

"How do you spell Weir?"

"Like 'weird', but without the 'd'," said Andy. She giggled and wrinkled her nose.

Andy shuffled his feet, cleared his throat. "Look," he began, "maybe you ought to consider ..." But he'd hesitated too long. She was gone, glazed, her body bereft of life.

Taking a seat, Andy slouched on the outer rim of a world dedicated to fragrance and beauty. Beneath atmosphere lighting, away from the frantic pace of the outside world, everything seemed different, quieter, voices hushed, pulses lowered. It felt like being in a kind of limbo, a transient, never-never land, somewhere immune from the gritty world of toil, trials and complications. Not heaven as such, but a kind of staging post.

He looked at the customers, two women outstretched on white leather recliners, bodies softened and cosseted by semi-translucent sheets. They seemed contented, resigned, perfectly at ease with their part. They bathed in the soothing ambiance, amidst the rhythmic snip, snip, and meaningless back and forth murmurings. The clinicians in their white, flat-soled shoes, moved easily and silently. Another truck passed, its great weight causing a dull resonance, but it couldn't break the spell of the sanctuary within. Occasionally a clinician would pause, reach out for a brush or for a spray or to change position, but these were mere embellishments to the therapeutic rhythm.

Andy started. A bustle of movement broke the spell.

"Well! Look what the cat brought in!" boomed a wide-girthed woman with a helmet of tight, blonde curls.

The snipping and primping ceased, the ambiance blasted away. Heads turned.

Andy, like a startled rabbit, tensed and froze.

"Hi, Daisy!" he croaked, forcing a twisted smile.

Daisy, robust, had taken the middle of the floor, feet apart, hands on her hips. Andy grinned back, trying to keep his cool as Daisy, like a gun-slinger, narrowed her gaze.

He hated this, hated being the focus of attention, hated shrivelling beneath stares and having absolutely nothing to say. Later, reliving the indignity, he'd think of half a dozen rejoinders, but by then it would be too late.

"So, Andy," she said, brow raised, "what can we do you for?" Andy opened his mouth, but the reason, the real reason, couldn't be tossed out in front of strangers. He started to scramble for something plausible, some reason why an unkempt, never-darken-a-salon kind of guy happened to be standing there now. Come on brain! Something sharp and snappy. Okay, forget sharp and snappy. Plausible—what the hell's wrong with you? Something! Anything ... !

"Excuse me," said Robyn, hesitant, head cocked to one side, "but the gentleman asked for a style consultation."

Andy winced. How could he have forgotten that?

"Style consultation?" mused Daisy, a grin on her face.

"Yes," confirmed Robyn. "That's what I put against his name."

"Name!" laughed Daisy. "Name! Now what would that be? Hah! Oh, no, no, don't tell me!" said Daisy, holding up a thickset hand and raising her eyes to the ceiling.

"Let's see—who could he be? Franz ... Johnny ... Ziggy ... Warren ... Duke." The girl shook her head and bit her lip.

"Maybe Doug then. I'm guessing Doug. That's his casual ID, his messing around town persona. No?" She raised an eyebrow at the girl. "Well, what is it then?"

"Jim ... Jim Weir," admitted the girl.

"Hah! A new one. So you're still at it," exclaimed Daisy, a wide grin on her face. "Another day, another ID. Must cost you a fortune, Andy—or do you hack them up yourself?"

"I ..." began Andy, but Daisy didn't wait for a reply.

"Andy's got profiles like a stray dog's got fleas," said Daisy, conversational, casting an eye around the salon. Then, becoming grave, she nodded grimly, as a doctor might when diagnosing cancer.

"Can't help it, the dear. Fragmented. Schizo-ID. Whatever happened to the name your mother gave you—God rest her."

"Daisy. I know who I am. I'm solid. Totally clean—not even a console. Three years. Look!" He held his hand out, keeping it steady. "See! Nothing. Come on—I'm just avoiding the loggers. I bet there's not one person here who hasn't fragged an ID?"

"I know, Andy. But there are limits. So, nobody's called you in—no supervision order—never been tagged? Glancing around, she shook her head. Then, resolute, she walked over to a viewscreen and pressed CALL. She lifted the translucent handset, then turned to Andy as if a thought had just crossed her mind.

"Andy, I just want you to know that I'm glad you came. Somebody, somewhere, has got to take care of you." She searched his face for a second, then, with another shake of her head, scrolled and tapped at the screen.

Andy's awkwardness turned to disbelief.

"What are you doing! Daisy, don't!"

Deaf to his plea, she put the handset to her ear.

"Hello. Daisy Galletly. Option 1 ... Option 12."

"Geez!" Fizzing, he made for the door.

"You want fries with yours?" She hollered.

Andy stopped dead and turned. Daisy exploded with laughter. With surprising agility, she skipped past the chairs and, grinning, gave him a big motherly hug. Looking over Andy's shoulder, she caught the eye of the girl.

"It's okay, pet," she winked, "Andy and I go back a long way. Known him since he was a babe. He's a good 'un. Harmless," then, wagging a finger, mouthed in a stage whisper that everyone could hear: "but u-n-r-e-l-i-a-b-l-e." The girl smiled, gave a knowing look, then pretended to concentrate on aligning a rack of dolphin-topped bottles.

"Right, let's be having you," said Daisy, leading him to the far end of the salon.

"Gents this end. Can't have a big lummox like you mixed in with the ladies." She swung the chair round for Andy to sit and called to her staff: "Ladies—time! I heard a rumour that some of you come here to work."

Andy swung up his legs on the recliner and leaned back. Daisy gave the chair a nudge and it spun round to face the window. She leaned over, her cheek close to his.

"Nice to see you, Andy. What's it been—five years? A card, a text, would have been nice." Andy grimaced, shrugged and began to mumble an apology.

"No grovelling," said Daisy. "It's no more than I expected. So—what's up?"

"I just can't do anything with my hair," quipped Andy fiddling with a stray end, putting on an effeminate voice.

"Andy, I've got five minutes. You want to spend it messing around—fine. If there's some reason you're here, you'd better spit it right out."

"Okay, okay," said Andy, defensive. "Just, well ... it's an idea I've been tossing around."

"I see," said Daisy dubiously. She looked over; a woman entered and hung up her coat.

"A consultation? Look at the state of those hands!" she blurted, loud enough for the others to hear. "You're not leaving here like that." Then, with her back to the rest of the salon, she muttered to Andy: " Miss Druber over there runs like clockwork. Ten minutes and you're out on the street."

She swung a table across his lap, filled a small bathing tank, brought it over, then fetched some bottles and a stool. She flicked a switch on the side of the tank, it shook with a gentle pulsating hum and, as she squeezed a milk-white 'emollient' into the water, it softened, like a mist, spreading throughout the tank. In a matter of seconds the water was evenly fogged.

"Check if the temperature's okay." He slid his hands beneath the liquid resting his wrists on the padded edge. The effect was pleasing; warm and tickling, tiny bubbles dancing over his skin.

"So," she said, keeping her voice beneath the background hum of the tank. "Talk!"

Andy asked about Neil, Daisy's eldest.

"He's fine! And?" she said, brusque. Andy looked evasive.

"Stop shilly shallying, will you!"

"Okay!" he said, closing his eyes, taking a deep breath. "The job's crap."

Daisy looked at him.

"So?" she said. "Join the club!"

"Well I was thinking of chucking it," he looked at her, checking her expression, "I ... I was thinking of resurrecting the band ... making a go of it. But all real this time. No virt. None. God's honest truth! We're not risking anyone. I'd never, ever go down that route again. Not even for top billing. It's not even that I wouldn't, I couldn't ..." He lifted a moist hand out of the bath and clutched Daisy's arm. "Makes me sick to ..." He gulped and stared, cheeks hollow as he waited her response.

Daisy's face had frozen. She looked shaken, uncertain, suddenly old.

"I never once blamed you," she hissed. "Matt made his decisions. That's over. But Neil—Neil has a family, a job, a good job! He's not giving that up for ..." She held back, aware of a background of silence when there should have been snipping and hair-driers and low conversation. She spun the chair round and beamed the eavesdroppers a defiant, mind-your-own-business smile, before returning to Andy.

"The band didn't make it, Andy," she said, hackles gradually coming down. "You've got to face up to that. You had your chance. There's a time to take risks, and this isn't it. I appreciate you coming to me first, but it's people's lives you're talking about. If you honestly think ... " She put a consoling hand on Andy's arm. "Andy, you've got to move on. You made your choices." She searched his face, trying to elicit a response. Andy stared flatly ahead.

"Andy, listen!" she pleaded, her emotions rising again. "It's not just Neil, it's his wife ... his little boy. He's a dad now, he can't just wander off into the unknown. Leave Neil alone, Andy. Do you hear me? If you start feeding him this fantasy ..."

Andy sat forward in the chair.

"Okay. I've got the message! Stay out of his life," he muttered, swinging his legs over the side and wiping his hands. "Pay at the desk?"

"Now hang on! We're not done yet," said Daisy, her muscular hand pressing him back into his seat. "Miss Druber over there can go rewrite her schedule. Do her good!" And she gave a dismissive buck of her head towards the belligerent client. "They've been messing you around, have they?"

Andy nodded. Daisy breathed deep, her barrel chest doubling in size.

Chapter 4 Friday

The bus jarred, it felt hostile, noise assaulted his ears. At times like this, Andy wished he'd kept some basics from his virtworld days: noise-cancellation, sleep timer, a few themes. It wasn't just the bus. Damned suit was like a straitjacket. Why'd he let Daisy talk him into this.

Andy glanced at his fellow travellers. At least half were carcasses, bodies in transit. Minds, like neglectful parents, off cavorting in virtworld. Commuting had degenerated into dumping bodies on a bus and picking them up at the destination. It made him uneasy, so many vacants packed in one place, like a meat wagon. Where were they all? Movies, resorts, out with their mates. The girl directly opposite laughed then, reflex past, resumed her po-faced indifference—implant. Her glazed eyes were staring right at him like they were locked on. Could she be feeding visual? Might be hosting a stalk. That would explain the laugh. He couldn't see, couldn't tell, but he could imagine it—the activity, the frenzy behind her dead-pan mask.

'Hey, guys, guys, guys! Got one! Come look at this,' she flags up 'open hunt' as she beams vid-feed out to her crew. A fraction of a second buddies start rolling in, building the pack

'So! What've you got?'

'Way to go, Suzy!'

'Nice one—Hey, everyone! Dork alert, Suzy's hosting!'

And that's all it takes, they're up and running.

'New suit,' observes one scrutinizing the feed from Suzy's eyes.

'That's not new, three ... four years,' challenges another as she books a seat. 'See the lapels. Way out of date. Trussed up in his glad rags for a special occasion.'

Having rounded up a posse, the host sets the ball rolling.

'So, who's starting?'

'Interview ...' pipes up Zana, fast on the ball. 'Total frack zone. Shaking like a leaf—picking his nails. Suit he never wears, and the tie, see the logo—going to work. Technology company. T ... T ... Totalistic ... '

'Okay! I'm being generous. Five for the suit, five for the tie, five for Totalistic. Fifteen! Zana's left you girls standing. Come on! Move it, move it, move it!' rants Suzy whipping them on, aware it's not far to the terminal.

'Penalty!' squeals another. 'Screw Totalistic. That's Techdomestic.'

'Sure?'

'Absolutely!'

'Okay! Ten points Pat, Zana drops ten. Pat's in the lead. Any more takers?'

'It's not an interview," ventures a fourth. "He's getting fired, hauled up, something nasty. Look at him. He's got 'loser' written all over his face.'

'Okay, contention! Interview or firing squad. Any more? Calling time. Bus terminates in five. Chrissy? You've been awfully quiet.'

'Breaking up with his girl?'

Laughs of derision from the others.

'Get real!' A chorus of laughter.

Andy envisaged them scurrying off, frantically seeking a match, running trackbots and setting search snares in the hope of catching his trail. What did they have? The image from the girl's staring eyes. He was wearing mirrored vizars, dummies, to reduce his bio-D count. With the constantly changing lighting and the movement of the bus, the image quality wouldn't be great. Could match hundreds if not thousands. Need heavy filtering. Techdomestic should, by rights, be their best tag, but it would come up blank. He made a point of regularly mussing his work profile. His mugshot, tweaked in an image processor, might be passable to a human, but he'd fragged it—the facial proportions were all out, hair colour changed, different ears added in. The bio-D would have him and Rupert Bear vying for 2098th best match. His home address was currently that of a local Chinese restaurant. Other tweaks such as a typo in his surname, a weirdly accented 'A' in 'Andy' and his birthday listed as 01 rather than 10, helped muddy the water—whatever it took to keep the trackbots off scent.

They might try stuff like location and age, but that'd be too vague. Nothing would tie firm. He didn't for one minute think they'd strike. Even, if, by some fluke, they got close to a seam, like as not they would be lured down one of his snoop snares, pick up a virus or a few allergens on the way. Pack hunters in the heat of the chase seldom bother with hygiene.

Problem was their stupid antics left trails. The images they used would be touted all over the web, featured on Trackworld Unknowns and added to search stats. His face would be splattered across a heap of databases from now till eternity. In a few weeks, a few years, someone, somewhere would scan in his image and find out that the same, untraceable guy had been on this bus, this day, at this time, wearing this stupid suit and, because of the tie, tag him against Techdomestic. He did what he should've done from the start: loosened his tie and stuffed it in his pocket.

Andy felt panicky and weak. Another fragment of himself ripped out and laid bare, another unwilling sacrifice on the great altar of freedom. What right had they to tout his image around ... He tightened his jaw, stared maliciously at the girl. She stared back.

Guilt, like tepid water, flooded over him. What the hell was he doing?

He focused on his breathing, slowed it, fought to overcome the tremors. Wise up! Dammit! Check it out before you start the delusion. He took out his wallet, fished out a false holocard. Keeping it low, he began to fidget, flicking it back and forth between his fingers keeping the name partially covered. Averting his eyes, he focused on her reflection in the window. Twenty, no make it forty seconds—just to make sure. Come on. His eyes stung, he mustn't blink.

Nothing! Not a bite. She just stared resolutely ahead. No way they'd resist—a crew would've pounced on that card like starving wolves on a rabbit.

Andy snorted with disgust. Turned his mind to his current predicament, he stared out the window.

Techdomestic rose before him, a giant, white ovoid on stilts, too unwieldy, too precarious to be floating in a bleak winter sky. The building seemed to hover. Only when closer, did you notice tubular, transparent legs that doubled as portals.

A low walkway guided possible customers to an entrance and elevator in one of the legs nearest the street. The curved glass doors swished apart as soon as anyone came near. It reminded Andy of one of those jungle plants with the slippery-edged chambers where insects were lured in and slowly digested. Here, the customers was effortlessly whisked up into a breezy atrium, clean, uncluttered and calm, the marketing department's metaphor for what the product did to your life. Free to wander, they would cross the atrium, relax on the islands of comfy white sofas and open their nostrils to the aroma of freshly ground coffee. After a few minutes, a charming young droid would approach, fetch their drinks and chat, not about their 'problems' (a forbidden word), but about their ideals, how they wanted life to be.

The For You campaign with its muted, pale-grey lettering on an expanse of cool cream was a zero-clutter, zero-tension, zero-hard-sell experience—at least that's how it looked. But something was there, a presence, intoxicating, like an invisible gas, an insidious undercurrent that stripped away inhibition.

The advertising concept—emotion as the key to the brain—was as old as the pyramids, but it was the mastery that had changed. From the moment the customer's foot crossed the threshold, analysis began: gait, breathing, pulse, body language. The customer's initial disposition was acquired, an ID match was made, various financial, lifestyle and social databases were searched. Each person was profiled, categorized and behavioural triggers defined. That took 0.7seconds.

Individuals posed no problems, but within a family or group there could be conflicting views. The system's strategy here was to identify and target the decision maker, tilting the key features in their favour. As soon as was practicable, groups would be invited to wander then meet back later. Separated out, the system could optimize for each one. Little Jack would see his room as a 3D gaming emporium; his parents would see the same room as a high-end educational solution.

What to push, how to pitch, was tailor-made to satisfy deep-seated needs. To turn down the For You programme was to deny your very self.

'I'm here to listen,' was a typical opening line. The droid, male or female, whichever proved most effective, would mirror and empathize with the client, casual or business, excited or chilled, early adopter or consolidating conservative. The system adjusted constantly, sensing every little flicker of interest, registering every aversion of the eyes, noting every smile or momentary tightening of the lips. The customer was the salesperson, they sold to themselves.

Ethical? Legitimate? Such techniques pushed hard at the boundaries between civil liberty and exploitation. It was only by limiting the data capture to real time, each analysis being erased the instant the customer went out the door, that Techdomestic avoided prosecution. In Andy's view it would have been more honest to knee them in the groin and rifle through their wallet. At least they'd have known what was happening. Today, he was too preoccupied to manage his usual sardonic smile.

His suit, although he loathed it, made him feel efficient, business-like, part of the system. Perhaps because he was nervous, or just keen to get it over, he strode rather than loped, his heels clicking on granite. He didn't feel right about skipping the low wall; instead he walked directly towards the main entrance. This, the biggest of the portals, was situated directly beneath the building's suspended bulk, the umbilical cord from its belly that connected it to mother Earth. Magnanimous corporate doors and flagrant glass opened onto seating expansive enough to accommodate baby hippos. In the building's shadow, Techdomestic's logo, a futuristic silver and black hologram, hovered, mod-Gothic with ice shadow. Not for him, not for the menials. Guests and senior management, big-guns like Hannah. He thought of her clicking her way over the polished tiles, all pert and smiley and brimming with caustic ambition.

He veered left taking a walkway that led towards another portal at the back, one that neither flattered nor pandered. 'Staff Entrance H' it said without enthusiasm. Toughened glass, steel inner door—fire-escape chic.

He'd been through it a thousand times. Over time he had come to see his behaviour as rat-like. First, finding his way to his tunnel, then scurrying off along the warren of corridors. He was a poorly trained rat. The employment process had, in its incremental, surreptitious way, tried to saddle his soul, condition him to doing tricks for treats. He just didn't fit.

He skirted 'the pond', a perennial puddle thanks to the fact that the local water course didn't feel obliged to comply with the construction company's drainage plan. Stopping beside it, he ducked down and dipped his right palm into its dark mirror surface. Water dripped from his fingertips as he stepped up to the doorway. Inside the outer glass door, he slapped his wet hand on the sensor, squinted into the eye scanner and feigned a coughing fit as he gasped out his name. An alarm sounded and a display flashed 'PLEASE WAIT'. Hurriedly, he wiped the sensor dry. The door he'd come through had locked behind him, the one in front was yet to open. The 'please wait' message was superfluous. Unless he could punch his way through fifty mill steel, reinforced concrete or toughened glass, there wasn't much option.

From a concrete passageway a security guard appeared and loomed behind the glass partition. His voice sounded through a speaker grill.

"Well, well, well—what have we here? An imposter!" he grinned.

"Yup, that's me," said Andy. "Never miss a chance to impost."

The security guard twisted round to the control screen, reset the alarm and put on a show of being serious. Whilst his back was turned, Andy took a couple of deep breaths and shook out his shoulders like an athlete limbering up.

"Geez," said the guard, staring at the readout and shaking his head. "Overall 40 percent. Not one of your parameters came in over 70." He squinted at Andy, puzzled. "No point putting you through again." He tapped at the screen.

"It's a while since I've been in," offered Andy.

"Yeah. Looks like you need to log in more often. System doesn't think you work here anymore. How do you spell your second name?"

As Andy spelled it, the guard called up his profile.

"Strange. All here. Can't see why it's not ..."

"Bio-D's probably corrupt," suggested Andy. "Happens a lot. I'll check when I'm upstairs." The guard dithered some more in front of the panel, shut down Andy's profile and selected the 'visitor' option.

"Right young fella, who're you going to be?"

"Chaplin."

"If that's Charlie Chaplin, sorry, he's been in already."

"Okay. How about how about something more sinister. My first name is 'Count'."

"Count?" The guard squinted, tapped the screen, hit 'enter' and said, "Yeah, 'Count' is okay."

"Second name ..."

"Dracula."

"You want to access ..."

"Young maidens ..."

"Any particular floor?"

"I'll start on the parapet and work down to the dungeons." The guard looked up with a weary eye. "Fourth floor," conceded Andy.

"Floor four," said the guard. "Reason?"

"Come on. Can't you see how pale I am?" said Andy, baring his teeth

"I'll put that down as 'unscheduled meeting'. Okay—now the security questions. Now make sure you remember your answers or you could be stuck in those dungeons for a very long time."

"That would never do. I must return to my castle before dawn," said Andy.

"A favourite place?"

"Transylvania."

"T-r-a-n-s-y-l-v-a-n-i-a," spelled the guard. "And your mother's maiden name?"

"Mmm ... tricky ... have to go back a few hundred years. Countess ... no ... actually she wasn't a countess at the beginning, she was a maid—I think it was Gertrude or, Gerty though she preferred to be called Countess Valhein."

"Valhein?" said the guard puffing his cheeks with air then expelling slowly. "That's?"

"V-a-l-h-e-i-n."

"A significant date?"

"Let me see. Ah, yes ... I once escorted the most beautiful young lady—Arianna was her name—to a midwinter masked ball. She was truly enchanting ..."

The guard harrumphed and gave a world-weary sigh.

"Oh you mean 'Date' as in 'year'," said Andy, "I see. Better make it my birthday—1623."

"Right, Mister Dracula, we're admitting, you but stick to the rules: three hour time limit, report here before leaving." The security guard dropped his business-like tone and gave Andy a look of fatherly concern. "Okay, so what's the big deal?"

Andy faltered for a second. Had he over done the flippancy, too much joshing around? Or had the guard sussed that he'd deliberately flunked the scan.

"Big deal?"

"Yeah! The suit. Maybe that's what threw the scanner." Andy felt relief. Of course, the suit! Obvious.

"Giving the moths a day out," he grinned.

With the misgivings of one who knows when not to probe further, the guard activated the release. The slab of metal and glass shifted a few millimetres, hissed, then swung briskly over to one side. Andy, with a mock salute, stepped through and into the lift. As the door slid shut, he pressed 'hold' and glanced at the pulse readout on his watch. Heart rate 92. High. Had to get it down Breath slowly, think of something peaceful. Tip 100 and total monitoring kicks in, push it to 120 and you get a security guard, a paramedroid and a lie down in the first-aid room.

At least he didn't have to worry about voice stress. For all the profiler knew, Count Dracula could be as squeaky as a bat. Andy released the hold option and leaned his back against the lift wall.

"Which floor?" The attendant was smiling at him from the wall screen, alert, bright, eager to help.

"R and C, floor four" Andy instructed. Different profile from last time—a dark eyed brunette. He wondered if they'd upgraded the stuff under the hood and how long it'd take her to start up a conversation. The current fashion was for sympathetic and concerned. They'd ask stuff like how you were doing, if they could help, were you in good health. He'd been throwing them something stupid as a kind of protest at the superficiality. 'Yeah, thanks, could you help me change my car tire?' or 'I've got my heart set on becoming a whale?' The thing was, they took everything so seriously. Whatever you said became the starting point for a 'meaningful' conversation. He tried feeding them false information, just to see if they'd pass it on, check with the bots a day or two later. He got a rumour going that a professor at Cornell had discovered a process for turning circles into squares. Huge advantages: you could measure the circumference by 'squaring' and using a standard ruler. No need to multiply by pi. Easier to transport, easier to stack, no rolling about in the trunk on the way to mathematical conferences.

"Quiet today," said the brunette.

"Yeah," said Andy, staring at the floor.

"You haven't visited us before, Mr Dracula?"

"Not in this life, no."

"Well, I do hope you find your meeting productive."

The lift stopped and Andy exited with a curt thanks. He pretended to study a display for a moment. Once the lift had moved on, he checked the corridor was clear, nipped along to the gents and put on his tie. Five minutes later, he walked smartly back to the lift, pressed the button, only to hear a door open along the corridor. Footsteps approaching. Drat! He moved away from the lift, crouched low, pretended to tie his lace. He glanced up as a woman, vaguely familiar, walked by. Too busy with her digi-pad to be bothered. The suit was a good move, like a camouflage jacket in a leaf-strewn jungle. Back along the corridor, the lift pinged, and the door opened. Andy sprung up and darted towards it, slowing at the last minute, preparing to walk by if it was occupied. It wasn't. He asked for floor five, but, as soon as it started ascending, he changed the request to floor seven.

"I'm sorry!" said the brunette. "Floor seven is not accessible to …"

"Access code theta: Hannover—Four—Theodore—Seventeen—Juniper—Ninety-two—vinegar, " he said, holding the up and down options at the same time. Every system had an override; the trick was to treat it like your last dollar.

"Acknowledged," the brunette smiled. Andy closed his eyes and sucked in air. Made it! Past level six. He released a loud breath. His pulse could do any damn thing it wanted. Senior management came with privileges, one being that you're vitals could rocket and you could drop dead without any rude interruptions.

Floor seven flashed up on the display. The door began to open. He knew what to expect, but it still flooded the senses. Warm air, gentle breeze, the rush of waves rolling in. Enviro III, top-end realism, the lifestyle of choice.

He didn't get a foot on the sand before being intercepted. "Are you sure you're on the correct floor?" asked the blonde beach-droid on duty. She lifted her legs off the sun-lounger, leaned forwards, and came out from under the parasol that constituted 'reception'.

"Yes—I am," said Andy.

"Wait here, please," she said, and she bounced back to the parasol to make her checks.

Andy blinked and stepped onto the warm sand. Sun, like a golden, life-giving fluid, infused his pale city skin. He looked into the expanse of blue sky. He'd love to have lain down, let the warmth work on his body, stretch, breath, allow wisps of sea breeze to caress his skin, but this wasn't for him. Eyes adapted, he began scanning the beach. Up amongst the fringe of palms lay clusters of work islands, awnings, verandas and canopies whose shade proved impenetrable when set against the sun's glare. He squinted, could just make out people wearing suits, pretty peculiar given the setting. No one out, all under canvas; the sun would be too much for view-screens.

Over to his left lay an expanse of ocean, or at least a wall screen so detailed and so well integrated that it looked as real as didn't make any difference. Azure mounds of water topped by tumbling, playful waves. The rolling, rhythmic foam mesmerized and massaged the soul.

If anything it was too good. In real life there'd be the occasional bit of flotsam, a washed up detergent bottle here, an abandoned sandal there. And the sky, you'd see vapour trails, a little reminder that pretty soon it'd be over and that you'd up there yourself, dirty washing in the case, stuffed inbox at home, bank statement waiting to give you a sharp smack on the wrist.

What were they selling here? It was attractive, he'd give them that, but what was it exactly? Was it a substitute for something people really wanted or did people want this, the illusion, this sanitised, customized version where the sand wasn't gritty, the sun need never set and you controlled everything with a remote. There was something slightly obscene about it, like having a virtual lover, a betrayal of the real thing.

Taking longer than expected. At last, from the chair and parasol and palms, the bikini-clad droid reappeared. Moving languorously, hips swaying, her toes dug into the sand as she lilted bare-footed towards him. "Sorry," she called. "Just checking." She stood before him, smiling. Security, reception and data-terminal rolled into one.

Andy tried to give an air of being serious and efficient. Ironic, he mused. Pseudo business guy meets pseudo beach-babe, the laid back trying to look ultra-organized, the ultra-organized trying to look laid back. Maybe it was appropriate, maybe it's what should happen on a fake enviro-real beach.

"Who did you want to see?" she said.

"Miss Gish ..." said Andy, "I er ... just called in. I've a message for her, a personal message."

The beach babe tilted her head and gave a cute half smile. "I see. Count Dracula with a message for Miss Gish ..."

"Actually, there was a security flaw. I signed in as a visitor, that's where the Dracula thing came in. I'm Andy Naismith. I'm actually an employee, floor 4. Hannah was trying to get hold of me this morning. She wanted to see me, but, with the security crash I had to use another name. It's Andy Naismith. Just say it's from Andy."

"Mmmm," she said, drawing in her lips in a perplexed but sweet smile. Her voice became soft and apologetic, like she was breaking bad news to a kid. "I'm sorry, but you are Count Dracula. Andy Naismith is an employee who, I'm afraid, is not in the building right now."

Andy raised his eyes to the heavens. AI at work. Droids work on data feeds, reality's an inconvenience.

"Yeah, that's what I was saying ..." He ran his fingers through his hair then decided to change tack. "Yes, you're right. I didn't explain that too clearly. I've got a message from

Andy Naismith—from Andy Naismith. It's personal. I've to pass it directly to Hannah Gish."

She smiled as though delighted. He couldn't think what at, but then she spoke and he knew why.

"I'm sorry, but you haven't an appointment?" The smile was compensatory, a mix of no-hard-feelings but you're-not-getting-in.

"Yeah, but this is a message ..." said Andy, "if you just tell her I was here—say that Andy was here."

"But you're Count Dracula."

"Yeah. Look, just pass on the message that Andy wants to meet up."

"I'm sorry," she smiled, changing her stance and tilting her hips and giving him an ambiguously welcoming smile, "but Miss Gish is fully booked today and I'm instructed not to disturb her." She shifted to cute but sad, consolatory, as though he'd just dropped his ice cream.

Mannerism shuffle's too high, registered Andy.

"Perhaps later in the week," she said, suddenly bouncy, like an enthusiastic puppy.

"Look," Andy blurted, ignoring the body language, "all I want is for you to go over there and tell her that Andy's here and that there's a problem with the fridge. Is that so difficult?" Andy scowled at the beach babe. So smooth, so lithe, so soft to look at, but that meant nothing. She was the latest Midas class 2, not to be messed with, he'd seen the ad. It opened with her as a kindergarten teacher, homely, cute, dabbing a little girl's nose with a tissue and settling her on her knee and recounting a story. Next up, the exact same model standing to attention, sharp blue police uniform, walks up to a sheet of wood and WHAM! Punches a hole clean through it. Then she picks up a metal trash can, crumples it into a ball and tosses it away like a disposable cup. In the last scene she looks sporty but normal, in a running suit, happily jogging' along, then the camera angle widens and you see she's jogging along the freeway, keeping up with the cars. 'Gentler, stronger, faster,' ran the tag line.

Overkill for a receptionist, but this was about impressing the clients.

His options? Dodging past, overpowering her—totally out of the question. Persuade her by arguing—fat chance. She'd her orders. Humans reconsider, droids restate facts.

He looked across the expanse of sand to where pockets of business people milled around and consulted beneath gently billowing canvas. Hannah was across there somewhere, in the shade, at a desk, in some meeting or other. He couldn't shout over, the place would be divided into sound zones. Noise cancellation would replace his yelling with Pacific island breeze.

What now? Here he was, stuck, human-squishing beach droid blocking his way. He smiled dolefully at her, shrugged, wondering if there might be some sort of clever programme subroutine in her that might empathize with his plight. She just stood there, straddling the sand, friendly but with a vague touch of menace.

"Look, he said, "is there someone else on this floor I could see? One of her colleagues. I could run a few names past you ..." He reached into his pocket for his organizer

"Chisick, Chorizo, Coleridge," he began, scrolling indiscriminately through the employee register. Andy paused and gave a plaintive smile. "We're drinking buddies. They asked me to drop by."

"I'm sorry," the beach babe was saying, swaying a little and pushing back her wind-tussled hair, "but you need an appointment to see anyone on this floor".

Andy snorted. Well, Daisy! This is it! A little taste of just what it means to work here. Bikini droid and sand and a big, fat dead-end. Did every darned thing, just as you said! Every last friggin' step. Suit, tie, blagged it all the way in. Dammit! He pulled out a folded sheet of paper, felt his face redden as he ran down it. Embarrassing! Daisy really treated him like a kid. Check list. Right! Done it, done it, done it—just this last one. No! That's just stupid. He turned his beleaguered eyes towards the swaying beach babe. He had to ... Daisy would ask!

"You gotta pen?" he asked the beach babe.

"Digi-pen?" she queried.

"No, a damn write-on-a-piece-of-paper-pen."

She swayed over to the sun lounger as if to a samba beat, opened a large cooler-box, then swayed back with roller-point in hand. Andy scrawled a few words on a piece of note paper, stuffed it in an envelope and handed it over.

"This is a ... a present, for Ms Gish," he said, fully expecting to be stone-walled.

She took it, smiled, and with a pert 'Okay!' trotted off.

Dreeber was more jaded than Andy had expected. He looked as if he'd like to yawn but just couldn't be bothered. This was the legal conveyor belt. Clients, the base commodity, trundled past, fell off the end, that was all there was to it.

Andy described his problem, prattled on, started and stopped, waffled and, when he'd run out of ideas, repeated himself. Dreeber, leaning back, fingers forming a steeple, listened with the infinite patience of one who charged by the minute.

Andy wasn't really bothered, his only concern was reception.

"Are you expecting someone?" said Dreeber, mildly curious.

"No ... no. It's just I left my phone with your receptionist. Expecting a call. Too important for voice mail. I hope you don't mind. I didn't want it interrupting our meeting."

"No, no ... not in the slightest," Dreeber drawled with tepid conviction. "Bring the phone in. Take the call here. Really, I don't mind."

"Thanks, no. Somebody I need to talk with after this meeting. But thanks." Andy, continued, outlined his 'difficult' situation, meandered and eventually came to a stop.

Dreeber raised a ginger eyebrow. "It's very much up to you, Mister Naismith. Of course, as a lawyer I'd have advised against any involvement—but, seeing as you're already entangled, I rather suspect such advice would be superfluous. I'm no judge, but, from the current climate, I'd say you're looking at ..." and he studied the ceiling as if himself passing the sentence, "35 years tagged—the remainder of your life monitored through comms. You're not already ...?"

"No, nothing," responded Andy.

"Mmm," mused Dreeber, eyebrows lifting. "You won't be wanting that then. As to your second point: no, they have no right to pressurize you, but, having already implicated yourself, that somewhat muddies the issue. It would be wise to tread warily. So far, it's all confidential? Your words against hers ... apart from the delivery?"

"Yes."

"Its contents, if we assume it is what you say, would constitute evidence—but opening to check, considering what you believe it to be, would in itself be a violation—a complex situation, I'm afraid." Dreeber leaned back in his seat, lids drooping, heavy, as if building towards total despair.

"As you say, setting the police on your employers could prove to be awkward, but I think it's the only way if ..."

Andy leaned forwards, twisted in his seat.

His mobile ringing! He'd set it on loud. Then, though muffled by the door, he could make out the secretary taking the call, announcing 'Dreeber, Ralsten and Walsh', confirming that she would ask him to call her back. Finally silence, the deed was done.

Andy grinned profusely. Daisy, yah beauty! First time in his life he was calling the shots. He could see Hannah right now, tight lipped, gripping her mobile like she was trying to squeeze the eyes out of a rabbit.

Andy froze, intense cold. A shiver, a chill, unexpected, like a stiff breeze from the Arctic, ran through his very bones. Hannah would be pissed off—totally pissed off.

Dreeber was still talking. Andy blinked and looked but was unable to tune in. He was done here, he had to get out.

"They couldn't fire you for not opening it, not since you suspect it's illegal." Dreeber's eyes were closed. "They may well look for something else, rustle up some misdemeanour, a poor productivity record, instance of late coming, mistakes, theft, deviations from company policy, subordination." He opened his brown, placid eyes and settled them on Andy. "Mmm? Could they use those?"

Andy, squinted. "Huh?"

Dreeber repeated the list.

"Would they need the full set? Cause they couldn't get me on theft."

Dreeber frowned.

"I see—In that case, it would be better if we took action first—before they fire you I mean. If we allow them to take the initiative and terminate your employment, you'll be seen as a disgruntled employee. Of course for us to prosecute, we'd need ..." He looked at Andy with wavering insipidity. Andy had stood up.

"Perfect, Mr Dreeber. Good advice."

"I was about to say ..."

"Sorry! Gotta shoot." Andy moved briskly through to reception.

"That lady called," said the secretary, officious and brisk in her shade-of-black suit. "Your caller sounded anxious." She fixed Andy with a coercive full-intensity stare. "I assured her you'd get back to her as soon as you'd finished. You will get back to her?"

"Of course. Yeah. Absolutely," said Andy, tapping the power option and watching the phone die before slipping it into his pocket.

Out on the street, Andy paused and took stock. A bit early for the restaurant, not long enough for anything else. Move anyway. Hannah might turn up, try to get him out in the open. Off the thoroughfare, down a side street, he switched his phone on, glanced at it, switched it back off. Two more missed calls— Two in 10 minutes. Still biting. Daisy was right. 'Get her attention, rattle her cage, then have her come to you.' Daisy understood people, knew how to steer them, put them right where she wanted. He guessed it came from having to fight her corner. Independents like her had to fight to survive.

What now? He tried to recall Daisy's words. 'Lure her in, take control'. He'd done that, the first bit anyway. 'Then, when you're good and ready, start reeling her in.' Andy's brow furrowed. It had sounded so easy, Daisy building his ego, him lolling back in a big padded couch. Reeling her in had sounded like it might even be fun. It was like being at the cinema, seeing it all second person. Someone else, some guy, some James Bond-type character up on the screen, smooth, assured, everything falling into place because the script said it had to. But the realization was sinking in: it wasn't some guy, it was him, Andy. Daisy may have knocked up a script but this was turning into reality TV. Andy doing hand to hand combat with a corporate man-eater, one that was vicious, fizzing, out for his blood.

Trance-like, barely registering, he kept moving along. Don't think about it. Just take the next step, take one more—step—step.

Art-nouveau. Wrought iron strangled the stairwell, black, contorted, like writhing snakes. The carpet, green and heavily cushioned, silenced his steps, an upholstered swamp, a place where you'd expect to find things dead in the water. His troubled eyes lifted, drawn to the high ceilings, the fussy clouds of baroque ornamentation.

A waitdroid, traditional version, dinner suit and bow tie, came to meet him at the rail.

"Welcome, Sir. Have you a reservation?"

"Huh. Eh ... Yeah—Naismith. There's two of us." The droid scanned the space behind Andy.

"The other person, Hannah—I mean my colleague—is just coming. She should be here soon." The droid flickered a stilted acknowledgement and guided Andy between islands of white tables and through a stream of high-brow chamber music. With a sharp flourish, the droid indicated the lone table that was his. It was in one of the window alcoves, heavy crimson curtains on either side, private and apart. The centre tables were busy. Groups, business lunches, animated chattering. Cutlery clinked relentlessly, the throng of conversation dipped and swelled. He pulled out his phone and glanced at the display. She'd given up trying. Probably on her way now. Any minute. Better be ready, keep an eye on the door. It was glass-panelled; he could see through the decorative etching, ghostly arrivals, faint, then bolder, then the door swinging as another newcomer strolled in.

"Sir?"

Andy jumped. The waiter was hovering at his shoulder.

"She's running late. Give it ten minutes."

"Certainly," the waiter nodded, smoothly traversing the cushioned carpet on high-gloss leather-look shoes. Andy's eyes followed it to where it joined a posse of white-shirted, bow-tied droids in a little coral, all waiting to be called. He stared at the glass door for a minute or two then turned to the menu. It was a reactive-screen affair, but instead of the usual easy-wipe screen on a stand, it lay flat, had a hinged cover, like a leather-bound book. Apart from the exorbitant prices and fancy names, it was the usual: menu options, video-feed from the kitchen, connoisseur blurb, nutritional breakdown and stats.

Andy was too uptight to concentrate. Instead, he looked down at the street. Mottled, patchy, the rain that had threatened all morning had started in earnest. Car lights gave the darkening tarmac a flittering sheen of red and white. It occurred that he might see Hannah arrive, catch her little yellow sports car, cute, toy-like, down on the street. He fended off the waiter once more and, melancholy and resigned, gazed out upon a dank, leaden world. Eventually, he spotted a flash of yellow, assertive and surreal in the shabby blue-grey of the street. Darting, the car cut across the oncoming traffic causing oncoming autos to slow and bunch up, then the clatter of the parking ramp on her descent into the bowels of the building.

In the minutes that followed, he envisaged her slipping off her yellow gloves and laying them parallel on the dash, sliding out, blipping the fob. Then the handbag, the sharp energetic steps, the purposeful stare. As the thoughts ran through his mind, he looked at the other diners, prattling, chewing wodges of steak, cracking their lobsters. He had no concept of time. Two bodies approached from across the far side of the room, he knew it was her. He pretended his attention was taken up by something out in the street. He yawned, feigned indifference.

"Mister Naismith ... Miss Gish has arrived." The waiter stood, feet together, awaiting Andy's attention. Andy paused for a second before responding. This was it. Be strong. Don't mess this one up. He stood, looked to the waiter and to Hannah, then forced what he hoped was a confident smile. He wasn't a minion, an anonymous worker in the boiler room of technology, someone to shove and bully and cast aside at a whim. She'd already admitted as much, she'd cleared her schedule to be here. He held out his hand. His grip was firm, controlled, he pressed her palm strongly and for long enough to make his point, but couldn't help notice the warmth and smoothness of her skin, the delicacy of her bones.

"Hannah!" he said, as their eyes briefly met. He was trying to pick up the signs, and what he picked up didn't seem right. She appeared to be peaceable. Where was the taut-lip? Where was the steely eye that skewered her victims to the wall? Her cosmetic profile forbade anything too overt, true, but there were no indications whatsoever of the bubbling vitriol that must be flowing in her veins. Even the outfit was lighter. It wasn't the usual geometrical, blue and black power gear, but a soft, beige, two-piece suit, the blouse creamy white, silky, feminine.

"Well, Andy—this is a surprise." She studied his face, her eyes steady and watchful. The waiter pulled out her chair causing her to break eye contact. She took her seat, adjusted her jacket. Andy felt a tightening in his throat, a stiff, awkwardness come over his body.

She ordered wine, efficient, casual, without consulting the menu, then waited till the waiter withdrew.

"Glad you could come," offered Andy, neutral, testing to see how she'd respond now that they were alone.

"Yes. Good choice, my favourite restaurant."

Andy tried hard to detect the sarcasm, the acid edge to the seemingly innocuous comment, but there was none. She sounded ... generous. She stroked back a loose strand of hair, took out her mobile, laid it on the table and propped her handbag against the inside of the alcove.

What was happening? This was meant to be the showdown, the scratching, biting, wrestling power struggle, her with her authority, him with his killer-punch lawyer. He glanced across just to make sure. She was studying the menu in a good natured, isn't-this-nice sort of way. Geez! What happened to the vitriol. Did she siphon it off or something—maybe she had some kind of switch, or maybe she had a double, a nice, humane, considerate twin-sister that she used as a stand in when things got too busy.

Andy picked up the menu and flipped it open. He peeked at her over the top edge. That strand of hair that had escaped her hair clip—that was unusual. She hadn't stopped at the cloakroom on the way in. She caught him looking.

"Traffic heavy?" he blurted, feeling a need to say something.

"Ten minutes," she said. Andy went back to the menu and fought the urge to pick at the folded leather. It was a relief when the wine arrived and the waiter went through the performance of showing them the bottle and letting them taste before pouring each a generous glass. Hannah said something about the region and the type of grape and the importance of the volcanic soil. Andy didn't hear any of it, he only knew it was expensive and that his bank balance, like the wine, would be dry and red. The waiter retreated. Andy studied the menu, kept his eyes locked on it, avoided making eye contact.

"Andy," said Hannah, "I think we've something to toast."

'Toast?' thought Andy. What was she on about? He observed her warily for a second, then turned his eyes back to the menu. "Nearly got my choice sorted out."

"Andy! Look at me for a moment," she persuaded. "You've invited me here, I think it's an excellent idea, but you seem to be avoiding me—surely you're not shy?" There was a mischievous glint in her smile. "Now lift your glass—no, don't look at the glass. Look at me. That's better." He did what he'd been avoiding, he looked directly into her eyes, complex, vibrant, a vivid green, the perfect circle of the pupil like the darkest, coldest, winter night.

"Andy?" He blinked and looked. The two glasses were touching.

"Yes?"

"Here's to you, Andy," she beamed. "To the future!"

Andy stuttered in confusion. "Yeah—well!" This was the time to put a halt to all of this, lay down he gauntlet. Their glasses clinked, hers against his, him following her lead, and then they drank.

"Taking the initiative, Andy. Excellent! That's what it's about!" She nodded her head in approval. "I'm only surprised you didn't do it sooner—get legal advice I mean. You have to know the rules to decide when to break the rules—that requires confidence, intelligence, a special type of person." Gripping her glass by the stem, she held it up again, poised, ready to make another toast. Andy faltered, but felt obliged to respond. He held his glass.

"To us!" she said, clinking her glass against his.

"Us?" said Andy, with some dubiety in his tone.

Hannah closed her eyes and breathed. "Andy, I know there are times ... times when we've had our differences, but we're a team now. This is too important to let the small things get in the way. We sink or swim together. Surely you realize that?"

"Yeah—I suppose," he began.

"Excellent!" she enthused.

The wine was velvet soft, infinitely-layered, easy to swallow.

"Last toast! I promise. Don't want to get carried away," she brimmed, her delicate hand raising her glass once more. "To the project!" She touched her glass gently against his, leaning it against it, like two bodies pressing together.

"To the project," he said in a low voice. Eyes locked, they raised their glasses and drank. Andy's Adam's apple lifted and fell till he'd upended his glass. She smiled demurely and tilted the bottle to refill his glass. "You know?" she said, frowning at the strand of hair, undoing the clip, shaking her hair out. "If you're ever wondering what to buy me when your bonus comes in—a clip. One that works—that would be perfect. Anyway ... I'm having the Thai prawn," she said, touching the image on the menu, then laying it down. Andy ordered something with chicken, and listened passively as, with undulating voice, Hannah talked of his future. He was in a position to negotiate now, he should know that this project was just the start. There were limitless opportunities for those with skill and ambition. Amidst the bonhomie, bathed in the glow of the wine and the comfort of the sumptuous food, Andy finally struggled to voice the issue he'd come about, the danger, the possibility of stopping or delaying the review, but it came across as shallow, unfocused, without merit or conviction.

"Andy, look at it this way," she sighed. "Would you say that standing on a cliff top constitutes an unacceptable risk? Of course it doesn't. People go there, they enjoy the views, they have a picnic. It's simply a matter of not stepping over the edge. It's exactly the same here. The goods themselves don't pose a risk. The task doesn't pose a risk. The procedures are standard, it's just common sense. Follow them, stay within the flat, and the risk is negligible. Is that really so difficult?"

"No," said Andy, digging a cherry out of his desert. "I guess not."

"Andy," she said, "I can't—I'm driving," and she topped his glass up with the rest of the wine.

The drive to his flat was fast, blurred and, for Andy, almost horizontal in the reclining seat of her vintage car. A BMW, hydrogen fuel. No computer programmed conveyance was going to dictate Hannah's route. He felt like a sack. He lolled, he lurched, he swayed, and, frequently, he close his eyes, as Hannah, with rally-cross flair, barrelled hard into junctions and scudded along empty back streets.

Chapter 5 Friday

The suit lay strewn on the bed, abandoned in favour of a sweater and jeans. To shake off the languor brought on by the food and the wine, Andy fixed a strong coffee. Away from Hannah, alone in the flat, he had time to review the morning's endeavours.

Kick-ass Andy. Taking control! Really showed her—yeah! Buy her lunch—Ouch! Bet she's quivering in her boots. Please ... please ... don't buy me lunch again. I can't take any more of those expensive free meals. No! Not the oak-conditioned Pinot-Noir, not the Scottish smoked salmon roulade, not the braised lamb and mint sauce with baby Jersey potatoes. You swine! How could you!

So, what had come of it? Besides giving her the opportunity to massage his ego, work on him with those dexterous fingers of hers till he was sufficiently pliable and putty-like to be dumped back on his doorstep, he'd come away with some vague, instantly-forgettable, assurances about bonuses and team-work and career trajectories. Think about it, how's that going to work? If he's the anonymous source of this review, the author of a mysterious report that just happens to land on her desk, how's she going to arrange payment? How's she going to team up and make a partner of Mr Anonymous? Why, for no apparent reason, would she put a rocket under Andy and blast him into the big time? That's going to look helluva suspicious—and she knows that. None of that's going to happen. Net achievement? Two massive dents in his wallet.

Forget it! Forget her! Do it, get it over with. If this review works as she says, she'll be promoted into the stratosphere and out of his life. That's the bonus. Downing some of the coffee, he faced up to the box and cracked his knuckles. It was big. Little boxes were okay but big ones, big as this, were daunting. There was no rational reason for his uneasiness, he couldn't argue it away. It was subliminal, primeval, the same animal instinct that drove pagan tribes to erect standing stones, make sacrifices and gaze into the sky. He was just a caveman with fancy toys. He shook himself. Stop putting off the evil moment. He stooped for his coffee, sipped, and surveyed the monolith with a determined, narrowing stare.

This was it. No witnesses, no ceremony, a new era for the civilized world and not a soul to record it. That's the way these things happen. Someday they'll do an official version, one for the records. But history, real history, is just as likely to happen in a back room or a deserted field when the world isn't looking.

He slid a pen knife from his pocket and sliced down the security tape. All along it, the words 'sealed', holomarked in green, vanished and the words 'opened' in vibrant orange took their place. He put the mug on the floor. Reaching up, it was quite a stretch, he split the tape along the top. Squatting, he slit it at floor level. The panels at the front of the box sprung open a few centimetres; the pressure of padding from behind. He opened them fully and removed the shock absorbing foam to reveal a cream-coloured cabinet. He'd expected khaki green or grey, something military. It looked like standard office equipment, a tall metal storage unit, flush handle at chest height, a card-reader just below. The instructions, the access card and so on, were in the usual hologram-sealed pack.

It all looked pretty standard. He freed the access card from the sealed pack, pressed activation, held it, and the finger scan was done. One side of the access card was a screen. It lit and flashed menus. Andy checked a couple, got bored, then stuffed it in his back pocket.

The next stage was critical. Starting the kit up wasn't usually an issue. But this time there was no helpline, no sending it back under guarantee, no logging on to forums for geek expertise. 'Hey, anyone got tips on booting a mark 3?' He grimaced. Nope, he was completely on his own. If he got stuck, Hannah would crucify him.

A quick check through the rest of the pack. Important to look out for special warnings, lockout alerts, any special protocols? Zilch.

Okay. He slid the listen-up card from its envelope, squeezed it and propped it up on the hall table where the sound quality would be better.

The output was terse, technical, no congratulatory fanfare a complete absence of promotional drivel. Marketing would want to sort that. Half-listening, he skipped through the unwieldy terms and conditions and voice-signed his acceptance. There was other stuff, general consumer warnings, product advice. Stuff it! He could spend the whole weekend going through this.

Inserting the access card in the slot, he stood back and the doors, with silent assurance, swung open. A soft sheet, like a shroud, clung gently to the form within. Carefully, he peeled it back. The face was that of a young woman, eyes closed, untainted, like a child blissfully asleep.

Andy stood and considered with a critical eye. Bland, characterless, disappointing. The physiotech guys had held back, played it safe. Okay, you don't want a giant nose, grossly irregular features or a mass of spots, but when you go too far towards perfection you get something else, the semolina syndrome, a pale, pasty, artificial pallor. About as realistic as a marble angel. Point one in his report.

Andy felt better now he was working. This was his thing. Forget the office politics and the power struggles and just get on with the job.

He thought about the report, he'd need a couple of paras on physical. Once she was up and running it would be more difficult, too much moving and talking to see the fabric beneath. Proportions good, natural, but then that was to be expected. Height a tad below average, slight build, nondescript suit, shoulder-length hair, blonde fairly thick, a bob. He wondered what it was like in the finishing stages at the factory, getting their clothes on, styling their hair, finding them the right size of shoes. Dressing up for big kids.

Overall—nothing special, not any better than the market leaders. He was surprised, considering their background. He'd certainly have no trouble telling she was a droid. Until activated, there wasn't much more he could say. No point touching her. She'd be cold, unresponsive, limbs stiff and impossible to move.

He lifted his coffee. It was cooler now; he took a couple of large gulps. Preboot time and he was feeling his usual twinge of reluctance. Sure, he wanted to see what she could do, but he felt a kind of responsibility. He started up new stuff all the time, no probs, but droids—one minute they were cold slabs of technology, next they were walking and talking and fixing you dinner. It was like raising the dead from the tomb.

He shook himself and cracked his knuckles. Okay, anything else? Well packed, arms and legs held by mouldings at about fifteen degrees from the vertical. Deactivated androids were surprisingly difficult to manoeuvre: awkward, top heavy and almost impossible to balance. Even leaning them against walls could be darned tricky. You really didn't want to lie them down, they were a dead weight to get up off the floor. The trick was to get them running in basic, then they would stand without falling and you could guide them around.

Andy pressed and held the module. It took five seconds for her eyes to open. Hazel brown, blank, staring. Her limbs moved, almost imperceptible, but you could see she was supporting her weight. Her chest began to rise and fall gently as if breathing, and that was it! Straightforward enough. Andy took another swig of coffee, popped through to the kitchen for a biscuit, and chucked the wrapper on the floor. No point having a droid and clearing up yourself.

Codes in hand, ready to move on, he stopped. Something was different. Had he been too hard in his initial assessment? There was something about her basic physio, something different, a change in character—he wasn't sure. He studied her more closely for a moment. The bland store-model features were gone. Most droid faces were pre-moulded plastics with smart rubber on top. Throw in a bit of mechanics, the jaw, the eyelids, and a few hydraulics for basic movement, and that was it.

But this much more subtle, more fluid. Micro-hydraulics, he guessed, nano-texturing of the skin for fine detail. He looked more closely, at the fine skin around the eyes, at the coating of fine hairs on her cheek, at the lines in the soft puffy flesh of her lips. It's funny, maybe he hadn't looked close enough before— but now the skin seemed good, excellent in fact. Must kick in during start-up, like a kind of profile-creation stage. He'd have to ditch his first impressions.

He reached out to touch her, but stopped short. He felt reluctance, like it was violation of her privacy. He knew it wasn't, she was just a piece of technology, but the feeling was there nevertheless. It was like an optical illusion: you know the facts, but your brain tells you something else. He shivered, and, pushing himself, stroked the back of her hand. Skin was one of the trickiest things to emulate. This looked completely natural, not too perfect, fine hairs, pores, faint blemishes, tiny wrinkles at the wrist, just the right balance of detail and imperfection.

He shivered, stood back. What else? Pretty? Yes, but kind of—demure. No supermodel. Overall impression: a little reserved, never stays out late, a home bird rather than a party animal. But that could all change. Character was the domain of her psycho-designer. Physios and psychos, different disciplines, different departments. Appearance and character didn't necessarily have much in common.

Andy stuck out his bottom lip. So far, she was as good as was rumoured, but static was the easy bit. Credible human behaviour ... that was the Holy Grail.

Taking a last draft of coffee, he set the mug on the floor. Time. He'd two days—Tillington and Davids would want two months. They'd put her through the Turin, Ground-House and Majorek tests under controlled conditions, see if she'd manage the 0.7 threshold or whatever. That would take a month for starters. So Hannah had got Andy, an employee whose special attribute was leaving everything to the last minute. It was a seat-of-your-pants job. Suss her out, box her up, have her ready for uplift on Monday.

Andy interlocked his fingers, then stretched his arms above his head till the knuckles cracked. Two days, no disturbances, no distractions—need to keep moving. He pressed the blipper three times. Her eyes blinked, her chest rose and she inhaled deeply as if awake but dazed.

"Ready for initiation," she said, her voice a monotone, her face expressionless. She stepped forward, extricating herself from the moulded shell, correcting her balance.

Andy stooped till they were face to face and pressed the palm of her hand. She stared intently, searching his eyes. When she was done, she blinked slowly, indicating the retinal scan was done. Andy exhaled loudly through his nose, waited. A flicker of life, she moved her limbs, swayed. Her eyes focused on him, took in the hall, then, lifting her arm, she gazed at her hand.

"Ah! Diana. Take a seat—How are you?" said Hannah, half-rising from her desk. Diana settled herself into the washed canvas chair and felt the unfamiliar scuff of her soles on sand-gritted wood decking.

"Fine, thanks, but busy!" she hastened to say. "Putting the finishing touches to the guide. We launch in under two hours."

"You've delegated?"

"Yes, of course!" nodded Diana, emphatic, but resentful at Hannah's implication that it didn't come at a cost. Delegated? She'd delegated alright, delegated to someone busy before, but frantic right now, someone scanning so fast that if they so much as blinked they'd miss a whole line.

"Good—then you can relax—breath in the atmosphere enjoy a bit of time out. It's your first time in this enviro, isn't it?"

"Yes." Diana leaned back, tried to believe it was a treat but such deception didn't come easy. Hannah didn't called you up for a chat. Diana forced herself to sit back in her seat and pretended her intestines weren't contorted.

"Coffee?" asked Hannah. Diana accepted the offer. As Hannah linked through to a droid, Diana racked her brain for possible causes for the invite. Nothing she could discern—things appeared to have been running as normal.

A beach babe arrived with a tray neatly laid out with a carafe of fresh coffee, white porcelain cups, saucers and tiny foil-wrapped biscuits. Very neat, typical Hannah, thought Diana. And the biscuits, no wonder she stays slim.

Hannah did the pouring and stirring and presented Diana with her coffee and a platter of tiny biscuits. Diana suppressed a wry smile. She recalled the pretend tea parties of her childhood, friends kneeling in some corner of the garden, making a big thing of the process, pretending to be ever so polite. Five minutes later they'd be fighting like hyenas over a doll and tearing it limb from limb.

"So," said Hannah, "no problems? Level five's getting on okay?"

"Yes," said Diana, her insides coiling tighter. "Fine, absolutely fine—we're all, just ... you know ... working away."

"Gabriella's getting on alright? Her and her partner ..."

"Yes, as far as I know."

"And Dermot ..."

"He's fine too. Sue's expecting in the summer.

"Oh, lovely!" said Hannah, switching to a sympathetic, cooing tone. "That's so nice. They are such a lovely family. That'll make three won't it?"

"No, this is number four. There's the oldest one, David, he's six and then the twins. They started to walk about a month back. Dermot gives us daily reports."

Hannah sipped her drink as Diana spoke. She swallowed, and looked thoughtful, then spoke.

"Lovely. And what about Andy?"

That's the one, thought Diana, the coffee cup jarring against her teeth. The other stuff was padding, the dissection begins now.

"As far as I know, Andy's fine—Just the usual." She made a point of keeping her response low key.

"Mmm ... Do you really think so?"

"Well—we don't actually see him that much ... but he's still working away. Does his appraisals at home. I suppose, with having his own office, and nobody else to annoy, he doesn't often need to come in." Hannah nodded and waited, wanting more. "But I think he's fine," reassured Diana. "Just dodging along. Same old Andy."

"Yes, of course—same old Andy," said Hannah, her voice trailing away, as though reciting something she no longer believed. She sat forward in her seat, her voice confiding. "It's just that I'm concerned that he's become isolated, too cut off from the group." She finished with a tentative, worried smile then looked to Diana for a caring response.

"Maybe you're right, I really don't know," said Diana. She took refuge in peeling the foil from a biscuit.

"Maybe I'm barking up the wrong tree," said Hannah, less conspiratorial, leaning back in her seat. "Andy does live alone?"

"As far as I know."

"So, no girlfriends?"

"Again, not as far as I know—not since ..."

"Alice." Hannah tilted her head back and stared towards the billowing canopy. "Alice—yes. We all know about Alice." She drew a tight little smile.

Diana took a drink and, in the process looked warily at Hannah. A tiny sliver of truth, a hurt, a regret, a chink in the formidable Hannah defence. Diana couldn't stop herself fishing for more.

"Yes, I wonder if she still remembers us, if she ever thinks of us still working away here. To think she couldn't configure a droid when she first started."

"Mmm ..." Hannah gazed, but for the briefest of moments. Her eyes snapped back into focus, her body straightened.

"She's done very well for herself," she breezed. "Good for her, that's what I say." She took a moment to align her cup precisely on its saucer. "Now! Andy. I'm not trying to pry, but I thought you two were—close."

"No—not really," said Diana, attention turning to the flapping canvas of the door. Hannah waited. "We are friends— were friends would be closer to the truth. Andy keeps pretty much to himself these days." She smoothed out her skirt.

"That's a pity!" said Hannah with a momentary frown. "And there's no one else you know of—someone outside of the company ... friends in other circles."

"Perhaps—I don't know. Look, why don't you just ask him?" Diana looked at her hands, feeling precarious at having openly challenged Hannah.

Hannah sat quietly for a moment, finger touching her lips, thumb pressed lightly against her cheek. A short vow of silence. At last she tilted back her head and stared into the rippling canopy above.

"I'll tell you what it is, Diana: Andy's a nice, easy going guy, but I feel ... recently, that he's been struggling."

Diana looked at Hannah cautiously, not wanting to commit.

"To be perfectly honest," explained Hannah, "I've asked him to do a job, and—well ... I wonder if it might be too much for him. It's a pre-launch, I've signed a confidentiality agreement. I'm afraid I can't disclose any more."

"Andy's more than capable," said Diana. "If there's anyone who can ..."

"Oh, no," said Hannah, smiling and flicking up a hand to stop Diana in her tracks. "I'm well aware that he's capable. That's why I asked him. I just sense he's a little low at the moment—a bit fragile."

Diana tensed inside but limited her response to a look of muted concern. She could quite believe Andy was in trouble. Andy was the kind who coasted, eyes shut, into minefield and swamp. If there was anything unusual in all of this it was Hannah. Hannah being concerned? That was way out of character. Hannah wouldn't interrupt a phone call if you tripped and splatted your brains on her desk.

"From what you say, Diana, he doesn't appear to have anyone. I wondered if you wouldn't mind popping in to see him, over the next couple of days." Hannah had shifted to bright, forthright, scheduling clearly her thing. "Obviously, your discretion would be appreciated. Take him something round—use a pretext. I just think someone should see how he is." She flashed a smile. "Now I know it's an unusual request, but I'd never forgive myself if something happened. Woman's instinct. Just to put my mind at ease." She gushed a full-spectrum tsunami smile, the kind she used to obliterate resistance.

Diana didn't rush her response. Yes, she'd had some laughs with Andy, but that was all. Andy socialized in a sporadic, now you see him, now you don't kind of way. Inter-department squash, office night outs; he'd say he'd come then wouldn't, or that he wouldn't then wander in at the last minute. They were always trying to find him a spare ticket for an event or up against a team one man short. It jumbled along like that for a couple of years until Alice arrived and mopped him up. Diana tightened her lips. Now she was the 'contact', the person who 'knew' Andy.

"I hope I'm not pushing you into this," gushed Hannah. "You're perfectly entitled to say no. It's just a matter of checking he's okay."

"Just checking," said Diana, sipping the coffee, taking her time to lower the cup.

"Yes," Hannah said. Diana took another sip before responding.

"Okay. I'll pop by."

"Great!" said Hannah, gushing. "I'll book a taxi for three. Anything you want—pop home, change of clothes, make some calls—that's perfectly alright, but be back here by five ... earlier if you can. Oh! And the pretext. I was thinking a hamper, something foody. He looks like he never gets a decent meal. I'll set it up, have it delivered to reception by two forty five. That'll give margin. You know how these ..."

"Sorry—I thought we were talking about something casual."

"But it is! Just a quick visit, see how he's doing. He might be in trouble, why wait? You never know what might happen over the weekend." She threw Diana a scrutinizing look. "Good. As

I was saying—I'll order the hamper. Just pick it up at reception, will you, on the way out. Tell him it's a prize. His name was pulled out of a hat. Healthy eating initiative, that kind of thing. Andy never knows what's going on, so that shouldn't be a problem. When you're there, set the taxi to wait. I'll see you when you get back. Find out how he is. Shouldn't take—Oh, what? ... A couple of hours. Okay?"

"What if he's not in?" said Diana, taken aback at how 'popping in' had taken on military precision. "I thought I'd wait till I was going that way. I'm over in his neck of the woods on Wednesday—my yoga class."

"Nonsense! In your own time? See it as a company perk. Oh, and one last thing. Report back directly to me, in person, not a word to anyone. I wouldn't want my concerns to blot Andy's record." Hannah sat tall, she checked her watch. "Goodness! Must go. You'll want to clear your desk." She didn't say 'chop, chop', but it was there in the tone.

Back at her desk, eyes distant, Diana slipped off her shoes and shook the sand into the bin.

Chapter 6 Friday

"Hello! I am android model: Atlanta mark 9S. Serial number: A000 000 000 027. My usage is dependent on your accepting controller terms and conditions."

"Skip 'em," said Andy.

"I'm sorry, but registration is only possible if you ... "

"Okay, okay, just do it!"

"Shall I recount the terms and conditions now?"

"Yeah, run through them. Fast forward at max," said Andy. Her lips a blur, a high-pitched mosquito whine followed. It stopped.

"Accept terms and conditions," Andy blithely responded.

"Accepted. Would you like me to run through my features and operating instructions?"

"Skip features, skip operating instructions."

"You are my sole operator," she said casually, as though commenting on the weather. "I will take your remaining biometrics whenever you are ready."

"Yeah—okay," said Andy, apathetically. There was no real alternative.

He held his hands close to her eyes so she could record his finger prints, recited a standard sentence for voice recognition and walked back and forth up the hall so she could register his gait. Finished, she stepped back, very straight, almost at attention.

"Biometric record complete. Please provide a name for this operator."

"Andy," he said.

"Surname?"

"No entry. All other profile entries to remain blank."

"Accepted. Moving to my profile," she said.

Now it was Andy's turn to set her up, name her, 'Droid baptism' they called it. He needed an ID. Traipsing through to the office, he shuffled through a small bundle of ghosts. He had one for her. Heinz, his ID 'advisor', had responded to the request for a female ID much as Andy expected.

"Woooohoo! Here you go, Dorothea my girl! You will look lovely. Get your hair done, find something shimmery and slinky!"

"Not my style," said Andy. "I'm after a flowery pinafore in the Debby Web sale."

Andy stared, lost for a moment in the hazy blue of Heinz's marker-pen scrawl. He blinked, refocused, eyes settling on the serial code. He nipped back through to the droid, a rueful smile on his face. Hannah would have a heeby-jeeby, but then Hannah didn't need to know. This wasn't about rebelling. Running droids on factory defaults was like painting by numbers—boring, predictable and, when you're dealing with high-end kit, totally pointless. To push the limits, you need a unique profile, and to set that up without fighting your way through a forest of 'INVALID PROFILE' warnings, you need a genuine, eighteen-carat, Heinz-knocked-up ID. It made no difference. In two days, the whole lot, including the droid, would be shredded and ready to send back. For Andy, ID fraud barely registered on shit radar: he was already deep into just-don't-get-caught terrain.

"Righty ho!" he said, with forced jollity. "Profile begin. First name's Dorothea. Middle name's Janine. Surname's Hope. Friends will call you Dorothy ... Dot ... no ... too techno sounding, just keep it at Dorothea. You'll introduce yourself as Dorothea Hope. Your title will be Ms, so for letters and forms or for more formal introductions to associates or in a business situation you'll be called Ms Hope." Andy flicked the plastic card with the data and looked up to see how she'd taken it. She gave an eager to please smile as their eyes met and said: "Fine! Dorothea Hope. Dorothea to friends. Ms Hope in formal situations." Oops, though Andy. Autopilot. For a droid that wasn't meeting anyone, that was a tad superfluous.

"Thank you" she said, then, after a moment's hesitation, added: "I like 'Dorothea', it's a good name.

Strange. He'd expected a non-committal drone. Her character modules must have auto booted. Probably defaults. He'd look into that later. It was important with a droid to choose a personality that wouldn't drive you insane.

He remembered the Belinda mark 3. In the early days of 'character' droids you just got what they came with, no cut off, no options, just endless prattle from your 'HumanReal soulmate and friend'. 'It's so nice to be able to sweep the floor—and such FUN! Can I sweep the floor any time I want? Really? Are you SURE?' Andy cringed at the memory. He gave up after a few hours, had to wade through the menus, sort it out using advanced settings, something reviewers don't do till at least 80% through the assessment.

His attention drawn, he studied her for a moment. She seemed thoughtful, silent, but not in the usual dumb, nobody's-at-home manner of your typical droid.

She broke out of her thoughts, looked up, then paused as though unsure whether to ask. Finally, she spoke up.

"Andy, may I ask if you are a friend or an associate?"

"Well—I guess I'm a friend," said Andy, not quite sure what to say.

"Thank you! Thanks ..." she said with a pensive smile. She relaxed her stance a little and added, "It's good to have friends."

"Yes, it is," said Andy. She waited quietly and watched. Andy felt awkward. He busied himself, stuffing the blipper and the registration bits and pieces inside the delivery case, closing the door. He wondered if that was a good idea, it might look like he was trying to cover it up. He recalled Hannah's instructions. Fall back position, Andy: it's just a mix up in the review programme. Someone's delivered the droid instead of the fridge—as far as you know the job's been changed and you've to assess an advanced level 2. You're doing your job, you're not guilty. You are keeping it private because there's a confidentiality agreement.

Andy glanced at her. He wasn't so sure. You'd have to be an idiot to think this level of kit was a jumped up level 2.

"I realise we already know our names," she said, "but do you mind if we introduce ourselves. I'd like to practice."

"Yeah—why not," said Andy.

"Andy Naismith. Pleased to meet you."

"Dorothea Hope. Pleased to meet you, Andy." They shook hands and Andy noted the warmth, the softness of the skin, the natural movement of the handshake. Damned perfect! The lack of droid clues was starting to get to him. Normally, even at this stage, he'd have noticed a few limitations, minor glitches, something to mention in his report. Instead he was fighting to retain objectivity; he was having to tell himself that she— this—was not a person. The awkwardness he shouldn't be feeling was that of strangers confined together, at a loss for words, and with nothing particular in common. He had to snap out of this. She is a droid, period! Now push on with the programme.

"Dorothea, would you make me a coffee?"

"Sure—no problem," she responded, looking past him, her eyes taking in her surroundings.

"The kitchen's over there," he pointed. "Watch your step. Place is a minefield."

"I'll watch out. White?"

"Yeah ... no sugar." He decided to leave her a couple of minutes then go through to see how she was getting on. It was basic stuff but there was no point in overlooking the obvious. The coffee initiative test could be remarkably telling. He recalled an early encounter with a Belinda Mark 5.

"How much coffee?" was the first question.

"A teaspoon."

"A rounded teaspoon, a level teaspoon or ..."

"A rounded teaspoon."

"There are three different sizes of teaspoon in the drawer. Which would you prefer me to use?"

"It really doesn't matter."

"How much milk would you like?"

"Just a splash."

"About 10ml then?"

"Hell, I don't know. I don't measure it."

"Sorry, but how much?"

"Oh ... just make it 10ml and we'll see."

That was just the start. She'd still to ask him which mug he'd prefer, how full he liked it filled, what temperature he'd like the coffee, how many stirs—if any—she should give it, whether he'd like it served on a tray, a plate or with a napkin, carried through to the living room, placed on the counter top, and so on. Making a sandwich, another barrage of questions. Questions, questions, questions. Every task, no matter how simple, was always the same. The Mark 5, if you could stick with it, learned as it went. In theory, it would become more independent, need to ask less. Somehow it never quite worked out. As soon as anything changed, like the coffee not being left in the right place, a designated mug going missing, any minuscule change in the set up, and the whole barrage of questions would start up again. A bunch of visitors was an absolute nightmare. Some people actually liked the Mark 5, but they tended to be ultra-organized types whose lives were as controlled and repetitive as the Mark 5 itself. His report on that one was damning and, even by his standards, brief.

Droidco overcompensated when they launched the Mark 6. It would hardly wait for the instruction to leave your lips, then it'd scoot off, barge around, never consult you on anything. If you asked it to clear the floor, you'd return to find the room cleared, bereft of everything, like you'd called in a removal team. If you asked her to walk the dog, the poor animal, unless you specified a limit, would get a 10 mile speed hike, no pausing to sniff or lift a leg. If you told her to wash your clothes, she would: she would wash every item of clothing she could find. Too bad about dry-clean only, your best suit, the new shirt that was still in the packet. The Mark 6 didn't pester you to death, but, unless you were very careful and very precise about limits, it would, with great verve, enthusiasm and unerring logic, destroy everything you owned. The Mark 7, the current model, was well-balanced, functional and dull. It did chores in moderation and only when asked, but it did so half-heartedly, slowly, without enthusiasm or feeling. Andy's report summed it up as 'the perfect appliance for the consumer in need of a drudge'. Despite its shortcomings, he much preferred the enthusiasm, determination and what-now thrill of the Mark 6.

Andy could hear the noise of the kettle boiling from the kitchen and the sound of cupboard doors and clunks on the counter. He'd given her a minute, perhaps it was time to see how she was doing.

"Find everything?" he said, peering through the door.

"Yes, fine," she said, with an obliging smile.

Andy had forgotten just how bad the kitchen was. His first instinct was to feel embarrassed, then he reminded himself, yet again, that she was merely a droid.

"May I have a glass of water—if you don't mind," she said, handing over his coffee.

"Oh, yeah, sorry! I should've said ..." He cut short the apology. There he was again, apologizing to a droid. "You use water?" he asked, business-like, trying to regain distance.

"Yes," she said.

Andy looked at her. "Maybe you'd give me a rough idea why—without getting too technical."

"It's okay for me to say?" she asked, looking concerned. Andy shrugged and said, "Yeah, go ahead. I've got Bugwatch. It's just you and me."

"Some of my functions—my eyes, cooling systems, hydraulics—use water. I come with a minimal supply, but I've a reservoir that's best kept topped up."

"Fine—okay," said Andy nodding. Any droid he'd known was topped up via a little refill cap, usually somewhere between the neck and the shoulder or behind a service panel on the chest. This one was more natural. Must have a mechanism that separates the ventilation and speech from the refill duct.

"No problem. I can stretch to water. But if I find any snack bars are missing," he joked, "I'll know where to come looking!"

"Actually," she said, anxiety in her stance, "although I don't need anything right now, I will have to eat eventually. I use a series of catalysts and chemical processes to extract energy and materials for my maintenance system."

"Maintenance system?"

"Yes! Nano-nutrition. As long as I eat reasonably regularly my nanodistrib unit will keep me topped up, not just with energy, but with all the elements and compounds I need for my maintenance cycle."

"Wow!" said Andy, letting his mug down heavily on the counter. He closed his eyes and pressed his fingers to his forehead as he struggled to let this sink in. "So ... you need food. Effectively you eat like a human. The food's like your source of energy and your basic materials for repairs, just like we need our carbs and our proteins. Geez, that—that really is something."

"Yes, it is," she said, a note of concern in her voice. "You weren't aware that I required food?"

Andy didn't seem to hear. He just stood there, massaging his brow with his hand, running through the significance of what she'd said. If she got the right diet she'd just keep going indefinitely. He shrugged to himself. Why not? The dissembler breaks the food down into its constituent atoms, the assemblers stick them together to make any material she needs. The separate processes are done every day in nano-recycling and manufacturing; the genius was in the miniaturization and the combination into one self-contained system.

"The amount of food I need will be minimal," Dorothea continued. "In fact I can eat leftovers and even some non-food products as long as I can break them down, and they're not corrosive or physically damaging ..." She hesitated, watching for Andy to break out of his troubled stance, but Andy was deep in thought.

Of course—it made perfect sense! She must have inherited that from the spydroid development programme. Out in the field, you wouldn't want your spydroid looking for an electric docking point every night. Bit of a giveaway that. As would topping up the hydraulics and ordering up spare parts.

He could just see it. 'Excuse me, Mr Nasty Terrorist Dictator, Sir, but my 10K service is due. Won't be long, just teeth floss, coolant top up, and anti-virus upgrade. Now, while I'm gone, no regime changing and no firing weapons of mass destruction—do you hear!'

Up until now, spydroid infiltration, despite its amazing potential, had been severely limited by the problem of keeping them running ... but this ... The whole thing must've cost a fortune.

"However," said Dorothea, as Andy broke from his thoughts, "if providing me with food is a problem, perhaps you should consult the distributor. They may offer a refund."

"Eh?" said Andy, puzzled. "A refund?"

"I was just saying that I can eat a wide range of things—even leftovers, scraps, but, if that's a problem, perhaps you could apply for a refund."

"No, no ..." said Andy, jovial, slapping a hand against her arm, trying not to feel like a real heel. "I can feed you, no problem. I was just thinking that you're—I mean this is a real leap forward ... in terms of droids. Light years ahead. Way ahead of anything I'd expect. Sorry, yeah ..."

He frowned. Dammit! There he goes again: feeling awkward. You don't feel embarrassed when you deal with a fridge, or a digiview, or a computer. So why feel embarrassed now? She was just a piece of high-tech equipment. He glanced at her, she looked away, and then he realized. It wasn't just him. She acted like she was feeling it too, the awkward gaps, the tentative but unsuccessful attempts at conversation. If she were to beam back at him with a big breezy smile, all robust and impervious, he could go ahead and treat her as a thing, a soulless object, technology on legs. The skin, the eating thing, the intelligence, massive advances though they may be, were just the tip of the iceberg. There was something different about her, something infinitely more important. Subtle character traits, vulnerability, empathy, emotion-laced logic, whatever it was, it was darned effective. She was playing on him, making him feel cautious, protective, see her as weak and feel that she needed him. Clever, very clever. Exactly what a droid would need if isolated and alone on enemy ground. Still, she was a droid. A clever droid, but a droid. Get that into your head, Andy. Droid, droid, droid, droid, droid, droid. He squinted at her through narrowed eyes.

"Right, Dorothea!" he said, picking up his mug. "Come through to the living room. We need to talk."

By three-thirty, Diana had arrived at Andy's. The visit had been okay; awkward, but okay. She'd gone hoping he wouldn't be in, but he was. So she kept it brief, gulped her tea knowing that the longer she stayed the more she learned, and that the more she learned the more Hannah would have to pick over. With deep misgivings, she returned to Techdomestic. A securidroid intercepted her in the foyer and, with droid implacability, escorted her to the seventh floor.

The weather had changed. Diana slowed to let the droid beach guide get ahead. She stopped, breathed deeply and felt salt-air scurrying past, pressing her clothes to her body. She scanned the sky. The sun was lower now, like early evening. She'd never studied enviro functioning and she didn't wanted to now. It would be hard to believe, to appreciate with your mind distracted by the technical gubbins making it work. But she couldn't ignore the practical implications. How many Pacific islands were suitable for enviro cloning anyway? Must do some kind of buffering, adjustments for time difference, limits. Headline: 'Admin Wrecked Freak Hurricane!'—didn't seem likely.

"Diana!" gushed Hannah, beneath the billowing canopy. Her finger slid across a control menu on the desk. The noise of wind and sea fell to barely audible, the pervasive, ebb and flow of the water and weather was quelled. It seemed empty, as if something had died.

"Getting a little blustery," said Hannah, nodding. "Don't want you straining to talk." She was too still, the smile too fixed. Diana sensed that she was struggling to hold back, that she'd have preferred Diana to talk without her having to ask.

"Manage okay?"

"Yes, thanks," said Diana, settling into her seat. She smiled and waited, forcing Hannah to make the next move.

"Well," smiled Hannah. "Did you see him?"

"Yes, he's fine."

"You didn't stay long."

"No. No real need. As I said. He was just fine—normal, normal as Andy gets."

Hannah's lips were tight, a twisted rosebud, slightly off-centre. This wasn't what she wanted. She raised her chin, looked serious, pushed for more.

"It's just—well ... he's such a solitary soul. I thought a bit of company might have done him some good."

"Actually, he ..." and Diana faltered, cursed herself. She'd come determined to offer nothing, to answer what was asked, not one iota more.

"Yes?" said Hannah. "He ...?"

Diana lowered her focus onto her lap. Silence. She looked up to find Hannah focusing intently on her, prepared, unashamedly, to push the embarrassment home.

"He ... he had company, that's all. Just a neighbour. I didn't like to intrude."

"Oh!" said Hannah, arching forward, animated. "That's nice. A neighbour—Good, good! Still socializing!" Tensed, smile fixed, professional. Hannah had taken on the manner of a dentist bearing down on a patient.

"Yes," said Diana with a curt smile. She wanted to end it there, she sought a diversion and, unashamedly, asked if there was any possibility of that excellent floor 7 coffee. The periphery of putting in the order, the tray arriving, the ritual, gave her a few minutes to think.

What on earth was Hannah up to? Was she building a case against Andy, stringing him up for wasting company time. Surely she didn't need this kind of stuff. Andy provided all the ammunition anyone would need. Then again, could be they've given him some kind of ultimatum. Could be shape-up or ship-out. Whatever was going on, she had to tread carefully. She made as much fuss about the coffee as she could and introduced what she hoped was diversionary conversation. Eventually, she had to stop; she dabbed the corner of her mouth with a napkin.

"Male ... female?" pressed Hannah, eyes glinting with impatience.

"Pardon?" said Diana, though she knew full well what was asked. Hannah stared; it didn't merit a response. "Female," said Diana, softly.

"Did they look like they were getting on okay?"

"Actually," said Diana, "he looked like he was working. She looked like she was borrowing a screw driver. She's from the flat down below. Brief visit."

"Of course. And her name?"

"Sorry?" said Diana.

"Her name?" repeated Hannah, tetchy, diplomacy wearing thin.

"Oh, her name! Victoria, I think she said. He barely knows her. She's new in the block, in fact most of her stuff hasn't arrived."

"Ah," said Hannah, nodding, as though somehow this made perfect sense. "And what was she like?"

"Like?"

"This Victoria. A nice, normal girl I hope ..."

"We barely met."

"Yes, but surely you got an impression."

"She seemed okay. Why?"

"I wouldn't like Andy to get hurt—not like ..."

"No, I understand," said Diana, unconvinced. "Well, from the few minutes we chatted, I'd say she was nice enough. Sympathetic, well mannered. Quiet—I think she was tired."

"Tired?" said Hannah, arching a brow.

"Yes, tired."

"When you say 'tired', what exactly do you mean?"

"I don't know. The way she spoke, she seemed ... she wasn't keen to talk."

"I see," nodded Hannah, satisfied with the answer.

Diana sighed inwardly, wary of the cat and mouse. Somehow, despite her best efforts, she seemed to be providing Hannah with what she needed. Maybe she should be ambivalent, vague. Perhaps that would be best.

"I could be mistaken. Maybe she was just shy. Does it really matter?" Her eyes wandered. The light was fading, the fluttering cotton canopy had taken on a warm glow. She imagined being out there, the sinking sun and the breeze. She dearly wanted to be alone, find a spot in the dunes, sit, sit and think, hug her knees to her chin.

"I see ..." pondered Hannah. She was leaning back in her chair, finger tips touching and rearranging her pearl necklace.

Diana drew her eyes away from the rippling canvas, let them settle on the big glass plinth that was Hannah's desk.

"Did Andy say anything about her, about Victoria?"

"Not much. He mentioned they'd only met this morning." Hannah paused, nodding.

"Did she say anything to Andy?"

"No. I think Andy was pretty busy—wanting to get back to his work I guess."

"Mmmm ..." responded Hannah with a sceptical narrowing of her eyes.

"And she, what did she say?"

"Hardly anything. She was only there a few minutes. She went out just after I arrived."

Hannah froze as if she'd been skewered, a steel rod rammed into her back.

"Out?" she snapped. "What do you mean 'out'?"

Diana shrunk back in confusion. What was wrong with going out?

Hannah's eyes, dark-rimmed and narrowed, locked on.

"Just to a shop ... a shop along the road."

Hannah threw her head back, closed her eyes, inhaled deeply. For almost a minute, there was nothing, just Hannah hyperventilating and the distant, almost inaudible shush, shush as the waves rolled into the beach.

Slowly, like a demon awakening, Hannah's head levelled and her eyes, burning, opened accusingly on Diana.

"You couldn't have got this wrong could you? You are sure ... you are absolutely sure?"

"Well ... I didn't actually see her going out."

"Ah," said Hannah, tilting her chair back. "So she might have said she was going out but not actually have gone."

"Well ... perhaps."

"Andy went with her to the door?"

"Yes."

"And then what?"

"He called something after her ... 'Milk'. He asked her to get him some milk."

"But she might not have been outside. It might have been a pretence."

Diana hesitated. What was she supposed to say? It occurred to her that Hannah might be insane.

"You're holding back, Diana. Tell me. I HAVE to know."

Diana stared away and felt empty, her body a sack of bones slung in the canvas curve of the chair. Anyone with a heart would have eased off, but this was Hannah. What Hannah wanted, Hannah got.

"Well ... I heard her calling back. She said 'Okay'. There was an echo, she must have been down at least one flight. There were her footsteps, a door slammed—"

Hannah stood up and started pacing back and forth, her arms crossed.

"There wasn't a problem," said Diana. Hannah stopped and stared, oblivious, face as frozen and cold as if had been carved out of marble. "She was just fetching a few items. They were getting on fine—really. Andy gave her directions. She said she was going for some bleach and she ..."

Hannah's eyes flickered. She looked at Diana.

"Go," she said in a flat voice.

"If there's anything I can do ..." said Diana.

"Just go!" said Hannah.

Diana gathered herself up and walked towards the exit. She pulled back the canvas and stepped out into a cool surge of air and an expanse of sand recently washed by the tide. The sky was red now and the ocean on fire. With brooding remorse she strode back to the lift.

Chapter 7 Friday

Ludd's eyes watched with acid disdain. A fallen star, neon pink, scuffed and defiled, lay abandoned on the floor. The amazing offer it once heralded had expired. It was worthless, curled and distorted, a putrefied starfish.

It had been on the floor a few days now, trapped in a corner, but now it was lying in the main thoroughfare. Ludd had watched its progress, with dull-eyed disparity. It had vaguely registered that, face down, sticky tab up, it might attach itself to someone's foot, be carried outside. It would save him the trouble of picking it up. However, with every day it lay there the chances of attaching itself deteriorated. The shop floor and the scuffing feet were degrading the stickiness; soon no trace of adhesive would remain. Ludd considered it morosely and twisted the sparse hairs on his chin.

"A tenner it lasts the day," he called. Vince, breaking off from serving a virt-raddled geek, followed Ludd's eyes and appraised the bereft star.

"Twenty," said Vince, "so long as I can raise you tomorrow."

Ludd stared, pasty-skinned, imperious.

"Done," he said, spitting into his palm and holding it up. Vince sniggered a dirty laugh, and, spitting into his own, slapped it hard down on Ludd's meaty pad. Ludd's Asian lady customer turned away with revulsion.

He looked past her, scowling at glassy-eyed virts and tetchy reals. Maybe he should stay at the counter for his break, send Vince through for a coffee. He wouldn't put it past Vince to help the star out the door the minute his back was turned. He could really do with a fag. Closing his eyes, he cursed and moved his heavy haunches on his seat.

The phone rang, Ludd didn't register. Vince snatched. "Wise Buy—Yup ... Uh huh. Yes ma'am. No, he's busy. I can deal with it. There's no need ... Look, if you just give me your vidcam number ..."

Ludd, without turning his head, held out his hand for the receiver. Vince clung on to it for a moment, eyes defiant, like a mongrel defending a bone. Finally, he conceded and passed it across.

"Huh," mumbled Ludd. "Already? Packed ... we need the memory wiped. Security wipe." Ludd put down the phone and pouted his lips in what might have been a kiss were it not for the sourness of his bristly mouth.

"Finished with it already ..." said Vince, eyes, fixed on Ludd.

"Still pays full whack," growled Ludd. He was uncomfortable, grim features a shade grimmer, scowl less upbeat than normal.

"Problem?" sniffed Vince.

"Freaked out. Liability."

"Typical! Typical!" said Vince, as the techno-geek he was serving, hair like an Afghan hound, drooped and deliberated over an audio upgrade.

The part Ludd had been waiting for came through from the store; he took the Asian lady's payment and stared morosely as she snapped her handbag and left.

"Excuse me," came the confident voice of Ludd's next customer. The man, big, strong browed, with the air of one accustomed to getting attention, moved forwards and began a well-rounded request. "I wonder if you can help me. The problem is my autodrive. It's somewhat erratic. Now I could get it repaired at the dealer or I could buy a stand alone ..."

Ludd ignored him with practised ease. He turned to Vince.

"You hold the shop—I'll sort this in the office." Ludd ducked his head and pushed his way through the curtain of plastic strip on his way to the back shop.

"Excuse me," the man called in vain. Then he addressed Vince, brows working overtime, tone stroppy, but with a whiny edge. "I take it the lines are going to merge. You know I've been waiting forty minutes."

Vince leaned to the side so he could squint down the shop. In his queue, behind a big bumbly looking guy and a nerd was a smart city-suit female. She looked feisty, he liked feisty. In Ludd's queue—kids, a few guys, nothing to speak of.

"Nah!" he grinned, beady eyes squinting at the man. "No point."

The man began to argue, but, as Vince grinned bemusedly at the man's efforts to apply reasoning to the system, Ludd arrived back.

"Sorted?" Vince asked.

The man with the heavy brows interrupted. "Excuse me," he said. "I was just saying that ..."

Ludd twisted his mouth in a bitter grimace. Shoulders hunched, nostrils flared, he glowered at the offender with blood-hot eyes. Ludd was not a member of staff in the technological service industry, he was a warrior, a harbinger of death, a volatile psychopath who, at the slightest provocation, would wreck and destroy anything and everything to alleviate his hell-tormented soul.

"Sorry! You ... you go right ahead," said the customer, visibly shaken. "I'm happy to wait."

Ludd swung his big head a fraction towards Vince. "Sorted," he said. He jutted his bottom lip in dour appreciation and sniffed, as though trying to combat a nasal drip. "Pick up the goods this evening. I've taken that off the books. Permanently ... everything."

"You mean?" said Vince.

Ludd batted his eyes and, opening his big meaty fist, revealed a cigarette lighter. He glowered in the direction of the store room as if sniffing something unpleasant. "I think there could be a problem in the back office," he said. "Faulty drive." He paused for a second then picked up the phone. "Seth. Check the drives. Probably shorted. Check B-drive ... Believe me, it is B-drive. Yeah ... Chuck it out the back, don't want it smoking the place out?"

"Terrible!" chuckled Vince, "the past month's transactions, gone! Just like that. I'm crestfallen I am." And he gripped the edge of the counter and beamed delightedly across the shop as if the customers should all share in the joke. "How will we manage!" Jubilation cut short, he whipped round—a noise right behind them. The curtain rattled and Seth appeared.

"How'd you know it was B drive from out here?" said Seth "I was staring right at and it looked like it was C ... the smoke was drifting round the back."

"Ludd's psychic," said Vince. "The big man's friggin' psychic!"

Dorothea's fingers flitted in the air as she worked the menus. Andy had left her the Net, basic interfaces, sensory input and a screen.

She had no particular mission to complete. Any data could be relevant, there was no way of knowing. So she used the albatross method, randomly wandering, picking up whatever she happened upon: the Green Corn Dance used by native Americans, a status report on a Milwaukee 1969 Dodge Charger rebuild, a NARF blog written in Spanish, terms and conditions for an OptoMizer Lighting Audit System. Page after page, downloads, video clips, books, networks, whatever there was.

The screen flickered like a strobe light in the darkened room, a million views every ten minutes, each logged and stored and cross-referenced. It was subliminal, slotting into her memory but barely registering with her conscious thoughts. With her spare capacity she analysed live data she'd acquired that day, considered her mission, her purpose, her place in the wider structure. Most of Andy's instructions were about what not to do: don't draw the blinds, don't answer the phone, don't open the door. The rest was disconcertingly vague: 'Use the net, see what's going down, you can tell me what you found later.' He did, however ask her to find out how to keep milk fresh without a fridge. She was pleased to have something definite to do. In less than a second, she'd come up with three alternatives: use ultra-heat treatment (UHT), lower it into a cold mountain stream, keep it in the cow. On her own initiative, she researched and compiled a list of fridges to suit the space in the kitchen, should Andy opt to buy one.

Throughout her searching her sensory log kept running. It classified humans as priority 1, local communications as priority 2, immediate environmental conditions as priority 3, and social, political, cultural, technological and news items as priority 4. Everything else was logged as priority 5.

She was getting to know Andy. He was her only profiled human. Physical aspects were 80% complete. Everything from height to body odour had been sampled and recorded. Fast food wrappings in the bin, defrosting food, no cold food storage system; she'd marked him as gastronomic 2.7. In his psychological and social profiling there was still plenty to do. At first the criteria filled up steadily: 43.5% in the first hour. Then came the discrepancies. She'd taken the lack of references to other humans in areas such as belongings, audio-visual material, room layout or domestic provisions, to indicate limited family and social networking. Forensic evidence backed this up with scent, fingerprints and DNA showing little recent evidence of anyone but Andy. She'd allocated him a social rating of 3.3. Then, within a matter of 10 minutes, he had a visit from Victoria, a neighbour, whose audio she'd been tracking in the apartment below, and then someone called Diana, a work colleague in what, it seemed, was a semi-official call. She upgraded him to 6.2. An hour later the phone started ringing, stopped ringing, started again, stopped, started. Andy totally ignored it. Did he know who was calling and want to avoid them, was he reclusive? She was about to downgraded him to 4.8 when he announced he was going out to meet up with a friend. She'd decided to wait for more data before settling on a value. He hadn't said when he'd be back.

She tapped and processed and monitored as the light faded. It was late evening when the footsteps sounded outside.

She stopped typing and optimised her audio. Two men speaking. A van door. Footsteps moving towards the main security door.

'Naismith—that faded one, top left ... 4a.'

Andy's buzzer sounded. This she ignored, as Andy had instructed. A metallic sound, a grunt, the security door opening. Heavy steps in the stairwell, closer, closer, footsteps louder as they ascended the stairs. Breathing outside Andy's door. The buzzer sounding again.

She did nothing. 'You're not here. No answering the phone—or the door. Keep away from the window.' He said he'd explain later. She'd accepted that without question. Now, it seemed important to know.

Visitors, but what kind of visitors. They hadn't known where he lived and they'd referred to him by his surname, so they were unlikely to be friends. They'd used some sort of bypass system to get through the security door—possibly illegal. The snippets of conversation between them were business-like, serious. They pounded on the door a couple of times then one of them used a mobile. She tapped into the call.

"Yeah?" the person answered.

"We're here. Nobody home. Quiet as a morgue," said one of the men at the door.

"Sure you've got the right place?"

"Yeah. Right street, right number, name on the door. Should we go in anyway? We could pick up the goods and ..."

"Are you crazy! You can't just break in and lift it. Better get back. We'll have to check what went wrong."

"You're calling the shots, mate. Whatever you say." More shuffling, doors banging, then the van bustling off along the empty city street.

Careful not to be seen, she watched their departure through the slats in the blinds then went over and sat at the desk for a while. The event had triggered several trains of thought.

The obvious questions, 'who they were' and 'what had they come for', were top of her list.

First of all 'who'. She'd already tracked the call, knew the mobile numbers, the phone models, their IMEI codes, the telcos who issued the SIM card. Now it was just a matter of checking the databases. So that nothing traceable was sent through Andy's optics, she set up her own wireless link. The phones and SIM cards first. She got the companies okay, but both phones were unregistered. The SIMs were PAYGO and also unregistered. Nothing. She sighed.

Next, the vehicle. She scanned her memory for the registration, paused whilst she set in motion a back door link into the massive bank of DVLA records. The vehicle was registered to a Mr J Gunning, proprietor, Clacton Rentals, Exmouth industrial estate, unit 7. She tapped the company name into the Net. Strangely, no telephone number, no company profile, no entries in vehicle hire listings. Anyone could have rented it. Another dead end. She felt a little unsettled. Perhaps this was normal, perhaps these methods weren't as effective as sources made out. In any case, Andy probably knew exactly what was going on. She frowned. She'd mention it when he got back.

The next big issue wasn't about the men or about Andy, it was about her. The incident had taken her by surprise, but she had reacted swiftly and without consultation. No need to seek advice. It was instinctive, inbuilt. Data, procedures, sensors and faculties, many she wasn't aware off, had kicked in as the situation evolved. That was what was bothering her. Why were these things there? That she was able to speak, to communicate, to use body language, was necessary and not in the least surprising, neither were human support functions like preparing food, organizing clothing and so on. But the abilities she'd just used, the phone tapping, the hacking into databases, the stealth techniques, where did they fit in to her life?

She'd gathered a substantial amount of general data, now she focused on droids. Droids were widespread. You could order them online, check their specifications, see how they fared on review centres or watch videos; the most highly rated showed them doing stupid things. One thing was somewhat puzzling: although expensive and sought after, droids fell short of human needs and expectations.

Perhaps she too was a disappointment, perhaps that's why Andy had disappeared. He said he'd liked the coffee, but he'd seemed troubled. He said he'd tell her about her role, why she was there, yet he seemed reluctant to talk about it. Humans were difficult to read. Why introduce a topic that you'd rather not talk about? Perhaps he'd said that as a trigger. She had the ability to deduce and respond and decide. This could be her first challenge. Andy had raised the issue then left her here alone with the Net. Her first real task could be to use her deductive and reasoning powers to understand not only the world, but herself. Of course! It made perfect sense. She needed to understand both. How else could she integrate and functional fully?

Her expression brightened, she knew exactly what she should do.

Chapter 8 Saturday

The 'Billiard Club' lay still and defensive in the chill morning sun. Solid and low-ceilinged, a leather saddle sat next to a pith hat, campaign medals faced an animal hide shield, a clutter of Victorian bric-a-brac barricaded the windows. The once mighty empire was now a gastro-pub theme.

When it was quiet, as it was now, the musty collection and hushed ambiance worked well. A group of tourists tucked into their 'full English' whilst a scattering of regulars, like bit-part actors, sank into seats, read papers and snoozed.

Behind the bar, in a beige safari dress, a girl busied herself polishing glasses. She checked with a keen eye, cleaned and racked them overhead, bobbing down, stretching up, nimble on the well-trodden boards.

Andy, amidst a surge of rush hour clamour, pushed through the door and ambled over to the bar.

"Bruce around?"

The girl pulled herself up for more height and leaned forwards to see past the ice buckets, her focus finally settling on the swing doors that led to the billiard room.

"He's probably through there." She nodded her head. "Veranda's your best bet. It's straight through, then to your left."

Andy nodded, stuck his hands in his pocket, made to go, but stopped and turned back to the bar.

"When you're not busy, could you fix me a latte?"

"Regular, large?" she said.

"Large, and could you float a chocolate flake on top."

"I'm not sure a flake will float."

"It can be done alright. Takes practice. Just keep adding them, eventually you'll get it to work."

She gave him a dubious look. "I'll see what I can do."

It took Andy a few minutes to adjust to the onslaught of light.

"Now, we're entering the natural habitat," said Andy in a hushed, wildlife reporter voice, "of the lesser-freckled Aussie."

"Give over," said Bruce, without opening his eyes. He lay, languid and sun-drenched, on a fully-extended steamer chair. Clumps of jungle plants, palms, ferns, creepers, lurked in corners. Big slow fans stirred the air.

Bruce had his own variation on British Officer dress. His stone-washed cotton and desert boots swung more towards desert rat than officer elite.

"They pay you to do this?" said Andy.

"Yup!" said Bruce, with a grin. "Beats the hell out of working." His eyes looked sleepy. Stretching a golden-haired arm up, he massaged the back of his neck then, with an effort, twisted round to check a clock—Victorian, ex-railway, an ambient energy-powered reproduction. He opened his eyelids a crack and rolled his head towards Andy. "You're early. Locked out?"

"Might as well be," said Andy easing himself onto another chair that lay slightly askew and a few-feet further along the parquet-tiled floor. "Boss is on a manhunt, or should I say 'Andy hunt'? Laying low."

"You camped out last night."

"Yeah. How'd you guess?"

Bruce made a harrumphing sound. "You're here before 11."

"Ok ..." admitted Andy. "Obvious."

Bruce raised an eyebrow. "Why don't you just rent out the flat?"

"Maybe I should." Andy considered the suggestion for a moment, then squinted his eyes. "Actually, I like the flat; I've got it set it up the way I want—no junk, it could even pass as minimalist. Abstract art, a few big, graphic pieces, nothing fussy, guitar ... and clear open space. The absolute basics. No IoT kit, that's for sure. I've never understood why people flog their life to the corporations?"

"They are told what happens to their data," said Bruce. "I guess they don't care."

"Hah! Told? Told as in told the truth!" said Andy. Then, mimicking the regulatory line at the end of every IoT web ad, he put on a sassy, you've-got-it-sorted, voice: "'Your data may be shared with carefully selected grave robbers, pimps and blackmailers. Terms and conditions apply.'"

"Is that the new 'transparent, above-board, ethical' version they've been talking about," said Bruce. "Anyhow, the problem isn't the flat..."

"No, the flat itself is fine ... it's life that's the problem ... it's too complicated. Work schedules, bill payment cycles, registrations, feeds, servicing programmes, renewals. It feels like I'm drowning in a sea of itsy-bitsy, pointless tasks that suck every ounce of motivation out of me."

"I didn't know you had any motivation to suck out," yawned Bruce.

"Look who's talking. Don't strain yourself reaching for that cup. As I was saying ... up on the roof I ditch all that. It's just me and the sky."

"And the hammock."

"And the hammock."

"And the rechargeable space blanket."

"And the rechargeable space blanket."

"And those old discs."

"The valuable late 20th - early 21st century CD collection, if you don't mind!

"And the crate of whisky."

"Okay, okay! And the odd bottle of Scotch. You know what I mean, Bruce! When I'm up there, I can forget all that whiny, update-me, hand over-your-data, stuff. It's just me, the sky, and empty space. I could get up and walk away and never look back. I feel like I can get out. It's like ... a kind of departure lounge."

"Departure lounge?"

"Yeah."

A silence grew between them. Bruce gazed up lazily at the ceiling fan. "Last time I flew, I could barely fight my way through the departure lounge there were so much merchandise in the way."

Andy, eyes closed, began breathing more quietly. Neither spoke for a while. There was no need.

Andy lifted his feet up and adjusted the cushion behind his head. "You know I could get used to this. If you ever find this gets too much for you." Bruce laughed and cleared his throat.

"Long hours, Andy. Very long hours. Just keeping my head above water."

At that moment the girl from the bar came through. She set the latte down over to one side, brought a table over next to Andy's chair, then placed the drink at his elbow. Straightening, she hovered, looking towards Bruce.

"Coping?" she said.

"Just about."

"Everything okay on the front line?" he said. "Natives behaving themselves?"

"Very quiet."

"Aha!" he said with a magnanimous sweep of his hand. "Don't let that fool you. There could be an uprising at any time. One minute it's clear to the horizon, next minute a coach arrives and they're six deep at the bar. By the way, Rowan, this is Andy, Andy—Rowan. He's hiding from work. His boss is after him. Don't let anyone know he's here."

"Hi Andy," she laughed. She gave a little wave, then she was gone, her bob swinging out as she made a brisk turn and went through to the bar.

"Boy, have you got it made!" said Andy. "Waited on hand and foot—free food and drink—delightful company."

"Delightful company? I hope you're not referring to yourself."

"I was talking about her, the new girl. Seems nice."

"She's what's known as an employee, Andy. A person with feelings and ideals and who happens to work here. You've probably forgotten about that concept. It's old-fashioned, I know, but before robots took over the world, that's what people did. There were people and there was work and the people and the work got together ..."

"Yeah, yeah, yeah ..." said Andy, waving away Bruce's rant. "Like you know about work. Hail, Bruce! Defender of the working man. The patron saint of slave drivers, selfless dedication to keeping others gainfully employed. Personally I'd much rather have a machine than some subjugated human."

Bruce retaliated, Andy argued his point. Eventually, Bruce laughed and reached into the chest pocket of his shirt for a phone.

"Rowan, if you're not busy, could you pop through here and settle an argument"

She appeared, smiling, a few moments later.

"Rowan. I want you to answer honestly. I want you to forget for the moment that I'm a slave-driver. Okay?"

"Certainly, Mister Conlon."

Andy laughed.

"Don't hold back, Rowan. Go right ahead. Tell him what it's like being bossed around ..."

"Whoaa!" said Bruce. "You're tampering with the unbiased third party. Let her make up her own mind!"

Rowan appeared bemused as they bickered over who should ask the first question. Bruce pulled out an old penny. Andy called. Bruce tossed and won.

"Okay," he said, "I want you to imagine that I came in one morning and announced that I was going to give you the sack—instead I was going to get in a droid to serve in the bar. How'd you feel about that?"

"Well ... obviously, I'd not be too happy. I'd miss the work and the money and ..." she paused and wrinkled her nose. "And I'd feel, I suppose, that the work I'd been doing hadn't been valued."

"Exactly," said Bruce, snatching at the air as though trying to hold onto her answer.

"Wait! Wait! Wait! ..." said Andy, "that's just one side of it. Forget that just now. Clear your mind and tell me—how do you feel about Bruce here ordering you about? Don't you feel that it isn't quite right that he gets to lie around here while you do all the chores? I know there's money involved, but you've got to admit, this is, in a way, a mild form of slavery."

"Hey! You're telling her what to think. Ask her a straight question or don't ask at all." Bruce winked at Rowan, making out he was trying to protect her. She smiled back and waited for Andy, now stalled in his line of argument.

"Okay, let's put it this way. You could have someone come to your house, clean up, do your washing, all the menial stuff, or you could get a droid to do it. Imagine yourself, at home. You've got to go one way or the other. You're too busy to do all the stuff yourself. What would you do?"

Rowan tilted her head to one side, concentrated, then looked over at Andy.

"Is this a long term arrangement?"

"Yeah, let's say it's long-term," said Andy.

"I think I'd get a person in to help. You can relate to a person more easily ... I guess. Actually," she said, as if beginning to understand it herself. "It'd depend on how the person felt. If they were happy in their work, I'd much rather have a person; if they kind of trudged in and looked like they hated it, I'd consider the droid. But if they were pretty much the same and the only difference was the droid/human factor, human ... definitely."

"Excellent!" said Bruce. "Look out for a bonus at the end of the month." She grinned then moved towards the door.

"The customers," she said, making her excuse. "Better see if anybody is needing something, oh master." She bowed to Bruce in mock deference, and, as she rose, threw a got-to-humour-him look towards Andy.

"Be gone!" boomed Bruce, legs wide, basking in the watery midwinter sun, and then, in a French accent he announced 'un point', licked his finger and marked up his victory on an invisible score board.

"Okay, but you're on home ground," retorted Andy. "How am I supposed to win in a zero-tech stronghold? Anybody who works here is biased right from the start."

"Life's tough," said Bruce. "Anyway, you're beginning to sound like you've gone pro—strange coming for a foam-at-the-mouth phobo." Bruce eased himself back on the recliner and stretched his legs in turn. "Can't figure you, Andy, how can you work for them." They sat quietly for a while staring glumly at the blinds.

"You might not get away with this any longer," said Andy, in a low, despondent tone.

"Jealousy!" said Bruce, breezy. "I'm doing fine. The owners couldn't care less. As long as the cash keeps pouring in, I'm as solid as old Kitchener's whiskers." At the far end of the veranda, a framed poster of the British commander in chief glowered down with manic intensity. "Anyhow, look at you!

Getting paid to play with the latest gizmos. Don't come the workaholic with me. You've got a cushy number yourself."

Andy held back. This wasn't something he could lay on his friends. Just knowing about a class 3 would put Bruce on the spot. It would leave him two choices: either turn Andy in, which of course he wouldn't, or become complicit, guilty of the concealment of unlicensed AI and of undermining national security. If the shit really hit the fan, Andy could be mind-ripped and every memory, every conversation, including what he told Bruce, would be trawled over in court. He sipped his latte and stared straight ahead.

"You okay?"

"Yeah. Tired. Didn't sleep that well."

"You ought to try sleeping in a bed, a roof over your head. Geez! It's the middle of winter! I'm surprised you haven't frozen to death."

"Maybe that'll be my way. Glass of whisky, the stars, not a bad way to go."

"Probably be cloudy," yawned Bruce. "You know what it's like."

Excitement and anxiety were vying in Dorothea's mind.

"Everything okay?" said Andy flinging his jacket through the bedroom door.

"You missed seventeen phone calls."

"But you didn't pick up."

"No."

"Good. It'll be Hannah. Keep ignoring them."

"And two men called yesterday evening."

"Two men ... You didn't answer?"

"No."

"Good. Did they leave a card?"

"No, nothing."

Andy stopped in the middle of the hall. "It's all Hannah. She just doesn't know when to give up. Unbelievable! She must've sent round some guys from the work. You know when Diana came ... the woman who came with the hamper?"

"When the doorbell rang, I went through to the bedroom. You told me to keep out of ...."

"Yeah, anyhow ... you heard her. That was no social call. She was sent. Hannah, my boss, she's trying to keep tabs on me."

"How can you be so sure? Maybe she just wanted you to get a nice surprise!"

"Hah! I don't think so. The last Friday of the month, two hours to deadline, Techdomestic's in chaos. Are you trying to tell me that Diana ditched the zillion and one last minute things before launch and went: 'Hold everything! Stop! That Naismith guy won the absentee-of-the-month hamper. And you know what? This tin of ham's only got six months left on the label. Screw the deadline, screw the formatting, screw the editing. I've got to get that hamper to Andy right now'." He gave a hollow laugh. "Goodwill missions to Andy Naismith. Geez. Diana hasn't spoken to me for about a year, and she ain't after my body. Hmmm. Why was I top of Diana's to-do-list? She was forced, that's why. You could see it in her eyes. Hannah had the frighteners on her."

"The men who called didn't appear to know you."

"They didn't? Probably newbies—guys who've only been with us a few years. I'm a rare sighting at Techdomestic since I got my get-out-of-work-free card. The lesser-spotted Naismith, occasional winter visitor."

"Well, okay. I just thought you should know," she said. "There was one other thing. My position—I could do with knowing what I'm supposed to do."

"Yeah, okay. Look, I'll have a shower. Why don't you fix me a coffee."

"Let's grab a seat," said Andy, rubbing his hair with a towel, steam tumbling into the hall through the bathroom door. Dorothea followed him into the lounge, set his coffee on the window ledge and sat, upright and tense, on the sofa. Andy perched himself on a stool next to the window, took a gulp of his coffee and fastened the buckle of his belt.

How should he begin. Should he just give her a list of instructions like she was class 1 or class 2, or aim higher, have a two way discussion, a kind of droid-human heart to heart. No, forget heart to heart. Too messy. He gave his hair another quick ruffle and resolved to stick to the basics.

"The situation here is ... a little delicate," he began, glancing across. She looked tentative.

"First thing, you're not official. Don't go calling product registration or request updates or hand over contact details. Don't tell anyone that you are a droid or use any powers or comms or stuff that might cause suspicion. Generally, you don't tell anyone anything. If pressed, the story is that you're a web friend who happened to be in London for a few days. I don't know much about you, you don't know much about me—it was web-talk after all, the usual inanities. You're a bit shy. You don't like getting involved. Don't tell anyone anything about me or Hannah, or say anything to any visitors, or pass on anything you see or hear or learn about me, my associates or Techdomestic. Okay?"

"Okay." Dorothea took a sip from the glass of water she'd brought through.

"Andy?"

"Yes."

"Why am I unofficial?"

"It doesn't really matter. Stuff. Political, regulatory corpcrud." He took a slurp of coffee.

"Andy?"

"Yes?" She was sitting towards the front edge of her seat.

"I've got certain abilities that—well—that concern me. It's difficult for me to know when it's okay to use them when I don't understand my role."

Andy sighed. Why couldn't things be straight forward? He swallowed more coffee, unwrapped the chocolate biscuit that Dorothea had thoughtfully provided, and took a bite. He chewed then stopped.

"Okay. You're based on a military droid. That means you've got some extra bits. Surveillance stuff. I wouldn't worry about it."

"Military?"

"Yeah, military. It's not a problem."

"Actually, that does make sense. When the two men arrived, surveillance systems kicked in; I didn't even know I had them. They just happened. I'm not sure I can override them. They were triggered by my environment. I suppose I could try to ignore them."

"Okay—if you can, stay away from that stuff. See if there is a way to switch it off. You can erase the data can't you?"

"Yes, but what about the thoughts and ideas that spring up between me detecting something and erasing it? As soon as I know something it influences other things which in turn ..."

"Okay, okay, okay!" said Andy, holding up his hands. "Let's keep this a simple as possible. Just do your best to ignore them. If you do pick up stuff, try to pretend it didn't happen. Right. Any other questions before we move on?"

"Andy, will I get training?"

"No. Maybe later."

"But ..."

"Yes?"

"Don't military droids have the ability to kill?"

"Well—they kind of kill ... I suppose ... some of the time ... but only in very, very special circumstances—and not that often. Look I really don't think killing's going to be relevant."

"But, what if something happened, say a threatening situation arose, and some kind of inbuilt killing ability gets activated."

"Just do like I said for the surveillance stuff. Shut it down, ignore it."

"But if it happened automatically and I killed someone before I'd a chance to cancel—I don't think it would be appropriate to just pretend it didn't happen."

"Look, let me make it simple. You won't be in that kind of situation. If anything were to happen, don't kill anyone, okay! Just don't. Period. You get the urge or the trigger happens or whatever, you stamp on it right away. It's an absolute no-no. Understand?"

"No."

"What do you mean no?" remonstrated Andy. It was the first time a droid had ever defied him. He was stunned. Veins in the side of his neck started to throb.

"Sorry. I just mean that I don't understand," she said, sensing his shock. "I will try to follow your instructions to the very best of my ability but, without any background information or a full appreciation of what I am and my circumstances, I would be lying if I said I understood."

"Just hold it, will you." Feet flat on the floor, leaning forward, Andy clasped his hands and, gathering his thoughts, resolved yet again to get the job done fast, but resigned himself to filling in more detail.

"The basics—let's see. You might know some of this already," he muttered, brow furrowed. "There's a lot of this stuff on the net, tell me when I'm wasting my time. Okay?"

"Of course."

"A few years back, technology imploded. Big problem, two big problems, implants and androids. If it were just the one, it might've been okay, but they hit about the same time. People started getting spooked, questioning where technology was heading." He glanced up. She was still perched on the edge of her seat.

"You okay?" he said.

"Yes, fine—the water's nice," she said holding up a glass she'd fixed for herself.

"Anyway, there were problems. The implants affected people—some started acting like class one droids, others went mad. Generally, implants, the early ones, weren't a good move. Then there were the droids ... and the accidents. Some people got killed. Androids got a bad name." Andy's face twisted in a half smile, puzzlement showing through. "I'm not being callous, but humans are so darned illogical. Autodrive isn't infallible, cars crash every day of the week." He looked up and she nodded to show she was still with him. "They're responsible for a couple of hundred deaths a year, but there's no outcry, no major enquiry." He shrugged. "For some reason autodrive is seen as an acceptable risk. But when an android's responsible for a death, it's dealt with like homicide. Maybe it's something to do with androids looking like people. They'd never take a washing machine to court." Andy put on a pompous legal voice: "M'lord, the washing machine pleads innocent." He shook his head, grinning at the absurdity.

"Anyhow, the manufacturers and the androids ended up in court and there was a big hullabaloo. The press had a field day, the government couldn't ignore it, so they came up with legislation, tried to clarify the boundary between technology and humans. The upshot was droid classification. Class 1 droids, basic level, they only follow direct orders and geographically they're loosely restricted. Whoever gives the order is responsible for the resultant actions. Class-2 droids, they make decisions, mostly at a basic level, but they're restricted to one location, like within a home, or an office or a factory, stuff like that. Someone in the workplace, or home if it's a domestic, is responsible for running it and defining what it can do. They have to be licensed.

Then there are class-3s, like yourself. Class-3s make decisions and aren't restricted to a particular place. They do have a controller but they can be away from the controller for days, even months, working autonomously. They're pretty much illegal except for the military and intelligence services. Strict regulations prohibit anyone getting their hands on them. With them being autonomous and able to make decisions, and make mistakes, who's responsible when things go wrong? Society's not ready for decision-making droids loose wandering the streets. Class-3s are too close to humans, and too capable— I guess the bottom line is that humans don't trust anything that's too much like themselves."

"So I'm not permitted ..." she said, looking at Andy, perplexed, focusing on him intently.

"Don't worry—it's okay." Andy held up his hand in a placatory gesture. Slugging down some coffee, he wiped his mouth with the back of his hand.

"You want to know where you come into this, don't you?"

She mouthed 'yes', but it was barely audible.

"The military wanted the perfect spy. Human spies have one serious limitation: you can't design them specifically for the job. They're limited to human frailties, they can't be significantly improved on. How do you get ahead of the opposition when you can't upgrade your operators? If you use androids, 'spydroids', and made them realistic enough to pass as human, you can kit them out, upgrade them, design them to do anything you want. You could have them eavesdrop, not just on regular conversations, but on subsonic, ultrasonic and stuff that is too faint to be audible. You could fit them with telescopic and infra-red vision and have them pick up radio, microwave, TV, just about any kind of signal you could think off.

"If they were caught, you could have them self-destruct and erase everything. No point interrogating a melted lump of plastic. You could give them superhuman strength and endurance, the ability to withstand cold or heat, go underwater, travel in a depressurised aircraft hold, withstand radiation, hide them in a compartment for months at a time. Sleepers wait, sneak out just when you need them. You can use them for counter terrorism, even as assassins. You could even have them emulate other people, face, voice, hair, mannerisms, biometrics, the lot. Androids, if you could make them realistic enough, would be much more versatile than humans." Andy rubbed his fingers through his hair and looked up to meet her eyes.

"The question was: could anyone do it? Well, the military have budgets commercial companies can only dream of. The NA approached Armandroid, one of the smaller cybertechnic centres, but reckoned to be at the forefront, and financed a new high security plant. The military gave them the specs, resources, a pile of cash and a deadline. You're the result."

Andy stood up and walked over to the window. It was blustery. A bus passed at speed and the rush of air lashed the branches of a tree into a frenzy of motion. He scratched his waist-band and faced into the room.

"Sorry," he said, annoyed at himself. He'd already said more than he wanted. "You probably know most of this already."

"No, I didn't. Please ... do go on." She was staring at him, deadly serious. He found it unnerving.

Andy picked up his coffee and observed her for a moment over the top of the mug. He knew from experience that droids were good listeners. They could sit for hours without so much as a yawn. But experience also taught him that prolonged explanations didn't necessarily produce any return. They seemed happy to let their recording systems churn away and then, when you were finished, stick the file in some archive never to be opened again. He sensed Dorothea was different. Maybe it was just over-active body language, but she looked anxious, bereft, like some kind of pathetic orphan deprived of the anchor of knowing who she was or where she belonged.

What was this? He wasn't a history teacher, he wasn't a frigging counsellor. He looked over at her, at her searching eyes, at the tentative, hopeful, sensitive expression. Maybe he should tough it out. Tell her to stop looking all snively and give her something to do. He paced back to the window, put down the mug and glanced back. But that could mess up the review. He was squeezing into minutes an orientation process that should probably take days, maybe weeks. Having brought this fancy bit of AI into existence, could he deny her the basic requirement of knowing why she was there, expect her to blindly ping into action and perform to her full ability? That's class 2 level thinking, she had to be treated as a class 3.Like it or not, he would need to plough on. He continued but with less impatience.

"Armandroid, that's your parent company, they actually did it. They made the first android spies. At least that's what people say. Most of this is classified. Stuff on the net only lasts a day or two—blog and run. A team of NA security officers wipe military indiscretions, plug up leaks, try to find out who's responsible. They stonewall. 'Do you use droids in the Agency?' 'No.' 'But I just passed some droid cleaners on the way in.' 'You must've been mistaken.' That's what they're like.

"But people know! It'd be nice if they'd admit it. I suppose the way they see it is that if you give the press the basics they push for the next thing. Even if a piece of information's not strategic, it moves public knowledge one step closer to the stuff that actually matters. Anyhow, nobody's admitting what they have. A couple of droids were caught, but they self-destruct, nothing left but a charred shell. Quite a shock for the people who thought they knew them. One of the first ones was decked out as a delivery guy, another was standing in as a PA. "There's other stuff. A terrorist leader, Lee Chu, was, according to accounts, taken out by a spydroid. She, or should I say 'it', impersonated a female member of staff. Lee Chu, instead of a mid-day massage, got a mid-day strangulation. She walked out, bullets flying everywhere, guards, barriers, nothing stopped her. Apparently a car tried to ram her. She jumped, landed ten feet beyond it. She's probably on a beach somewhere sipping a Martini.

"There could be lots out there, going quietly along, soaking up information, reporting home. Who knows. Some people think they've replaced real people; face, voice, physique perfectly matched. Kinda spooky. Somebody you know, trust, maybe even love, turns out to be a droid. Anyhow, a new era of spying began. These would've been a model or two prior to yours. Near ancestors."

Andy winced. Technology! He found it hard to stop rambling on. He glanced at her to see how it had gone down. She was still looking at him, waiting. If anything, she was more concerned than before. Andy ran his fingers through his hair. He'd just told her she was descended from a bunch of self-destructing spies and assassins. What would that do for her esteem? Did she actually have esteem? What did esteem mean anyway?

He closed his eyes for a second. This was harder than he'd thought. Before, with other droids, it was just information, they weren't personally affected. He could only guess what this stuff meant to her, but, looking at her, it seemed it was hitting pretty deep. Maybe he should try to be more positive, upbeat. Give her some confidence. He wandered over to where

Dorothea was seated, sat up on the arm of the couch, casual, friendly, but not too near.

"So, Armandroid did it, developed some amazing spydroids. Problem was they'd neglected their traditional market. With all their R and D focused on spies, their domestic side was non-existent. The military are phobic about techno-obsolescence, so it was all short-term contracts. Armandroid had become dependent on a very volatile client. They needed to change strategy. Why not bring some of their class 3 developments over to the domestic market? Of course it would be quality, hi-end stuff—for the seriously rich, but at least they'd have something if the next military contract fell through." Andy walked over to close the door and then stood in front of her, his hands in his pockets.

"Obviously they planned to leave out the spy-specific features. You don't need an assassin wandering around in your kitchen—not unless you bring home a live turkey." Andy forced a laugh and looked to Dorothea for a smile. She drew back her lips, but it was more a grimace, perseverance rather than joy.

Andy bit his lip. Had he upset her feelings? Wait a minute. Feelings ... what feelings? Why couldn't he get this! She's just a droid. Andy rubbed the palms of his hands on his T-shirt. He was sweating.

"Anyway, their timing was mince. A Techalliance agreement limited the use of Class 3s to a few highly restricted areas: national security, nuclear or biohazard emergencies. Now the military had more than they could legally use. Armandroid was stuffed. Nobody's sure how far their spydroid-based domestic got. They were bought over by Droidactics. And that's where you come from."

Music, faint but clear, began filtering up from the floor below. Classical, it sounded like a cello.

"I'm not military?"

"No. Like I was saying. Based on military, but a domestic version."

"So why can I hear Victoria?"

"That's normal. I hear her too," said Andy. "She must play in an orchestra ... I guess."

"Can you hear her breathing, her heartbeat?"

"Er ... no. Can you?"

"Yes ... and that of an older man in the apartment across the hall. His is slightly irregular. I can also hear a woman across the street, a Mrs Jennifer Hill. She's trying to arrange transport for her daughter's wedding. The man she's talking to on the phone is called Charles. He's based in Huddersfield. His phone number is 01666 245 7619. I can hear a vehicle 1.85km away. It's approaching at 43km/h, slowing to 37km/h, now at 1.76km and veering, accelerating again, back up to 48.2km/h and 1.43km away ..."

"Okay! Stop!" said Andy. "Right—so your hearing's way better than mine ... That's not really a problem."

"But isn't it considerably better than what's required by a domestoid?" she said, her voice clear, unerring, the point impossible to skirt round.

"Yeah. Well. Looks like they might've left some of the sensory stuff in there. They probably figured it wouldn't do any harm—unless the owner's the town gossip." Andy grinned and shrugged.

She looked at him with a still, evaluating stare. He sensed that she could see through him, cut through his superficiality with a laser scalpel. He didn't like the feeling of being laid bare.

He was losing patience. What was this? Why was he pussyfooting around with a jumped up domestic appliance?

Droids were droids. Sophisticated or not. Glaring at her, he resolved to show her up for what she was. Emotional incongruity, that was the one. He'd get her on that. Droids were pretty good at body-language reciprocity. You smile, they smile back. You frown, they look concerned. Not quite mimicry, but the response is based on visual cues. Some of the more sophisticated class 2s recognize emotion in speech. She'll be more sophisticated yet, but, if she was like any droid he ever knew, she'd have to prioritize conflicting information: data content of speech came top, then visual cues, body-language, and finally tone, volume and intonation. If the first two agreed but the third didn't match, she'd simply ignore it. Emotion, as such, didn't really exist. The stuff he was seeing was just sophisticated feedback. All he needed was proof.

Casually, he walked over to the shelf, stood with his back to her, angled himself so she could only see the back of his head. Right, honey, let's see how good you are.

"You want to know why you are here?" he shouted, aiming for an angry, bawling, roar. He turned round to face her and gave as warm a smile as he good muster. That was the first set: dialogue neutral to positive, visual highly positive, tone highly negative. He faced away again. "You don't know, do you." he barked. "What a pleasure, what an amazing, out-of-this-world pleasure it is!" he yelled. He glanced back, she was looking at him, eyes wide, concerned—or was it confused. He gave her another cheery grin then turned away.

Combining hostile vocal tone with friendly body language was difficult. He threw her one last beaming smile and, pretending to find something of interest sauntered over to the bay window and, continuing to stroll, moved round the back of the couch till he was standing behind her. This made life easier. No visual clues. One last blast of innocuous dialogue delivered in a diabolical tone and he should have enough for a convincing result.

"I can tell you this," he snarled "answering your questions is an absolute JOY. Really—totally makes my day." He filled his lungs for one last blast. "What would I do without you? I REALLY DO NOT KNOW!"

Test over! Now for the results. Taking a moment to catch his breath after his vocal exertions, he peeked over her shoulder. To keep it fair he should see her without her seeing him, otherwise his current expression, whatever it was, could mess up the result. At Techdomestic they'd use a camera or a one way mirror, but, by leaning over he'd just about manage to observe her without being seen. He peered over. Slight technical difficulty: her head was tilted forwards making it difficult to see. But, so far the signs were good. No flare up, no break down, no whining or being offended. Gottcha he thought with a lop-sided grin. Didn't register the tone, did you girl. Good old emotional incongruity. Another human wannabe bites the dust. All he needed was to see her happy little face for the final confirmation.

"Dorothea?" he said. No response. He leaned over to one side. No use, her hair shrouded her face. Then he noticed something, a little spot, dark and severe on the grey of her skirt. Water, he thought, must have splashed some when she was drinking, coordination a bit out. Then he noticed a drop of water nestling on her lap, glistening, a little globule he hadn't noticed before. And, as he watched, he saw it shrink, soak in, making another dark spot appear. Strange how it had just been sitting there, hadn't soaked in earlier. Then he noticed a tremor in her shoulder—something wasn't right.

"Dorothea?" he said reaching out and gripping her shoulder. She looked up, eyes red-rimmed, water tracks on her cheeks.

"Hey, come on. I didn't mean it. It was just a stupid joke—a kind of drama role-play thing. If I sounded a bit harsh it was just ..."

The doorbell rang. Someone was out on the stairs.

"The door," she sniffled.

"It's okay. They'll go away." The bell rang again, and continued, long, demanding, forceful rings.

"It sounds urgent," she said, struggling to read him through watery eyes.

"Look, just forget the door," he said.

The caller, impatient, kept their finger hard on the button.

"I think it's Victoria from downstairs," breathed Dorothea.

"Look! I said forget the frigging door!"

The ringing stopped. Andy paused, felt relief. Then the pummelling started, fists drumming hard on the door panels. It stopped only to be replaced by loud yells. The pummelling started again.

"Don't move. Right! Just stay here."

Andy went out into the hall. The door was vibrating in its frame. He tiptoed over and looked through the spy hole. It was Victoria. He could see her stepping back and looking at the door.

"Open up!" she yelled. "Open up!"

Andy waited and watched, tried to suppress his own breathing.

"Okay, that's it. I'm phoning the police," she bawled. "I've got a phone here in my hand. Open up or I'm calling them right now!"

"Friggin hell!" blurted Andy. He closed his eyes, braced himself then pulled the bolt.

"What on earth are you up to?" she blurted, pushing past him.

"It's nothing..."

"Who were you shouting at?"

"I was just ... doing some drama. You know, pretending ..."

"Pretending?" She stared at Andy. "So there's no one else here."

"Yeah—Of course not," he remonstrated. "Just, me. Wait! Don't go in ..."

She marched past and through to the lounge. When Andy came through, she was already kneeling in front of Dorothea.

"It's alright ... it's alright," she was saying. She drew Andy a dirty look.

"I'm fine," Dorothea murmured.

"He has no right to shout at you like that," said Victoria in a firm but soothing voice. "That's abuse. You do not need to put up with it." Victoria stood up and, sliding onto the seat by her side, put an arm round her shoulders. Andy watched, guilty, moving uneasily from foot to foot.

"I didn't mean to upset her."

"You were yelling at her like a bloody maniac," she glared.

Andy looked sheepish and shifted awkwardly.

"Sorry," he muttered. "I didn't say anything nasty. It was just ... like ... a bit loud. Never know how loud I am."

"Okay. We'll talk about this later. What's her name?" breathed Victoria.

"Dorothea," said Andy, eyes down-turned, as if making a confession.

"And who is she?"

"She's ... just visiting for the weekend. We connected on web chat."

Victoria studied him for a second, sceptical, then turned her focus back to Dorothea.

"Dorothea!" she said quietly. "How would you like to come downstairs for a nice cup of tea ..."

"She'll be fine here," said Andy, a little too quick.

"Andy, I asked Dorothea! Dorothea—can you hear me?"

Dorothea looked at Victoria, faltered. Eyes questioning, she looked to Andy for approval.

"Dorothea. Look at me! I'm asking you. It's not up to him."

Dorothea looked down abruptly, confusion on her face.

"I'd better not," she said.

Victoria stood and came over to Andy. "She won't even leave the flat," she hissed. "What on earth have you been doing to her?"

"Nothing. She's—em ... she's free to go. She's just a bit shy!"

"Don't insult my intelligence! You've told her to stay here, haven't you? You're keeping her cooped up so you can intimidate her."

"Of course not!" He stared back, defiant, but it was hopeless. He was torpedoed below the waterline, sinking fast. Bedraggled and weary he crouched before Dorothea.

He had to drag the words out, force his lips to move and form the sounds that simply had to be said. His shell-shocked, flabbergasted brain was resisting like hell, screaming stuff like 'No!' and 'You idiot!' and 'What the hell are you saying?' But he said it anyway.

"Look! Why don't you go ... with Victoria ... for a while. It's okay ... Go on. It's perfectly alright."

And then his brain dished him up a replay of Hannah from a few days earlier, Hannah sitting at her desk like a spiteful mannequin, her metallic voice, slow, meaningful, like she was talking to some kind of primitive life form. 'No one's to get involved. Have you got that?" He nodded. 'No one's to hear or see or talk to her.' Another nod. 'No one's to know you've got a droid in the flat.' A pained etch-that-into-your-brain stare. Then came the biggy, the absolute 'no-no'. He could see that imperious, manic, on-the-edge look in her eyes, knuckles whitening, like she wanted to pull out a nail gun and staple the message word by word onto his skull. 'She must never—under any circumstances—no matter what happens—step a foot outside your flat'.

He became aware of Dorothea watching him, uncertain. Victoria was watching him too but the look in her eyes said something quite different. Unless he was very much mistaken, her stare said 'you stinking, yellow, weasely scum-bag'. He'd have to work hard to retrieve this.

"Go. No problem. Have a chat," said Andy.

"Then what?" said Victoria.

"Huh?"

"Back to this. Back to you bullying her."

"Don't be daft. We're going out after, aren't we, Dorothea. We've a heap of stuff to pack in over the weekend." Victoria detected a flicker of confusion on Dorothea's face.

"What other stuff?" said Victoria.

"Things ... stuff ... We hadn't decided on any specifics yet. I was thinking we'd go for a drink, take in a museum or two, maybe some galleries ... culture ... you know." Victoria eyed him dubiously. "Honest! That's what we're going to do."

Dorothea wiped away a tear, a smile lit her blotchy face.

"Yes, Andy," she said. "I'd like that. Is it okay if I go with Victoria first?"

Stunned, Andy nodded, watched, then listened as the door shut behind them. He staggered to the couch and clasped his head between his hands. How'd that happen? He'd let her out! A friggin' class 3. Out there. How the hell could he have ... Hannah—she'll go bloody ballistic!

He hauled in a few deep breaths, tried to slow it down, use his asthma techniques. Get to grips, Andy. She's just gone down for a 'cuppa'. That's all. What's the harm in that. He stood up, went over to the window, looked down at the leaf-strewn pavement.

Who was he kidding! Cuppa? Cuppa was girl code for in-depth interrogation. They could be walking out that door any minute, Victoria's arm round Dorothea's shoulder, taxi to the police station. Ten minutes till he was stuffed. Or Victoria could be on the phone right now, social services, medicare, victim-support or whatever they call themselves now. He could just see it. 'Dorothea? There's something wrong. They can't find you on the national database.'

Andy fidgeted at the bay window, paced up and down, fidgeted, paced some more, looked at the winter sky. He heard the noise of a vehicle, a van pulling up outside. He breathed out in relief. It was just a courier. But then the doorbell rang. He froze, rushed through to the hall. Some courier guy at his door! Only then did it click. The fridge, the replacement fridge he'd ordered ... before he'd gone up to the roof. So much had happened he'd clean forgot phoning it in.

The delivery process was like a dream sequence, the guy talking, Andy nodding, barely taking in a word he was saying. There was the tote droid, then there was the big box in the hall. Andy stood like a zombie as the data was entered into the logger. When the guy was gone, Andy stared out at the receding van then trudged downstairs.

"Better give Dorothea this," he said to Victoria, holding out the key. "I'm going out in about ten minutes—in case I'm not in when you're done."

It wasn't wonderful, but it was the best he could do: the chance to find out if Dorothea was still there, maybe get invited in so he could steer things away from trouble, Dorothea might even offer to come with him. But that was too much to hope. Even if none of that happened, it cast him in a better light. Jailers don't generally hand over the keys and tell the prisoner they're going out.

"It's Andy," said Victoria; she didn't step aside to let him in. Dorothea came to the living room doorway, a silhouette. She called 'Hi'. He asked her how she was doing, exchanged a few words across the hallway. Victoria had thawed, Dorothea must have allayed her concerns. Victoria even joked a little, made out they were ganging up on him, warned him, but in a playful way, that he'd 'better watch his step'. But no invite to come in. Conversation ran out and it became awkward to stand there. So he said 'Bye'. He'd found it strange to see Dorothea there, part of someone else's life. She seemed distant, amazingly distant, more distant than if she'd been shipped to the other side of the world. There was nothing more to do but go upstairs and begin packing stuff into the fridge.

Chapter 9 Saturday

"We don't have to go out!" said Dorothea.

"Yes we do," sulked Andy.

"I don't mind. Really, it doesn't matter," she pleaded. "Why don't we go back."

Andy walked on, then, without warning, cut across the busy street. She hung back, chose her moment, then broke into a trot to catch up.

"Andy, please!"

He stomped along, hands stuffed into his pockets, baseball hat tipped low, shielding himself from the onslaught of lights and shoppers as if it were storm-driven rain.

"But why—why can't we go back?"

"Because," he retorted, "Victoria is fully expecting you to have a weekend of fun and parties."

"I don't have to go. I don't need to get new clothes."

"She will ask."

"I could say I couldn't find anything I liked."

Andy stopped for a second, rubbed his chin, made a show of giving this serious consideration.

"Let me see. She knows you're totally up for this. She pumped you full of fashion advice, armed you with a list of this season's essentials and pointed you, like a clothes-seeking missile, straight at a square mile of boutiques—Zilch! You just couldn't find a thing." Andy scratched his head. "Mmmmmm ... What happened there? Were the stores empty or something. Did all that fashion frenzy just evaporate the moment you stepped out the door. Or maybe it was something to do with Andy, fashion's Neanderthal man, that club-wielding moron who lives upstairs. I mean, if I really am the kind of guy who slaps his girl around, would I go along with the touchy-feely, retail experience thing? No, of course not. It's like this, if you don't come back stuffed to the gunnels with fashion gear, she'll decide I'm not just a bully, but a no-good, lying bastard, and, that, my little shopper, would be the last nail in my coffin. Bye, bye, Andy, hello social services."

"What if I pretended I did get some things but said that I'm not wearing them tonight?"

"You're joking!" said Andy, striding out again, shaking his head in exasperation. "If you don't rush back, chuck it all over the bed and get glammed up tonight, her antennae will start tingling."

"Antennae?"

"Yeah, woman have this special instinct. They sense things."

"Wait, Andy!"

Andy forged on, then veered left, cutting down a light-starved alley, a tunnel, a dank, gritty worm hole, connecting one dazzling retail street to another. "She'll want all the details," he called, voice echoing off the dripping brick walls.

"We never arranged to ..." called Dorothea.

"Didn't you hear the way she was talking? You are her protégé. She sent you on a mission. Go forth and shop! You have to report back."

"Andy, I'm sorry. I didn't realize."

"Why the hell did you tell her you'd no clothes?"

"Not with me," she corrected. "She asked if I'd come from a meeting—because of the suit. If I said I did have other clothes she might have asked to see them."

"Are you crazy!" said Andy stopping, half-way down the alley, street noise subdued, conversation easier. He took off his dark glasses; there was no need in the alley. "I can just hear her.

'You have clothes! You will show me them to me now!' Women never ask to see each other's existing clothes. Rifling through someone's old togs is an absolute no-no, it's invasion of privacy. New clothes—the rules are the exact opposite. Everyone's expected to pick them up and feel the material and check the labels and say how great they look. And the new owner gets to give a blow by blow account of what they'll match with and all the occasions you might wear them and where you bought them. Don't ask me to explain. It's some kind of female ritual thing. "

"Andy, I know I got you into this, and I've been silly—but will you forgive me?" She bit her lip and looked coy.

"Stop that!" he griped.

"Stop what?"

"That—that grovelling, apologetic stuff. It's just stupid."

"Andy!" she gasped, eyes filled with concern.

"I said stop it! Look, I just want you to be normal. That's all. No pathetic looks, no poor-little-me dramatics."

"Truly, I'm sorry. I didn't mean to ..." she said, hurt, looking straight into his eyes. "I'll try hard. Really, really, I will. I didn't realize I was doing something wrong. It just happened—I'll try to change. Truly I will. "

Her eyes became moist but she stood very still, eyes wide, staring, chin brave. Her bottom lip trembled. She realised, compensated, tried clenching her jaw, face muscles taut, but the welling in her eyes became too much. A globule tumbled and ran down her left cheek. She shivered, eyes fixed, unblinking, then she could hold it no longer. Her head suddenly dropped. She buried her face in her hands, sobbing, gasping for air.

"I'm sorry ... I really am," she blurted. "Just take me home. I can't ... I can't do this."

"Darn!" muttered Andy. "Look ... here." He put his arms around her, cosseting her. She collapsed into him, leaning, sobbing against his chest.

"It's okay," he said softly, caressing her hair. "It's just ... it's me. You're great. Honest. You haven't done anything wrong. It's me. I'm just a selfish bastard."

"Don't say that, Andy," she said. "Don't. It's not true."

"Yeah ... well," he sighed. "I'm no angel, and I kind of freaked out there. It's just tension. Work—sometimes it gets me."

Her head jerked up. Eyes, despite the tears, intensely searching his face.

"What is it Andy?" she sniffled, easing an arm from his grasp, fumbling for a tissue. She blew her nose and hastily wiped the tears from her eyes.

"Is it those people?"

"What people?" said Andy, puzzled. He stopped, they were getting near to the open street. "You mean the ones Hannah sent round? Nah. Some rookies from floor 6. They'll just have to break her the bad news. I'll phone Hannah in the morning. Tell her I took an early night. Conked out. On sleeping pills ..."

Andy flinched. He couldn't be sure what happened, but he realized, even in the alley's gloom, that Dorothea had moved quickly, like frames clipped out of a video, a discontinuity, a shift. Dorothea was slightly further away, her left leg extended out to one side. He was sure of the sound though: the brittle crunch, then the tiny high-pitched whirr, like a bee's wings, but, unlike a bee, the sound winding down, slowing and the final tick ... tick ... tick death rattle.

"Oh!" was all she said, mild surprise on her face. "I've stepped on something. I—it just happened. I felt an urge to ..."

Andy looked down. Skewered on her heel, black and jagged with its needle legs twitching was what looked like a spiky black toy.

Andy kneeled to study it more closely.

"Roach," he said, glancing up. "Surveillance gizmo. You must be helluva fast. Never seen one live, never mind catch one. This one's wrecked."

"Is this going to be a problem?"

"No. The less of these the better. Darned pests. They're illegal. They're imported by low-lifes for snooping around, black-mail, sleaze, or maybe a dealer checking out a rival's patch."

"Is it okay to ...?" she said.

"Yeah," he said. She lifted her foot but the brittle casing was skewered onto her heel.

"Wait! You could rip your hand on that edge," said Andy. He did a quick scout, fetched a discarded drinks can and, gripping the back of her shoe, tried to prise the device off. "No use!" he muttered. "Okay. Try putting your foot down. See if we can loosen it first." The shell crunched on the gritty concrete.

"Right! Now twist—Geez these little critters are tough. Titanium casing."

"Andy?"

"Huh ..."

"Let me do it. I think I can manage."

"You sure?" he said, standing. "Be careful. It's razor sharp."

"I'll be careful," she smiled.

Deftly, she removed her shoe and held it up for inspection. "Mmmm—Interesting." She wobbled on one foot. "Can I lean on you, Andy?" Strange, thought Andy, top-spec droids have excellent balance; but then she was spydroid—emulating human behaviour was the norm, high-tech kicked in to harvest data.

"Yeah, sure." He moved to her side and looped an arm round her waist.

"Better?" he asked

"Much better," she smiled. "Now ... how to free it."

Using her thumb and index finger as pincers she began wiggling it.

"It's tight. I'll have to snap it. Oops!" She wobbled and Andy grabbed at her to stop her falling over.

"Sorry."

"No, it's okay."

"Look, if I turn like this it might work better if I ..." and she twisted towards him, reaching her arms out, one on each side, over his shoulders. They were face to face as lovers stand before their lips touch. Her eyes gazed steadily into his.

"Andy? Do you think ...?"

Andy gulped. He was aware of her warmth, what felt, like—though he couldn't be sure—the caress of her breath on his cheek.

"Yeah ... what? " He said, clearing his throat.

"Could you hold onto me? I need to use both hands on the roach."

"I suppose—yeah!" he said. She was looking into his eyes. Andy returned the look, gazed back for a second, before flustering. "How's it going? Getting anywhere with it?"

"The roach?" she said. "Yes ... right! Let's have a look." She tilted her head to one side and began to study the shoe.

Andy was aware of her closeness, her body pressed against his, her hair brushing against his neck. And he could feel her arms flexing, tussling, pulling, as, behind his head, she tugged and twisted. A high-tensile snap fractured the silence, a scattering of small parts ricocheted into the void. Dorothea remained pressed against him.

"That's it," she said, quietly, pulling back and looking into his eyes again. "All done."

"Good," said Andy. "I—Well, I guess you can put your shoe on."

"One minute," she said, and she moved her head to one side, cheek close to his, doing something behind his shoulder. He could feel her arms moving again, something going on behind him. "I just want to check ..."

Andy loosened his arms round her waist and twisted to see what she was up to.

She was rotating the roach slowly in one hand, studying it, holding it a few inches from her nose. Turning the split underside towards her, she extended her tongue and touched it to the exposed terminals of the chip.

"Geez, Dorothea!" gasped Andy, reeling. "What the hell are you doing?"

"Tasting it," she said with open-eyed innocence. "Before the data seeps way."

"But it's ... it's so weird!" Andy stepped back, pushed her away.

"Andy!" said Dorothea, letting the roach drop, wobbling, reaching down to slip on her shoe. "Wait ... Andy." Putting on his shades, he was striding out of the alley into the noise of the city street. "Andy, please! You don't understand."

It was dusk. They came to a stop and stood in a corner he knew had a CCTV shadow. The sky inky blue, the city lights brash, attention-seeking, were overpowering the lingering vestiges of day. Andy felt a taste in his mouth, like blood. Putting his hand up, he touched his tongue, then looked at his fingertip. Nothing. He swung round. Fighting to be heard over the noise, he waited for a lull in the stream of shoppers to give her instructions.

"That's it just ahead. See the old-fashioned green door, the Victorian junk in the windows, that's where we'll be coming tonight. The scanner's inside in the hallway. If the screen flashes 'sorry, no entry, tech-free zone', you just turn round, go to the next shop along and have a look in the window. No fuss, nothing to alert the street cameras."

"What will we do then?"

"Don't know. But better to find out if the alarm triggers now. Victoria's suspicious enough as it is. You setting off the alarm would have her asking more awkward questions. And then she'd want us to find somewhere else. A potential minefield."

Searching, her eyes settling on the spot fifty yards further along, she gave a dutiful nod. "Ok," she said, "I see it."

"If you get in, and I'm pretty sure you will," he said, taking a step back into the surveillance shadow, "go to the far tables on the left-hand side, the ones amongst the palms. I come to this place a lot so I have to be really careful. You and I going in together wouldn't be too bad if that was the whole story. Victoria, unless she's into surveillance avoidance, will be totally trackable. That's a big issue seeing she lives right below me. I need to do everything I can to minimize correlation. Anyhow, I'll get a newspaper, the kiosk is just across from the door—that's normal, they don't do news feed in this place. I'm not abandoning you, remember that, I'll only be a few yards away. Just enough to break connection with you on the cameras."

"It's some kind of bar isn't it?" she blurted, wanting to keep him engaged, to keep him with her. She stretched and stood on tip-toes as a dense mass of shoppers obscured her view.

"Yeah! Why, is that a problem?" he said.

"No. It's just—I thought ... it doesn't matter."

"Look, I'll only be a few seconds behind you. It's better you go in first than have me go in leaving you out on the street, isn't it? I'll go ahead, then I'll stop like I'm window shopping, you walk right on past and into the bar. Ok?" He looked at her straight for a few seconds, slipped on his dark glasses and headed in the direction of the kiosk. He chose a specific spot to stop, a pawn-broker's window, his back to the street. Instead of looking in at the goods, he peered diagonally up over the rim of his shades to the silvered globes above the door. It took a few seconds to make her out, but there she was coming along the street towards him, a tiny figure in the globe's all-encompassing world ... closer ... closer ... slowing down ... stop. She was standing a few yards behind him, she made to go, hesitated, then continued on. Even in the distorted reflection of the sphere he'd clocked her facial expression, her body language, her faltering movements. Droids were logical. She wouldn't fake something for no reason, she wouldn't put on a show that he couldn't see. A heaviness came over his heart—she was capable of fear.

"Got you a wine," he said, sipping his beer as he sat, paper under his arm. He was keeping it matter of fact, like this was a daily occurrence. He'd looked over when he came in, saw the relief on her face, the beaming smile, but had responded with a non-committal wave, acknowledgement, nothing more. Whist he'd been waiting at the bar, he'd reviewed the situation. Maybe she was a sentient being, maybe she really did have emotions, maybe a whole heap of touch-feely baloney was true, but that didn't change the fact that he had a job to do and that by Monday morning she would be gone, wiped, packed and shipped back to some high-security warehouse.

"Well," he said, "that's the first thing that didn't go belly up today."

"Andy, I don't know what you mean."

"Getting in here. It's called pre-emptive fun. If I hadn't gotten in first and told Victoria I was taking you here, she'd have arranged something else—probably a cosy night with bouncers, ID checks, and wall-to-wall IoT, the kind of evening where you sit back and relax whilst all your vitals get streamed to the combers. At least when you come here you leave all that at the door. The drink here's top-notch too."

"Is it?"

"Yeah. You can't go wrong," he said, wiping beer froth from his top lip and nodding at her drink. "Bruce, that's the guy who runs it, he's into small family-run vineyards. He tours France during his holidays, cycles around on an old black bike and talks to the locals. Turns up unannounced. If he likes the wine and the people, he orders a hundred or so cases. Shakes hands on it, no contracts, no bureaucracy. Connoisseurs come a long way just for the wines you get here."

"Thanks," she said, eyeing the glass. She looked up. "What are you drinking?"

"Beer."

She picked up the glass by the stem, but hesitated to bring it to her lips. "I've never tasted wine. What kind is this?" Andy took another mouthful and wiped his lips with the back of his hand.

"Red," he said, laying down the paper. "Okay, there's a few things we need to sort out."

"Is it safe ... safe to talk?"

"Yup. That's why they have the scanner. Bruce runs a zero implant, zero digi-wave, zero droid, set-up. You're the only piece of tech inside these four walls."

"The scanner at the door is meant to keep me out?"

"Yup, but I guessed you'd get through. You're spydroid based—I mean, what use is a top-end spydroid if it can't get through security."

"I see ..." said Dorothea, glancing round at the other customers with a slightly furtive air. "So, I'm not meant to be here."

"No."

She flicked back her hair and sat a little lower in her seat.

"Andy, I'm worried. I know we need to sort things out, but is this wise? Just my being here could get you into trouble."

"We'll get to that later. On the way over here, a few things cropped up. Seeing it's safe to talk, we might as well clear 'em up." He inhaled and looked purposeful. "Some key points. One: you need to stop freaking out every time something comes up."

"I'm sorry, Andy. I really want to do better, much better. And I have tried. It probably doesn't seem like that, but that last time when you asked me to ..."

"Woaaa! Wait," said Andy, holding back the flow of apologies with his hands. "Let's just forget everything that happened before. Begin again. Fresh start. Okay?"

"Can we? Oh, Andy! That's wonderful," gushed Dorothea. "Do you mean it? This means so much to me. The worry, the guilt. I've been feeling so ..."

"Okay ... okay ... okay! What did I just say? What did I tell you, huh? What was number one?"

"Not to freak out ..."

"Exactly. And what are you doing right now?"

"I ... I'm freaking out, amn't I?" she said, crestfallen. "But I ... I just ..."

He simmered for a moment, but couldn't hold it for long. "The problem, Dorothea, is you're so darned sensitive. Every little thing turns into an emotional roller coaster. It's driving me crazy!" He leaned back in his chair and pushed his splayed fingers back through his hair. "Right. Okay, sorry," he said, tight-lipped. "Fresh start. You're going to be calm. I'm not going to lose the rag. Deal?"

"I'll try very hard," she said.

"Good," Andy nodded. "And I'll try too ... and we'll get on just fine."

Dorothea bit her lip, reached out and gave Andy's hand a brief squeeze.

"Okay, I'm ready," she said with a determined glint in her eye.

"First of all, instead of battering straight into this, let's practice. We'll try to chill for five minutes. Sip your drink, soak up the atmosphere, let your mind drift."

"Okay," she said. "Great idea!" She bit her lip. "Sorry!"

Putting the wine to her lips, she took a first tentative sip.

"Oh!" she gasped, hand to her mouth. "It's ... it's just not what I expected."

"You don't need to drink it," he said.

"No ... it's ... it's interesting, and quite complex. There's the obvious flavours, the tannins, the acid, the sugars, but ... yes," she took another sip, "there are so many layers, degrees of subtlety and they interact, almost infinite variation. I see why people enjoy ... Oh, Andy, I interrupted you reading. Please, please continue."

Andy lifted the paper again and tried reading an article, but he couldn't concentrate. He glance over at Dorothea. She was looking aimless, awkward, sipping her drink but looking lost, like she'd been stood up by her boyfriend.

"Here," he said, "you take the paper. See if that helps." She opened her mouth to protest but, thinking better of it, took it and began earnestly to scan the front page.

Andy just leaned back and stared at the ceiling. He was good at chilling but it wasn't easy knowing she was there across from him trying her damnedest to stay calm. He sat up again and gazed across the room. Two women a couple of tables nearer the bar were drinking coffee and conversing. He wasn't trying to eaves drop, but with nothing to occupy his mind, he couldn't help noticing. The older one, short mousey hair, wiry frame, was sitting with her back to him. The younger one, mid-twenties, Hispanic, was facing him. They looked like they might be work colleagues. The Hispanic one was doing most of the talking.

"Swear to God!" she enthused. She'd an American accent that carried clear above the background noise yet had a wonderful chocolate-smooth quality. Square-set, face broad but feminine, a black tumble of curls hung level with the neat point of her chin. The older one must have said something, but it was completely inaudible. "I can get her twenty or thirty," continued the younger one. Another gap. Then, unforced and smiling broadly: "I love that woman!"

Andy was half way through taking a draught of his beer. He stopped, put down the glass, and looked over. That was quite a declaration. Simple, refreshing, a natural, expression of true affection. There was something heartening about it. No reward was being sought, no vested interest to serve. Andy slouched back and stared blankly towards the ceiling. Why did it matter? He wrestled with the thought. He realized, sadly, that it mattered because it was rare, and because it had truth and because it held the undefinable value of those things that can never be bought.

And what about her, thought Andy, looking over at Dorothea. Where was the truth in her? Was she a fake? Does she even know what it means to be true? Could she be fooling herself? Who really knows. Victoria probably knew her better than he did ... but then again, maybe not. When he challenged Dorothea about why she'd let Victoria start scheduling stuff for her weekend, she replied that she had no past, only a future ...what else could she talk about? It was true. She had so little to go on. She was just finding her way.

He snorted. Talk about Dorothea being a fake, what about good old Andy—all the stuff he was hiding under the carpet. He didn't exactly hold the high ground. Sighing resignedly, he geared up to face her.

"Time's up. Let's do it."

"Okay, Andy," she said and she folded the paper carefully before putting it down. Andy leaned forward and huddled over his glass. "First up, you're here partly because of me ... so I figured you need to know a little about what I do and where you and I stand."

She nodded. Andy took a resolute gulp of beer, held it in his mouth, swallowed and laid the glass down with an air of finality. "This is the official version. I'm a technological consultant. I assess technology and try to see how it fits into domestic life. I also meet with clients, troubleshoot, design or adapt stuff so it fits in with their needs. I don't do much of that last bit any more. Management thinks clients and me are safer apart. Anyhow, my job's mostly product assessment. That's how they put it." She was watching intently over the wine glass. "Now, about you: you're here so I can find out what you're capable of, see if you can do things like running a home, gardening, buying food, child-care, just general living. Once I've checked you out, I'll write a report."

"You'll write a report on me?"

"Yes."

"But ..." she said, confused. She lay down her glass, hands twisting in her lap.

"I didn't realize. Do friends write reports on each other?" She looked at him wide-eyed.

"It's not as if it's something I want to do. I hate it," moped Andy. "But it's part of my job."

"Andy, you didn't answer my question. You said you were my friend. Do friends write reports on each other?"

"Er—no ... not usually."

"I'm sorry," said Dorothea, sitting up straight. "I'm finding this difficult, Andy. I'm a friend, but you're not treating me as a friend." She narrowed her gaze.

"Well—it's like ... You know when I said ..." Andy's mouth shut tight and his eyes locked onto the table, staring right through the dark soul of the wood. At last he looked up. "Look, there's things you ought to know about me, just for the record: I'm disorganized, unreliable and, if I'm honest, I'm pretty darned lazy. Most of the time I am way ... way out there on my own, don't ask me where. I don't know what the hell I'm doing, my life's a mess, work home—whatever. So, like, when you start asking me these really logical questions, and you want it all to fit together and expect the bullshit I say one minute to fit right in with corpcrap I say the next, well ... I'm sorry, that's just never gonna happen." he glared at her before lowering his eyes. "Just so you know, don't expect too much." He put both hands round his glass and stared into the thinning froth on what was left of his pint.

They sat quietly for a while. A couple a few tables away asked a waiter about peanut allergies, then decided to play it safe and ordered wine and a sandwich. A rabble arrived and migrated to a far corner. One went to the bar with a long list of drinks, the others dragged two tables together and rounded up extra chairs.

"Andy ... Andy?"

"Huh!"

"I understand."

Andy looked up with a flat despondent gaze.

"If you do, you'll be the first."

"I think I do. We have certain things in common. You're unsure of yourself and your position and, as a result, you feel lack direction and out of control." Andy remained silent not acknowledging her words. "If we, both of us, could find the answers to the things we really need to know, perhaps we'd feel more secure.

"So?" said Andy.

"I've been thinking about training. I was wondering ... maybe ... and I know you're not a droid ... but maybe some kind of training could help you to ..."

Andy exploded with laughter. "Training. Geez! ... Training!" He threw his back head, his eyes watering. "Training. Do you know what training is? It's like a list of instructions. Do this, do that, do the other thing, done! You complete the steps, they give you a certificate. That's it. Training's right up there with procedures and consultations and vision statements. If you've got the right person with the right drive they don't need the training. If you haven't, tough, the training's a waste of time You do it for one reason—to get the protocol police off your back ... and promotion ...and for the free sandwiches ... and to get out of the office. That was three reasons but you know what I mean."

"Four reasons," mouthed Dorothea, barely audible, face downturned.

He looked at her. She looked small and unwanted.

"Hey, look. It's okay," he said, leaning forward, laying his hand on hers. "You weren't to know. You're good, you're fresh, you're funny. It's kind of nice to hang out with someone who isn't as pissed off and cynical as me. "

"I'm stupid, Andy," she said, blinking, eyes averted.

"No, you're not. You're great. There's a friend of mine who says life's about learning, recognizing your limitations, being humble enough to know what you don't know, then building from there. We're all stupid some of the time. It's ironic, but it's the ones who can't see when they're stupid, that really are. Anyway, you made me laugh. It's good to laugh. I needed that." Her face brightened fractionally, a shadow of a smile, a flicker of hope. "And we have things in common." He frowned, unsure how to justify that claim. "It's ... it's not easy for either of us. I guess we're both kind of lost. Yeah, some people know exactly where they're at. So goddamned logical, always on top of things. Me? Geez, there's so much incoming shit. People are always pushing me, pulling me, and I'm screaming inside 'just leave me, leave me alone, give me a chance'. I mean, like I'm trying to get my head round important ideas like whether or not I exist and what this Universe thing is all about and in amongst it someone's pestering me to attend a quality assurance meeting. Can you imagine?"

"Andy?"

"Yeah!"

"If there's any way I can help ..."

"Yeah, thanks. I'll think about that ... let you know."

"And Andy?"

"Yeah."

"Even if you're not able to be my friend ..."

"I didn't say that!"

"Andy, I've no right to expect you to—I just want you to know that I'll be a friend to you ... I'm here if you need me. Always. I really mean that." She reached out and grasped his hand, eyes locked on his, unflinching, fragile yet certain. Andy's eyes connected for a second then, buckling under the intensity, he looked away.

"Yeah—likewise," he said, inwardly cursing himself. Commitments, like razor wire, were coiling round, limiting his movements, ensnaring him in an inescapable future of remorse.

He hunched, scrunched himself, bracing himself. There was something else this bullshitter hadn't told her, something insidious. It was there, waiting, like an explosive charge, a landmine. Soon there'd be no option but to lead her towards it, make her step on it, watch it rip her apart. His mouth was dry. Do it now! Tell her. The longer it goes on, the worse it'll get. What's wrong with you. Just say the damned words. 'You've a day and a bit left, honey. Shutting you down Monday morning. Yeah, sorry. It's short ... too short, but, like I say, that's it. You won't feel a thing.' He tightened his hands into fists, ground the knuckles hard together, wanting the pain to erase what was plaguing his mind. Say it! Dammit! Say it! Say it! Say it!

He glanced up, and looked quickly away.

"What is it, Andy!" she asked.

"Nothing," he said, unable to meet her eye. "Just, you know ... thinking."

"Are you sure?" she quizzed, watching his reactions, looking for confirmation.

Andy took a deep drink of his beer, swallowed it fast, downed it, almost choking in the process. She stared. He checked the clock on the wall.

"Hey, it's getting late. Better hit the shops. I'm going to the gents. Meet you at the door."

"Okay," she said, picking up her wine, swirling the last drops then finishing off the glass. She stood and pushed in her chair then began slowly towards the door. When Andy came out, she was sitting at the table nearest the door. Damn! He'd meant for them to meet outside in the lobby. He looked over to the bar. Bruce wasn't there, it was okay. He walked directly towards her, avoiding looking left or right.

"Andy, there's something—before we go."

He looked furtively at the noisy huddle just across from them.

"Heard the one about the pole-dancing nurse?" blurted a thick-spectacled guy who looked strangely inanimate like some kind of mechanoid joke machine. Only his mouth seemed to move. Another guy, flushed, pink, wasn't going to be left out. He whooped, slapped the table and bawled:

"Brilliant joke—Brilliant! Wait till you hear this!"

Andy tuned out, sat down stiffly and looked edgy.

"Not too long, huh! Better hit the shops before it gets late."

"You know how I'm not supposed to be here," she said in a low voice.

"Yeah," said Andy, eyeing her warily.

"I'd just like to know—is this the only one?"

"Sorry?"

"Is there anywhere else I'm not meant to be?"

Andy closed his eyes.

"There are some others. Look can't we ..."

"Andy, I need to know. Please."

"Well—yeah, there are places ... To be honest, pretty much everywhere." He glanced back towards the bar, Bruce had appeared! He was conversing with someone as he poured out a drink.

"Everywhere!" gasped Dorothea, face white.

Andy reached out and took her arm.

"Look, it's no big deal. Let's go," he muttered.

"Andy!" she hissed, distraught, pulling her arm free.

Andy surveyed her for a moment then leaned over, his head almost touching hers.

"Don't worry. We can work round it," he whispered huddling, keeping his back to the bar. Standing up now would only draw attention.

"But there must be places," she mouthed. "Your apartment ..." Andy shook his head. "What about outside, in the street?"

"Afraid not," said Andy. "I'll tell you later." She stared into space, bereft, speechless. "Look, tell you what, if I tell you now, do you promise to leave it there, get the shopping and go home?" She nodded. "Okay, it's not as bad as it sounds. There are places, in fact there are whole countries."

"What countries? Europe, the United States? Canada?" She looked, waited, but Andy didn't confirm. "China ... Korea ... Australia ... Indonesia? Where, Andy?"

"I can't remember exactly which ones. I think there might be one in Africa, or is it the Middle East? And one or two of those countries near Russia, ones that end in 'stan'. You know that area, north of India and along a bit?" She looked intently at him. "I admit it tends to be places that are a bit—well, kind of maverick: totalitarian regimes, unstable governments, terrorist controlled areas, but some have really nice scenery and ... Look, it doesn't really matter."

"Andy," she clutched at his hand, "how can it not matter? I don't have the right to exist!" She looked down into her lap then up into his eyes. "Andy, I so want to help, to understand, to belong, but just being here—it's wrong. Can't you understand?"

A roar burst out from across the way as the nurse joke reached its conclusion. Andy glanced over. The guy with the specs hadn't even smiled. He had them rolling, gasping for breath, yet he looked like he was just sitting there waiting for a bus.

"What! Yeah," stuttered Andy. "But you've got to see it in perspective. Laws aren't always right. People have to look at the laws and, if they're wrong, they have to push against them, change them. Suffragettes had to fight to get the right to vote. The law was wrong, they broke the laws, they fought and they won. Same with slavery, discrimination, stuff like that. Laws are made by people and sometimes people are wrong. Class 3s aren't bad, they're just new. In time people will see that and the law will change"

Dorothea paused for a minute, considered, then the concern and anguish were washed away by a flood of awe and respect. "Oh, Andy!"

Andy squinted back, suspicious. She oughtn't to be wearing that big gushy smile. She was reading stuff into this, stuff that had no right to be there.

"Thank you," she said, eyes half-closed, lips pulled back thin in admiration, as if dazzled by a sun god. "It's an honour to be part of this."

"No! Geez, wait! You picked me up wrong. I'm no hero. That is NOT how it is! Forget the suffragettes and anti-discrimination and stuff. Bad analogy. It's more like—more like ... wait a minute ... When cars came in, and people were scared and they brought in a stupid law that said someone had to walk in front with a red flag. Now see that guy, the jerk with the red flag—that's me. I've been roped into carrying the flag. No hero. Okay? Big difference."

He splayed his hands and squeezed shut his eyes, aghast at having been so misjudged.

Dorothea observed him with a dubious eye. Her voice was low but vibrant "You may say that, Andy, but I know you are running considerable risks, and I understand now why you're so edgy and nervous. You're playing it down, you're being modest. I just want you to know, Andy, I'll do my best not to let you down."

"Yeah ... No ... Whatever. Look, I'm not big into sacrifice. As far as I'm concerned, we play this right, no one needs to be brave, no heroics, no one ever knows. You just do your bit; the main thing for you is to avoid being suspicious. Don't stand out, just act like you are a real woman, and we've got a pretty good chance."

Dorothea leaned forward.

"Andy!" She touched his arm. "I'll try. And Andy ..."

"Yeah?"

"Am I doing okay so far—as a woman?"

Andy, disconsolate, looked into her eyes.

"I don't understand you, I've no idea how you'll react or what you'll do next, so yeah—you're doing a pretty good job."

He felt the presence of someone behind him, saw the shadow, knew who it was.

"Excuse me, Ma'am. Is this guy causing you trouble?" Bruce stood tall, grinning, his thumbs hooked into his belt. "We've thrown him out three times this week."

Dorothea looked enquiringly at Andy but played it safe, smiled and decided to ask him about that later.

"Aren't you going to buy the lady a drink?"

"Hi Bruce," said Andy standing up. "Bruce—Dorothea. Dorothea—Bruce. Actually, we've had a drink. Just going.

Trying to catch the shops. Don't think we could fit in another, I'm afraid."

"Slippery so and so," said Bruce. "Sneaking in and out without so much as a hello."

"Where were you, anyway? Didn't see you when I came in."

"Like that ever stops you." Bruce gibed. "Dorothea!" He studied her carefully. "You must be a very special lady. Wild horses couldn't drag Andy into a shopping mall. Tell me, how do you do it?"

"I liked him," said Dorothea. They walked side by side over the mall's matt silver floor.

"He tries."

"He seems keen for us to come to the party ... it's through in the function room isn't it?" she said, barely audible, watching him carefully out of the side of her eye.

"Yeah, the Club House is just at the back of the bar. Bruce runs a lot of social events there. I'm not sure what ...I don't generally go." They weaved their way through the congestion caused by a mobile jewellery stall. Finally they reached a quieter stretch. Andy slowed. This was as good a place as any.

"Let's talk strategy!" he announced. "We go in, we get the goods, we get out. Clean and simple. I'm there for backup, nothing else. No mulling over stuff, no trying on a dozen things you'll never actually buy, no ferreting out the items missing from the rails. It's grab and go. Okay?"

"Okay. You're the boss," Dorothea chirped. Her head was up. She was looking around. "Just being here is amazing."

"I thought you'd know about this kind of thing. Isn't it— you know—familiar?" He was avoiding references to 'pre-installed knowledge' or 'databases' now that they were out in public.

"But it's not the same," she gushed as they walked forward, her stride making full use of her heels. "When you experience it yourself it's ... it's just so different. You know it's real. Happening right there. You see it, hear it as it happens. And there's something ... it's ... it's yours. You see it from your viewpoint. When it's recorded, it's been selected, edited, it belongs to somebody else. I'm the only one seeing just what I see, smelling exactly what I smell, hearing the sounds that I hear. Don't you see how wonderful it is!" She was animated, her expression one of excitement, eyes roving, darting, frightened she might miss a thing.

"Wait!" She slowed and extended an arm to him signalling him to stop. "That gorgeous smell—that ... that's new leather isn't it. Yes, I'm sure—Look!" She pointed. "It's coming from the furniture in that store. There are other ones—quite different, sharp, tangy ... citrus ... apple ... banana ... that'll be ..." she twisted her neck, scanning, "the milkshake bar. Smoothies! The fresh fruit," she bubbled.

"Right, right. I get the idea," Andy glowered. "Let's, you know, just calm it down. We don't want it to look like they let you out for the day."

"I'll try," she said. She began walking again but more slowly, the spring in her step gone. Andy trudged along a little ahead of her.

"About Bruce's invitation," she said, drawing abreast, calm, even and formal. "I take it we're not going. I'm not trying to press you, it's just—I need to know if I'm choosing clothes."

"No, we'll keep it simple," said Andy. "Stick to the plan."

"That's fine. I'd have quite liked to go—but that's not a problem. Perhaps another time."

They walked on silently. A kid with a balloon ran into them, giggled up at them then bounded away to where a slow-moving grandparent was delving into a bag. He saw Dorothea's eyes momentarily follow the burst of motion, then pull back, gaze blankly forwards. They were sad eyes, trapped, suppressed, pitiful, the cowed gaze of a slave.

Is this how it was going to be? She had a few meagre hours of existence and she was going to live them as a bored, unemotional drudge, thwarted at every turn by her kill-joy 'friend', Andy. Soon, as her executioner, he'd pull the plug, drop her, her hopes, her curiosity, her desires, into the big black bin bag of eternal oblivion. And he'd be left with the memory of having been a heartless sod.

A big boutique lay ahead, one on Victoria's hit list. Andy stopped.

"Changed my mind. We'll go to Bruce's party, see what he gets up to. You go in, get something nice."

"Oh, Andy!" she thrilled. "Thank you, thank you ..."

Her voice trailed off and, her body, momentarily bunched like a coiled spring, grew slack and subdued. She hauled herself back, eyes narrowed and pained as if distraught at having smashed a fine dish. "Sorry, Andy!" she murmured. "You sprung that on me. I forgot."

"No—That's okay. You be yourself. Have fun," said Andy. "Sometimes, Dorothea, I'm one massive pain in the butt."

"Andy," she murmured, "I don't know you that well, but I know you are a good person."

Andy threw her a pained look. "You don't know me at all. You don't know what I'm capable of."

"Andy. Please!" she said, confusion in her eyes. "You're frightening me." She stood staring and fragile whilst Andy scuffed the silver flooring with the sole of his tennis shoe.

"Forget that. Forget all of it. It's just—I don't want you making a big deal out of any of this," he said. "Okay?"

"Okay," she said meekly.

They walked around for five minutes, directionless, lost souls between self-assured mannequins that flounced and swayed and pirouetted to the fashion beat.

"Got any ideas?" said Andy at last.

"Victoria gave me a few pointers. She thinks I'd suit green."

"Green? Is that it?"

"Well there's 'Sherwood'."

Andy looked blank.

"Mid-thigh length skirts, hung on the hips, leather belt, fitted stretch tops a couple of tones lighter, half sleeve with button fronts and neat rounded collars, calf-length boots, everything suede or washed cotton, base colour green, forest colours, fern, hi-lights in russet browns, natural. For smart casual it's pleated skirts and wide-collar, greeny tweeds with flecks of stone, shoes suede but heeled and narrow, blouses calico. With the right kind of extras, the style can be pepped up to be that bit smarter or be played down and made ethnic, but at its heart it's the kind of smart-casual you can wear day to day."

"You sound like a fashion promo."

"I do?"

"Yeah. Anyhow, this green, foresty stuff—that's what we're looking for."

Dorothea bit her lip and looked.

"It's not party wear."

"It isn't?"

"No, for a party you need something with a little more zest. Something sharper, figure enhancing, more feisty and fun. This season it's geometrics. Barbara Shrimpton influences but less constrained. Splashes of colour give it the individuality that allows you to ..."

"Dorothea!"

"Sorry. Another promo." She looked vaguely around before turning back. "Andy, what do you think I should get?"

"Huh?"

"Have you got any ideas?"

"Look, the way I see it, clothes are materials that cover your body. Get the right size, get the right shape, cover the right bit, and you're 90% of the way there. Okay, I know there's a whole art, fashion, image thing going on—but, personally, I couldn't give a monkey's." He looked at Dorothea and detected a warning tremble.

"But don't get me wrong!" he said, holding up his hands. "I appreciate that some people put in a big effort and really look great. I admire that, I admire them. It's like ... an artistic contribution to society. I like works of art, I go to galleries to see them, but that doesn't mean I want to paint them myself. See all these racks of clothes ..." he indicated them with a half-hearted wave of his hand. "... the same style, but in different colours, the same colour but in different sizes, the same size but in different styles—it drives me crazy. It's like I'm sartorial dyslexic. When you buy a piece of tech, you can work it out. You look at the specs, check out some reports, figure out the stuff you want it to do, match it up with what you're willing to pay and hit the 'BUY' button. Simple. But this stuff, this is a total nightmare."

"You want me to choose," she said.

"Yup."

Andy followed her past bleached lime counters, solid, expensive. Big chrome conveyor feeds swung endless outfits across the expanse of floor, and sprouting selection buttons enticed you to select from the fashion industry's fruits.

"See anything?" said Andy.

Dorothea picked a skirt that consisted of rustic brown panels each finished to a slightly different height and angle at the hem. She held it up against herself and turned to Andy.

"What do you think?"

Andy knew perfectly well what he thought ... it was a skirt, it was brown, and if it was the only skirt in the world he'd give it a no-holds-barred 'yes'. But it wasn't, she was young and lively and even he could see that she needed something with pizazz. This was the only time she'd ever do this, might as well do it right.

"Tell you what," he said, "this woodland thing might not suit everyone. You want something that's about you, your personality, not what some style juggernaut is bunging into the stores. There's an indie design place around here somewhere. Custom. They come up with a concept, knock out the gear on the spot. Never been there myself, but my ex got some really sharp kit there. They'll sort you out. And you won't have me moping around in the background."

They arrived as ZaZaZee and he gave her free reign, took the opportunity to lounge around on a leather sofa, the aroma of coffee and waxed-paper cup wafting around his nostrils. Dorothea chatted with a couple of designers, tried on some templates, then went into the rendition room. Eventually she came over wearing what they'd created: a neat, clean-cut, 2020s-influenced dress—a zingy green and black job with matching green and black knee-high boots

Andy nodded his approval, but as he did so, the sound of approaching steps could be heard, direct, business-like steps. Andy knew what was coming. When they arrived at ZaZaZee his reverie on the couch had been threatened by a roving mall droid. Identifying Andy as a lapsed consumer, the droid attempted retail injection: 'A bloody mary in a crystal Apis shaker? Frog slippers? Nat Now subscription? A micro drone? Cowboy-Mayhem 3D, Total Tone skin cream ... any of the ten pre-black Friday discounts?' He sent her off on a promising errand, now she was back with an apologetic smile.

"I'm sorry, sir, our droid attendants have searched every store in the mall, but none stock off-the-peg jeans with exactly 98 zipper teeth. Yakawaks, at the top end, have 106 teeth— eight more than you require, but that's an extra-large fitting. I don't think it would suit." She switched to bright breezy mode.

"Perhaps, however, I could interest you in StarGetBuy's Golden Toro range. They come with between 66 and 88 copper-plated zipper teeth, matching copper rivets at the stress points."

"No," said Andy. "I had my heart set on 98."

"We might have something other than jeans that would suit your zipper requirements. A sleeping bag, a dress with a zip fastening?"

"Thanks, but I'll try somewhere else." The droid retreated. Dorothea, nose scrunched, looked on in puzzlement. "Why 98?"

Andy shrugged. "Why not?" He drained the last dregs of coffee, crumpled his cup and tossed it in the bin.

Chapter 10 Saturday

Hannah would need a shower when she got home, she knew from the instant she touched the greasy door handle, she was doubly sure when she inhaled the fug that hung inside the door. She wasn't willing to brush against Wise Buy's motley assortment of customers so, amidst clarion calls of 'excuse me' and 'if you wouldn't mind', she manoeuvred her way to the front. Having traversed the tacky Lino, she took a mental note to wipe her shoes before getting into the car.

"Excuse me," said Hannah, for the last time, and she cut in in front of a pallid youth who was hovering in front of the counter with a poly-bagged lead in his hand.

"Missus," said Vince, pulling himself up, "this is the front of the queue. Up there's the back. That's where most people start."

"I'm not most people," snipped Hannah. "I've a car outside and I don't intend leaving it out there one minute longer than necessary."

"Got a point she has," said Vince squinting at the youth. "You know what, just take it. No charge. We're big-hearted we are." The youth took a hesitant step backwards then, dumfounded, loped away.

Hannah lowered her dark glasses and, peering darkly from beneath the brim of her hat, gave Vince a narrow-eyed permafrost stare. Vince wriggled inside his leather jacket. The past couple of hours had been a drag, suddenly the tide had turned.

"I want to speak to the manager," Hannah declared, the usual edge to her voice. Vince's face broke into a moustachioed-bandit smile.

"Didn't you hear me," Hannah spat, impatient, "I want to speak to the manager."

"That's me," said Vince.

"The manager responsible for distribution and logistics," she added with pained clarity.

"That's me," grinned Vince. "Ain't it Higgs?"

Higgs looked dumbly across from the other half of the counter, face pasty and white.

"Uh?"

"Sure I'm the distribution and logistics manager? Me, the manager. Tell her Higgs." Higgs looked dopily at Vince as though he'd never seen him in his life. "Yeah, he's the—manager thing that he said."

"Look, sonny," Hannah said, mouth drawn into a bitter line, "you may be a shop manager, but you are not the manager I spoke to on the phone ... not unless you've recently been castrated."

"Oh that," said Vince, bobbing his head gleefully. "My phone voice. Listen." He inhaled deeply and puffed out his chest. 'Manager ... Wise Buy Computing' he rumbled.

Hannah grew rigid. "Look, I don't know who you are, you little squirt, but ..."

"Whooaa. Stop right there missus," called out Vince, hand in the air, taking on the stance of a referee flagging up a foul. "That's sizism that is. Sheer unadulterated sizism. I've a dozen witnesses. You all heard?" he called to the dreary souls waiting behind. No one confirmed or even registered he was talking.

"Okay—Higgs? Higgs?" gasped Vince.

"Huh?"

"Sizism."

"Huh?"

"Sizism. Discrimination—about being small."

"But you are small."

Vince squinted at Higgs with incredulous disdain.

"Stuff it. See that?" He nodded to the ceiling. A blue light flashed inside a smoked glass dome. "Surveillance. State of the art that is. Picks up every whisper, every heartbeat. I could sue the pants of you."

"It's a Yako 120," Hannah responded in a bored tone.

"Yeah—so?"

"State of the art? It's obsolete."

"I didn't say when it was state of the art!" blurted Vince, bottom lip defiant above the untidy fuzz on his chin. "Doesn't matter anyway. The thing is you're nailed."

"It's not connected."

"What the hell are you talking about. Look! The light's on. There's a wire ..."

"There's only one wire, the power line. There's no data link. If you want to record, I suggest you connect it to an appropriate device, such as, let me see—a computer." She gritted her even white teeth and leaned over the counter. "Now stop wasting my time you pathetic little gnome," she hissed, voice barely audible. "If you don't get me the manager right now, I'll have Datatrawl investigate every second of your pathetic little existence."

Vince wriggled behind the counter, panting and bobbing.

"Hey! That's extortion!" he jabbered. "I'm just doing my job. It's my job to take over when Ludd's on his break. Still got twenty five minutes. Doesn't like being disturbed. But ..."

"But what?" she scowled.

"You won't want to see him yet—wait till I tell you about these amazing new deals!"

Ludd was laid out on a bench like a whale on a mortuary slab. It was his break and he wasn't going to jump to attention for a paranoid customer who couldn't wait her turn in the queue.

"A communication issue," glowered Ludd, eyes staring like a dead fish.

"That's correct," said Hannah, standing stiffly a few yards into the workshop. The downward-directed light gave the room the moody ambience of a smoky snooker hall. "The technician doing the assessment is fully aware of the security issues," she added. "No phone records, total discretion. Our problem is merely that he's been overly thorough. I couldn't get through to him. As a result he didn't get the message about the new collection time."

"Yeah! What's with the change of date?" said Vince, squatting cross-legged on a metal box near the centre of the room. His eyes roamed over Hannah, but his hands fidgeted with a remote. Behind Hannah, leaning against the wall, a tote-droid, naked, save for rigger boots, flicked open its eyes. Vince slid his finger on the remote's touch pad and it lifted one arm vertically into the air.

"As sometimes happens," she continued, "we finished earlier than anticipated."

"Six hours instead of three days?" grumbled Ludd. "Big difference. You know they're still charging full whack." Vince tapped an option and slid his finger side to side. The droid behind Hannah began to wave the raised arm side to side as though waving goodbye. Vince sniggered

"I understand." She lifted a shoulder casually and stretched her neck. "We allowed for more time than we needed—as a precaution. But now we're finished. There's absolutely no point us hanging on to an expensive piece of technology when it could be useful elsewhere."

"Is that it? Are you sure this fridge thing isn't too hot?" said Vince, chortling and wheezing at his own joke.

"Actually, no!" she snipped, throwing him a fiery stare. "But we are professionals. As I see it, there's no sense in retaining a sensitive item any longer than required."

"Professionals, huh!" said Vince, and, pressing some buttons, rotated the droid's head from side to side in an emphatic shake of its head. He stifled a laugh. Hannah, puzzled by his continuing bemusement, threw him a look of disgust. She turned her full attention to Ludd.

"It was a simple misunderstanding."

"Maybe, but the couriers were pissed off," said Ludd, bored. "And you know what's further up the chain. They're not the types you want to mess around."

"Mister Trout," snapped Hannah, shoulders hauled back, arms folded, cheek muscles taut, "are you trying to intimidate me?"

Vince smirked at her use of the name 'Trout' and looked eagerly to Ludd for a caustic response. None came, so he got the droid to fold its arms and roll its eyes, mimicking Hannah's behaviour. He was loving it.

"Lady," Ludd exhaled wearily. He moved a big foot and rubbed the toe up and down the inside of his leg. "I'm just giving it to you straight. When we picked the 'fridge' up we were told to return it to the warehouse Monday 11am. I phoned about arranging an earlier time and they said okay. Warehouse is open 24/7 today—tomorrow, as long as it's there by Monday 11am. They're being patient. Running back and forth for stuff that's not ready looks kind of suspicious. You got a problem?"

"Of course not!" said Hannah. "My people will have it ready. As I was saying, we'd actually prefer to have it back sooner, if we can arrange it."

"Something tells me you **are** having a problem," said Ludd.

"A problem? Don't be ridiculous." She choked out a nervous laugh. Ludd lifted his big head then dropped it back onto the bench, a surly twist on his lips.

"Actually, the reason I'm here in person is to make absolutely sure that this uplift goes smoothly. I'd like to arrange it for tomorrow, 3pm same location. And I'd like something for discrete communication—two ripped mobiles. "

"Ripped mobiles," said Ludd. "Take it there's just the one guy. He's on his own."

"The fewer people involved the better," said Hannah. "I want to maintain the highest level of security. No point leaving tracks."

"Yeah," Vince gibed. "Tracks leading to you. Bet there's plenty leading to the technician."

"Vince?"

"Yeah, he said, perking up, eager to be included.

"Shut it!" said Ludd scratching his fluffy beard.

"And, I'll take something to put on the records. It doesn't matter what, as long as it's plausible and legitimate," said Hannah.

"You do that," said Ludd. "I've another half hour. Vince, you're still on. Sort it."

"Do you think he's capable?" sneered Hannah. "He has delusions of grandeur. Did you know he goes about telling people that he is the boss?" Ludd closed his eyes, his chest rose and fell. Vince stroked the remote and the droid made a rude sign behind her back.

"No problem," Vince said. "A legit gadget for the lady. Let me see—how about Motovac. That's a good one." Vince hummed a couple of introductory bars from the web ad and began raucously singing : "Motovac ... motovac! Car's all clean when you come back. Do..do-de-do..doo..." As he did so he slid his finger on the droid control causing the mechanoid to roll silently forwards till it was inches behind her.

"What a star," said Hannah sarcastically. She swung round to go and walked straight into the parked droid.

"Oops!" said Vince. He tapped the controls and the droid's arms raised up forming horizontal barriers blocking her exit. Hannah shrieked and shoved.

"Get this thing off me!"

"You walked into it! Countered Vine. "Ought to look where you're going. It's just trying to stop you falling over."

Ludd, wearily propped himself up. "Knock it off—now!" Vince's eyes, mischievous and glinting, darted from Ludd back to Hannah. "I said, NOW!" yelled Ludd. Vince flicked at the control like a petulant child; the arms fell down by the droid's side.

"You moron!" she hissed. She flew furiously at Vince. Vince responded by hunching up, his arms over his head. She stopped dead. "You little rat! I'm getting an order on you. See that snigger, well you'd better enjoy it. I'll rip your tiny little mind. You won't be able to think without me. Do you hear! You've lost it, you stupid little moron. Lost it!"

"I don't think so," growled Ludd, nostrils twitching, blood-rimmed eyes fixed on Vince. "You need us, we need you. Vince here is about to apologize."

"Oh, yeah. Sorry," said Vince, casual as if it were so trivial it was barely worth saying. As Hannah stalked off, he flicked and stabbed at the control and the droid swivelled its head and leered after her with a grotesque mechanoid grin.

"That's all we need!" muttered Andy, a cold sweat on his brow. Elevator doors gliding open, they stepped out into the expanse of Parking Level 2 and gazed upon shoals of shiny vehicles in the mall's cavernous insides.

"Andy?" frowned Dorothea.

"What?"

"We didn't come by car ..."

"Shshtt!" he hissed, quickly grasping her hand, pulling her round and hugging her close as in a lovers' embrace.

"Don't say a word!" he gasped, pressing his lips to her ear. "Trying to lose the surveillance cameras." He glanced up at the nearest surveillance stalk. "Visual tracking. Audio triangulation. Stay close. When I give the word, take off your heels."

They walked between the rows of cars, holding hands, slow, but measured. Dorothea could feel the tension, was aware that, despite their meandering unhurried progress, Andy was on knife edge.

He stopped to duck down, made out he was tying his shoe lace, waited, poised and watchful, next to a camper van and a pillar. A car was approaching, growing louder. The car drew nearer. Andy grasped her hand and pulled her down beside him. As it passed, its shadow over them, he pulled her sideways into the gap alongside the camper.

"We've broken visual," he whispered. "Heels—ditch em. Stick them in the bag. Not a sound." She slipped them off and waited as they squatted besides the pillar. His breathing seemed loud in the silence. "Fast and low," he mouthed "Ready?"

Bent double, they moved along the side of the camper van and rounded the front of the cab. Before them lay a narrow, irregular channel between the line of parked vehicles and the outside wall. Scrabbling along, bent double, their fingers pressing the ground for support, they began working their way back in the direction they'd come. Most of the parked vehicles were out from the wall the standard auto-sensor gap, but some were pulled up close. For these they crawled underneath, half under the car, half under the safety barrier, Dorothea clutching the bag to her chest.

Reaching a heavy concrete pillar, they stopped and straightened, their backs against its cold mass. In front a big metal grid window, like a prison door, beyond which lay the vicious icy, black of the city. Noise rose up from the streets, random snatches, a yell, overlapping voices, warning beepers.

Andy breathed heavily, dropped his head and rubbed his closed lids with his fingers. He stared out, gaunt, bitter, shivering, lips severe and thin. Dorothea looked out with him, and waited.

"Are you okay?" she whispered after a few minutes. He said nothing. "Andy?" She reached a hand out to his cheek.

"Yeah ... yeah," he muttered, flinching, pulling away as if her touch was burning his skin. "I'm okay—alright!"

"What about ...?"

"Shhtt! Face out, dammit! Send the sound out, lose it in the street."

"Right ... sorry," she said in a hushed tone, eyes drawn away from him. "Think we've lost them?"

"I bloody well hope so," he breathed. "When that nosey bampot gets the lost-track alert, he'll do a step back, see where the cameras lost us. If this works, he'll guess we got into a car, drove out. He'll start checking the registrations and the exit cameras, try to identify us by scanning footage of cars that left the building. That'll keep him busy. But ... he might keep half an eye on what's up here .... But, if we're really unlucky, he'll suss that the car thing was nothing but bluff."

"So he could still be scanning this floor waiting for us to reappear?"

"Yeah, that's about the gist of it."

"So, what do we do now?"

"Wait till he gets bored. Call someone with a van to come get us out. Hell, I don't know! I'm making this up as I go along." His voice became hard and low. "You want to know the answer, you want to know what we do? We don't get into this situation in the first place."

They looked out into the night. His breathing began to slow, but she could still hear the tremor in his voice.

"You'll be okay, Andy. I don't think they got enough. The hat and the shades hide a lot." She waited a while longer, watched and listened to the flickering lights and the clash and clamour of the city before trying again. "Did I do the right thing not letting him past?"

"Yeah, thanks—for stepping in," he muttered, eyes glancing briefly towards her. His voice had come down a notch, he sounded strained rather than frightened. "These security guys think they're a law unto themselves. It's like they've got a God given right to take your biometrics."

"It's illegal to force people, isn't it?" said Dorothea, shaking her head in disbelief. "Unless they've actually committed a crime."

"Yeah, but try telling them that."

She reached her arm out sideways and clasped his jittering hand.

"Andy, I hope you don't mind me asking—but why this? Why come all the way up here? Why not just go back home. All we were doing was buying clothes. We didn't need to run. They couldn't do anything, could they?"

"Couldn't do anything?" echoed Andy, shaking free her hand. "You don't see it do you. All you need is to get noticed, to stand out. If they realize you're not on the database, it's like 'Who is this guy? Why is he not registered?' Once they latch on, you are in deep shit. 'All we need's you're name—Oh, yeah, here it is. Thanks ... Oh, and your email ... Great ... And the first line of your address ... and your geo code.' Before you know it they're onto the rectal examination and the DNA swab. Can't ever get enough, pick you over like vultures. All they need is that first lead. Could be from work, at home, travelling, retail outlet, anywhere." Andy rubbed his palms against the denim on the front of his thighs then folded his arms tight across his chest. His breath created a cloud of mist that hung for a few seconds then dissipated into the chill night air.

"Who are they?" said Dorothea brow furrowed in consternation.

"Who? Who aren't they! There's tons of them. Generally starts with some lowlife, a geek, a stringer, someone like that security guard out to make a few bucks. They sell you on to a dealer who polishes you up, pays some combers to flesh out your profile. When they're ready they cash you in. Do you know how much the big five pay?"

"I don't. No," said Dorothea, serious, studying his face.

"Up to a thousand, even tens of thousands, depends on the profile. Seems a lot for a bit of poxy data, but they base it on all the crap they think you'll buy in your lifetime: mortgage, credit cards, services, pension, funeral arrangements. Birth to grave— they want a piece of your ass every inch of the way. Commission, it's all commission and incentive schemes." He cupped his hands over his nose and his mouth and breathed through the gaps in his fingers. "Darn, it's cold!"

"Andy," said Dorothea, tentative and concerned, "these registers, they're only for marketing and finance and services, that kind of thing. It's promotional. I don't think they're vindictive."

"They use you. How vindictive is that."

"But isn't it standard. Lots of people—most people—live perfectly normal and happy lives ..."

"For God's sake, Dorothea! Define 'normal'. Define 'happy'. Most people I know are chasing their tails night and day. Why? To keep up with the payments. Who to? To one of the big five."

"But there must be others like you."

"Guess there is. Maybe I should start up a social club for paranoid reclusives."

"I see what you're saying. But surely ..."

"How many people don't have a single credit card?"

"I suppose there'll be some ..."

"Or a club membership, or a service contract or a mortgage?"

"But your wages, they must be paid into a bank account."

"Internet, taken out with false ID. I use pay as you go, cash-cards, prepay. No names, no tracking."

"Electricity?"

"Swipe meter."

"Insurance?"

"Don't have any?"

"Doctor?"

"The emergency drop-in centre—and I use fake ID."

"The apartment. You must have your name registered as owning the apartment."

"In my mother's name. Never changed it when she died."

"The phone line?"

"Company's. Listed as theirs."

"But why?" Dorothea shook her head. "Why do you want to be ... so ... so ... apart from everything?"

"Because," he said, vehement, jaw tight, "I see how it works. It's all profiles. Your life becomes one big profiling exercise. You build up a profile, you get measured by your profile, you live for your profile. It takes over. Soon you're life's all about upgrading your profile. Builds up over years. Before you know it, your profile takes over. They don't bother to ask you, see who you are, they just check your profile. Want insurance, a food delivery, tickets for a concert ... we'll just check your profile. I mean ... really! Don't bother talking to me guys. No, my profile will tell you. What's my profile saying now? Oh no, it says I'm not right for this. Gotta work harder, get more points, bend that back, build up that profile." He paused his tirade and became listless and subdued. "That's how it is, Dorothea. Classed, pigeonholed, walled in by a pile of crap."

"But hasn't that always been the case, Andy. People tend to group, create classes. It's happened through history."

"Yeah, but now it's different, now people live for their profile. Internet of things, good old IoT means the machines don't need us to tell them anything. They talk to each other. Great! What are you guys saying? Washing machine ... have you been talking to the energy company about me? Every darn thing you do, open the fridge door, eat a tin of beans, press a button, get a positive ID on a camera, take a photo, have a shower, it all adds more profile."

He fell quiet at the sound of approaching footsteps. They continued past.

"You know how money started, don't you?"

"As a means for trade," said Dorothea.

"Yeah, well that's not what it is now. You live, you spend, you create profile. Money, profile, people... they merge to become the same thing. They use secret algorithms to tie it all together."

"But I didn't think you cared about those things, Andy," said Dorothea, above the noise of doors slamming and a pick-up whining as it passed behind the pillar. "You could just ignore it. Do you really have to isolate yourself like this?"

Andy hunched up his shoulders and pulled up the lapels of his leather jacket.

"I can't quite explain it, but it's about—I don't know. I guess, deep down, it's about truth. Truth should be about what is, what's actually there. Money and profiles ... it's all false. The system replaces real stuff with data. The people who are good at manipulating the data then manipulate the real world. The ones who figure out how to get a really big number in their bank account, or rank high in some rating or poll or who get some fancy letters after their name, get treated as uber important, the world revolves around them. If you have zilch in the data categories you're a nobody, you get pushed around, ignored, you have no voice."

Dorothea thought for a while, let him calm before asking her question. "So what is truth, what is real?"

Andy laughed. "Philosophy-Course 101!" He rubbed his hands briskly up and down his arms to try to warm them up, then stuffed them back inside his jacket and became still again. "I won't even try to answer that. Let's just say: you're real, I'm real, the floor's real, this moment in time is real. I know it sounds stupid and totally obvious, but that's not what goes down out there. Nobody takes anything at face value.

"Andy?" said Dorothea. She hesitated before continuing. "Andy, I know you do everything you can to avoid it, but you were born, you went to school, you must have a profile."

"So?" said Andy, kicking at a discarded bottle cap. It flew against the low wall then ricocheted off, silver, spinning, careering across the tyre stained concrete and rattling to a halt under a car.

"Is there something wrong with it?"

"Huh?"

"Is there a problem with your profile?" Andy looked sharply at her then stared out at the bitter night. "I want to understand you," she continued softly, "I want to know the real you, Andy. I can't know the real you if you hide things that matter."

Andy considered for a moment, thought about the big secret he was keeping from her and the half-truths he'd fed her so far.

"One of my mates snuffed it," he breathed. "We were playing a gig. Virtworld Mega Tour. He wanted to stop at 24 hours. How was I to know he'd just done a straight-shift. I signalled him to man-up, chucked him a can of Ultra Kaff. He died, I got to watch that in real world. "

Dorothea didn't comment other than to say that she was sorry. She sensed it wouldn't be appropriate to talk any more so she gazed out into the night. She was becoming aware that woven into the fabric of the bright colours and the fascinating smells and the excitement of the world, there was pain, tragedy, hardship and cruelty. It was there, in the things around them, in what they were and how they'd come to be. Andy, when he spoke of what was real, made it sound simple, as if the present was everything. But, it was clear to her that past events had formed him, shaped who he was, and, that being the case, the present, this time they had now, each decision, each event, held within it the power to determine what they were to become.

"Geez it's cold," said Andy, as if to himself. He clapped his arms round his body a few times and peered round the pillar. "Stuff it, let's go."

He had to find something to wear to the party. That was a tough one. There were two shirts he used to think of as stylish: the curved collar, pearl buttoned one; the shimmery red, night-clubby thing. Nah! Hated them both. Collapsing onto his bed, he pulled off a tennis shoe and chucked it across the room. T-shirt, jeans. He wasn't getting ponced up like some male-gigolo-debutante kind of thing. Shave, shower, that'd have to do. Do the T-shirt hunt later. He grabbed a towel, jeans and leaned against the bathroom door.

"Mmph! What the ..." The darned thing was locked.

Inside he heard a movement and the dying hiss of the shower.

"Sorry!" called Dorothea. "Just be a minute! ... Andy?"

"Yeah?"

"Can I borrow your robe?"

He grinned doggedly. It was a few years since he'd had to wait his turn. The bolt snapped back. She was quick. Shrouded in a cascade of warm, moist, perfumed air, she padded by, damp feet traversing the rug.

"I haven't held you up, have I?" she enquired, tying the robe, entwining the belt loosely around her waist. The towelling, thick and comforting, clung to her wet skin. "You said not to keep asking. I thought I'd freshen up before we went out."

"No problem." said Andy.

"I'll leave you to it then!" she smiled, walking past, her head piled high, the towel tilted precariously to one side.

Andy just stood there. This was the future—Mark 3s. Everybody thought about big stuff like the implications for society, impact on commerce and business, legality, balance of power, world order. But the reality for most people would be day to day stuff like jockeying to see who'd be first into the shower. They see human-real as a nirvana. The reality was this: compromises, mine fields, strategies to follow for the sake of a peaceable life. Just look at himself: press-ganged into taking her shopping, escorting her to a party, waiting for her to vacate the bathroom.

Dorothea came wandering back through with her dress clutched against her. She held it up by the straps and surveyed herself in the hall mirror. "Do you think I should wear my hair up?"

Andy shrugged. "It'll be informal. Maybe leave it down." He assessed his 'partner'. She was going to look classy, sophisticated.

"Decided what you're wearing?" she chirped, as she sidled past.

"Still working on it," he grumbled.

"Want me to look you out something?" she offered, hanging back at the bedroom doorway, dress draped over her arms. "I could lay something out while you're in the shower—if that's any help."

Andy felt his bristles rising. Since when did he need someone running his life, picking his clothes, deciding how he, Andy Naismith, would appear to the world. Who did she think she was?

"Appreciate it," he said. As always, his lethargy outbid his indignation. As he closed the door, he felt a tinge of guilt. That was a tough call. He wondered if she realized what she was letting herself in for.

Victoria had booked the taxi and, by accident, or by design, got one that had been hacked—it double-parked, dropped them right at the door saving them the cold slog from the rank several hundred yards up the street. Andy had his strategy figured out: instead of exiting the cab, he faffed about with his prepay card, then checked around the floor under the pretext that something had slipped from his wallet. It helped that it was raining, the kind of short, sharp shower that can have you soaked to the skin. Victoria and Dorothea, overcoats pulled up round their cheeks for added protection, crossed the pavement, and, on seeing that he was delayed, sheltered inside the Billiard Club outer doors—perfect: out of view of the street cameras. With the rain reducing visibility, his hat, his shades, and the time-gap between them, there'd be near zero correlation between Victoria and himself. He let the girls go ahead through the scanner and inner door. A moment of tension as Dorothea passed through but, as in the earlier test run, the green 'Enter' sign flashed up. Bundled in their coats, they emerged, slightly disorientated, into the oil-lamp gloom and muggy warmth.

The Billiard Club atmosphere was very different at night: the lamps gave out a warm, but meagre, amber light, like glowing coals, and the table tops took on a black liquid appearance as if they were pools of still water surrounded by bunches of palms and ferns—the dominant decorative feature. Most of the place was in shadow, jungle shadow. Andy was feeling awkward. He was the reluctant host, the guy who knew the place but hadn't wanted to come. Struggling with initiative or enthusiasm, he let Victoria and Dorothea make the first move—the inevitable, totally predictable 'let's get a drink' step. As the girls chatted at the bar and waited to order, he kept half an ear on the conversation. Would it be painfully awkward, or revelatory ... the kind of thing that would require sudden and drastic intervention. He was on standby, ready to interrupt problematic conversation with an enquiry about the purchase of crisps. Victoria spoke about the orchestra having to practice on Sunday evening— something to do with venue availability. Dorothea's response was general commiseration, and the view that work shouldn't be allowed to encroach into weekends and holidays. Then a pause, a gap, that junction where a conversation can plough straight on, or take a completely new direction. Victoria wasn't ready to change course.

"It's not the extra work, it's the loss of time to do your own thing that really irks." She'd had her gripe, she turned the conversation back to Dorothea: "Does that kind of thing ever happen to you?"

Andy grimaced. The girls' earlier confab had resulted in a mission to shop and a list of must-do touristy things—that was problem enough—how was Dorothea coping with this kind of probing, tell-me-about-yourself questioning. Should he leap in with crisp enquiries? That could look suspicious. Earlier attempts to curtail Dorothea's response had spectacularly backfired. Better wait. She must have dealt with stuff like that over her cup-of-tea inquisition.

Dorothea paused, a thoughtful expression on her face, as if trying hard to recall. Victoria took a couple of sips of her drink.

Andy waited, tension levels ratcheting up. Why didn't she reply? Was she stuck! Was she suffering an algorithm collapse, some subroutine careering round and round in a non-executable loop? At last she deigned to speak.

"You know, you've had such a tough time, Victoria, what with moving house, all the unpacking, starting a new job ... I feel we shouldn't even be thinking about work. Let's just try to unwind. What do you say?"

"You're absolutely right," returned Victoria. "Let's switch off. It's Saturday night, for crying out loud!"

Andy supressed a quiet smile. He was totally impressed. Without fuss, and with impressive regard for the enquirer, Dorothea had completely put a stop to all work-related questions. Instead of being evasive and simply not telling, she was being helpful, kind, considerate, and keeping her trap shut. He inhaled slowly. He shouldn't have got so keyed up—she was Spydroid after all, kitted out with combat-ready, wriggle-out-of-that-one defences. In fact he was quite envious. He could do with some premier league avoidance skills. He took a long, satisfying draught of his beer and smiled admiringly at Dorothea as she continued, effortlessly, to converse with Victoria. One day out of the box and her communication skills had noticeably developed. Dorothea sensed his look and cast him a fleeting glance, a quick smile. It might have been his imagination, but in that brief exchange, he thought he detected the tiniest trace of a wink.

As the girls passed him back his drink and turned back to the bar to pick up their own, it occurred to Andy that the Hannah's total lock-down strategy had been flawed. Keeping Dorothea locked up, a secret prisoner, was a sure fire way of drawing suspicion—this morning had been a pretty close thing. Dorothea had no difficulty passing herself off as human ... the strategy ought to play to that strength. Treating someone who appeared to be human as a Class 3 only drew attention; the strategy hadn't been viable from the start. How on earth could he guarantee no one would ever come into his flat; Hannah had sent people round herself—for heaven's sake! Having found that the programme had been ill-conceived, it was up to him to adapt, come up with a workable alternative. Having Dorothea out of the flat was part of that alternative. At some point Hannah would have to be told ... she'd just have to get her control-freak head round that. Once the uplift was done, he'd break it to her ... even better, he'd bung it in the report. Fait accompli. Anyway, what could she do? Come thundering down from floor seven with his 'anonymous' report and slam it on his desk. That would be a bit of a giveaway, wouldn't it? Yeah, things were starting to look up.

But right now he had the Victoria conundrum. His guess was that she was looking on Dorothea as a naïve, emotional and vulnerable young woman. Whatever she thought, she was involved, and involved in a way that was undefined. Was she a vigilante social-worker, a chaperone, an adopted big-sister, a friend? What about himself, his position, how did Victoria view him? He might have upgraded his reputation from this morning, but questions remained unanswered, awkward conversations about the Andy-Dorothea relationship, the kind of question that he'd rather fend off with a suave confident response instead of choking red-faced into his beer. Best plan was to avoid the topic if at all possible; if need be, have something plausible at the ready. From what Victoria was saying, she'd be fully occupied Sunday evening, so if he took Dorothea to a museum in the morning, that'd minimize contact till Monday—deletion day. End of the whole sorry business.

One thing hadn't changed: Victoria could not be told. Cyber-law was pretty draconian no matter the level of involvement. No, he'd dug himself a deep hole, he'd no right to drag Victoria in too.

Time to move things along. He'd committed to the party, he might as well get it over with. At his suggestion they squeezed past the growing throng in the direction of the Club House. Victoria spotted someone she knew, an old friend from university, and called to Andy and Dorothea to go on ahead and that she'd catch up later.

The Club House acted as the Billiard Club's reception suite, a space that could be hired out or, as was the case tonight, used for open-house parties. The decor wasn't as heavy as the main bar, more rattan and ceiling fans, less mahogany and aspidistra. So far the clientele consisted of a few insular groups dipping into finger foods and talking in secretive tones.

"It's an interesting style," said Dorothea.

"This bit's more colonial, Indian Raj," said Andy. "When the Brits moved in to tropical climes, they sent in the troops, the canon, closely followed by the billiard tables and the gin and tonics. Once they'd subdued the natives they set up clubs for the officer types. Apparently they looked something like this. Need another drink?"

"Yes, thanks," she said unbuttoning her coat and folding it over the back of a chair.

As they sat in the table-lamp glow, she asked him about his favourite things: books, films, food, places. He said his bit then she asked for more, asked about reasons, what made them so special, where you could find them. Despite himself, Andy began to enthuse, open up, which he hated. He was drinking too fast. He wanted to keep his mouth shut, he hated blubbering nonsense. There was a sudden increase in the noise level and, amidst it, Bruce's laconic, good natured drawl.

"Bruce!" Dorothea said.

"The man himself. Him and his entourage. Bruce with a coach load of pals. Good at drumming up business is old Brucy-boy."

Andy took a deep draught of his beer.

"He is very outgoing, isn't he?"

"Yup."

"He's not from London, not originally?"

"Nope. Middlesex. Went for a two week holiday down under and came back red as a lobster and crazy about everything Aussie. I think it was sun stroke that did it. Watched every movie they ever made. Turned from a limey into a typical can-of-Fosters, life's-a-barbie, no-problem, Australian. Calls a kangaroo a kangaroo couldn't cares less if it's a wallaby. I'm thinking of nominating him for the stereotypical Aussie award."

"Do you think he'd win?"

Andy blinked and looked at her, as if he'd become disconnected. "That was meant to be a joke or facetious or something," he said.

"Oh, sorry! I'm not good at telling ..."

"No. My fault."

Dorothea sipped at her Perrier water and ice. "So," she said, "where did you meet?"

"At a barbecue, would you believe? Some society or other, can't even remember which one. Wait—must've been geology ... yeah, that's right. We went in the geology department mini-bus. Geologists are like Jekyll and Hydes: they're either amazingly boring or off-the-wall loopy. Anyhow, they do this insane Christmas party thing: east coast, middle of winter, a big bonfire on the beach. You get roasted by the fire on one side and frozen by Arctic gales on the other. To avoid third degree burns and frostbite you had to keep twirling round—not an easy thing to do when you've downed a few cans."

"It sounds primitive."

"It was, and the sparks were amazing," recounted Andy, with a flourish of his hand. "I've never seen such sparks. Crazy. Shooting into the sky like supercharged rockets, tracer bullets, huge streams of them. I guess they fizzled out over the sea. And the sea, the sea was really weird. It was just so amazingly black. I remember I had this notion that the sea at night would be romantic or atmospheric or something, but it was actually quite scary."

"I'd like to do that sometime," said Dorothea quiet, distant, imagining what it might be like to stand in the glow of fire with the night all around. Andy glanced at her, took a deep slug of beer, and changed the subject.

"Want something stronger?"

"No," she smiled.

"Crisps, peanuts, Bombay mix?"

"No thanks."

"So you bumped into Bruce at that barbecue?" she enquired brightly.

"Yeah. It wasn't actually a barbecue, just a bonfire. I can't even remember how the bonfire got there—if we brought wood or someone else built it or what. Whatever, there were sausages and rolls and stuff. The geologists were skewering sausages and cooking them over the flames. I use the term cooking loosely, it was more like incinerating. Bruce goes 'Whoaaa guys! That ain't how you do it!' He did his survival guru cum master chef act; showed them how to rustle up something that a student could happily bung in a roll and smother with sauce. Anyhow, some vegetarian chick brought potatoes, but Bruce didn't know how to cook 'em. I did. We used to do it when we were kids. Gang huts, nick a few spuds for the fire. Bruce started yelling 'roll up, roll up!' like we were running a hot dog stand at the fair. Next thing we'd a queue of customers. People acted like we were the caterers. After that we got requests from other clubs, a kind of barbecue double act, Bruce grilling and flipping, me doing the less usual stuff like fish or grilled bananas—most of the times I was guessing. We earned a few bucks. Bruce never looked back: ran a mobile party trailer for a couple of years, then he got this."

A surge of laughter came at them from across the room. Andy glanced over. Bruce of course. He hated this, the sitting around, the waiting-to-be-discovered moment. He started flipping up beer mats and trying to catch them in mid-air. Bruce was working his way round, shaking hands, a nod a wave, an amusing comment. A party appeared at the door and hung there, not sure whether to enter. Bruce strolled over and took control.

"Looks like it could be busy," commented Dorothea.

"Yeah, it takes a bit to liven up."

"Andy?" said Dorothea.

"Yeah," he said, suspicious, sensing something was coming.

"I told Victoria that we were friends."

"Hmm," said Andy, sitting there, wanting to affirm but unable to conflict word and intention yet again. Picking up a beer mat, he floated it, like a raft, on top of the puddle of beer. He was vaguely aware of interruptions, saying 'hi' to Bruce, inane meaningless conversation, Victoria arriving, making a big thing about Dorothea's outfit. Then Victoria taking Dorothea over to talk to some historian friend of a friend—apparently Dorothea had been interested in iconoclasts and the reformation. Victoria returned to sit beside him soon after. Andy's suspicious mind reckoned the whole thing had been a ploy to get him on his own.

He'd expected a one-to-one with Victoria to be awkward and argumentative, but she was easy to talk to. She managed to make basic, non-controversial, mundane things interesting— the company that serviced the flat, the strange paint marks on the bottom hall floor. He was able to provide background, tell her about the area and the quirks that come with living cheek by jowl with people you never really know. Reluctantly, inevitably, she steered them onto rocky ground.

"So ... you took Dorothea to ZaZaZee?" she began.

"Yeah."

"Expensive! I hope that wasn't because of me ..."

"Huh?"

"Out of guilt after this morning. Dorothea explained what happened."

"Explained ..." said Andy.

"Yes, about the misunderstanding ... the drama thing you were doing." She raised an eyebrow and held her gaze a fraction of a second—in case he thought she was totally convinced.

"She told me she just got carried away, that she over-reacted." Victoria looked at Andy as he slouched into the corner of the bench. "I was pretty hard on you."

"No, it's okay," said Andy. He waited for the next instalment, he knew there'd be more.

"You don't seem to know Dorothea that well."

"You're right, I don't. If you want to know: somebody at work asked me to put her up for the weekend. Only known her since Friday."

"I thought you said you met her on webchat."

"Just to set it up. It was just a favour, really ... to do with work. She's heading off on Monday."

Victoria fell silent for a while, reassessing the situation.

"You'll be seeing her again?"

"No, I don't think so."

Andy braced himself.

"Andy, I'm concerned. ... I think you might have a problem."

"Huh!"

"She's very young. I think you know that ... And she thinks the world of you." Victoria paused, trying not to push her opinions too hard. "When she's talking and you're not there, it's all Andy this and Andy that. I'm not saying she's totally infatuated, but it's certainly heading that way ... I think there could be a problem if you try to end it abruptly."

Andy didn't respond. Victoria became aware of an acute silence, a darkness in his eyes.

"If there's anything I can do to make it less ..."

"No," he said. "Thanks, really. There's nothing anyone can do."

"Ok" she said, "but the offer is there."

Victoria tried to make small talk, but now she sensed that it was intrusive; Andy had become too preoccupied to engage. As they sat side by side and Victoria tried to make sense of the situation, she became aware of Dorothea approaching from the far side of the room.

"That was so interesting!" Dorothea beamed, too excited to wait till she was sitting beside them. "Did you know that..." but her voice faded to nothing. "Andy?" She stopped abruptly, leaned forwards to get Andy's attention. He didn't look up. A tremor ran through her voice: "What's wrong? What happened?" Victoria gave a desultory shrug of her shoulders.

"Andy," Dorothea pleaded. "Look. I'm here. It's alright!" She squeezed round beside him and leaned forward, her head in front of his to try to see into his eyes. "What is it, Andy? Is it work? Is it those men? Andy ... Look at me. Why can't you look at me?" She coiled her arm through his arm and clenched her fist tight into his. Her voice lowered and she spoke with her mouth close to his ear. "Whatever it is, Andy, we can work it out. Andy ... Andy."

A waiter came up and said 'Hi, I'm Geoffrey. Can I set up this table for you?' Plates of food started arriving: tandoori chicken, vegetable korma, rice and poppadum and Nan bread. Excusing himself to top up his beer, Andy made his way to the bar. When he got back through to the Club Room the lighting had dimmed: a classical guitarist was setting up under the bathing glow of a spotlight. As the recital began, Andy stood in the shadows and listened to the mellow tones of a country he would never know.

He couldn't return to the table. Sliding through a louvre door he escaped into the cool darkness of the veranda, its black shadows made intense by thin lines of light gliding through the slats of the shutters. It was very different from the morning— the sun god had moved on and, as the day ran its course, Andy had crossed the river into the kingdom of Hades.

He gazed out at through the big panes at the night and the turbulent clouds, and his thoughts turned to Monday morning and all the possible scenarios, combining them, adjusting them, like a newsreel cutting room, running them again and again in the labyrinth of his mind. He was captive in this world, he couldn't shut the images off; in his mind's eye, in his ears, a barrage of disjointed stills and enactments flashed and stuttered onto the screen. Him, Dorothea, the path stretched out before them. He knew how it went, he'd wiped dozens of droids: procedure, options, confirmation, always ... always, the blank face at the end. Doing the same with Dorothea—him reading out her death sentence, her trembling, crying, struggling not to cry. She'd recite the endless list of options. And he'd have to respond with 'shred', 'security-level', 'no back ups', 'delete data', 'delete memory', 'delete personal attributes', 'delete appearance'. She would help create her own sentence, offer him the choices, each one a chance to save her, to save something and he, relentlessly, would spell out her damnation.

But he couldn't do it like that, he couldn't go through it like he would with any other droid. Faced with her standing there, waiting, cold, bereft, eyes searching but not finding, he wouldn't be able to rattle through it like she was some kind of household appliance. At some point he'd have to comfort her, kiss her forehead, hold her in his arms. And when it comes to the bit where she asks if that's what he wants, he won't just bleat out 'confirm', he'll have to explain that he has no choice, that it has to be. When they've done all that, when they've gone through all the options and she seeks his final confirmation and she asks if he's sure that's what he wants because the next step is irreversible, he'll have to lie to himself and to her. The final act. Whispering the fateful last word, releasing the drop of poison into her ear, letting it seep, black, treacle-like, to invade the depths of her being. For you, Dorothea—oblivion.

The beer glass cracked, and, as it fell, cold and clear amongst the cascade of liquid, its razor edge sliced, silent and efficient, into the warm flesh of his hand.

Chapter 11 Sunday

The tumbler was ice cold, the juice sharp-edged and tangy. Orange with bite. Breakfast in bed, sun flooding in, big white bandage round his palm—he felt different, heroic, like a war veteran. Propped up, sitting straight, the juice infused his body as he swallowed it down.

"Better?" said Dorothea watching from a respectful distance.

"Yes, thanks," smiled Andy, grateful.

She crossed the bedroom floor and laid a hand on his forehead.

"I hope that's not a regular occurrence," she said, withdrawing her hand, retreating, going over to the window and straightening the curtains.

"Most saturday nights, except when there's a stag night or a birthday booking or something. Bruce has to make a living."

"I meant Accident and Emergency," she said, her gaze earnest and unflinching.

"No. That was a one off. Saturday night A and E isn't my thing."

"Andy," she said, with a touch of reproach, "you should've come for help instead of using the fire-exit."

"I know, but it was the quickest way out."

"But you were losing blood. I was half expecting to find you slumped in the street." She came over and examined him again as if she might have missed some of his symptoms. "You were very talkative at the hospital. Perhaps you suffered some kind of concussion?"

"Just me blabbing. Can't hold my liquor," he said. She didn't respond.

Andy poured himself some coffee. It was a relief to be awake. The night had been a mix of hallucinations and anxiety dreams, a quagmire of sheets and fever and pain killers. He'd been up four times. Sleep, if he could call it that, had taken its toll.

"You make this fresh?" said Andy, studying the glass before setting it down. He surveyed the rest of the breakfast tray. Ten out of ten for presentation. Not over the top, not overly presumptive. Appropriate. The juice in a glass tumbler she must have unearthed from the back of a cupboard, the bowl ready for cereal should he want it, a cafetière filled with fresh coffee. He didn't have the heart to tell her he hated breakfast in bed.

"Yes, I couldn't find your citrus squeezer. I just did it by hand. Is there a problem?"

"No, it's great. Nice, very nice," he said, taking a dutiful gulp, tasting, nodding appreciatively.

Sun shone in through the trees, the wet branches shivering, the sky a clear, pure, translucent blue.

He looked at her sympathetically. During brief interludes in the night fever, a notion, a hope had come into being. It might be possible, just possible to save Dorothea, or at least to extend the trial beyond Monday. But he needed a good reason, a fantastic reason, something a heck of a lot better than his normal, measly, need-more-time excuse.

Dorothea appeared with fresh clothes.

"Now, just say! I'll put these straight back if you'd rather choose them yourself." Andy looked at them. They were typical of the motley selection he would have chosen himself. Even the socks didn't match. She was observant, and happy to follow his preferences, but how long would that last.

"Great, just dump them on the bed," he said.

"Okay. If you don't mind I'll just wait here till you're finished your breakfast—perhaps you'd like toast."

"No, I'm fine."

She went over to the window, sat on the wicker chair and looked out, silent and calm, as if in deep thought.

Where was he? Yeah ... Hannah. First up, he'd have to make out he was getting somewhere with this report. Maybe he could use stuff like this. An account of what it was like living with a level 3. How much initiative they showed, how often they surprised you ... and whether or not that was a good thing. What about consistency? Would it be perfect breakfast after perfect breakfast, or human-level variation. If she truly was 'human-real', how far would that go? Unreliability, arguments over who's going to clear the table, mood swings.

He leaned back to consider. Yeah, that was a good point. If her base profile was still that of a spy, realism would be paramount. Being permanently upbeat and helpful, a human who, morning after morning, was all sunshine and light—how realistic was that? To go deep undercover, a spy would have to do the full range: bolshie, tetchy, demanding, the works. Maybe this was just the honeymoon period. In a few weeks she might be nagging him, burning the toast, waking him up in the small hours because she'd been out partying and had forgotten her key. This idea, this great quest to make androids indiscernible from humans, was that what people really wanted? It'd be like taking in a lodger, a stranger living in your house.

The customers, top-rollers, presidents, industrialists, celebrity brats, how would they cope if their zillion dollar droid had off-days, told them to 'go shove it', pointed out that if they wanted the house vacuumed they could move their precious butts and do it themselves. Wouldn't work would it? The human-real features of your spydroid would go down like a lead balloon.

And what about her other specs? A phone antennae inside her head, the ability to hear a mouse fart on the other side of the street, knocking out a titanium roach with a flick of her heels. That ain't domestoid.

Andy closed his eyes and let out a low murmur of joy. Geeeeeez! That's it. He needed more time—not because he was a lazy sod, true though that may be, but because there were fundamental issues at stake. This wasn't a droid level 1 or level 2 performance check. You could do them in a few hours. You told them to do something, they did it the same way time and again. You'd meet them in the hall or the kitchen or whatever, at the precise instant, doing whatever was programmed into their schedule. Dorothea was different. He needed to look for day to day variations, monitor her for a week at least ... even a month. Hannah had to give him an extension. He'd tell she was great, of world-shattering significance, but point out the complexity, the vast pile of unknowns, tell her he couldn't even begin the report unless she gave him a couple of weeks. More time for Dorothea, more time to think of a solution. Hannah, sorry, but to try to review a level 3 in a weekend is to deny what you've got. You can't apply level 2 assessment to kit that's a hundred times more sophisticated. Not my fault. Impossible time scale. The job spec was flawed, that's down to you, Hannah.

He took a final swig of the orange and glanced over to where Dorothea was sitting, swinging a leg under the chair, peering inquisitively at something outside. He followed her gaze. A crow on the rooftop opposite hopped a few steps. Eye bright, it cocked its angular head and heavy beak in a sharp, almost mechanical manner. He suppressed a shiver as he emptied the glass. He had to make this thing work.

The latch he twisted with his good hand, his left; the door handle he pushed down painfully with the bandage-protruding fingertips of his right.

"Andy?" Dorothea called from the kitchen.

"Just ... just popping down to check the post," he called, reaching for the post box key to add authenticity.

"Can't I do that?" she said, leaning out into the hall, concerned, a crease on her brow.

"Nah! These stairs are about the only exercise I get."

The heavy entrance door clunked behind him. He was outside, outside and free. He stood at the top of the steps and, with pleasure, inhaled the stale city air and felt a few spits of rain on his skin.

Somewhere out there was Hannah. Hannah doing what? In bed perhaps. He found that difficult to imagine. Probably be up now, having breakfast, brushing her teeth, on the loo? She was human, just a person, no better than he. More organised perhaps, more drive, more focused, more connected, more ... Forget the 'more' stuff, she needs to get used to controlling a tad less.

He stretched his arms up, reached his hands down behind his head and flexed his elbows back. The stillness of the buildings, the long, dripping chasm created by the flats on either side of the street, moss sprouting from crevices, algae-tinged road signs, rivulets gurgling, muddy gutters, drains bunged up with decaying leaf litter. Although it was the city, it was natural, like a gorge, as if the hand of nature had touched every stone.

He went down the steps and, selecting carefully, picked up a single round pebble from the gravel below the bay windows. Bringing it back up, he placed it on a little stone ledge near to the door pillar. It'd stay there for now. Tonight, or tomorrow morning, when it was over, he'd come to this same spot, he'd take the pebble from the ledge, carry it upstairs and place it inside the spherical glass bowl on the mantel piece. It would be over.

On the way back into the hall, his eye caught the protruding flap of his post box. There was actually something in it. He scowled. Strange, nothing ordered. It was a small package, brown and plain and slim. No postmark, no sender details, just a white label with his name and address. The format was familiar. He took a few minutes to register, then, guessing what was inside, ripped it open as he ascended the stairs. A noise from above, the second floor, Victoria's door swung open.

"Not expecting to see me?" she said.

"Eh, yeah. No. I ..."

"Are you alright?"

"Yeah, just a couple of stitches. Popped round to A and E."

"Would've been nice to have known you were back, that you were alive, something like that," she said as she leaned against the door frame.

"Sorry. The beer glass fell to pieces in my hand. Weird."

"Really?"

"It does happen. There was a guy I knew—kind of knew—I didn't know him personally, a wine glass broke in his hand at a lecturer-meet-student function. He ended up bleeding over some professor's car on the way to the hospital."

"Not like you then?" she said, voice brittle.

"What do you mean?"

"He didn't disappear. Vanish ... leaving a big pool of blood."

"I ... I'm sorry. It just happened. I thought I should get to the hospital as quickly as possible."

"First you vanish. Dorothea didn't know where you were. We started searching, then we found blood and glass all over the floor in some back room ..."

"That was the veranda. It was mostly beer."

"There weren't any lights on. I thought you'd been attacked, that maybe you were mixed up in something. Dorothea had said something about some guys—I didn't know what to think. Dorothea ran off out of the fire escape, not a word where she was going. I was left standing. I didn't know what to do. I called the police, Andy. What else could I do? I spent an hour and a half filling in police reports. Then Dorothea phoned from the hospital. A minor accident. Couple of stitches. Well, you know what the police are like. They just looked at me like I was some stupid, saturday-night drunk. They'd already cordoned off the 'crime scene'. Forensics were on their way." She inhaled painfully, throat constrained with emotion. "Andy, they were half-right. I wasn't drunk, but I was stupid—stupid to have got involved."

Andy watched, helpless, trying to think of something to relieve her distress. Nothing came

"You know something, Andy!" she struggled. "You like your secrets, life's one big secret isn't it—you, Dorothea, whatever the hell you're up to. Nobody else matters. Well, that's fine by me. Count me out, Andy. Count me out period!" She slammed the door, the stairwell reverberated and the hallway windows shook in their frames.

Andy, stunned, stood and stared at the wrinkled blue paint on her door. Geez! Where'd that come from? He had a ton of shit to deal with, he damn well didn't need any more.

"No problem!" he yelled at the door. He squatted down and pushed the brass letter box open half an inch. "Nobody invited you anyway!"

"A task?" said Dorothea.

"Yeah, a kind of challenge," said Andy, throwing himself back on the sofa, trying to calm himself down. "See how it goes.

Options are pretty slim. You need certificates and stuff for all the professional roles—doctors, nurses, teachers. You could always do something business related, take the helm of a major corporation, run a consultancy, but then you'd need to know the right people to get in." He crossed one leg over the other and swung his foot up and down.

"Andy, I'd be happy to try anything, but with it being Sunday, isn't most of that offline?"

"Yeah, that's an issue. We need something that runs seven days a week. Hey, what about child care! That's important, that requires responsibility. Yeah, and ... taking a kid to the Natural History Museum would keep Victoria off our back. That's on her to-do list. We'd kill two birds with one stone. You mentioned you wanted to see some galleries and museums—well, here's your big chance."

"What kid?" said Dorothea.

"Well, that's the thing. I don't have a kid to hand. I know people who have kids, kids to spare really, but it's not that easy to get one at short notice. In any case, with you not having any experience, it might be a bit iffy to hand one over for training purposes. I'm getting enough flack without looking for more. This is about giving you practice ..."

"Practice for what?"

He rubbed the palms of his hands over his jeans, paused, considered how much he should tell.

"There's something I haven't told you—about where you fit in. Your job. What you'll do in the longer term. How long you'll do it for."

"Okay," she said cautiously, her back to the bay window, patchy cloud beyond.

"Yeah. More experience means more opportunities."

"Opportunities?"

Andy didn't like being deceitful but how could he tell her that the opportunity he had in mind was that of surviving past Monday.

"I don't know exactly what your run time is, but I've been thinking—if I ... if we could come up with some evidence to show how fantastic you are, then we could make a case for a longer run time rather than a shorter one. I've been trying to think of a task that gives you responsibility. Something important. What's more important than bringing up a kid? "

"So, you think this might help?"

Andy shrugged. "Who knows? There's always a chance. Look, if it was up to me, I'd let you run forever, but my boss, Hannah, she calls the shots. We could change her mind. Tough call though. Hey, here's a thought! What if we go above Hannah, take it out of her hands?"

"There's someone higher?"

"Yeah ... must be. This is risky and mega expensive. Hannah's stitched up tight as a baseball. Control freak. She doesn't do messy, ass-on-the-line stuff. She's loathing every second. Somebody put this on her plate. Had to come from above."

"Has she mentioned anyone?"

"Nope, and she's not likely to either. See this? Came in the post." He pulled a mobile and a slip of paper out of the box. "Disinfected, digitally scrubbed. I've to take it to some public place, switch it on, pick up a text or a call or whatever, get my instructions. Maybe it's Hannah being cautious, or maybe it's someone higher up. Let's hope it's someone higher."

"But if you don't know who it's from, it could be a hoax."

"Yeah, but everything that goes through this is bleached, that's the whole point. Even voice will be masked. I'll have to go on what is said. If it makes sense, if it sounds right, I'll take it as genuine."

"If not?"

"Then ... I don't know. I guess we're in trouble." Andy stuffed the phone and the slip inside the box and propped it up on the table in the hall.

"Okay, before we phone anyone, we need a report that says you're utterly fantastic at child care. You're the grown up, I'm the kid."

"Starting when?"

"As soon as you're ready, I suppose. You'd better plan out the day. We'll run it, say, till two in the afternoon."

"Fine. I need to check a few things on the net," said Dorothea, leaving Andy to himself.

Taking control felt good, mused Andy reaching over for his guitar. He could still strum a little with the tips of the fingers protruding from the bandages, but it had to be very light and it was awkward to get the right angle. He managed a gentle lilting melody as he vaguely considered their moves.

Hannah would fight tooth and nail to stop him going over his head. That was a given. The thing was how to take it a stage higher. Wouldn't be easy, but he had a few ideas.

"Andy!" Dorothea frowned, as she reappeared at the door. "I don't think that's such a good idea."

He stopped fingering the chords, the guitar fell silent. He'd expected the research to take 10 minutes; it had taken less than two.

"But I'm keeping it real quiet."

"Not that! Your hand," she said. "The stitches might open if you start using it too soon." He paused, resisted the temptation to retaliate, and stood the guitar upright against the end of the couch.

"Good, Andy. Now we're going on a little trip and you'll need to be appropriately dressed. The air temperature's to be about 12 and there's a 90% chance of precipitation." She put her hand up, touched her forehead and frowned. "Sorry, I'm forgetting something." She turned to Andy again but with a cheesy smile and a lot of eye contact.

"Andy, it could be a bit chilly out there, and there's a good chance we'll get caught in a shower. Can't have that, can we. I'd like you to find something nice and warm to wear ... and a jacket, rainproof if you have one. Do you think you can manage that?"

"Yeah," laughed Andy. "You've really caught that momsy tone."

She looked puzzled.

"I'm sorry," she said. "I thought we'd started."

"We have. It's just I ... it doesn't matter. I'll go get some clothes."

"Good. Now I'm going through to the kitchen. I want you to come through and see me in five minutes with those things done. That's 10.15. Do you know how to read the time?" Andy nodded.

"Yeah, learned that in year five."

"Good! In five minutes then."

Andy switched off the amp, gathered up a couple of things, planted a baseball cap on his head, and jacket slung over his shoulder, went through.

"Well done, Andy!" she gushed. "You're through in plenty of time. Now there are one or two things I need to go over before we go out. This should only take a couple of minutes, so I want you to listen very carefully."

"Okay," said Andy hoisting himself up onto a bar stool and resting his elbow on the work surface.

"Right!" she smiled, coming closer. "First, have you brushed your teeth?"

"Yeah, of course I have!"

"Andy, please! Don't be offended. I'm sure you brush your teeth every morning, but I just wanted to check. After all, you might have forgotten. Everyone forgets sometimes, don't they?"

"Okay, okay. The way you're talking, Dorothea, it's kind of pissing me off."

"Andy, language! That's not acceptable, especially for a seven year old!"

"You can talk! This seven year old is finding your language pretty nauseous."

"Well I'm sorry I'm annoying you, Andy, but either I behave as though you are a seven year old or I don't. I don't see how I can do this if you still want to be treated as an adult."

Andy grimaced and became resolute. "Okay, but this sure as hell isn't easy. I was thinking of this exercise more in terms of you, the responsibility, the decisions, that kind of stuff. I didn't really consider what I was letting myself in for."

"Well, do you want to continue?"

Andy skulked for a minute and pulled at his ear lobe. He didn't want to admit it, but what else was there? "Yeah, okay." Andy narrowed his eyes. "Before we start: you're not putting me into day care are you?"

"No, of course not. I'm assuming that you're new to the area, and that you're an active seven-year old boy of average intelligence. Actually, likes and dislikes are two of the things on my check list." She paused, the bright smile she'd been using was all gone. "Andy, you asked me to do this, and I really am trying my best. Maybe I'm just not suited to looking after children."

"No, no—I think you're doing great. It's just not easy being treated as a child. You forget. I suppose when you're a kid you get used to it."

"I've never been a child, so I'm afraid I can't help you with that. You decide, Andy. I won't continue, not if you don't want me to." She watched him, reading his body language, seeing if it matched what he said.

"I survived being a seven year old for a whole year, I guess I can manage a few hours more." He rubbed his hands together, rolled his shoulders and loosened his neck as if limbering up for a mammoth task. "Ok. Let's do it! No chickening out!"

Dorothea smiled again, as she prepared to address him. It may have been Andy's imagination, but he reckoned the smile was slightly tainted, not quite the unfettered, saccharine-sweet version she'd used before.

"Will that jacket keep you dry?"

"Yes. It's okay for the odd shower."

"Good. Now, do you take medicine before you go out in the morning?"

"Nope."

"Good. And are there any medicines we might need to take with us?"

"Inhaler ... asthma. Got it here in my pocket."

"Good and do you have allergies to anything in particular—cats foods ... sprays ... anything?"

"Nope."

"Okay—last of the medical ones. Do you have any illness or medical condition I should know about?"

"Apart from the hand?"

"Apart from the hand."

"I sometimes get a flare up of dandruff, but I generally pull through."

"That's okay." She smiled, ignoring the flippancy. Instead, she paused a second and toned down the smile to something softer and more empathic. "Now Andy, I want you to tell me: is there anything that scares you, anything that you really have to avoid?"

"Mmmm ..." he mused. "Just department stores, especially the one we had to escape from yesterday."

"You're teasing me, Andy. You shouldn't do that. It's not nice."

He mumbled an apology and Dorothea checked the phone and added medical centre numbers to the contact list. "Nearly ready. Can you think of anything else we might need?"

"Prepay card."

"Of course, thanks. I'd better hold on to that. Let's go."

Andy unfolded his Oakley's and stepped out onto the street.

"

"Wait right there, Andy," said Dorothea, catching him up. "A few ground rules. You must stay close to me at all times. You must try to remember your manners. You must do whatever I tell you. Do you think you can do that?"

"Yeah, I suppose," said Andy, hang-dog. If it was bad in the flat, it was going to be ten times worse in public.

"Good. Now we're going to visit the Natural History Museum. Won't that be fun?"

"I guess," he said, scuffing the pavement.

Undeterred, Dorothea chatted brightly as they approached the first junction.

"Now, Andy. I want you to take my hand when we cross the street. Your left hand of course. I'll keep to this side."

"Hey, c'mon. We don't need to do that!" Andy made his protest in a low, warning growl, whilst thanking the heavens there was no-one to hear.

"We do, Andy, we really do. Do you know how many children of your age are hurt each year because they misjudge when to cross?"

"No, I don't," he said, glum and surly as a convoy of vehicles hummed by.

"Well it was far too many," she said. "And it could have been easily avoided by children holding their parent's hand."

"But I'm old enough to cross myself! I've been doing it for ages!"

"Well I'm very pleased to hear that, but until I know you better, and I have your parent's agreement, we'll take this extra safety precaution. Okay?"

Andy cursed inwardly and wondered whether to stick to his guns. As they stood waiting, a shop door swung open, and a man, tall and black, cruised up beside them, smoothly athletic, with Jimi-Hendrix cool. Andy's heart sunk. Dammit! New tactic. Pretend they're a couple holding hands. He reached out. Dorothea grasped his palm firmly and hitched her handbag higher onto her shoulder.

"Well done, Andy!" she exclaimed. "We're going to be good friends, aren't we?"

The guy tilted his head, Andy could tell he'd tuned in. Pretending he was checking for a break in the traffic, Andy snatched a quick glance. He was watching alright; their eyes met. He was squinting at them, inquisitive, slightly bemused. Andy returned a weak smile and shrugged as if to say he didn't understand either.

"I know!" said Dorothea. Andy winced and looked straight ahead. "Perhaps you'd like to show me what you've learned. You could tell me when you think it's a good time ... but you have to wait. If I agree, if we both agree, we'll go. Would you like to try that?"

"Let's just cross the road," said Andy, flatly. He glanced over at the guy. He was chuckling, struggling to contain it, face split ear to ear in an uproarious smile. Andy stared forwards. With the free hand behind his back, he tried, despite the bandages, to make a rude sign.

The streets weren't busy. Sunday morning doldrums; no workers or shoppers to clutter the place up. Even parent's and toddlers were yet to come out in force. Andy barely noticed. He was busy deliberating how to pre-empt the next embarrassing moment.

"One adult and one child," said Dorothea at the museum turnstile. The woman sat higher in her seat and peered down over the edge of the counter.

"Where's the kid?" she asked.

Andy closed his eyes and let out an exasperated breath.

"Excuse me," he said, leaning forward and cutting in before the conversation got into uncharted waters. "There's been a misunderstanding." Putting a hand round Dorothea's shoulder, he guided her away. "Can I have a word with you, Dorothea—in private?"

"Certainly, Andy," she said, "is there something bothering you?"

Huddled in a corner of the vaulted entrance, Andy hoped that anything incriminating would be lost in the echoing din from the street.

"Look, Dorothea. We're pretending that I'm a kid, but you can't expect everyone else to pretend."

"No, I suppose you're right."

"So, when we're dealing with everyone else, you need to treat me as an adult. You understand don't you? I mean that woman's never going to allow me in as a child, is she?"

"No, okay, Andy—I see what you mean." He felt a pang of sympathy. She was trying to make this work, this flimsy, half-baked attempt at saving her existence. She was putting her heart into it, not knowing how imminent the precipice, or how heartless the judgement.

Inside the museum, it was better than he'd thought. A lucky break. It was a place where he could run and play about, a safe indoor environment with almost no need for intervention. Andy was free to skip and whoop (within limits) and press all the buttons, but Andy played the part of a lethargic and melancholic child. Dawdling along, he was contented with looking at stuffed animals and fossil displays. It was, in fact, something of a nostalgia trip; he hadn't been since he was a kid.

There was plenty of new stuff, but he homed in on the familiar, the 3D interactives on global warming, the reinstatement of the rainforest, the giant models of zoo plankton.

Dorothea kept their conversation to a fairly basic level, explaining and commenting as they went along. To Andy's relief, the dialogue wasn't embarrassingly juvenile. As Dorothea studied the exhibits, Andy couldn't help notice her expression, the wonder in her eyes, her eagerness to move to the next gallery. The whole darned thing should be inverted: she was the kid, naïve, fascinated, taken up with the experience, and he ... he was the jaded, world-weary adult.

"Look, Andy. To think that these were the tools that people used right at the beginning," she said, pointing at a display of flint axe heads. "The people who made these were at the forefront of human technology."

"Yeah," said Andy, "at the cutting edge." He cringed.

"Very important. They'd cut skins, wood, make spears, hunt animals they wouldn't dare tackle with their bare hands. They went on to use copper, bronze and then iron, but for that they needed to discover new skills. See! There are some bronze age examples over there." She pointed and they drifted across. "What's really fascinating is that although they fought over things like land and precious objects and power, it was the skills, the knowledge and the beliefs that survived. Most of the material things are gone: their homes, their boats, their furnishings. But the ideas, the skills, they've been incorporated into our lives, the things we do each and every day."

"What about dugout canoes? Don't make many of them these days," said Andy, not entirely convinced.

"We may not make them, true, but that's exactly what I mean. It's the skills and the knowledge that survive."

Andy frowned. "You mean like how to dig out a tree and make it hollow."

"No, silly!" She chucked him under the chin and ruffled his hair. "How to make boats. Before canoes they would have had rafts. You do know what a raft is?"

"Doh! Of course I know what a raft is!"

"Andy! Don't get stroppy. I was just checking. A dugout canoe would be so much better than a raft. The idea of a boat is something we all know about. We know hollow things float, but someone had to discover that. Mastering a skill was important, skills like how to melt metal, weave cloth, make pottery, grow food from seeds, create fire. They'd guard these, pass them on to their children and their grandchildren, but eventually, of course, the skills would spread. Andy?" She turned and, with a sugary smile, put her nose close to his. "Have you any idea how these ideas were passed on?"

Andy huffed, threw her a loose-jawed what-do-you-take-me-for look. "PowerPoint presentation?"

"Now, Andy, I can see why you'd say that," she said, relentless positivity quelling everything in its path, "but that's much more recent. This was before presentation software, before computers, before any kind of technology."

"I was just being ..." began Andy, but there was no point. To survive the next couple of hours, he had to dig deep, stick to straight truthful answers, predictable and factual. He felt small and weak as he gave the answer she wanted. "They were passed on by word of mouth and example ... families, tribes, trade routes, stuff like that."

"Well done! That's right. No books, so no written records, but we can make deductions from artefacts and carbon dating. Occasionally there are clues in the ..."

"Dorothea, can we just leave it there. I am just a kid."

"Okay, Andy. Perhaps you'd like to do something else. There's Find the Fossil at the sandpit and they're doing a Colour that Flag activity in the History of Nations room ..."

"No thanks."

"I know, how about dressing up in a medieval costume. You could be a knight or a jester. Now wouldn't that be fun?"

"Somehow I don't think so," he said, closing his eyes. "The costumes won't fit."

"We could always go and ask ..."

"Dorothea," he said, fighting back exasperation, "I'd just like to wander for a bit."

"That's fine," she said watching him, letting him move on by himself. "But be sure to stay within sight."

Andy moseyed over to a display of early spearheads but his mind was on Dorothea. He wasn't too surprised at her knowledge of history. Androids could load an encyclopaedia in milliseconds. Data, raw facts, that was the easy bit. It was the fudgy, hard-to-define stuff like common-sense and creativity and humour that caused headaches. She'd some limitations there. Didn't she see there might be a problem squeezing him into a kid's costume? Couldn't she see that pulling on bright yellow pantyhose and skipping around wearing a jingly hat might be a tad embarrassing? Should he mark her down for that? Or was it the exercise that was at fault? If he had been a kid then he'd probably have jumped at the suggestion. On the other hand, she should have taken into account that he was a somewhat diffident, lethargic, over-sized kid and by suggesting that he try something that wouldn't be suitable was surely a mistake. But then he'd told her to pretend he was a kid even though he clearly wasn't. The pretence could include physical size and development as well as interests. So how did she score? Was that a plus or a minus? He'd have to work that out later.

He looked back to where she was studying an arrowhead collection.

Andy hadn't expected her to be interested in ancient artefacts. At a basic level they were just chipped stones and crusty old bits of metal. Perhaps their significance lay in what they represented: the resourcefulness and ingenuity that had taken humanity on a route that deviated from all other creatures on earth. Maybe that's why she was so fascinated. She was the ultimate machine, a tool. Flint axe heads were just the first of many steps that, through thousands of years of development and discovery, resulted in her. In a weird kind of way, those angular piece of stone were her ancestors.

If she was merely a tool, a highly sophisticated tool, why was he so strung up about deleting her? The lump of flint and her, what was the difference other than the level of sophistication. But then you could argue that about people. A bunch of chemicals that got beyond themselves, became sophisticated, convinced themselves they were special.

He stopped at a 3-D display of a tribe working around a camp fire. Dorothea caught up with him.

"Can we stop for something to eat?" he said.

"Of course!" She stopped, checked the museum floor plan. "We're due a break." They walked side by side now, covering ground, Andy trudging along, hands in his back pockets, Dorothea, straight, relaxed pausing every now and then to let him catch up.

"Skills are incredibly important. Some were lost, some are lost," she continued, casting a chummy smile as they stepped into the lift. "They had to be rediscovered. It could take centuries. The Romans discovered how to make concrete. They used it a lot in their building. When they lost their empire, the skill was lost. No one made concrete for over a thousand years. Did you know that?"

"No—no I didn't," said Andy, his attention minimal as the doors opened and the museum's café bar appeared before them.

"Ah! Here we are," announced Dorothea. "Now, what would you like?"

There was no queue and Andy moved forwards, the suppressed feeling of being a junior briefly forgotten.

"I'm going for a ploughman's lunch and one of those craft beers ... Seven Giraffes," he said searching the glass display.

"Andy! You're teasing ... you can't have alcohol! How about a nice, fresh fruit drink?"

"Ok, forgot. Make it a double-shot Americano." Turning towards the counter, voice low, he muttered: "Look, I need something if I'm going to pull through." The checkout was manned by an oblivious droid, but a group was queuing behind, and at nearby tables eavesdroppers who could easily log in.

"Andy, did you know," said Dorothea, facing him, caring but softly assertive, "that these coffees pack a whopping 200mg of caffeine? Did you know that you can become hooked on caffeine, and it can make you hyperactive?"

Andy detected a silence behind him in the queue. Ears had pricked up. At the nearest table a man stopped with his coffee half-way to his lips and peered over the top of his tablet.

"Look!" hissed Andy. "Skip the health lecture. You get what you want, I'll get what I want, we can discuss it once we are seated."

"Sorry, Andy," she said, tautening her lips. "This is important. If we can't agree, I'm getting you mineral water."

"I don't want mineral water!" Andy grated.

"Well, I'm sorry, but it's that, or a healthy alternative." She fixed Andy with a resolute smile. He glared back.

"Very well," she said, turning to the droid. "A still water please, a cranberry and melon juice, a bagel, hot, with honey and cream, and a cheese and salad panini. Thanks."

Andy, helpless, traipsed over to an isolated table; he'd given her charge of his paycard. When she arrived, he didn't meet her eye. The pack of crayons and colouring-in sheet she placed on the table elicited a twinge of guilt. She was sticking to what they'd agreed, trying, at every turn, to make this thing work. Sullen, he opened the water, took a slug and chewed on a mouthful of bagel. Quit? But what else did they have. What if they limited the scope? That would involve demarcation lines: what counted, what didn't, when it would apply, where the boundaries were. Too messy.

Their isolated table wasn't isolated for long. A group of what looked like students came across, plonked down their bags, and did some toing and froing with food stuffs and chairs. Andy worked through his bagel and observed them with a desultory glower. They were a strange mix. He always noticed the common element in a group. Families were easy: similar physical traits and mannerisms and the kind of conflicts and power differences only families could survive. Other groups had their social commonality, or their peer group identity, or their workplace repartee, but this one ... the only thing they seemed to have in common was their mid-20 age spectrum. A big girl with a loose, black, cotton outfit, was sitting half off her seat, anxious not to be left out. Beside her was a relaxed, mister-average, plain, calm and mild, in fact so plain, calm and mild that he seemed a little unworldly, like he'd been trained by some intelligence agency on how not to stand out. Another, a compact, assured Londoner, was the focus of attention; he was relaying from his mobile news that a celebrity had named her baby 'Cruz'. 'Guess she was on a cruise when it happened,' observed a peripheral male, turned sideways, feet up on a chair, too engrossed in his phone to bother looking up. 'After the city Santa Cruz?' a girl tossed in, her short tight curls storage for her wraparound sunglasses. Another big girl, slightly older, late 20s perhaps, seemed less at ease. Like a police photo-fit picture, her features were strong and perfect but big and somewhat askew. The vibrant green coat—knitted, double breasted, with big lapels and giant buttons—looked like fashion-house couture. To top it all, she'd an amazing head of rolling ginger curls. Any one of these would've made her stand out, but all three—

totally awesome. The strange thing was that it worked; she looked really good.

He took a swig from the bottle and held the liquid in his mouth. Something ... something was nagging at him, a distant voice calling in that vague no-man's land between conscious and subconscious. A warning? A cry? He couldn't tell what. He cast a sideward glance at Dorothea as she sipped her fruit juice. She was watching without staring, waiting for him to come to her like a horse-whisperer, ready, when he finally accepted, to make up and move on.

Andy looked from her, back to the group, to her, to the group—then it hit him full square.

Her face, her appearance! He had his cap and his shades, but what about her? He'd treated her as he would any droid, assumed ID tracking wouldn't matter. But she wasn't a mass produced clone. Her spydroid biometrics might be catalogued, they might have her model profiled. Hannah had insisted she didn't go out. Maybe that was why. But they'd been to the shops, the party ... surely they'd clocked her by now. Not necessarily: it had been dark both times, artificial light, mobbed with shoppers, wherever possible they used alleys ... they might have scraped through. But this morning, full daylight, quiet streets, AI tracking woud have picked her up this morning, for sure. His eyes darted to the nearest camera. Multi-lens. Could be looking anywhere. Hannah—damned Hannah! If it hadn't been for her, he'd have scoped it properly, figured out the safe limits. With regular droids, this kind of thing just wasn't an issue.

He slumped low in his seat. If they had clocked her this morning, for some reason they hadn't picked her up. He paused, brain churning feverishly. Could be playing the long game. If cyber-security have locked on, they may opt to track rather than arrest. What use is a nobody who's cavorting around with dodgy goods. Better to see how high it reaches, link it to Hannah, take it higher, some corrupt official who loans out unlicensed level 3s.

What have they got? With his hat and shades, he'd be low correlation. They left the flat via the alleys. They might have sussed the area they'd come from but they wouldn't have the street or flat number. The key thing was to get back without them linking Dorothea to him or to the flat's precise location. He glanced around, tried to weigh up the odds. Of course, he could be panicking. Maybe they were fine ... tracking and data-trawl was the great unchartered ocean. You could never tell who was out there, or what they were hunting. The tiniest scent, a fragment of data that ten years ago, or ten leagues away, had seemed an insignificant ripple, could trigger the pursuit, and set the gargantuan number-crunching behemoth on its relentless, to-your-door, quest. Yeah, he could just ignore it, it might be nothing, but he'd not one valid reason to make that assumption.

Dorothea offered him a napkin. He stared at her face, seeing her now, not as a person, but as a bunch of geometrically aligned features. She said something, he didn't hear. He was focusing on footsteps behind. He pretended to be getting something from his jacket on the back of his chair and looked round. Just a soft-bellied guy with a jogging suit and a tray. He went back to sipping his water. What did that tell him? They don't send in obvious muscle; they don't send in guys with trench coats or flak jackets to track miscreants down. It could be anyone ... anyone but the girl with the giant-buttoned green coat and the flaming-ginger hair. There was only one way to get out of this.

"Ready?" said Dorothea.

"Huh ... eh ... Going to the toilet first."

"I'll come with you to the door," she said, beginning to tidy the table.

"No, please," said Andy, picking up the crayons. "You have to let me do something. I'm big enough to go myself." She considered momentarily, then gave him permission.

"Thanks," he said. Through the swing door, right next to the toilets, was the fire escape.

Why feel guilty? It made perfect sense. They had to get back fast. No discussions in front of the CCTV, no faffing about, no arguments, home like a rocket. It wasn't like he'd abandoned her. She'd see the 'Going Home' he scrawled on the toilet door, she knew the way back using the alleys.

Andy was walking fast, half-jogging. His main problem was speed, he didn't want to confront her out on the street and she'd almost certainly catch up. Solution? Shelter. Take cover ... let her go past. He looked around. Estate agent? No. Big open glass window. Office block, shut on Sunday. The flower shop, Oh So Pretty, Florists. Perfect. Wait till she'd passed, meet her back at the flat.

The little brass bell jingled, Andy blundered into a melee of perfume and colour. A little wizened bird of a lady, in black PVC and chains, twinkled a smile from behind the counter. Andy nodded, said hi, then headed over to the foliage-filled window. Dorothea could be there any minute.

"For yourself? Or for somebody in particular?" the lady called over.

"Em ... a ... a neighbour," he spluttered, still facing out.

"Good neighbours are a blessing aren't they?"

"Yeah—I was a pain in the butt this morning."

"Oh dear. We all make mistakes don't we. It's what we do after that counts."

"After?" He glanced round, a cynical twist on his lips. "What if it's mistakes right down the line."

"You can't go wrong with flowers, luv." She said, detecting his bitterness, letting him be alone for a moment. After tidying a few blooms she tried again. "Any preferences?"

"Huh! I don't have a clue what she likes."

"Tulips perhaps," she offered, her black PVC-gloved hand trembling as she indicated the sinuous stems and the perfection of their bulbous heads.

"Yeah, nice," he said, obliged to look round. He surveyed them with puzzled abjection. "A bit, I dunno—jaunty."

"Too colourful ... Mmm? Any particular mood in mind, luv?" Her eyes twinkled, sharp and grey in the solid black tomb of her eye liner.

Andy shrugged and dragged his eyes away from the leather peaked cap with its jagged armoury of chrome badges.

"Lilies?" she suggested, biker boots clunking, chains on her waistcoat swaying as she crossed the shop.

"Nah! Too formal. Aren't they, like, for funerals," he said, searching the street again, squinting, resisting the urge to clear back a swathe of foliage to improve the view.

"Flowers can mean different things, luv. All depends."

He squeezed past a cascade of delphiniums to get a view further up the street. No sign.

The lady observed him with the sympathy of one who knows suffering, thumbs, like claws, hooking into straps on the side of the jacket, skin soft, puffy, finely wrinkled, almost white against the utter black of leather and lipstick and eye liner.

No sign. Maybe he'd missed her, or maybe she's taken another route, hard to say. He'd give her five minutes to make sure. He abandoned the window and wandered vaguely, brushing past white clouds of gypsophila.

"What is she like?" said the woman. "Perhaps, if you told me about her, I might be able to suggest something suitable."

Andy shrugged and blinked. "She's—she's considerate ... sensitive I suppose, but bossy. Plays the cello. Gets strung up about things, gets involved in other people's problems."

"Your problems, luv?"

"I guess."

"It sounds like she cares about you. Forgive me for being so forward," she said, eyes scrunching with twinkling devilment, "but do you want this to go somewhere?"

"Pardon?"

"Are you in love with her?"

Andy laughed. "Love! I don't have time to think never mind love. I'm struggling to survive."

"Sorry! The reason I ask is that flowers can send a message," she said, straightening some stalks in a carnations display. She put her hand to the black line of her lips as if apprehensive. "People only know the obvious ones: red roses—the sign of love. But there are others. White, can indicate purity, but white roses mean 'I don't love you'. Do you have a message you want to send?"

"I don't know really," said Andy, wrinkling his forehead. "We fell out over something stupid. I cut my hand and went to the hospital but I didn't tell her. Just beat it. She walked in and there was this blood and stuff on the floor—you can imagine. Anyway, I appreciate that she cares ... or used to care, and that I shouldn't have yelled stuff at her through the letterbox."

"Oh dear ... and you look like such a quiet boy!" Her hand moved from her lips and fingered a safety pin on the side of her cheek. "You can't send a message as specific as that ... not in the flowers themselves. You'd have to put some of that on the card, or on the wafer."

"The wafer?"

"Yes, the digi-wafer. They come in all sorts of storage capacities and colours and we have lots of different themes—congratulations, sympathy, welcome, friendship, love, thank you, bereavement—then you personalize it, add your own special touch."

"Have you got something for damage limitation?"

"I think you'd be best to write 'sorry'. Most people add something to the outside of the wafer, a short message, an intimation, then the name of the recipient, that sort of thing, then record something more detailed inside. You don't have to use a digi-wafer, you could use a card, but most people do one or the other—a written card, or a digi-wafer. There's a booth over there if you do want to record something—you choose the background, the music and so on. Or you can connect it to your mobile, load a personal diary onto it, or video. Whatever you want. You hang them—the wafer or the card, whatever you choose—on the ribbon. It's very easy; they get the beautiful flowers and the personal message at the same time. But it's up to you. You choose what you want: the type of flowers, the message, the wrapping. We've got a nice selection of wrappings over here."

"How fail-safe is this?"

"Pardon?"

"What are the odds a bunch of flowers will do the trick?"

Andy heard the click of the door. His head jerked round. Dorothea. She took a moment to fix him with her eye, to make him squirm. "Andy, why did you run away?" she asked, constrained but clear.

"Dorothea," he blustered, "you don't understand."

"Understand what?"

A vacuum grew as Andy's explanation failed to materialize. Seconds passed, the vacuum grew deeper. Andy blinked then, hangdog, stared down at the floor.

"Excuse me," said the old lady, chains clinking as she moved between them. "I don't know either of you very well, and I don't want to interfere, but I do know that this young man came here to make amends. I think, if you don't mind, we should let him continue. Then, when he's finished, we can see how things go. What do you say?"

Andy viewed the blue door with misgiving and cosseted the flowers to his chest with the bandaged right hand. He gave the door a soft rap with his left. Flowers! He was beginning to feel like a darned delivery droid. Dorothea had hers, she was on her way up to the flat with a big bunch of magnolia. Victoria was about to take receipt of a big bunch of peonies. Should have got something for Hannah, hemlock, something like that.

He gazed down into the flowers and rotated them so the card was directly to the front. The 'language of flowers' thing sounded a bit iffy so he had backup, words of apology scribbled onto the card. The blowzy fragrance rose up, suffocating him; he fumbled for his inhaler, sucked in counted to five, then rapped again. Movement! Drat! Now he'd have to confront her. Was it better to talk, say something appropriate, or let the flowers do the talking, stand there, like a simpering idiot. Perhaps he should wait to be asked in, but she might not ask. Better to hand them over fast, see how she reacts, get ready for a hasty retreat. How long did it take a bunch of flowers to take effect anyway? Were they like a stun grenade, lob them at the hostile forces, count to ten, move in. Or was there a kind of time delay, a few minutes, a few hours? There ought to be instructions, guidelines, for this sort of thing.

Victoria pulled back the door and paused.

"Yes, Andy," she said, hostile, edgy, "what is it?"

"Hi ... I just wanted to say ... I er ... It's on the card."

She bent forward and scrutinized it.

"Sonny?"

"That's 'sorry'. It's meant to say sorry. Had to write it with my left."

"... for ..." She peered hard. "... hot something."

"... not ... it says not ..."

"... being ... con ... con ... consolidate?"

"... considerate."

"Oh, right!" she said straightening up, jaw tightening, eyes clashing with his. "So this is going to make it alright?"

Andy clung to a deflated smile. "I guess not ... Thought it was worth a go. Didn't hold out much hope really. I mean to say ... flowers!" He brightened a little, holding them out. "Maybe you'd take them anyway. They're playing hell with my asthma. Or if you know someone, someone who might like them. You'll actually be doing me a favour, not that you need to do me a favour. It doesn't mean like we've made up or anything like that."

She glared at him and then at the flowers and took them and held them against her breast.

"You big sap!" she said, stepping forwards, hugging him close. The pungent aroma of crushed peony rose between them, thick and sweet; Andy held his breath. As she let him go, he took a puff of his inhaler and counted.

"Friends?" he said stuffing the inhaler into his pocket.

"Yes—friends," she said, her voice uneven, eyes lost in the flowers.

Dorothea had the magnolia unwrapped, stems soaking in the kitchen sink, when Andy arrived. She'd improvised; a tall container intended for spaghetti was washed and sitting on the draining board.

"Good idea," said Andy. "Never needed a vase before."

"Andy ... " said Dorothea, picking out the flowers, laying them on the chopping board and cutting the stems to length with a bread knife.

"Is that how you do it?" he said.

"I think so," she replied. "Andy, the flowers ... they were a lovely surprise, but there's something we have to discuss."

Andy braced himself.

"Andy, I didn't do a good job of looking after you this morning, I admit that, but ..."

"I wouldn't say that," said Andy, picking up a lemon squeezer and practising his Frisbee swing, "you were pretty good."

"That's not true. I was responsible for you and you ended up wandering the streets."

"Yeah, but I was a devious, sulky little toe-rag."

"I wouldn't put it like that. 'Difficult', perhaps. You weren't interested in anything. I thought the chance to dress up might have worked but ..."

"You're kidding!" said Andy.

"No. I thought you'd jump at that."

Andy laughed, the disbelief and the absurdity flooding his face. He grinned with incredulity. "You have got to be joking! Come on, Dorothea. That was a wind up." He beamed.

"Speaking of which, Andy! That beer and then the double-shot Americano you asked for ... you must have known those were unsuitable!"

Andy blustered back. "Dorothea, I was desperate! Cut me some slack. A frigging Americano ...!"

"Language!" intercepted Dorothea, wagging her finger.

"Language? I'll say what the hell I want!"

They faced up to each other, grim and intense. Andy, through the defiance, narrowed his eyes. A thought flickered across his mind.

"Dorothea—what age am I?"

"Seven," she said. Andy looked into the stern, censorious, cool of her eyes and snorted a laugh.

"Dammit, Dorothea. It's over. The stupid exercise is over."

"Is it? Oh, thank goodness!" she exhaled. "That was so difficult!" As the tension fell from her body and her eyes met with his, she offered a wearisome smile. She shook her head incredulously. "I couldn't believe it. You were so intransigent, so unwilling to show interest in anything. You were unlike any child I'd envisaged. You were just such ... I don't know"

"A little rat bag?" offered Andy. They both burst out laughing. The pressure was off, they no longer needed to make the impossible work. As they relived the events, and picked over the absurdities, they took turns at ribbing each other. Eventually they were done. It was peaceful, sitting and chatting, or not chatting, just sipping coffee, looking out of the window, not doing anything but watch Sunday's afternoon sun filter into the kitchen.

A shadow entered the room. Perhaps it was an awareness of the passage of time, or a fear of losing the precious moment, but Andy shrank into himself and grew profoundly silent. An obstacle, a huge barrier, lay before him. To surmount it was nearly impossible, the penalty for trying was harsh retribution.

He spoke in a low, unemotional voice, told her why he'd run, about the cameras and the bioscans and his fear that she'd be discovered.

Dorothea clasped her hands together, her face bright with hope, as she explained a recent development in droid-tech known as droid DNA. Her physical features, her personality, were generated randomly at initiation. Each initiation was unique. No one, not the manufacturers, not the programmers, could predict what a model would look like within certain parameters. Bioscans wouldn't pick her up, there would be no definite match.

She looked keenly at Andy, expected him to be relieved, happy, overjoyed that there was nothing on record. Instead, there was no response, not a movement except the flickering edge of the net curtain. At last he spoke.

"Your personality?"

"Yes, that too."

"And if you were deleted?"

"What do you mean?"

"You couldn't be brought back. Your blank could be rebooted, but, with the nano-materials and this droid DNA, the new droid wouldn't look like you or behave like you, would it? It'd be somebody else."

"True, but don't worry. I'm tough and, you'll have noticed, I'm pretty persistent!" she beamed, trying to lighten his mood. "And they allow one backup, as well as the active version. No twins or clones or whatever. That would defeat the whole point of droid-DNA But then who would want another like me?" Andy managed a weak smile and, deep in thought, got up, made another coffee and went through to the living room and the couch, where, knees up, he stared into his cup.

"You can tell me, Andy, she said, after she'd left him alone for a while." She spoke quietly. "I'm stronger than I was yesterday. You've been trying to shield me—I know that. But I have to face what's ahead. Don't try to carry this yourself. Tell me ... when?"

"Tomorrow—tomorrow morning," he said, lifting his head to meet her eyes, knowing what it would do.

She inhaled and tightened her lips.

"How much?"

"Everything."

"What about the backup?"

"They'd hunt it down, delete it—I'd be lying if I said it was an option."

"I see," she said. They sat for a while in silence, the sound of the city, muffled, like distant waves. A clock ticked in the hallway. Someone opened the bottom door, climbed the stairs, entered a second floor flat. Out front, further along the street, a dog barked then stopped and, throughout it all, the barely perceptible sound of a washing machine, the low thrum as it rotated then paused as it moved inexorably through its cycle.

Chapter 12 Sunday

Dorothea approached the sleeping figure and, with some hesitation, sat at the far end of the bench. An open book lay on his chest. The dog by his feet lifted its head and raised its ears. Having decided she wasn't a threat, it lay its head back down on its paws and watched with intelligent eyes. Loosening the knot of the headscarf, she slid along a little and, reaching forwards, stroked the dog's head. It snuffled her hand with her muzzle and gave an appreciative lick whilst the chest of his human companion rose and fell easy with slow, comfortable breaths.

As people passed and dry leaves rustled and scattered, she considered her situation. She wasn't alone but, in an undefined sort of way, in the care of a man—not any man, but, according to Andy, a philosopher. The term intrigued her. The fact that this man, this philosopher, knew nothing about her, was strangely liberating. What would she say to such a person? What would he say? What kind of man was he? A non-conformist—a garrulous rebel—a deep thinker—or, according to her eyes, a dishevelled, sleep-sodden tramp?

As she was considering this, Cornelius' eyes opened. He surveyed her for a moment, then, without judgement or fear, closed them again. Contentedly, he resumed his nap. She was struck by this and reached out again to stroke the dog. He was different, but it was difficult to understand how. She paused, reviewed, tried to put it together. The people she'd met, the other people, there were obvious contrasts: clothes, jobs, wealth. But it was much more than that. They were part of a system. Caught up, driven, haunted by problems, obsessed with conforming to expectations or cultural notions or terrible pressures. She sensed that this man, this Cornelius person, was very different. He was free. There was peace in his weariness. Just looking at him, she could see a complete lack of concern, freedom from obligation. What had he to worry about? No possessions, no home, no technology, no profile. The simplicity was beguiling.

She paused and inhaled the air, grass-damp and autumnal. Why had he chosen this life without possessions or comfort? He just lay there in this wide open space, sprawled and slumbering as if in his own bed. Others sheltered in buildings, lived in cramped little boxes shuttered away, but he'd chosen a carpet of grass, curtains of fluffy clouds, a blue sky ceiling. The world was his home. He belonged to it, it belonged to him. Weathered, touched by sun and rain and wind, his clothes were as rumpled and faded as the brown autumn leaves.

And where did that leave her? In her brief existence she'd been conforming like crazy, racing, pushing, every millisecond an opportunity to 'progress'. What good had it done?

Andy would be making the call about now. All her sensory powers, and her intelligence and she couldn't tell if her own life was about to end. It was a strange set-up, a deal in which she was the bargaining chip. They'd get her back in return for extending her life. She scanned the sky to the east trying hard to find a star. Andy's plan was flawed. She could see that, she suspected Andy could see it too.

Right at the beginning, Andy had told her to find her place, to discover who she was, he gave her the freedom to exist in her own way. Was that what she'd done? Had she achieved anything? She'd learned a lot—true. She could converse intelligently in countless fields, she could estimate and calculate and explain and convince, yet, as she faced the end, what did it matter? What had she been doing? Running, running fast, two days on a treadmill, hectic, grasping at all manner of things as they flew past, desperate for everything, yet, somehow, gaining nothing.

Her eyes gleamed with sadness and she turned and considered Cornelius. She desperately wanted to talk. She would wake him. She moved to reach out, to touch him. The dog lifted his head, pricked his ears, curious, head to one side. She hesitated.

No. That was the old way. What was she planning to do? Bombard him with questions that she would then file and cross-reference. No, she will be content to be there; that would be enough. It didn't matter whether they talked now or talked later.

There was a pile of books next to him on the bench. She took one and looked at the cover. More data, just in printed form. Should she flick through it, absorb it? No, not now, just put it back down. She inhaled, closed her eyes and let herself sink back against the bench. That was it. Slow down, slow the thought process down. You are more than a data processor. Perspective, you need space—and distance. No distance, no perspective.

She took in the expanse of sky and the orb of the sun on its fiery, plunging descent towards the horizon. Automatically, with precision and speed, she began to estimate when light levels would drop below ambient atmospheric haze and light pollution, and at what time with her above-average perception, the major order stars would become visible. She cut herself short. That was the old way. What did it matter? Day would run its course. The stars would be there in the night sky whether she calculated or not. All that was required was patience, patience and awareness. The urge to calculate was symptomatic, part of the urge, the insatiable need to know what lay ahead. The future was infinite, such a need could never be satisfied; amidst the deducing and predicting and forecasting, the present was slipping away, the seconds dying alone and unheeded. She may not have much time, but she should live what she had, appreciate the moment, value the experience of being.

She reached her hand out and picked up the book, rubbed her hand over the cover and felt its dry woody warmth. When she felt ready—if she felt ready—she would read the title of this book, maybe read a few lines, but, for now, she'd limit herself to no more than one thought, and she'd turn that thought over, let it stay with her for a while, and, like a pebble on a beach, consider it, carry it with her, and then lay it down.

"Andy! Is that you Andy?" He gripped the phone as if it were a burning coal. "What in God's name are you playing at!" screeched Hannah. "Dammit! Andy—how could you?"

Andy slunk deeper into the surveillance shadow of a Charing Cross Station vending machine.

"But I can explain ..." he spluttered against the rampage.

"Shut it Andy! Just shut the hell up. I'm sick of explanations. Do you know that? Sick to the teeth." Andy grunted something but didn't dare speak up. "Mess up your own life—fine, go right ahead—but you're not messing up mine. I was at Covent Garden last night, La Traviata. It was Mattacchioni's last performance, and you know what I was thinking? Do you? I was thinking: 'That little louse! The dirty, stinking, snivelling little rat bag! Castration—No! Castration would be too good for him!' Mattacchioni? She might as well have been singing 'Happy the Hamster'. Three double G and T's couldn't clear the crap out of my head. I took it out on my date. I get to sort that one out later. First, Andy, I'm sorting out you." She stopped. Andy stared glumly at a man who'd abandoned his case and was helping himself to a cup of soup from the vending machine.

"Andy, listen carefully. This thing ends now, right now, you hear me? You clear out the fridge, you box it, you have it ready for uplift. Got that, Andy? Nothing else. No excuses, no delays, no complications. I'm telling you to do it, and you will do it right now!"

"But ..."

"I said no buts, Andy. I don't want to hear anything but 'yes'. That's all. Then you go do it. I mean it, Andy. I want to hear 'yes'."

"But ..."

"ANDY!!"

"I have to get her first!" said Andy, prising his confession into the gap. Silence followed. He could speak as much as he wanted now, except, of course, he couldn't. She was a fizzing stick of explosives. The fuse had been lit, in seconds detonation would occur. Andy felt intensely and uncomfortably aware of himself, a lone figure, in this big processing factory of a train station, holding, clinging, clutching pathetically at this little box of tricks. He gazed at the scene before him. Bustle, smell, clamour. The public address system blurted something that resonated like a heaven-sent decree upon a world vaulted, not by stars and space, but by glass and iron.

"Andy—tell me I didn't hear that ..."

"That? It was just an announcement. Some train about to ..."

"Not that. You said something, you said you had to get her. Andy! She is in the flat?"

"Yeah. No. I—I mean," said Andy, sweat oozing as his confidence turned to mush. "But I've got her—kind of. She's just not—I didn't want to drag her around. I can get her. But, Hannah, there's stuff you need to know."

"Andy—stop it! Stop it right now! I don't need to know anything. I don't give a frack about the report. I don't want it, it's for further up the line. I didn't want this project, but it landed on my desk. I didn't want you either, but that wasn't my call. But I have a reputation, a reputation for getting things done. I am NOT—do you hear me—NOT going to throw my career on the scrapheap for you, or for a droid, or for any other stupid reason. So forget the whining and the excuses and the reasons. This finishes right now. Do you hear me? Now!"

"Yeah, okay. I hear what you say—It's just it's not that easy."

"Andy, for once in your pathetic, messed-up little life, listen! IT IS THAT EASY. You get her, you do it, you phone me back . . . You still have the codes?"

"Yeah, of course ..."

"So ...? Do it."

"She—she's an amazing person."

"Andy, it's not a 'she', it's an 'it'. It—it—it—it—it. Have you got that? It runs software. You think the software is amazing. Wow! Whoopseedoo! Got that! Now, you turn the software off, you end the programme, that's it."

"Honest, she's so real. And she gets so upset. I mean she breaks down in tears as soon as I mention it. You have to see her—it—I mean."

"Andy!"

"Wait, Hannah—wait one second. Just listen. I can't pull the plug right now. I can't just walk in and say 'that's it, time up, I'm wiping you'. Maybe if she had time to get used to the idea ... or if we could at least make a backup. Restore her when this is sorted."

"Andy," Hannah sighed. Her voice suddenly lowered. "I'm going to let you into a little secret to help you with this. She has something called ICE programming. Programmed independence, programmed conscious awareness, programmed emotions. It's in there at base level. She doesn't sit around calculating optimal body language or tear flow rate or what level of outburst will get the best results. It's automatic. The equivalent of instinct in a human. Got that? Very clever stuff, granted. But, Andy, it is still programming. And, she still has to follow direct commands given under admin mode."

"So, that's why she reacts so naturally ..."

"Exactly! She is built to do that. But it is just technology. You are dealing with a complex piece of hardware and software. Sure, she'll get some valves to pump out a few tears in difficult situations. You think the tech guys can't put a sprinkler system in and rig it to some sympathy-quotient subroutines. At core she's a spydroid, right? Tough as nails. These things don't just roll over and die. She's got a whole armoury of techniques. She follows core commands, like not to leave the flat. But, beyond that, she will fight tooth and nail to survive. Looking vulnerable ramps up the sympathy quotient. That's a desirable outcome. It's all base level, it's droid instinct ... that is what you're reacting to, Andy. But you must realise that inside ... it's not a heart, it's not a soul, it is ICE."

"I see ... I see what you're saying. She's just so, so realistic. Enthusiastic, innocent ... like a kid."

"Andy, if there's one thing we've learn here it is not to let these machines into anyone's hands without a pre-installed command structure. Circumstances resulted in you getting a raw machine; maybe that was a mistake. But what you have to realise now is that she won't think twice, not for one nano-second, about giving herself up for deletion. It's built in. Only a direct command from someone with admin rights can overrule that."

"I see," said Andy softly. "And that's me".

"Or we could transfer the codes. I'll give you two minutes more, then we move on. What I'm saying is simple fact. Think rationally. Name one thing she did that wasn't about getting you on side."

"She came to the hospital and took me home."

"Hospital?"

"Yeah. I was at this party, a friend's. He's got a bar, and I ripped my hand on a glass—an accident, pretty bad. The glass just burst in my hand. I went to A and E, ran all the way. You know what taxis are like on Saturday night. They did all the tests and stuff and they gave me stitches. It could have been serious if I hadn't ..."

"Andy, did I ask for your life story?"

"Okay. She came to the hospital. She took me home. It—it took me home."

"Right! But she has the Asimov-Zamyatin basics. That's AZ-H: duty of care. It has no option but to take whatever steps are ..."

"Actually, that doesn't apply."

"Of course it applies! Why on Earth wouldn't it apply?"

"Because, well—you know the whole licensing and restriction rigmarole? She was only running for a couple of days. Didn't seem much point, really. Could've spent the whole weekend just going through the zillion and one options. Crazy! They make it so complicated. Terms and conditions that would turn your brain to jelly. I'd still be ploughing through it when it came time to wipe her. You know what it's like. Hannah—Hannah? Are you still there?"

Andy looked out from his corner at the churning, mingling throng of bodies. Why was he the one. Look at all those people. Those dammed smug got-it-together people. They're not tortured by this kind of stuff. They're not harangued and hounded and pulled in half a dozen different directions. Nothing he did was right. What wouldn't he give to go back to last month. He had a life. Yeah, he'd been stuck in a rut—a cosy pointless, no decisions, no commitment rut—a rut he wanted to be in right now.

"Andy—tell me—this isn't real," said Hannah, choking, breathless, struggling to get the words out. Andy didn't like this unfamiliar aspect of Hannah. She was at home with lambasting and berating, and, if it suited her needs, turn on a we're-all-in-this-together routine. This was Hannah down to the raw, delicate, underbelly. Hannah didn't do raw, delicate, underbelly.

"Hannah," , he offered, "don't worry, honest. She wouldn't hurt a flea."

The only response was strained breathing. Hyperventilation. A scuffling sound, then scraping, then a clattering noise as the phone slammed into something hard, the desk, or the floor or the wall. He wondered if she'd walked out, or fainted—and how long he should hold on before hanging up. As he waited and sweated and looked sheepishly out into the crowds, the phone rattled and scraped back to life. He could hear a long, tremulous inhalation.

"YOU MUST BE OUT OF YOUR BLOODY MIND!" He lifted the phone away from his ear. "It could do anything, Andy. It could kill. It could cause a massacre ... Don't you realize what you've done!"

"I know, I'm sorry. BUT the thing is she hasn't done anything like that."

"How can you say that? You don't know. She could be puddling about in somebody's inner organs right now."

"She's too nice to do that ..."

"Nice! What does that mean. Nice means nothing. There are a hundred and one situations where she might not be nice. She might find it convenient to drop someone off a skyscraper to check the acceleration of gravity."

"No—no. She's not like that. She's sensitive—thoughtful. That's why I didn't want to delete her. You'd see that too. You would, Hannah. I tell you what—Come and see for yourself, just to see what I'm saying."

"Andy, I don't want to see her, not for one nanosecond. What I want to see is a delivery confirmation note."

"But she is special, and helpful."

"Andy, I've had enough of this. Just shut it and listen. Who the hell is her controller?"

"Me, why?"

"So—who's the only person who can close her down, shred her and sterilize her profile?"

"Me."

"And?" A pause, impatient. "God, why do I have to spell this stuff out. She needs you on her side, Andy. She could rip someone else's head off to get a better view at the cinema, but, with you, she has be 'nice'. Don't you see! It's tactical. Now go, eliminate her, and get us out of ..."

"But it's not going to be that easy ..."

"Not that easy! Not that easy? Are you so deluded you think there's some other option? Look, Andy, I don't give a shit how you end up—apparently you don't either—but I'm telling you, delete her, get her packed. You've got one hour! Bye, Andy ..."

"Wait!" blurted Andy. "Okay. I'll do it. I'll hand her over, but ... I want you to extend her run time ... then you get her back. It's not much to ask. I mean a couple of months, something like that."

"Andy, don't start messing with me!"

"Just a bit longer ..."

"You are so, so deluded. I'm wasting my breath here."

"I'm just trying to make a deal."

"Andy, do you want to know the truth? I've tried to order, to persuade, to use rational arguments, but you should know I'm done with this. It's not me anymore."

"Who then?"

"You know I can't tell. I can tell you that they're really pissed off. They're pulling it. They want everything."

"Yeah, I understand. And they'll get her back. I accept that, totally but ..."

"Not just her, Andy."

"The report? Yeah. I mean, no sweat. I could have it done this week ... Tuesday."

"Frack the report, Andy. I told you to keep her in the flat. I told you to keep her away from people. You ignored me. You trashed the comms and ignored me. Now they want everything. They want her, they want you."

"Why me? I'll put it all in the report."

"They don't trust you, Andy They're deep trawling you. They'll go in and get it themselves."

"No! Look, no! You could tell them ..."

"Tell them! Tell them what, Andrew darling? That you ignored every instruction I ever gave you. That you took every imaginable risk with their property. That you're whole attitude has been: 'stuff you, I don't give a shit'. What, exactly, should I tell them. Mmm, Andy? These people aren't crap merchants, they don't give crap, they don't take crap. Do you think I'm going to pass on your lame excuses? And another thing, they don't waste time. I reckon they'll contact you within a couple of hours. Sometime very soon a technician will be strapping you down for neurorip. Bolt gun. Implants. Bang, bang, bang. Link, sift, encrypt, mail. They'll get it themselves."

"H-a-n-n-a-h!" groaned Andy, slumping against the wall.

"I'm sure you'll find it very interesting—they do go through a lot of peripherals—brains congeal on the electrodes, gums them up. At least, that's what they say," she gloated. "The pay's nothing special, but the perks ... The contractor only wants the official stuff. What they do with the rest—I suppose you could call it recycling. Have a nice childhood, Andy? Girlfriends, your Mom, your mates, personal thoughts, fantasies. Imagine— every detail, every personal, intimate embarrassing moment, streamed out and grubbed over by hordes of drooling pervs."

"Hannah! Don't—that's sick."

"It's consequence! Something you might have considered before you fracked everyone off."

"I didn't mean to. Don't let them. Please, Hannah. I'm begging you!"

"Andy, honey. It is not my decision."

Chapter 13 Sunday

"I do see your point," said Cornelius. "Try to get hold of the Cult of Information by Theodore Roszak. Somewhat dated, but written during the early days of the data explosion." They'd reached the top of the steps and were facing the heavy doors that stood defiant and black in the ornate arch of stone. "After you. It takes a good push."

"Are we allowed to talk?" said Dorothea, as wide-eyed as a child beneath the high vault of the cathedral.

"Quietly, yes."

They waited patiently at the back as a sparse straggle of people filed towards the door, every footstep, every scuffle resonating against the austere expanses of stone. Some remained, kneeling, standing before statues, lighting candles, their lips uttering words for the immortal to hear.

"It's very atmospheric," hissed Dorothea. "The height. Doesn't it make you feel small."

"Yes, some have argued that this architecture is form of psycho-manipulation by the religious hierarchies—people made to feel insignificant in the presence of God."

"And is it?"

"I dare say it may influence certain individuals in that way, but, as a basis for a conspiracy theory of coercion and suppression of the population, it doesn't stand up to scrutiny." Cornelius paused for a moment to listen in case the dog was whining outside. "Is that Mishka?" he said. "My hearing isn't what it used to be."

"No. Do you want me to check he's alright?"

"No. He should be fine."

"Yes, the alcove, and the blanket, he seemed quite settled." They moved slowly across behind the pews. Cornelius stopped. They looked down the centre aisle. "You were saying it doesn't stand up to scrutiny."

"Yes. For one thing, some of the strongest religious followings occur in impoverished areas where the church building, if there is one at all, is little more than four walls and a tin roof. Historically, cathedrals and churches tended to be built by the local population, often over decades and using pooled resources. Coming from the people, I'd say it indicates a commitment to their belief rather than subjugation from above." He wiped drips of rain from his forehead with a soft chequered handkerchief.

Dorothea stared alert and enquiring, her nostrils picking up the woody tang of old varnish and the fungal earthiness of cold stone.

"Whatever your beliefs," chortled Cornelius, "it acts as a shelter for those, such as myself, at the mercy of the meteorological vagaries of this isle."

"Sorry?" said Dorothea, eyes drawing away from a mischievous face carved into a circular wooden plinth.

"Ah! You must excuse my verbosity," Cornelius chuckled, stifling the sound, dabbing his handkerchief to his lips. "Rain! This is a convenient refuge in foul weather. More spacious than a bus shelter, more impervious than a tree. Over where they light the candles there is even a soupçon of warmth. But I blabber on. You see, it's not often that I get to talk to a pretty girl. The old fool that you see here was once a boy, a youth, a young man whose hopes and ambitions are now scattered like straw in the wind, whose smooth, fine looks have been encrusted by the hoar frost of time, whose frame, once strong and lithe, stoops, brittle and dry, like the autumn grasses. But there remains here," and he beat his chest with a wiry fist, "some of that spirit, that inner flame, not wild and bright and dangerous as it once was, but still there, sputtering, flaring up, flickering erratically, and, ready, in due course, to succumb to that final extinguishing draft."

"You mean death," said Dorothea, face like porcelain, a grey shadow turning away.

"I do," he said, noting her aversion. "Does it upset you?"

"Yes. It does," she said.

"Why so? A young woman such as you has much to look forward to. If I were that young man, I'd plead with you to come with me right now, this very minute, to dance unsparing all through the night, greet the morning and the world with unflinching eye, and travel, and laugh and live, and never for a second look back. But do you see the irony? Here I am, my life mostly spent, and I AM looking back. Haven't I learnt a thing? Knowing and doing are such different things. We say we love freedom, but then we are so readily bound: responsibility, common sense, the practicalities of life. Animals and young children run with sheer pleasure. They don't see the need for reason or planning. The future, what is the future? We only exist in the present. Live now, death will come in due course and, when it does, all that is left is the hope of meaning, that we are part of a plan too vast and grand for the dim human eye to see, and perhaps a God, and even a means by which we might continue, if not in body, in soul, in spirit, or whatever one cares to call the essence of being that remains when the physical self is stripped away." He looked for a response but she seemed distracted, then, having decided, she turned earnest eyes to his.

"May I?" she said, indicating the front of the church.

"By all means. Take the full tour. Southwark is underestimated. The ten marble figures are deemed to be ... "

"Sorry—I mean is it alright for me to pray? Someone, a friend, asked me to pray to God. I think I ought to whilst I'm here."

"By all means my dear ... by all means," he said, taking a step to the side and gesturing to the isle with his arm. "Just as long as you want."

He watched her grow small as she walked steadily, resolute, to the distant altar. She knelt at the rail and bowed her head. After quite some time, she went over to the candles, lit one and stared into the flame.

"Thank you for waiting," she said, having come round by the side aisle, where she'd paused and at the carvings and inscriptions and the colour-tinged black of the stained-glass windows.

"It was a pleasure. Waiting is something I excel at. Impatience, that's where anguish lies." They stood for a few moments whilst Cornelius, hesitating, caressed the white bristles on his cheek. "Pardon the intrusion, my dear, but I sense a great sadness. Something weighs heavily upon you."

"Yes—I'm not very good company I'm afraid."

"Nonsense! I only wish I could help. Perhaps someone is ill?"

"No," she said, pursing her lips.

"Then what? Are you seriously indebted? Have you committed some heinous crime?"

"No—It's not that."

"Troubles, troubles, like most things, are magnified when seen from close to. In a year's time you probably won't even remember ..." She closed her eyes and shivered. "What, then, if you were to give yourself space, go away for a while, start afresh? If you want distance, why not the Antipodes: Australia, New Zealand. Fine countries. Or South America. They have wondrous rain forests, magnificent plants, exotic animals, indigenous species that not only amaze and delight, but ask remarkably few questions."

"I can't. There's someone else ..."

"A young man?"

She hesitated to respond. He must not connect her with Andy. For his own sake, he must not know. She uttered, as if making a confession, 'Yes'.

"Ah—but a man who brings great sorrow."

"It's not his fault!" she remonstrated, suddenly feisty. Then she closed her lips tight for fear of saying more.

"Very well. But there exists a complication, a tie, a connection, and through it your life is troubled. I cast no blame, but I say: let him be, let him sort himself out. Is it not his place to take care of his life and yours to take care of your own? You must be wary of being shackled by extraneous things, of always wondering what so and so will think, or how so and so will manage. The world beckons each and every one. You have life; don't, in God's name, squander it. Everything in creation has the urge to grow and to flourish. Cut yourself free from that which suffocates and imprisons. It is the duty of all things to survive, to grow to fulfil their destiny."

"It is?"

"Absolutely. Now go."

"But ..."

"But?—But? There is no excuse for living."

"I can't!"

"Tell me, in complete honesty, without excuses or buts or vacillation, that you can't walk through that door and never look back."

She looked at him, eyes urgent, hands tight, grasping, knowing in that second that she could pull back from the abyss. She opened her mouth as if to call out, but could not speak.

"I see that you can!" he boomed, the echo reverberating around the dark alcoves. He clasped her to himself and then, with great warmth, pushed her away. "Now go! Go while you have the strength!" he beamed. "Go now!"

Andy slumped over the guitar and strummed a slow, meandering rhythm, whilst his left hand, absent-mindedly, lurched from chord to chord. He was dog tired. Baseball boots and socks lay in a soggy pile seeping a widening pool of grime and water onto the varnished floor.

He'd run. He'd sought in vain, gasping, lean, confused, inadequate, the acid of Hannah's words curdling his mind. Where the hell were they? Okay, it was too early to meet back at the bench, but they had to be somewhere. They can't just vanish into the night. He strummed some more, lilting, breathing in time to the slow strumming. Midnight—why had he arranged it so late? If he'd made it eight, or even nine, he might have fobbed Hannah off, spinned her some yarn about shredding and codes and packing and stuff, but four hours, five by the time he'd got it done . . .

When the door bell rang, Andy registered the summons in a semi-aware robotic way. With leaden feet, he went to the door.

"Is this Naismith, Andy Naismith?"

"Andy shrugged in half-hearted recognition.

"Just the one item—a fridge," the guy said, straight, earnest, expecting no complications.

"Yeah," said Andy. "Afraid it's not ready yet. If you could come back tomorrow. Should have it ready first thing."

The guy looked at him, pained, as though a tooth had suddenly started to give him trouble. He was short, a square little power house of a man with a head that looked like it had come from a larger person, jaw angular, neck thick and well-muscled. His hair was cropped and neat and he looked organized and fit, the kind of guy who showered and dried off in four minutes flat and who had a workshop with all the tools clean and oiled and mounted on peg boards. Andy noticed the bulge of muscle in his cheek as he clenched his jaw.

"It doesn't work like that, Sir. This is Triple A: Absolute, Always, Assured. We guarantee one hour door to door."

He looked down at the logger.

"I'll have to contact the party that booked this. If it's not available for collection, they might choose another option. I'll see what they say." The van driver reached for the phone in his belt pouch. Andy guessed what was coming next; he wasn't going down that route.

"Okay, hang on a minute. If it's that important, just take it. It's here—through in the kitchen."

Andy stepped to the side and led the guy through. They asked for a fridge, well they could have a friggin' fridge.

"Stuff's still in it. Need to empty it first."

"You got a cool box?" said the guy.

"Nup," said Andy, opening the door, pulling out a tray and standing, aimless, in the middle of the floor. "I'll just stick 'em—in here," he said, going over to the sink. He tipped everything, bottles, packs, tubs, in on top of each other. "Don't want to hold up Triple A," he said, shoving the first tray back in and dragging another one out.

"Look, I'm just doing my ... Whoa, watch the—eggs," said the delivery guy but Andy trudged over to the sink and tipped the lot in an avalanche on top of what was already there. An open milk carton, upended, glugged its contents over the packets and tubs below.

"You might want to take it easy with that hand." said the delivery guy. "Want me to get the rest? I could stack it over at the side."

"Nah," said Andy, "nearly finished."

"It sucks, doesn't it," said the guy. "These recalls. How long have you had it?" Sympathy didn't suit him; it didn't fit well with his brusque get-it-done manner.

"A day," said Andy, swinging open the freezer and reaching in for the frost-coated pizza. He tossed them with his left hand, like Frisbee, across at the work surface. Three hit the target, one skidded and bounced into a precarious, half on, half off, position, and one flew high, slapped the wall and fell down the back of the cooker.

"Better not forget that one. Stink to high heaven if you leave it," offered the delivery guy.

Andy didn't respond. The guy scratched his head.

"I could get it, no problem. I've got a telescopic gripper down in the van."

"Nah," shrugged Andy. "Let it fester."

Andy chucked the fridge delivery box through from the spare room into the hall and the courier packed the fridge, rough, hasty, faster than required even for Triple A logistics. Andy noticed he had a limp, a limp he was well used to, no sign of weakness. Fetching a flip-down trolley he'd left in the hall, the guy swung it into position and, with an experienced tilt-and-slide movement had it loaded and heading stairwards in seconds. Andy watched from the window, the van, white, unmarked, the hydraulic ramp, the door shutting, and the tail-lights as the van receded. They were red, mesmerizing, alive, like glowing eyes in an infinite night.

That wouldn't hold them back for long. There'd be another knock, a harder, what-the-hell-do-you-think-you're-playing-at knock. He hoped against hope that it would come in the morning. It would have been so different in the morning, he would have Dorothea packed and ready. If they came now, he wouldn't have Dorothea, all he'd have was his favourite avoidance tactic: not answering the door, pretending he wasn't in. Failing that—excuses.

His favourite avoidance tactic lasted less than a minute. That's how long it took them to kick down the door and throw it, crashing and scraping, down the middle of the hall floor. Andy launched into his excuse for not opening up, blabbered something about being in the shower, which made no sense as his hair was dry and he was fully clothed. It was clear from the outset that this excuse, in fact any excuse, was pointless; they weren't listening. They just stood there, all pumped up from the exertion, straightening their suits, their big-chests sucking all the air out of the hall. The door had given them a buzz; they'd have been disappointed if he'd answered. Andy saw in their big-boy faces an underlying pride, a satisfaction in the crunching collapse, and as they stood there gloating, throbbing, blood like hydraulic fluid, surged in their necks.

Dialogue was minimal.

"Naismith?"

"Yeah ..."

"Andy Naismith?"

"Afraid so."

The heaviest one, blue tinged, like an overgrown kid who'd been dusted with iron filings, swivelled his big brown eyes on Andy and jerked his beefy head towards the door. His partner, with rockabilly quiff and lean, strung-out look, flared his nostrils aggressively.

The underground! Andy couldn't believe it. Where the hell was the limo! Public transport, an off-peak single. What was this? Bargain basement bozos! Intimidation on a budget. Nobody beats Thug Savers. You'd think they'd have stretched to a taxi. He peered down the length of the carriage overwhelmed by the ordinariness of taking the tube.

His bandaged right hand held against his chest, he juggled his ticket with his left, rolling it round from finger to finger, trying to break his record of three circuits without letting it drop. At least they'd paid. His tired eyes took in the jaundice-yellow seats opposite and the hint-of-slush white of the walls. On the promo-screen above the window a mango juice ad was playing: steel band, dancers bouncing, grinning insanely, their stomachs tight with a gut-load of tropical zest.

He looked to the guys on either side: po-faced and taciturn, rocking and jiggling in their white shirts and suits. Funeral suits. Save them changing if they come to pay their condolences. Could be a tradition for all he knew: for those we squelched, a moment of silence. The tube rattled and bucked. Rockabilly's ice-blue eyes met Andy's, and then they narrowed, alive and eager with sickly intent.

Andy thought about running, thought about waiting for the door to slide open, thought about bolting, pummelling along the platform, dodging and scrambling and slipping, nostrils wide with fear and skin clammy and wet. And then he thought about being slammed onto the tiled floor, a big hand circling his neck and a knee, like a steel piston, driving into the small of his back. The train stopped, the door opened, he watched it close.

As they jiggled and shunted along, he became aware of certain aspects of this set up. Being 'escorted' was, in a way, strangely reassuring. His life was no longer his responsibility. They had to make sure he got there. He was like a piece of luggage, nothing to decide, no need to act or think. If a feral gang piled into this carriage, he could smile right at them, give them the finger, goad them, it wasn't his problem.

"Ever thought of getting a Cross-City Rail Rover?" he said as the tube train shunted and clattered into the next station.

"Huh?" said Bristles, his big deep eyes confused. He was the talker. Rockabilly responded with a skin-you-alive sneer. Conversation was 'sissy', he liked his fun sharp and sweet. Andy could imagine him as a recalcitrant youth, dirt yard buzzing with flies, a flick knife, a squirming lizard, Rockabilly, the connoisseur, musing over which limb to lop next.

"Yeah, works out cheaper if you're a regular user." Andy's voice was high and wavering. "Takes you anywhere—you could even use if off duty. I don't know what you guys do but most folks ..." His monologue petered out. Andy wished he hadn't started. He wished he could shut the hell up. His hands were jittery. It was nerves talking, making him spew out stupid stuff, the kind of stuff that in normal times he'd have the sense not to say. He stared at the window and watched his swaying half-reflection.

They didn't exit the station by the escalator but hung back in the surveillance shadow cast by a long line of pillars. They stood, waited, then, during the tidal surge and back wash as the next train opened its doors, they moved smoothly to the far end and an access panel. Bristles slipped out a key and undid it with practised ease; behind lay a maze of service tunnels and passageways.

Andy, blind-folded, was led and jostled through the bowels of the city. Under the dark hood, his senses were heightened: the mains hum, the fume of plastic cabling, the hush of air conditioning, and the hard, unyielding echo of concrete and steel. Occasionally, like rays of light penetrating an overgrown forest, a flicker of life above would break through: the rumble of street traffic, an office door clattering, even a voice. Life, oblivious, carried on up above. Time and distance in this strange underworld, were almost impossible to judge. He had to use his bandaged hand to help balance, reaching out blindly, random waves of pain possessing his arm, a nagging portent of what lay ahead. Eventually, they climbed steps and stopped. When the blindfold was tugged off, the dim service tunnel glow was still too much; Andy shielded his eyes.

Rockabilly listened, not breathing, his bony skull pressed against the access door. A few minutes later, they were out, marching down a bright corridor with sky-blue doors, and then, just as abruptly, they stopped, and Andy, awkward, breathing heavily, stood between them, wondering what this blue rectangle with its aluminium bar handle and number 7 would mean in his life. As he waited there, senses ramped-up by fear, he tuned his ears, hoped against hope that he might make out something mundane and ordinary: office sounds, maybe a TV or a radio, people chatting or having a meal. He had a clear idea of what he didn't want to hear and that included sobbing or squealing, any kind of drilling or sawing, the clink of medical implements or the sharp snap of surgical gloves. Transfixed, face drawn, he listened intently.

A few seconds of what sounded like movement, barely audible, then a sharp whack, a strained yell and then an ominous heavy pummelling sound. This was not good. He glanced quickly at his minders, looked for a response, then hastily turned his eyes back to the door. Another whack, a grunt, more pummelling. His hopes of a bawling out over a coffee were being drastically downgraded. Comply. It was the only option. Pain wasn't his thing—there'd be no point pretending. They'd give him a chance to talk. Everyone got a chance. He'd explain how it went wrong. How he'd found it hard to see Dorothea as a droid because she was just so damned realistic. He was only human, fallible. But he'd sort it. Do whatever they want. He'd make that very clear. They don't start straight in on you. No point. They keep that for heroes who try to hold out. He was trying not to listen, but he couldn't stop. More shouting, a strained grunt, more hard, slapping noises. Again, again, again. Geez! Don't they ever let up? The escorts seemed immune. He guessed this was the norm. They just stood there, severe and still, like pall bearers. Andy picked at his nails.

"Will this take long?" he said, looking down the hall for an exit sign or a fire escape.

"Depends," said the black bristly one.

What the hell does that mean? Depends on what? Pain threshold—the amount of squealing—how long it takes to rupture your liver?

They stood silent for a while, then the noise pattern changed: mostly silence, a few prolonged bouts of muffled speech. Spilled the beans, or spilled the bodily fluids—one or the other. They'd clean up before he went in; surely they'd do that. Mop, disinfectant—maybe a stretcher, maybe not a stretcher—a bin bag. More talking: male, female. Moments passed. His mouth went sticky and dry.

The door swung open. Andy, rigid, didn't want to look. Like a wax dummy, his eyes fixed, he registered a face passing before him, a red face, flushed, sweaty, some guy in his late 40s. Andy waited till he was a good way down the corridor before he dared turn to look: white sports gear, kit bag, sports shoes. Andy was still staring blankly when, with a big hand on each shoulder, he was propelled through the door.

"Mister Naismith?" A crinkly-haired woman, wiry, with tanned limbs stood facing him. Andy nodded. With a curt nod, she dismissed the two escorts.

Andy looked dumbly at her, and then past her at the big white walls and the myriad scuff marks of smeared rubber, and at the high ceiling, and at the wooden floor with the coloured line running from side to side.

"Squash!" he mouthed. "You were playing squash." The body that had been strung together by tension and fear and bolstered up by the physical bulk of the minders on each side, became wobbly and limp.

"Mister Naismith," she enquired, "have you a problem?"

"No ... no," said Andy, struggling to regulate his breathing, "apart from the obvious—the situation ... you know."

"Indeed. The situation," she said, taking a mouthful of energy drink, screwing the top on the bottle and tossing it into her kit bag. Reaching into a side pocket, she unfolded a cloth and began rubbing down the racquet in brisk, efficient strokes.

"Yeah. I guess this is about the mix up," said Andy. "You see, some guy turned up saying he wanted my fridge. Funny thing was, I've just got a new fridge, and it's been acting up. I thought it was the uplift. I didn't realize it was the 'fridge' fridge, if you know what I mean." He snorted. "I know, it's really stupid."

"Mr Naismith ..."

"Honest to God. Hell of a coincidence ..."

"Don't waste my time, Mister Naismith."

"Weird things sometimes happen like that. It's not that I'm ..."

She turned away, took the racquet she'd been cleaning, lifted a ball from the bag, tossed it in the air and lashed out viciously. The ball rocketed through the air, a blur, it slapped hard into the wall.

"Sometimes these things happen. I should've ..."

The ball came back in a high arc. She was crouched, legs bent, warrior-like, every sinew taut. She grunted as she flailed out with hard, calculated precision.

"If the guy had just said—then ..."

She drove it back again powering it high.

"But because he said 'fridge' ...

She lashed again and again. Backhand, forehand, pressure, precision. Each tendon-taut drive making it rocket through the air. Finally, her hand shot up and she caught the ball dead.

"Have you finished," she said, head snapping round.

"Eh—yeah," he sputtered.

"Good. Because I get annoyed when my time is wasted— and that is not in your best interest."

"No. Sorry," said Andy. He felt his tongue thicken. Who was she, anyway? What was this? "You didn't mention your name," he said, awkward and clumsy under the bright court lights.

"No, I didn't," she responded, swinging her racquet lightly through the air, flexing, powering down.

"Or who you represent."

"Mr Naismith, I don't intend to give you any information unless it's essential to do so."

"So," Andy shrugged, "why should I talk to you?"

"Because people may get hurt if you don't."

"Is that a threat?" said Andy.

"It's an inevitability. Your fate and the fate of others depend on your actions."

"Sounds like blackmail—intimidation—isn't that illegal?" he said, daring to kick back.

"Illegal?" she said, a bemused look on her face. "There are many kinds of law: the laws of the country, the laws of science, the laws of life. Unfortunately, these laws can be harsh and uncompromising. I don't believe, when they happen to work against you, that you can class them as illegal."

"Maybe, but you're still threatening me."

"That's not true," she said. She tossed the ball, then flicked it high into the air. "Take this ball. Whether I want it to or not, it will fall back to the ground. Gravity kills construction workers, air travellers, babies, climbers. It doesn't care. No amount of pleading or argument will make it hesitate for one second." She picked it up, tossed it once more, and swung the racquet in a leisurely backhand causing the ball to fly low, almost horizontal, towards the back of the court. The ball impacted, rebounded back. She stood, stationary, not moving to meet it. It rolled, a small black sphere trundling towards the back of the court, using up its meagre vestigial energy against the junction of floor and wall. It came to a stop. She looked at Andy.

"The normal state—" she said, walking over, "is that things come to rest. In the case of living things—the normal state is that they die. They live for a while, some longer than others, but they only keep going ..." she flicked up the ball and swiped it up high towards the back wall, "because some force, some coincidence of life-giving conditions," she stepped back for the rebound, "combine to sustain it. If I do nothing, if I stand back," she said, "the ball stops, the game ends."

Andy looked at her slight frame and felt a chill sweat on his skin.

"Who will be affected?"

"That depends, depends on you, I suppose—and, to some extent, chance. Chance takes its part in any game." She studied the racquet for a moment, wiped down the handle a few times, picked up a matt-black case, and pressed the racquet into the moulded space within.

"Look," said Andy, his face twisted, screwing up his nose, "this is going nowhere. I've got to have a reason to talk, haven't I? You can't just haul me in here and expect me to spill the beans. You could be some rival company, a criminal organization—anyone."

"Okay, let's make a deal. You answer one question truthfully, and I'll tell you what organization I am with."

Andy glowered and scuffed his shoe on the floor.

"Deal?"

"Deal," he said, with a sideways glance.

"My question is very straightforward," she said. "Where is the class 3?"

"I don't know—that's the God honest truth."

"You haven't answered."

"I can't answer if I don't know."

"You've not kept your part of the deal. Mr Naismith, I'm not wasting any more time." She crouched to her bag, began tidying away the cloth and arranging the contents before zipping up.

"Wait—I'm new to this kind of stuff. I'll tell you, but you can't expect me to tell you what I don't know."

She stood and scrutinized his face for a second, then, leaning forwards, began to do a standing hamstring stretch on her right leg.

"These take two minutes, then I'm going. What did you instruct it to do?"

"What do you mean?"

"You must have told it to go somewhere, to hide, to wait for you—something."

"I—I just told her to take a walk ... to pop back to Hyde Park. I'd meet up with her at some point. Nothing specific. Later tonight. She'll be looking out for me."

"Do you have a photograph of her?"

"No."

"Might she return to the apartment?"

"I didn't tell her to—not specifically. She might."

"This is all very vague, isn't it?"

"Yeah, I'm like that."

"I've been informed that you initiated the droid without installing the standard directives. Is that true?"

"Yeah—she ... well ... she didn't seem to need any—and I was kinda short of time." Andy's voice echoed, sounded hollow as it deflected from the hard court walls. He wished there could've been some music, the hum of other voices, some clatter or buzz to soften the edge.

"You've allowed a powerful and dangerous machine to wander at will."

"It was the only way."

"What do you mean?"

"You can't stick a heap of limiting parameters on something and then expect to find it's capabilities. All you're testing are the parameters. The interesting stuff is at the limits. You've got to push the boundaries, see how far you can take it. That's testing, real testing." Andy became aware that he'd been waving his hands, that his voice had risen. He closed his mouth and thrust his hands into his pockets.

"And have you found any boundaries?"

"I dunno. I think we got near some. At one point she was afraid. In fact, I think she still is ..."

"Mr Naismith, thank you for being so open. You have more dedication than I've been led to believe. However, it's apparent that you have become emotionally involved. This is a machine, a highly capable machine, which we must retrieve ..."

"She's a heck of a lot more than a machine," interrupted Andy. "You don't know her."

"Do you really think you're the only one who's assessed this model?"

"Yeah, but with all the parameters, it proves nothing," he retorted.

"Actually, they did test her, I mean 'it', in a range of situations with different levels of parameter control. They set specific tasks and tried them both with and without the various parameters. Tests were carried out under a very wide range of conditions."

"And that's your problem," said Andy, arms wide, enthusing again.

"Sorry?" she said, her mousy curls springing up from her shoulder as she lifted an arm high. She tipped her body to one side in a long, slow, side-stretch.

"Tests—tests are just like limiting parameters. Does it do this? Yeah, tick the box. Does it do that? No, mark it with a cross. Speed to respond: 0.02 seconds. Accuracy of computation: 83%. The outcome is always limited by the test. Don't you see that? A test can't tell you anything more than what it's testing for. What about the stuff we can't test for, huh? What about the fuzzy stuff like goodness and compassion and trust and integrity! It's ironic: the stuff that's most important is the stuff we can't test. Imagine if we were summed up by our test results—you and me. We're biochemical machines aren't we. You could do physiological tests, rustle up some psychological ratings, get our DNA profile, a few acres of numbers and specs. On paper, we'd look pretty much like some mechanoid. Would that be us, would that sum us up?"

"Look, Mr Naismith. I think we're getting into semantics here. I believe you've told me what you know—and that you've been honest. Because I am a fair person, I will give you something in return." She stood still and looked directly at him for the first time since he'd come in. "Intelligence, I admit, is almost impossible to define, as is what it means to be human. We are very aware of the level of realism these droids achieve. The parameters are there for safety reasons—true, but they also ensure that class 3s exist as machines, not as sentient beings. A machine can be used as required, recycled and then terminated—but a sentient being, a sentient being on the other hand has rights and privileges that must be upheld and respected. Our world might just be able to cope with class 3 droids, it certainly isn't ready for an influx of sentient beings."

"So you're saying she is ..."

She closed her lips tightly. "Mr Naismith," she said, reaching, lifting her bag. "I'm saying that you created a problem, it's up to you to resolve it."

"Wait! What happens to me?"

Hanging the bag on her shoulder, she surveyed him with a piteous eye. "Mr Naismith, the best you can do is comply in every way that you can. After that, I really don't know. I do know that we can't allow her to exist. Goodbye, Mr Naismith.

"Eli, Hank," she said, as she pushed through the door, "nothing has changed."

Andy accepted the titanium wrist tracker without comment. It was a good sign. Trackers are for live bodies, no point tracking a corpse. He sucked in some air and let go, noticing suddenly the clamminess of his skin, the shirt so damp it was like it was straight out of the spin cycle. He followed them down into the service tunnels and, with the sack over his head, stumbled and bumped his way to the familiar hum of electrical transformers. They came out at the same platform and didn't have long to wait for a train. They rattled along, but it was when the guys started looking out their tickets that Andy realized something was up.

"We're getting off," said the bristly one. Andy's face crumpled in dismay.

"But my place is another four stops. If you guys want to head off—Fine! I'll make my own way back. No problem."

They didn't respond. Instead, as the train shuddered and rocked to a halt, in the few seconds between the announcement and the doors sliding open, they locked their arms through his and stood. Andy was pinned between them, overshadowed by their intimidating bulk.

"Hey! What is this? I'm supposed to go home!" blustered Andy. "She said we were done. Come on, guys—don't mess me about!"

"Wrong, sir. We have instructions."

"What instructions. She never mentioned any instructions. I just want to go home." People were starting to notice. "Somebody, help!" He twisted and squirmed. "Hey look ... look. I'm being abducted. Geez! Help! Someone. Contact the police. Somebody!"

Rockabilly leered, pulled Andy's forearm forward and, sliding back his sleeve to reveal the titanium tag, announced: 'medical'. It was the first word Andy had heard him speak. His voice was surprisingly smooth, cultivated. "This young man is being taken for treatment," he added, holding Andy's wrist high, the tag in plain view. Andy noticed the medical-logo. He felt as if he was looking down upon the scene as an independent observer, his body a separate entity over which he had no real say.

'Treatment?' he asked himself. 'What treatment?' He gazed in abject stupor up at his wrist. Rockabilly's kind of treatment. Eyeball squishing, kidney pummelling, face slapping treatment. Rockabilly, Rockabilly and his flick knife, playful—playful and cruel. He felt sick. He looked to the passengers again, but the few who had shown concern were nodding and pursing their lips and turning away, relieved at the excuse for not getting involved.

The hood went on again in an alley and wasn't removed till he was back inside a building and locked down onto a table. The straps holding his legs and wrists were in awkward positions, the table was too small, his head hung over the end and the edge pressed into the nape of his neck. Beyond the top of the table, a contraption with a headband was locking his skull. He had to roll his eyes to take in a bit more of the room. On the wall opposite, he could see kiddie posters, cartoons, a pictorial alphabet and Bravo Boy and Glitter Girl posters. That explained why the table was too small. A wall screen, positioned directly in front, was showing a cartoon: big-eyed, furry animals clinging precariously to a motorbike were being chased by an evil hippo and rat duo on a vicious looking ride-on lawnmower who, with absurd resourcefulness, were overcoming or shredding every obstacle thrown in their path. Behind Andy, well outside his range of vision, hovered people and voices, two, maybe three guys. As he tried to pick up on their conversation, the screen flicked to a log-in display. There was a pause whilst whoever was in charge of the remote had their bios scanned; a chaotic din flooded the room.

"Thought we'd missed it," barked Bristles as the volume ramped up. "Quarters?"

"Semis," yelled a voice he didn't recognize.

Andy looked up to see. It was something called 'Death Live', a subscription channel eliminator of the putrid filth variety. Andy's features contorted. He'd a notion that, in the underworld, there existed some kind of noble thug, workmanlike, do the job, no hard-feelings—and there were sickos. He'd no delusions about Rockabilly, but Bristles—he'd put his hope in Bristles.

Forget it. Turn your mind to—the posters, the bloated cartoon animals, distended features, sickening pseudo-human grins—the surgeon's lamp, clinical and white, passionless, hovering, silent witness to so many operations, the stupid dangling purple pony hanging from it, the screen, the pulsating, din-spewing screen. Nothing ... nothing. He closed his eyes; the screeching mayhem was baying for him, his audience, he was their sacrifice. He gave in, he looked at what was on the wall: the commentator, an unctuous sleaze-ball in a red and white checked jacket, teasing the audience, egging them on to a trembling blood-frenzy.

"Play! Play! Play!" the audience was chanting.

"But," he protested, pretending he might deny them, "we've only got three players left. Three brave lads. Why not give them have a little longer—think of their mothers, think of their sweethearts. Can't we be just a little bit nice?" And he rolled his eyes and grinned in delight as they bayed even louder.

The camera turned upon three crazed guys restrained in their traps, chests heaving, faces contorted by a palpable mix of fear, aggression and hate. Andy tried to avert his gaze, back to the kiddie posters, to the ceiling, but his eyes were drawn to the screen by some primitive urge.

"Well, well, well!" said the commentator with obvious glee. "Look's like you want to see more of our boys—but not too much more, I hope!" At the buzzer sound, the audience erupted. The screaming and yelling surged and fell and surged again as the action unfolded. Suddenly the clamouring din rose in pitch, then fell back into near silence, an occasional outburst cutting through.

"Oh my! Calamity! That is not the place to go—over the rail. Not good at all! The drop's bad enough—but the gears. We haven't seen the gear wheels since round three. But is that Lohan going down to help him—I'm sure he is? Come on Kevin—Kevin, climb up. Kevin! Lohan's coming!"

Andy squinted. Kevin was a big bloated lad, lots of muscle, but flabby with it. Too much steroids, not enough exercise. He could picture him in the streets, a head bigger than his mates, lording it over them. All the back alley talk and posturing building up his ego till he couldn't see the truth. And now he could see it, see it in the scorn of a vicious, tough-as-nails, pro—a human pit-bull who would never let go.

"Hang on son! Remember folks, some gladiators help their rivals up at this stage. Sportsmen, the chivalrous. For Kevin, surely for Kevin. Our boy's hanging on. What about it folks? Will we buy him one last chance. Will we beg for mercy?"

But the crowd were having none of it and were yelling: 'Go Lohan! Go Lohan! Go Lohan!'

"Oh dear! You do want to see more of Kevin—so cruel, so cruel." Kevin's desperate yells were like distant squawks above the roars.

"Lohan—Here's Lohan now. Is he going to help—Oh! Oh dear. Is that boy merciless, or is that boy MERCILESS! The way he swings that bar makes it look like it's alloy, folks, but believe you me, it is solid steel. Can Kevin's hands take much more of this? Can he? No! Down to one hand—surely ... surely. Oh, oh ... OH NO!" A hooter sounded.

"STOP! ALL STOP!" The commentator held his hands up to either side of his face. "Kevin—oh dear! Nasty, nasty, nasty. That's the gear wheels, folks. We stop them as fast as is humanly possible. It's the inertia, they just keep on spinning, until—well, You've seen what they do."

A fanfare was immediately followed by a chorus of wolf whistles and hoots from the audience as a troop of three micro-skirted models in heels swung onto the set and flounced along the ramps and stairways to a bouncy little tune.

"A big round of applause folks. The angels of mercy!"

Blowing kisses to the audience, a blonde, a brunette and a redhead tossed their hair, clutched their emergency bags and strutted, as if on a cat walk, towards the accident scene.

"First, Sinday, to assess his condition!" The redhead squatted down to reach him with a probe, rose up, and glanced at the display. Waving, she gave a thumbs up sign, then, swooping her arm out to the side in a theatrical flourish, she sprang up and held three fingers high. The crowd roared in appreciation.

"Well, there we have it folks! We've got a live one. Wonderful! Now you, the audience, and the viewers at home, get to decide. But first Trankillity, surely the most welcome of our three angles, will give him neural relief—and, boy, does he need it!" The blonde leaned down and, with a micro dispenser, pulsed medication into his neck. Kevin's frenzied spasms grew weak, his eyes milky with drug-induced stupor.

"And finally, Vanice. Vanice, of course, will make him virt ready." The brunette, who carried a larger bag, a holdall, took out a spherical cage-like contraption, lowered it down over his head and clicked a button on the collar causing it to contract and pins to penetrate his neck. Indicator lights flashed up on a panel on the inside of the cage. She stood, gave a pouting lipstick-thick smile and bowed low. The three, chests out thrust, stood side by side, curtsied, once to the camera, and once to the audience, then burst into a pirouetting, prancing walk, waving, blowing kisses, till eventually, with some reluctance, they flounced their way off stage.

"Lovely! Lovely! Maybe I'm misjudging some of the audience out there, correct me if I'm wrong, but I think some of you rather like these terrible tragedies—don't you—DON'T YOU! Come on—you might as well admit it!" A huge roar of laughter rose up and the commentator shook his head in knowing glee.

"Okay—okay! Enough! You know the game, folks. Those for physical retrieval of Kevin, maybe I should say 'what's left of Kevin', and the use of his earnings for rehab: green button. Red button—well, we all know what that means—collar's in place, he's chosen celeb-virt ... expensive. On his current point-level that would earn him one WHOLE YEAR! Imagine! What wouldn't you folks out there do to get celeb for even a day. Now get voting! One minute to choose. All you tender-souled lovies out there, and all you heartless scoundrels, get those votes storming in. Please, please remember, the more times you vote, the more your vote counts. Terms and conditions apply. See Death Live for details and costs for each call."

Andy, eyes tight, sick to his stomach, tried to hear no more, tried to blot out the presenter's mock sympathy and his putrid prattling as the votes piled in and, in the background, the swelling bloodthirsty chant. The buzzer sounded, the big cogs chuntered into action and Andy tried like crazy not to hear what he could hear, not to know what he would know.

The sound went dead. Andy opened his eyes: a mute symbol and adverts were showing on the screen. He became aware of them standing behind him and watching, waiting for the show to finish before getting to work on him.

"What a way to go!" said a nasal voice.

"Not gone yet. He's got a year."

"Yeah, and what a year!" said the nasally one. Andy heard an elasticated snap behind him, then another; that was the latex gloves. A click, a machine hummed and pressured up. A pause. Bristles laughed. "You've gotta be joking. That's your mask?"

When the technician leaned over, Andy understood. The technician was Yogi Bear, he was wearing a Yogi Bear mask with the mouth crudely widened. Through the gaping hole, Andy could see bristles and thin, weak lips; through the little round holes he could see eyes, wet and small and blinking. Close to his face, hovering round the periphery, hands, bony and unsteady hands, their gauntness emphasised by the tight white sheath of the gloves.

"NO! Don't!" yelled Andy, fighting against the head brace and the chair and the room, everything a blur, his mind screeching inside his skull, his body straining to tear free.

"I can give you what you want! I can ... I can. Just stop. Please. Whatever you want," pleaded Andy. Rockabilly sniggered with delight.

But even as he twisted and struggled, a nozzle swung down and pressed into his skull, hard to the bone.

A spit, a hiss and he felt a sharp sting and the recoil. The nozzle was pressed hard again, this time the other temple. Another spike of pain. It moved round to the side, just out of his vision.

"No—no more! I don't—I ... I ... Please!"

Then Rockabilly came into view and, grasping the side of the bench, leaned low till his face was inches from Andy. Grinning manically, he pulled himself back up, took the implant gun from the technician and, positioning the muzzle a few millimetres from his palm, pressed the trigger. A sharp burst of gas, a recoil, not a mark on his skin.

A voice came from behind, it was Bristles. "It's empty. Just to put you in the picture. You know what it feels like, this time tomorrow, we do it for real."

Rockabilly twisted his head round and signalled and snatched a clear plastic cartridge out of the air. He held it so close, Andy could barely focus. A line of tiny steel shafts with a coating of nano-electrodes so thin and fine they created a silvery fuzz.

"You see," said Rockabilly, whispering, his face close to Andy's, cold, snake-like, tasting his fear, "either you get it," he tapped Andy's skull with the cartridge, "or we get it ourselves."

Chapter 14 Sunday

Dorothea liked the docks. Perhaps it was the great open expanses between the hangers, or the proximity to the sea, but it felt good just to be there. Cornelius's encouragement, the call to explore uncharted waters, still dominated her thoughts. She pulled her coat collar up round her ears. Yes, this was right, it was the correct place to be.

She'd avoided surveillance on the way down. Now she was standing in a shadow, waiting her moment. An unfamiliar peace came upon her, she looked up. Gulls—noisy, flapping, screeching gulls. They were swooping acrobatically in the stark glare of a high central floodlight. Her eyes followed their movements, fascinated. They were so alive, so determined, so ready to fight for their place in the world. And so white against the dense black of the sky, like shrieking angels, wheeling and flapping in the great pool of light, but some, the ones who strayed further out, as if by magic, vanished, subsumed by the darkness, silent demons, careering to and forth, unseen, intangible, but for their cries. This she found disconcerting. Perhaps they went somewhere else? Perhaps they were the same ones who burst unannounced back into the light. She shivered and looked away.

Scanning the long walkway between the hangars, the stacked containers, the metal buildings behind, she could discern nothing, not a voice, not a footstep. She looked over towards the dockside. It was time to select a vessel, time to board and move on. Was there any reason for waiting? Hadn't she already decided? Yes, there was good, there was bad, but she'd balanced it up. Why keep returning to reconsider. She began to skirt the edge of a warehouse, taking care to keep in the shadow, avoiding areas exposed to the cameras. It didn't matter that much, they would be switched to night vision, infra-red sensing, which was ideal for her as she could turn her body heat off. However, there was one downside: if she were caught, her 'cold-blood' would give her away was a droid. Silent and smooth. Lingering a moment, she appraised her chosen ship: the Rio Marianne. It's digital ID, bleating like a lamb to its mother, indicated that she was headed for Argentina, the cargo electrical components and metal casings, and she was scheduled to sail at 11 am. The crew would be minimal, perhaps one or two humans, a couple of level 1 droids. She would find an obscure corner high up amongst the containers where she'd slide into a gap or under a tarpaulin. Like a chrysalis, she'd go into stasis, emerge in a few weeks, a new beginning, an exotic new country.

Stepping out into the open, she became acutely aware of the act of leaving, not just this country, but the people, the circumstances, the roots of her being. She hesitated. Her hand rested on the loading ramp rail; she looked up at the great structure of the ship. Andy was clever, he was flexible, he could walk away too. What people got themselves into, they could get out themselves out of—humans were resourceful, it was simply a matter of need. She scanned around one last time. Nearby, an infra-red camera remained idle, directionless, vaguely angled along the desolate length of the quay. She sniffed the air and, like an urban fox, slipped lightly on board.

Andy brought the tumbler up to his nose and breathed in the warm glow. He'd poured in a good measure of whisky, an Islay malt, and now he cupped the tumbler in his hand and gazed into its amber depth. A liquid time machine, the spirit of times past. Barley tossed and rustling on a windswept Scottish landscape, barley grown when he was a toddler, a kid tucked up in bed, his mind innocent, untroubled, mouth wide as he slept. Barley pelted all those years ago by rain from brooding cumulus, towering temples, gliding, majestic, invading the sun's realm, or plunged into mist by stratus, a great expanse of muslin, a burial shroud embalming the land. And that barley was gone, cut, harvested, but not quite gone. It had risen, transformed into this, a wondrous liquid that never grew old but, through passage of time, became ever more precious.

He glanced at the bottle then back to the glass. Tomorrow? Stuff tomorrow. This might be his last night on the rooftop, his last whisky, his last—okay, okay! Forget it. He needed a drink, but he wasn't going to rush it. Take it slow, savour. It was so much more than alcohol; it was a connection. When he drank, it became part of him, he became part of it; they were as one.

Andy's face split in a self-mocking grimace. Come on! Are you going to drink it or not?

"Cheers," he said, holding his glass up to a sky cleared by rain, the last remnants of cloud being ushered away by a keen easterly breeze. He took a deep breath, then drank. Lips moistened, he felt the fire, tasted the warming glow and the myriad essences of Kilchoman, a life-giving river of heat.

"That's better!" He nodded to a couple of stars like points of glinting ice. "So, you lot! How much did you get of this one?" he asked as if to a den of thieves. "Let me see." He picked up the bottle. "Fifteen years in the barrel. That's about 30%. Not bad seeing as you didn't pay a penny. Angel's share—huh? Some angels. Sly old bastards more like. One of these days they'll cling film the barrels and then you'll be scuppered ... If you want any, you'll have to pay like the rest of us."

He took a slow, considered sip and leaned back in the recliner.

"So who's drinking tonight? Anyone out there?" he yelled, cocking his head back wildly, peering up at a swathe of sky. No use. His eyes would take time to become accustomed. He closed them, breathed out heavily then took the opportunity for another slow, languid sip. The fire and the malty depths played over his tongue. He prised open his eyelids. They'd heard him, they were there, appearing, emerging, as his eyes searched. "Castor, Pollux—how's it going, lads. Orion— cheers!" He lifted his chipped tumbler and held it out, then grinned. "And the ladies. Mustn't forget the ladies—beautiful, sparkling jewels. Cassiopeia, Bellatrix, Virgo, Andromeda." He sipped again, his eyes a little less fiery. "Any ideas, girls, why she didn't turn up. Not like you ladies, not dependable. You wouldn't stand a guy up like that, would you? You're probably looking down on her right now. My protégé. Her little beating heart, or processor—whatever, is out there right now. She's calculated the optimal outcome, she's moved on, I'm redundant. She just did the rational thing—I don't blame her one bit."

He grew silent. His eyes roved from star to star and he thought of her out there somewhere beneath the same stars. And he thought of the bench and of Cornelius sleeping, considered whether to go out there and wake him, ask if he knew anything about a girl. But that could create a problem. Tomorrow, if they mind ripped him, they could pick up on that, a fresh memory, a strong memory, a link to Cornelius. Then they'd start on him, find out where she was, maybe where she'd been, drag more people into their clutches. He had to avoid thinking about any of that now. He had to run a whole lot of extraneous stuff through his mind, old memories, decoys, blind alleys, imagine stuff, recall stuff that had no consequence, sprinkle a few memories of Cornelius from past years. Mindrip was crap at chronological analysis; that was its big weakness. It wasn't linear like a movie but picked up long term memory pretty randomly, snippets tied to snippets, no date stamps on any of it. Keep Cornelius out of his short term-memory and there's a chance they'd leave him alone.

"Okay guys—how do I get out of this hole?" He glowered up at the icy blackness.

"We are here always," they said, "... from birth to grave, alpha to omega. We are here in our billions, lighthouses, beacons, shining, constantly guiding every existence. No storm can dim us, no catastrophe or hardship or pestilence can touch us. We are a constant. You must believe, you must trust. Your troubles are as nothing. Mountains will rise and subside and we, we will still be here. Your bones, the memory of you, every trouble that's ever agonized your mind, even the stones you walk on, they will all fade to nothing. Time washes everything. Your life is a mere whisper, you will be carried up and scattered by the wind, the Earth itself will burn up and turn to ash. Peace, peace will reign, the cosmos will absorb every strife, negate every decision, wash clean and heal every pain that existence can bring. You need not worry. Every trouble you can imagine will be swept away in the never-ending tide of time."

"Yup—" said Andy furrowing his brow and swigging a substantial glug of the Kilchoman, "same ol', same ol'. Ever thought of trying a different angle—how about being a tad more proactive! I mean, look at Andromeda there, she was in a tight corner. Perseus there stepped in, came to the rescue. Or do you just look after your own—are we humans too pesky to bother with." Andy stared defiantly up for a moment, then, frustrated, slumped disconsolately back in his seat. He sipped for a while before resuming his case. "I guess this doesn't matter a helluva lot to you, but it's my last chance. This time tomorrow the insignificant wad of grey matter inside my skull will be flushed into the rich, honking, babble of virt hell.

Flooded with crap. No more thinking, no more amateur philosophising ... be lucky to be sane by the end of the week."

He sipped and considered, then suddenly his restraint was gone.

"Give me a break, guys! So you're beacons—great! I love beacons, but beacons for what? I can see what you're saying: time ... eternity ... the big picture ... but come on guys, there's got to be a point, hasn't there? I don't think I'm being small-minded here, but I'm on my way to oblivion ... even a bit of grot gets to leave a stain on the carpet."

Perhaps he was asking too much of them, perhaps like lighthouses their message was simple, instead of marking out land and sea, the marked out life and death, a reminder lest we lose our bearings and forget the route. They don't come to the rescue, they're not like a life boat, they just encourage you to plot the right course, find your route from life to death, the big voyage. Andy drained his glass.

"I suppose that's it guys. No hard feelings. Watch out for me will you? Or I should say, watch out for my molecules, atoms, mostly carbon, hydrogen, oxygen, whatever—chances are they won't be stuck together much longer, not in the current Andy Naismith configuration, but they'll be out there, somewhere, dotting about. You never know, they say there might be a big crunch. If the Universe collapses, we might meet up in a few billion years. A humongous group hug with the rest of the universe." He poured another glass, held it up and left it on a stone ledge to vaporize into the freezing night air. "This one's on me."

Chapter 15 Monday

"I told you, I told you time and time again! What the frack's wrong with you!" said Hannah.

"Would you like the full list," said Andy, "or aspects specific to this case?"

She'd been pacing the sand, back and forth on her side of the glass desk, Andy facing her, slumped in a canvas seat. She stopped and leaned across, with her knuckles resting on the glass. "Don't blame me, you little rat! You screwed this up big time. If we end up in court, you'll get what's coming."

"And I'll admit it," he said. "I'll tell them it was me."

"You think that will be enough—don't make me laugh!" She pierced him with dark hateful eyes. "If you'd kept her in the flat, you could've used the delivery cock-up story. But it's obvious you knew what she was. A class 2 would never have left the flat. You paraded a class 3 all over the city, then, with no limiting parameters installed, you set her loose. A delivery problem is a minor blip. Smack on the wrist and move on, but what you've done—it's criminal, subversive, mind-bogglingly reckless. If we don't get her back, they'll issue a national alert, which means the media, a public outcry, embarrassment at high level, and heads on the block." She flounced over to the awning and yanked the canvas door tighter even though it was already fully shut. "They're not going to settle for a technician. I stuck my neck out for you, Andy: I must have phoned you a couple of hundred times, I met you for lunch, I sent Diana round to check up on you, and now you're here first thing this morning. It's damned obvious I'm in on it."

"You knew what I was like. Why choose me?"

"Because, Andy, you are a disposable, measly little minion. That's why."

"Hey!" snorted Andy, "you've been reading my profile."

The cat-calling and ranting raged for a good twenty minutes, then, like a boxing-ring bell signalling the end of a round, the phone sounded. They stopped and looked at each other. Hannah straightened the collar of her blouse and tensed before taking the call.

"Yes—speaking. Uh huh ... Really? Excellent!" She flashed a victorious smile. "Where?—Really! No, no, don't confront her. Monitoring, yes. I'll be right over—Yes, with her controller. That's right—Good. No, just what you've got ... Tell them you're retrieving a rogue class 2."

Andy felt a sickening lurch in his belly. He let his head loll back and saw the folds and the ripples play back and forth over the awning. He stared at the fluttering, restless membrane, immersing himself, moving with it, part of a rippling twisting dimension where ridges and kinks could appear and twist and vanish without reason.

'Andy!—I'm talking to you, Naismith! Don't you dare ignore me!" Andy finally came round, staring at her as if she were a total stranger. "We have her. You are going to come with us, you will decommission her, and there will be no complications."

Andy gazed at her darkly.

"And if I don't?" he mumbled.

"Instead of her meeting up with you for a cosy little end-of-line chat?" Hannah was suddenly sharp and efficient, the rage channelled into the vindictive grasp on the world she controlled. "There's another option: six Iron Fists wrestle her to the floor then we cut her open with an industrial laser. Hard reset, or a chat—which do you think she'd prefer?"

Seated on the red, flowing form of a repro-Verner-Panton chair, she seemed bereft, a lost child at the edge of a white marble sea. She didn't notice him at first but gazed, unfocused beyond the displays of the museum. Except for the occasional voice of a visitor drifting up from the levels below, there was an eerie, almost profound silence.

"Hi," said Andy as he drew near. He supposed the location was fitting: the history of computing section, dead electronics, a technology grave yard. Looking around at the displays, the cases, the familiar bits of defunct kit, he realised this place, this story of achievement and endeavour, would be forever tainted by his own cowardly contribution.

She looked up, proffered a smile, but it was thin, compromised.

"I'm sorry for not turning up."

"That's okay. London's a big place. I get lost myself sometimes. You're here now, that's what matters." He winced. The last bit sounded callous, like saying: 'we've got you now, so who gives a shit'.

"After, when I'd figured things out, I did go back to the flat. You weren't in." Andy shrugged, he was in no mood to explain. "So," she continued, her voice brightening a little, "how did you get on?" She looked upon him with searching, trusting eyes, but she knew in her heart, from the way he'd come over, and his posture and the tone of his voice, that he had nothing to offer. He shook his head. She looked away and, taking a few seconds to let it sink in, leaned forwards, preparing to stand.

"No, no! Sit. It's okay," said Andy. She didn't argue.

"Andy, it's okay. I know what happens now," she said.

"Yeah—well ... I'm glad they explained," said Andy, relieved that the groundwork had been done.

She looked up. "They? Who do you mean?"

"You know, Techdomestic—the authorities. Whoever told you to come here."

"Nobody told me to do anything, Andy."

"But—when they brought you up here, they must've said something"

"Nobody brought me, I came here myself. I don't have a key for the flat, so I wandered round for a while then I tried phoning you at work. There's a phone box in the foyer"

"Right ..." said Andy floundering. He squinted at his shoes for a moment, then stared blankly at a patch of wall above her head. This wasn't what he'd expected. Instead of a trapped fugitive, he'd a self-sacrifice, a martyr, an offering on the altar to the great god bureaucracy. He'd been deceived. Hannah had implied that they'd hunted her down. He supposed he could go downstairs and have it out with her, tell her to shove it, but what would that achieve. More arguing, Dorothea agonizing whilst he made a show of resisting. Then the deletion.

He looked down at her, her head dropped forwards, her hands crossed on her lap. She seem vulnerable, subservient. Maybe it was for the best that she gave herself up. Imagine if they'd had to drag her in, screaming, yelling, the Iron Fists holding her down whilst he called out the commands. She'd accepted the inevitable; it was her time to go.

"I wanted to see this," said Dorothea, meeting his eyes.

"Huh?"

"This, the history of computing. When we were at the Natural History Museum and we were looking at the stone tools, I realised that I had a history too." She looked up with an apologetic smile. "It's silly I know, but data storage, programming, processing, AI—it's my history, my evolution. I suppose, in a way, these are my ancestors."

"Yeah. You could see it like that," said Andy with an uneasy shrug. "Anyhow, it's good you've had the chance to look around."

"Andy, I waited; I thought we could do this together." She looked bravely at him, a tentative smile on her lips. "Don't I get one last wish?"

"I dunno," said Andy, rubbing the side of his nose. "Sure ... yeah. Why not."

She held out her hand. As their fingers clasped, he became intensely aware of the touch, the skin, the bond made between them. This was different. Before, everything, even the hugs, had been driven by outbursts of emotion, the kind of unthinking, reflex that just happens, that overpowers you, and almost as quickly is gone. This was deliberate, considered, every nuance of pressure carried meaning, a communication of trust, an integration of their lives. She held him lightly, her palm against his, her fingers curling and touching, gentle and tentative yet desperate not to let go.

They wandered over and, side by side, stood facing a display of number systems ranging from notched sticks to binary and hexadecimal readouts. He was pretending to look at it but was barely registering what his eyes were conveying. It would be tough closing her down, tough as hell ... and he'd feel guilt, terrible soul-gnawing guilt, but that would only last till the Mindrip. They say time washes away everything, well so does garbage, only more so; all the drivel seeping in through the neural probes would soon take care of the guilt. He would miss not having it—the pain and the loss, they were his, a way of making amends, his chance to pay off his debt.

Without speaking, they moved together along to the next display.

"You know anything about this?" he said at last, the words sounding harsh and abrupt. She shook her head. "It's a slide rule. I've always loved these. Technology without technology,

as it were. My uncle had one. Not like this, his was plastic.
Great idea. I think it was the abacus before this—but these,
these were so much smarter. They use logs—I think ... a special
kind of number. Wonder why they called them logs. Maybe
they called small numbers branches ... or twigs."

"Logs, isn't that short for logarithms?" she said.

"You're probably right. Nothing to do with trees then?"

"I don't think so."

They looked at it together, peering at the finely carved
graduations in the ivory slides.

"Andy, we don't have to see the whole floor. You won't
want this taking forever."

"No hurry," he said. They turned to move across to another
display and her shoe made a tiny squeak on the polished floor.
Just a squeak, a tiny random noise, but it registered in Andy's
mind with unnatural clarity. As they moved, he became aware
of her gait, her step, the way her weight pressed down through
the arch of her foot, the pressure on the ball of her foot acting
through the sole of the shoe and down onto the floor, the
lilting, counter balance of weight and motion, the adjustment
of her ankle as her heel touched down onto the floor, the
delicate tilt, the toes inside the fine stocking mesh splaying and
flexing and taking the rest of her weight. Her life, her body, was
there, right there beside him, moving and breathing, sharing
these same moments in space and time. Andy, without
realizing it, had been holding his breath; he inhaled deeply.
Dorothea gripped his hand turned to him, anxious.

"Are you okay?"

"Yeah—fine," he lied with tepid conviction.

At the mechanical adding machine with its brass cogs and
clever engineering, they commented on the workmanship and
the beauty of the mechanism, and, as they studied the two
hundred year-old product of Victorian inventiveness, it seemed
to Andy to come from a strange world of unfaltering certitude.

He watched her in the refection of the glass. Concentrating on the exhibition was near impossible.

Damn it! He fought to rationalize. He'd never felt an ounce of sympathy for any other AI. He must've dealt with dozens from thick-as-mince tote-droids right through to bumptious intellectuals. No matter how lofty and high-brow, no matter how impressive their intellectual capacity, they always seemed like high tech devices, kit, systems, not people. Sophisticated, smart, maybe too smart—but there was something missing. The smart ones had a kind of know-it-all smugness; they never needed to struggle, they didn't have to face the angst and contortions of surviving in a dysfunctional world. Some had been granted human-equivalence status, Eden-Certified, displayed the key facets of intelligent life—but was that enough? Certification was a man-made construct. Humans existed before certificates. The whole certification and analysis process was a man-made construct, a hurdle. You can jump without hurdles. Who could presume to know, who could define with any certainty what counted as human. Was it emotion? Feeling, rather than logic and reason—something like that. And then there was experience ... Experience, hah! She was hardly out of the box. But she'd tasted life, she knew what it was and she wanted it, wanted it bad, she had that hang-on-to-the-very-last-breath desperation. She didn't just carry out functions to a high standard, she interacted with life in the raw, the foot on the floor, the pain, the discomfort; she had a foothold and she was ready to fight for it ... He glanced to her at his side and sensed the cold of the marble seeping through the damp sole of his shoe.

"Andy?"

"Huh!"

"Were they?"

"Sorry, I was wandering." Andy blinked.

"Were they as revolutionary as it says?" They were standing side by side in front of a domed case. Inside, a slender, motorized, titanium bar rose vertically up holding aloft a porcelain-white eyeball that was in fact a video camera. The bundle of hair-like fibre-optics that sprouted from the rear of the eyeball were neatly clipped down the length of the bar eventually disappearing through a hole in the display base. Andy waved his hand. The eye followed, servo motors whirred and an image of his hand showed up on a screen fitted into the plinth.

"Yeah—the Hughes Lessing Reactive. Clever," he said, waving his hand again then hiding it behind his back, noting how the servo-motors tilted the titanium arm over to one side helping the eye peer round the corner trying to see where his hand had gone. "Up until then, perception had been clunky. A whole mishmash of programmes trying to decide what to do next. But what Hughes and Lessing did was to break down the software/hardware divide. Built it and programmed it at the same time."

"The sense of sight—it's so amazing."

"Yeah. So fundamental, and yet so complex."

She wiggled her fingers. The camera hesitated, turned, locked onto her moving digits but, after a few seconds, glanced back in case Andy's hand had reappeared.

"See that!" said Andy. "Anticipation, cognition, relevance weighting, all wrapped up in one neat little package." He smiled. "Four years without a break, garage workshop, an uncle covered their costs. Created a storm at the Hamburg show. I wish I'd been around in those days. Small guys tossing big multinationals clean out of the ring. It's harder and harder to do that kind of thing. These days it's all tied up. Every big advance is scheduled with a ten year plan and a humongous budget—most of it is spent on professional services, consultants and the like. The thrill is seeing how many gazillion it goes over. It's just so drawn out, so boring."

"I know," she said, squeezing his hand. "And then you end up with me!" She peeked at him, and flashed a brief smile.

"Geez no! You're great. Honest. I really mean it. I just mean that the system sucks. You are fascinating, distracting, addictive ... almost ... it's hard to ...."

"Addictive?" she said, puzzled. "I can't quite see that. However," she raised the pitch of her voice and tried for cheery and light, "on the plus side, Andy, this is one addiction you're going to have to quit."

Andy winced, began to pull his hand away. She wouldn't let go.

"Don't say that!"

"Sorry—sorry, Andy."

"This is so damned fracked up ...! If there was anything— any alternative, do you think I'd be doing this? Do you? Huh!"

"Andy, please! It's not as bad as it seems. I wanted to talk to you."

"Look, I'm trying not to even think about it," said Andy. "Can we just leave this? Let's just make the most of the time we've got left."

"Okay—if you think that's best," she said softly. She walked with him over to a display that took up a large stretch of wall.

"LEO. Funny—and yet tragic," began Andy, looking at the archaic computer display and pressing a big button. "Lyon's electronic office. Hard to imagine: a tea-shop chain so successful they were looking for computers before the damned things were invented. They rounded up some boffins, gave them the spec, and the guys came up with the kit. It was good, as good as anything on the market, but they didn't stand a chance. Imagine it, back in the early days, the big corporations lumber a junior manager with sourcing them one of those new-fangled computer systems. Which one are they going to recommend to the dinosaurs on the board of directors, a Lyons tea-shop spin-off or International Business Machines?"

"It's such a strange design!" said Dorothea, studying the controls.

"Doesn't much look like a computer, does it? Look at this," said Andy, pointing out an old-fashioned dial and some clunky levers. "No voice recognition, no keyboard, no touch-screen— at least not to speak off, no mouse. This is just the interface. The actual computer, the bit that did the calculations, would fill a whole room." Dorothea touched a display option and they listened to a recording of LEO's processor at work. The weird, urgent, pulsating sound, half-mechanical and half-electrical in nature, made the hairs on Andy's neck stand up.

"Kind of primordial!" he said, as he pressed the option to stop. He turned and looked at Dorothea. She smiled back. "What's the matter? You've barely spoken a word."

"Andy, we do need to talk."

Andy closed his eyes and braced himself not to flare up. He was good at avoiding: avoiding responsibility, avoiding the evil moment. He liked to pretend that no matter how near the dread moment might come, it would never actually materialize, the monster would stay just behind the curtain, always out of sight. It was a matter of bluff, delaying, hanging on, refusing to face up to its existence. To acknowledge its existence would be to pull back the veil. It was a weasely, dumb-ass strategy, and yet, more often than not, it worked. In the past two days the monster had ripped through the barrier and was firmly entrenched in his reality, glowering, breathing its foul breath on him, demanding he satisfy its vile appetite.

With an air of resignation, he walked her over to an interactive table and pulled out two seats.

"Let's have it," he said, meeting her with despondent eyes.

"Andy, I've no right to expect anything, and I am quite prepared, really prepared, for whatever comes, but—I had to ask ..." She snatched desperately, holding both his hands, full of urgency, her eyes locked on his.

"Andy, you've already given me so much—my very existence ..."

"Hey!" said Andy, frowning grimly, eyeing her with suspicion. "Just hang on there one minute. I've been upfront right from the start. Armandroid made you. The guys in their design department drew up the spec. They based you on the ideas and experience of a ton of earlier designs. You evolved out of billions of years' worth of invention and theorizing; money and sweat and lives went into making you what you are, thousands of prototypes, tests, improvements, upgrades. Where did I come in? Nowhere, that's where. I had zip all to do with it—so don't start with that I-owe-it-to-you baloney."

He looked at the ceiling, then, slumping over the table, cradled his head with his hands round the back of his neck. A minute or so later, exasperated, despairing, he lifted his eyes up to hers.

"You know what?" he said. "Hannah warned me about this. 'Don't start talking,' she said. 'No conversation, no farewells, just do it. Talking is where you go wrong.' And boy was she right. Here we are. Bogged down in another messy heart-to-heart. You're twisting this to make it look like I'm responsible for you, that you're mine. Given you so much? I've given you nothing ... NOTHING!" His eyes glistened with melting frustration.

"Andy," she whispered, tentative, "I wasn't talking about the hardware, or the software, I was talking about me ... me! I am what I am because of you. If you'd regulated me with the parameters, I would be a machine. My actions wouldn't have been mine, they would have been determined by programmes." She gave his hand a comforting squeeze. "Don't you see it, Andy? By trusting me, by letting me be free to choose, to think, to make decisions, you gave me the greatest gift possible: self-determination, self-determination not just in my actions, but in who I am, what I am, the chance to be me." She looked earnestly at him and listened to the weight of his breath and sensed the tell-tale struggle within. He slipped his fingers from her grasp, stood and walked away and leaned up against the wall, fists pushed hard into his jacket pockets.

"Dorothea, I don't want to burst your bubble, but try to see it for what it is. What makes you think these decisions weren't programmed in? You were designed to survive, find out stuff, integrate—it was built into your spec and you did it, that's all there is to it." Andy closed his eyes before continuing. "Look, I've got a boss, Hannah, heart like a kilo of granite, but she deals in facts, logic, you can't argue with her. She's been banging on about this since day one. She points out that you are a droid, you are a machine, but you've got ICE programming, similar to instinct in humans, and it kicks in at such a base level that you can't help yourself. And ..." he glanced up, wary of her reaction, "playing on my emotions was inevitable ... And I don't blame you —you were doing what you were designed to do. You do what your programming tells you, you are driven by logic! I mean that's what's in there. You can't deny it."

"But if I did?" She got up and, earnest and determined, stood to face him.

"Did what?"

"What if I did defy logic?"

"Em—I dunno," stumbled Andy, smelling a trap. "It depends what it was. I mean it might just be a mistake—a glitch in your programming."

A wry smile broke across Dorothea's face. Andy read her, knew what she was thinking.

"Hey! I'm trying to be fair. What choices did you make anyway? Whose fashion trend to buy into, whether to order a mineral water or a cappuccino?"

She laughed, a fragile, empty laugh that rose up, echoed faintly, and then was lost.

"Don't just laugh. Tell me!" he said leaning across, hands splayed on the table.

"It doesn't matter, Andy. Really. Just delete me."

"You did something," he said. "You did something and you're not telling me."

"Or, perhaps ..." she lifted her chin, and smiled with whimsical despair, "Perhaps I didn't. Perhaps I'm pretending I did something illogical so you won't delete me. But ..."

"But what?"

"Doing something illogical in order to survive is logical—and the kind of act that a machine, a cunning machine, a devious but logical machine, would try to do. Congratulations. Catch 22! You have every right to delete me."

"Don't make a fool of me," said Andy.

"Andy," she said, voice level, gazing softly at him. "I'm sorry. I was just trying to show you how impossible it is to ..."

Andy's breast pocket buzzed and a jaunty bleeping reverberated through the air.

"Excuse me," he said, fishing the phone out and pressing it to his cheek. "Yeah?" He knew who it was, why she was phoning, what her state of mind would be.

"Give me a chance, will you! I thought I'd show her the exhibits. Last wish kind of thing ... Well I am sorry, but nobody gave me a schedule! —I will ... yeah. Okay! No need to freak out!"

He lay the phone on the desk, carefully, as though it might explode. He looked over at her.

"It's fine, Andy," she whispered, reaching out and touching his arm. "It's hard ... hard for both of us, but I'm strong now, strong enough to face this. And Andy, you need to be strong too. Delete me—It's okay ... I understand."

Andy, grey and drawn, went over and laid his palms flat against the wall, his head pressing against it, breathing into his chest.

Dorothea stood, thoughtful and waiting.

"Okay, let's do it!" Sliding his hand into his inside pocket, he pulled out the digicard. Inhaling shallow and fast, he began selecting options on the touch screen, fumbling, overshooting the menus. When he started to speak, he croaked, coughed and had to begin again.

"Confirm controller. Andy Naismith. Delete codes. Klaxon, 0230, halo, 1477, alpha, 9188,"

Dorothea sat quietly at the table, hands in her lap, watched in silence. He held the card to his eye, it shook because of a tremor in his hand.

"Eye scan failed," came a tinny voice from the card.

"Dammit!" hissed Andy.

"Scan, second attempt in 30 seconds," the card advised.

Andy fidgeted with the card, then looked at Dorothea.

"You did something," he said. "I can tell. Where were you last night?"

"It doesn't matter," she said. "That's come and gone."

"Why are you keeping secrets from me? We are friends aren't we?"

"Cornelius took me to a cathedral."

"A cathedral?"

"Yes, and I prayed; you said that I should pray."

"Did I?"

"Yes. You said 'Pray to God this thing works' .... When you went off to negotiate. We talked, we went to the cathedral ... that's when I prayed, and then I went to a dance."

"You're kidding! You and Cornelius?"

"No. Cornelius took me to the cathedral. I went to the dance by myself. I just watched from a doorway..."

The card beeped and Andy glanced down at the countdown display, the background flashed a virulent, lime yellow.

"The dance ... it's strange, I know," she explained, "but Cornelius said I should ... Andy, it doesn't matter."

"What else did he say? Tell me!"

She dipped her head as if ashamed. "Live, dance through the night, travel the world. I just wanted to see what it was like. Andy, you'll get into more trouble. You're going to run out of time."

"The travel the world bit? You didn't go anywhere ..."

"Of course I didn't. How could I? Please. You'll run out of time."

"Stuff the time!" He narrowed his eyes. "Something happened didn't it? What about the rest of the night? After the dance?"

The card beeped a second time, the display flashed orange, a fizzing, attention-demanding orange.

"It doesn't matter. Just delete me," she pleaded.

"Tell me first."

"No," she said.

"I could command you. I could go back to your set up and make you do exactly as I say."

"I know," she said, looking kindly up into his eyes, "but you won't. You're not like that."

The card beeped, flashed red, and began to count down from ten on the display.

Andy walked away over to the balcony and held the card over the edge.

"If you don't tell me, I'll let go."

"Don't! Wait! I went to the docks, to a ship, but I changed my mind about going."

"Go on."

"I—I was just lying there looking up at the stars, thinking, thinking about the things I'd do, the places I'd go, the kind of person I'd be. That's when I realised ..."

"What?"

She hesitated and looked away, as if ashamed.

"Dorothea, please, we must be true to each other. At least we can have that."

"I realised—I realised that my first significant act, Andy, the first step in my new life, was to betray you, my friend, the person who'd set me free. I'd barely begun and there I was ... Anyway," she gulped, "I came away, Andy. I chose to be this person, the one that's here with you." She met his eyes. "Now you know."

Andy looked at her with an aching, helpless gaze. He looked at the card in his palm. It buzzed, angrily at being ignored. He let it slip from his hand, fall over the edge of the balcony. A faint clattering signified its impact two floors below.

Facing each other, emotional, drawn, there was nothing to say. They embraced, holding tight, grasping, at the edge of a precipice where time and existence and rationality were dropping away. Each second blossomed only to vanish, escape through their fingers and tumble into the abyss.

Distant footsteps sounded, numerous and hard, like the thrumming of hail on a roof. The air became hostile and tense, and then a black tide, a wall of bodies thundering towards them across the white tiles, black piston driven limbs, helmets, visors, securidroids like a plague of expressionless beetles. They encircled and, with their bodies poised and locked, positioned themselves to ensure no escape. The thundering stampede gave way to museum-hush silence.

Dorothea looked out, then turned her face sharply away. She peered up into Andy's eyes, their breath mingled, their lips touched lightly and pressed. The hostile world, with all its power and constraints, could not negate the simple act of a kiss.

"How touching!" taunted Hannah, breathing fast from speed walking, keen to get in on the kill. She pushed her way between the armoured shells of the droids. "Mister Naismith!" she said, "You've forgotten your code of conduct. Professionals do not get emotionally involved." She walked round them, smooth and powerful, like a panther surveying its prey.

They ignored her and held tightly together.

Moving back to the wall of bodies she stood perfectly straight and, arms clasped behind her back, addressed them.

"Let this go on record! Andrew J Naismith, this droid should not be here. As a result of an unfortunate error in logistics, the device was delivered to your address. An unfortunate error, but not your fault. However, since delivery, for reasons unknown, this droid has strayed beyond mandatory class 2 limitations. Consequently, it must be dealt with under Cyber-Law2058 legislation as an item of rogue technology. Appropriate measures will now be taken to protect the public. I formally request that you move away."

Andy did not react, but Dorothea loosened her grip and whispered into his ear that he must do as they say.

"Mr Naismith, I strongly recommend that you reconsider— for your own sake. I'm sure the device is very ... convincing, but recognize reality. You, as many others, have become infatuated with what is essentially a machine."

"I know what she is!" yelled Andy, his head jerking violently round to face her. "And so do you. That's why you hate her. You won't admit it, because that would mess up your scheming, controlling, money-fixated, little world ... She is sentient, she has spirit ... You can't buy her out, you can't manipulate her, that's it isn't it? That's what makes her a threat!" Andy's outburst subsided, the echo of his voice faded, and his head drooped. He clasped Dorothea's trembling body against his, caressed her hair, let her nuzzle into his neck.

"Andy," she responded softly. "It's time for me to go."

He lifted his head, his eyes met Hannah's and he spoke without anger. "You won't understand this, Hannah, but I don't feel sorry for her, I feel sorry for ..."

"Terminate!" rasped Hannah, cutting through Andy's fading words. "We've wasted enough time. Seize them! Separate them! Get the erase codes up here now!"

Chapter 16 Monday

"No thanks," snipped Miranda, tapping her car keys on the counter. Early 30s, honey-blonde curls, high-heel boots added several inches to her considerable height.

"But," said Vince with his roving kid-in-a-candy-store grin, "it's pretty much essential."

"Essential, my ass! It works doesn't it! I object to paying extra for things that ought to work in the first place." She sharpened the glint in her eye. "I want the module, just the module, nothing else." She stopped tapping the keys and flicked them up, catching them deftly in her fist.

"You sure?" said Vince.

"Of course I'm sure! Look, I'd appreciate if we could just get on with this. I'm meeting someone for lunch."

Vince sucked in his bottom lip.

"Could be a problem ..." he doodled a finger across the screen, "we don't—yeah, we don't actually have that module. We've similar ones, for other models, but not that particular one. We'll need to scout round see if we can get one."

Miranda stared at him, incredulous.

"No—No ... I don't believe this! You are joking! I've provided you with delivery data and contact information and listened to you nattering on about an extended guarantee and you don't even have the damned module! I don't believe this!" She shook her head vehemently and Vince gazed in wide-eyed wonder as the cascading curls bounced and swung in shampoo-ad slow motion.

Gorgeous! Drooled Vince. She had Luxbounce, hair like a goddess. Awesome! He had to see that some more.

How much time had he got? Squinting past her, he sized up the state of play. His queue, on account of this amazing specimen, had been static for twenty minutes. Three in his line, two virtgirls one virtguy, all hooked up and running. No problem there, he could leave them for hours. But there was a nervy guy at the back, bad skin, tremor, going into withdrawal. Could crack up in ten, maybe twenty minutes. That would spoil everything, they might have to clear the whole shop.

He looked over at Ludd. He was staring, with disinterest through a long-haired rake of a guy who was doing too much talking. If only he could switch the nervy guy into Ludd's queue—but Ludd wouldn't have it.

"Am I talking to myself?" glowered Miranda. Vince looked and saw the white of her eyes and the agitated rise and fall of her chest.

Vince clasped his hands and hunched his shoulders. "Yeah, sorry. Guarantee without the actual goods. That's normal, perfectly normal. In fact it's becoming standard practice. You can sell extended guarantees, it's kinda like insurance, you don't have to have the goods."

"That is ridiculous!" She stood tall and angular, scorn lines hardening her face. "What, I ask you, is the point of guaranteeing something that doesn't exist!"

Vince furrowed his brow. Getting there. That had riled her a bit, but not quite enough for her to toss around those wondrous locks.

"Well ..." he said, considering, watching her carefully, "it's, like, we sell guarantee packs, we sell tech spares. They're on a different code. We can sell one, sell both, don't matter really."

"But a guarantee's useless without a product, surely?"

"Not really. To activate the guarantee, all you need is a product code."

"What product code? You haven't even got a product."

"Yeah, but if you were to give us your module, donate it like, then we'd have a product and a product code. Then we could sell it back to you and sell you a guarantee to go with it. So now you've got the product, the sales doc and a guarantee. You give it back to us because it's not working, we send it off to Globe Mistro, they repair it, and you get a working part."

"You want me to pay money for a faulty module—a module that I already own?"

"Yeah, but we'll give you a good deal ..."

"Good deal!" she said, voice jumping an octave. "I've never heard such rot." She swished her head round so that the curls swung out behind her en masse, a big luxuriant swathe of flailing gold, piling over to one side, rebounding, then falling lightly down around her shoulders. She closed her eyes, exhaled bitterly and, tilting her head back, ran her splayed fingers through her tumbling locks.

Vince blinked and wriggled and sweated in his chair.

She took a measured breath, then skewered the perspiring Vince with her ice-like blue eyes.

"You have the audacity to suggest that I become involved in a scam. Just because you engage in criminal activities, doesn't mean ..."

"Wait—whoa ... hang on, lady!" said Vince, flailing his arms about in protest. "Us, illegal? No way! We're just astute, that's all. Why do you think Globe Mistro left a loophole in their terms and conditions? Companies don't go creating loopholes for nothing. They know they have to cater for the more knowledgeable customer. That's why people come to us; we're an important link in the chain. We work closely with companies like Globe Mistro to look after the more discerning customer, customers like you."

She gave Vince a frosty stare; she was not going to be flattered into some shady underhand deal.

"It's like this," said Vince, eager, "customers with more money than sense walk into a big flashy retail outlet with their dodgy-droid tale of woe. A sales guy rolls up, tells them that repairing their unit's going to cost 60% of the cost of upgrading to a new model—so they upgrade. He helps them feel good because by trading in the old one they only have to pay something like 80% of the normal price. That's only 20% on top of the repair cost and they've got a spanking new droid. It's a great deal."

"Great deal my ass!" said Miranda, eyes narrowing. "They're still paying through the nose."

"Yeah. But remember, they've got more money than sense. Splashing out cash is their way of solving the problem—and the flashy retailer helps them do just that. If it was the other way round and the customer had more sense than money, it wouldn't be a good deal. Intelligent customers, smart customers, they come to us."

Miranda wasn't convinced, but the fire in her belly was waning.

"You want a really good deal?" he said. She flicked her keys and aggressively arched her brow. Vince turned to Ludd. "Have we still got this month's golden handshake?"

Ludd looked at Vince with a dumb-ox glower. He was mid-glower when the phone rang. For a few heavy seconds, he observed it, hating it, then with obvious misgiving, lifted the receiver.

"So, how's that grab you!" enthused Vince, his attention back to Miranda.

"What grab me?" She said with a fresh flush of suspicion.

"Golden hand shake. We award one a month, like a prize. Gets you the best deal in the city." He smiled with childish glee, his teeth like small white pearls beneath the moist hair on his lip. "Deal so good you'll be in here every day of the week."

"I don't want a deal, I want a module," she riled. "Don't you understand!"

"No, you don't understand. That's top level club membership for zilch. Never have to worry about getting the best deal ..."

"Vince!" said Ludd, his hand over the mouth piece of the phone, "take a break."

Vince squinted at Ludd, his face twisted with anguish.

"Serving this lady," he said, panic in his voice, almost falsetto. "Where was I?" he resumed, giving her the oiliest of smiles. "Yeah, Golden Handshake. Gets you the kind of deal ..."

"Vince!" bellowed Ludd. "Get your hairy little arse over here!"

"Excuse me, ma'am" said Vince, sliding off his seat and jumping down to the floor. "What would these guy's do without me—Don't go! Be back in a flash."

Ludd was out of his seat and hunched like a moping giant at the doorway through to the back.

"I'm taking this through in the office. Stay here, we're going out."

"Out?" said Vince dragging his eyes truculently away from Miranda.

"Yeah, out," griped Ludd.

"Okay—okay. I'll just sort this deal while you phone ..."

"No, you wait here. The lads are on it," rumbled Ludd, sticking out his bottom lip as two back-shop workers sauntered past. Shug emerged first, blinking, his thick glasses magnifying the low-expectation in his eyes. Trev sloped behind, a fug of cigarette smoke clinging to his designer sports kit.

"Could be an hour," said Ludd.

"No probs," blinked Shug. "Anything we need to know?"

Ludd curled his lip. "Vince is doing the 'Golden hand shake'."

"Golden handshake?" said Shug, scrunching his nose so that his spectacles lifted up and bumped into his pock-marked brow.

"How long's that been going?" said Ludd.

"About 3 minutes," called Ludd, slouching off down the passageway.

"Yeah," said Vince. "New idea. Creative marketing. You just, like, find them the best deal possible. I was going over it with the lady. Tell you what, tell her to come back tomorrow and I'll sort it out then." Vince looked over, caught her eye, and tried a friendly little wave. She pretended not to notice and became transfixed by an outdated product recall notice tacked and squint on the wall.

"No problem," said Shug with mild indifference.

Vince, while he waited, hung back and gloated from the far end of the counter.

"This Golden Handshake thing," said Shug, peering at Miranda, "you'll need to wait till Vince gets back. Best come in tomorrow."

"I don't want a Golden Handshake," she remonstrated. "I want a replacement part, that's all, a part."

"This what you want?" said Shug picking up the module and holding it close to his specs. He lolled back in the chair and peered at what Vince had up on the screen.

"Yes," said Miranda. "Apparently they're difficult to get."

Shug leaned forwards, scratched the bristles on the back of his neck and peered again at the screen.

"Difficult? Depends what you call difficult. If you call walking through to the back shop and picking one up 'difficult', then you could say it's difficult."

"You've actually got one in stock?"

"One? Forty odd, mostly seconds—they're a tenner a pop. New ones come in at thirty five—probably worth it. Two year's guarantee and a new connecting link. Often it's the link that's the problem. Some folks are onto their third board before they realise. They twist, power link loosens—causes an intermittent fault. Anyhow, a module. Anything else?" But she had stopped listening.

"One moment," she said.

Her head whipped round, her ice-blue eyes locked on Vince, and her face, hard and skull-like became engulfed in a fury of curls.

Vince bit his lip.

She swung round, picked up an abandoned plastic stacking chair that had been shoved into a corner and, holding it horizontally at chest height, marched directly towards to Vince.

"Excuse me!" she said. The tall reedy guy quickly got out of her way.

"Hey ..." said Trev, sliding off his seat and moving away from the counter, "Lady, you don't want to ..."

She didn't falter. Eyes intent on Vince, she raised the chair high.

"No, wait," said Vince, backing away. "Woa—woa—woa! Hey, there's a complaints procedure. Wait till I tell you about the complaints procedure."

"You little rat!" she seethed, and she threw the chair at him. He ducked. One leg smashed a hole in the plasterboard wall and, clattering down on top of him, it wedged down into the gap between counter and floor. Out of the dust cloud, amidst groans and metal legs and plasterboard fragments, Vince coughed and scrambled and cursed himself back onto his feet.

"You all right, man?" called Trev, eyeing Miranda warily. "Want me to call security?"

"Don't be a dumb ass," Vince croaked, as he tested the movement of his arm, shook out his fingers, and shoved the stricken chair out of his way with a foot. "Golden Handshake needs some work ... that's all."

Miranda looked down upon him, impassive, situation resolved, then, with another sharp swing of her Luxbounce curls, went back to where Shug was sitting, transfixed, the faint glow of the screen reflecting in the heavy curve of his lenses.

"A replacement module, a new one, please!" she said, searching in her bag for a card. "That'll be all for today. Oh! and a brochure, if you have one ... special offers."

A black bird, bright, with yellow-rimmed eye, looked down from the dripping branch of a tree. Some thirty feet below Ludd was trudging a path, his lank balding dome glistening with rain drops, his big shoulders hunched under the insistent drizzle of rain. Vince, like a truculent troll, traipsed behind, pausing intermittently to fish fragments of plaster from his clothes and his hair.

Hannah, attired in a city dweller's version of country-set chic, was leading the way, at her side a brolly-wielding legal advisor.

"Isn't it horrendous! Simply dreadful!" she was saying as part of an ongoing litany of complaint. Her wax-cotton coat and hat were sodden and dark, the coat collar turned up, the wide rim of the hat sagging so that it obscured most of her face. "Foster, I do apologize for dragging you out."

"That's quite alright," he assured with tepid conviction.

She slowed, cautious, the path boggy and wet, her wellington boots with raised heel and smooth sole were more suited to pavements and drives. Foster held the brolly with outstretched arm, like a baton, an emblem of city and commerce. Without it, his soft mouse-brown hair would have succumbed and become a limp wet mat on his skull.

"A squirrel!" yelled Vince, sensing movement ahead. He scurried past, knocking Foster's elbow and causing the brolly to jump. "It is! I tell you! Over there. Hey! You're gonna miss it. Over there—there. Hey!"

"It's time to turn back," said Hannah.

"God's honest truth—you can't miss it," said Vince, cocking his head. "Just ahead. See that tree, the one with the cut off branch ... Hey, where are you going. The squirrel's there I tell you, it's just a few yards ahead!"

"As are the surveillance cameras," said Foster, guiding his brolly in a smooth, delicately controlled turn.

"What are you talking about," remonstrated Vince. "The camera's miles away."

"We don't have line of sight, granted," countered Foster. "But if one understands just how sensitive the surveillance microphones ..."

"Yeah and like you do understand," blurted Vince. "Bet you know it all. What do you know about Neodymium electrostats with infinite discriminatory amps? Wanna tell me their 60 dB range ... No? Their point source limit, free-air, zero-background? Come on—hit me!"

"Anyone can trot out a list of technical specifications," defended Foster. "What actually matters is ..."

"What actually matters, mate—" mimicked Vince, "what actually matters is that you're an ass hole! That's what actually matters."

"Could you?" said Hannah to Ludd.

Ludd, blotchy, hair pasted to his brow, inhaled distastefully.

"Vince," he heaved, "shut it!"

"Okaaaaaaaay," yowled Vince, as if his hair had been yanked.

"Look!" exclaimed Hannah. "You want out of this rain, I want out of this rain, let's cut to the chase." She fixed Ludd and Vince from beneath the dripping rim of her hat. "We've dealt with the droid: wiped, boxed, nothing to show. Now we're tidying up the loose ends. The technician who did the analysis—we'd like to do a neurological scan in case there's anything he's overlooked. Unfortunately, he's not implanted and he's reluctant to have it done—we need evidence for a warrant, something to put on the file." She sniffed and searched in her overcoat pocket for a tissue. "Obviously the evidence must be unrelated to the droid. We don't want to stir anything up." They moved slowly along the path, Ludd as sour as ever, was not admitting to his obtuse satisfaction at trudging through mud.

"Fortunately," breathed Hannah, "this won't be too difficult. He's surveillance phobic; he uses false ID. There's a mountain of evidence ..."

"Fragging? You're joking!" panted Vince as he weaved and slithered and tried to keep abreast. "You can't get a warrant for fragging!"

"If you'd let me finish. Last Saturday, one of your customers used false ID to ..."

"One?" guffawed Vince. "One of our customers used false ID! Geez! How did that happen. Must've slipped through the net."

"I'm talking about a specific customer, one who purchased a quantum hacking kit ..."

"We don't supply hacking kits," said Vince. "We do retrieval kits—it's not our fault if members of the public misuse them."

"I beg to differ," called Foster, who had a nagging feeling that his expertise was being underused. "Circumstantial evidence can be ..."

"Foster—please!" intervened Hannah. "I feel like I'm fighting to get this across. The hacking kit was used to log into some accounts. Unauthorized withdrawals were made from several Techdomestic accounts and deposits for the same amount were deposited into the technician's account. The kit was dumped as happens in such scams, but an oversight will result in the serial number being traced to the technician ... A receipt will turn up in his flat."

"A nice little stitch up," said Ludd.

"Appropriate precautionary measures," said Hannah. "Do you think I feel sorry for him? People take out a second mortgage to have an implant; he's getting this for free."

"You giving him a package—any extras?" said Vince. "Apart from the criminal record?"

"Can we keep on track! We need to know what he knows. This is not just for me, it's for all of us. I am being thorough, and that's to your advantage." Her step had become adamant, the rivulets of dirty water she stomped on splattered up as she strode. Stopping abruptly, she swivelled round. "It's simple really. We need some cooperation from you on connecting the kit to the technician. The evidence is in your transaction logs. The receipt links the technician to the kit, the kit then links him to the fraud. As a security precaution, we will delete everything to do with this case as soon as the implant procedure is over. The rest is in the contract. We want total control on this, so we're buying you out. Foster?" Foster fished out a data logger from his inside pocket but kept it beneath the brolly to shelter it from the rain.

Ludd, as if expecting something putrid, narrowed his nostrils and, shoving his head beneath the black dome, peered at the screen. His Adam's apple lurched in his throat. "Someone's got deep pockets," he croaked.

"See it as your retiral fund," commented Hannah, smug. "I think you'll agree, there's no need for quibbling. Once we have the warrant, we take ownership of your premises, erase any unnecessary records, close down the shop."

"How much?—How much?" gasped Vince. He pushed in between Foster and Ludd, and, pulling on Foster's arm, peered closely, his breath misting the screen.

"Ker ... ching!" he said, gazing in awe. He looked blank for a moment, brain struggling to take it in. "What could you do with that ..."

He came out from beneath the brolly, grinning insanely, unable to stand still. "Fancy a yacht, I do. Yeah—a big white yacht. Down in the Med. And staff, curvy staff, staff in bikinis, rubbing oil on my chest. Ooooyah—ooyah—ooyah!"

"What you do with the money is no concern of mine," said Hannah. "It is, by any standards, an exceedingly generous deal."

"So, what's the story?" sniffed Ludd, eyes wet, surveying Hannah with acid suspicion.

"Story? There is no story. We are simply taking precautions. The technician will deny the charge of hacking the accounts. If he can scrape together the money for the legal fees, expert witnesses and so on, he might try to mount a defence, come up with some implausible tale about a level 3 droid, argue that the bank fraud is part of a cover up. The panel is unlikely to believe him, but, if they did, it would lead to scrutiny, investigations, probing—all of it highly undesirable. To avoid that possibility, the evidence of fraud must be incontrovertible. You'll generate a holo-secured receipt for the hacking kit; I'll see that it turns up when the police search his locker at work. They'll check with the records at the shop. The missing money, the same amount in his account, the receipt in his locker—the evidence will be incontrovertible. We push for fast-track mind-rip, find out what he's been telling his lawyer, and clean up any loose ends. Soon after, your premises will open up as a grocery shop, or a café, whatever—there will be no trail to follow."

"So," said Ludd, eyeing her with gloomy distaste, "you set this up before the guy had messed up."

"The facility was put in place, it's been activated by his actions. I wouldn't feel too sorry for him. He went to a lawyer, he tried to strong arm a bigger deal. It became apparent from early on that he might go off track. I insisted that measures be put in place so that at the first indication of a problem we could close it down safely. It was precautionary. If he had fulfilled the mission as agreed, the payments into his account would not have been reported as fraud. It's ironic, but that was his bonus. He had every chance—he chose to throw it away."

"And us?" responded Ludd. "Do we have flaws? Is why you want us closed down?"

"No," she said, indicating the contract, "we are rewarding you for your excellent work with an extremely generous settlement. It's all in there. Read the terms and conditions if you like."

Ludd shifted his weight and looked to where Foster stood waiting. A shiver rose up through his great bulk as drips trickled through the fuzz on his chin. The rain was becoming heavier as they stood, the water dashing down in vindictive spikes.

Hannah scrunched her shoulders and stared through the deluge. "I don't know what else you could want."

Ludd hung motionless. "The story, the whole story?"

"Pardon?" said Hannah. She glanced momentarily towards Foster. "It's just as I've said. These are the finishing touches—it's all going well."

"So well that you're standing in the pissing rain handing out huge wads of money." Ludd looked at her steadily with red-rimmed eyes. Hannah's lips tightened. Ludd, heavy, wet, garrulous, refused to drop his stare.

"Foster, would you? A brief run down—some of the background."

"Yes—sorry! There might be some shelter further along, over by those trees." They walked, trudging, the mud reluctant to release their feet. "The droid's been wiped, thankfully, without incident," offered Foster. "Now we're erasing its trail, checking for backups, profiles, that sort of thing. Our first course of action was to track any contacts."

"Any profile or backup will be encrypted," piped up Vince. "You're not gonna find a file with a big label saying 'level-3 profile'."

"Which is why, for those three days, we are quarantining and erasing all files unable to prove they're of a legitimate nature."

"Just saying," said Vince as he dawdled along, his baseball boots oozing with mud, "with dodgy backups ... it's outta sight, outta mind."

Ludd nodded morosely; a drip of water trickled down his nose.

"We are aware of the situation," Hannah called forward. "Encryption's not a problem. And we're searching every possible location." She pushed up the brim of her hat and peered through the mist.

"Yes, such as contacts—we've been through CCTV and tracking," said Foster. "It appears to be just the technician, a neighbour and one other Techdomestic employee."

"This Naismith guy won't snap?"

"He's not cooperating," said Foster.

"Hence the stitch up," piped up Vince, tagging close behind Ludd and ahead of Hannah. He turned the conversation back to Hannah. "You're his boss. Why didn't you nail him—or put him on the board."

"We have tried—incentives, arm-twisting," said Hannah, faltering. "He's not your typical employee. And we can't afford to be too hard on him." She took a step up onto the rough grassy verge to avoid one of the deeper puddles. "He might run, disappear off the radar. Better to keep him close to hand."

"So you're after profiles—backups ..." scowled Ludd. "Seems like a helluva a fuss for stuff that might not exist."

"We have reason to believe they do," said Foster. He glanced back at Hannah but she was concentrating on the path. "The droid didn't put up much resistance when she was wiped,"

Foster stopped. "I'm not sure this is passable." A murky puddle spanned the full width of the path; thorn bushes lined either side.

"It's nothing," said Ludd, walking out into it, biker boots shrugging it off. "An inch at most."

Vince, feet already soaked, traipsed through with a jinky, couldn't-care-less walk, his PVC jacket pulled up over his head.

"Foster," said Hannah, "I've got wellingtons, but you really need to turn back ..."

"No! It's quite alright. If you could just hold this for a second." He passed her the brolly. "It's not far." He took a couple of quick steps and leaped, landing in the shallow edge at the far side. A sharp spurt of murky water shot out on all sides.

"Foster!" hissed Hannah as she surveyed her mud-splattered tights. She narrowed her nostrils and winced as the cold water soaked in.

"Way to go, Foster!" yelped Vince.

"I'm so sorry," Foster grimaced at Hannah. "I've a handkerchief, here—take this."

"No—No! Just leave me. It's done," said Hannah, cringing, splashing her way through the water. "Just get on with it. I have to change anyway!"

"Sorry!" said Foster. Hannah thrust the brolly at him, and strode out in front. "Yes, let me see," said Foster, with a pained smile. "Ah! Yes—the situation. The situation! If she does have a profile we will make sure that it's wiped. I mean it could be time-delayed, self-extracting ..."

"Foster, a brief account!" Hannah called back. She had reached the shelter of the trees and hunched beneath the meagre autumnal canopy that remained.

"Of course," said Foster approaching and standing beside her. Ludd and Vince caught up and huddled around. "It's not too difficult. We've flagged it up as an unknown and undefined threat and are using the full range of virus elimination options.

Everything not accountable is being tracked down and shredded. We've got that covered."

"What about the physical?" said Ludd.

"Yes. We're doing three fine-tooths of his flat. Nothing so far. With the neural trawl of the technician we'll clear all other possibilities."

"That's it. That is the story," said Hannah. "We sort the technician, we're clear, everybody's happy! Now, can we get with the contract."

"Sure, nice story," said Vince, eyes glistening in the shade of the trees. "Let's do it!"

Ludd glowered at Foster as who was offering him the logger.

"Think I'm an idiot?" he grumbled. "Still doesn't add up. Say he has got her profile—what's he gonna do with it? It's just a heap of raw data. He's not got a blank to load it on. It's worth nothing. Software without a system—it's just a waste of space. And even if, say in five years' time, class 3s get the go ahead and he rustles up a bundle and buys one—big deal! He reinstalls, he's got her back, but she's legal. That's gonna mean sod all to you. So, what I can't figure is why you're throwing a mountain of money at a problem that doesn't exist."

"Ludd!" yapped Vince. "What are you doing? You're talking it down. You're meant to be talking it up. C'mon man!" He turned his pleading to Hannah. "We're signing! Ludd's just a bit crotchety, deranged or something, that's all. No problem. Look, he's taking it now. See! Watch!" Vince snatched the logger from Foster and held it up to Ludd, but Ludd looked right through it. He stood like a colossus, an immutable, immovable statue.

"This is totally unnecessary, but since you insist ..." Hannah, eyes simmering, approached Ludd, her closeness adding force to her words. "Yes, it is about more than regulatory infringement. We need closure. Total, absolute closure He hasn't just risked us and countless innocent lives, he risked a whole industry. He allowed the droid to go beyond its design limits. The profile itself is dangerous. The knowledge that such a profile exists, or even that such a profile can exist, is dangerous. The limits we set were there for a good reason, but he ignored our express instructions, he thought he was above the system; he created a problem and now he'll have to suffer the fallout." A set look in her eyes, she turned her attention to Vince.

"Vincent," she said, with a smile saccharin sweet, "you've already decided. Why don't you go ahead? Sign!"

Vince stared at her and, in a rare moment of perception, saw the intelligence and guile behind the assurance of her mask. Impressed, he fixed his eyes on the screen and gazed lovingly at what was described as the 'remuneration'. His eyes ran back and forth over the zeros, counting them, meandering back and forth over the long, beautiful chain. He could see himself stepping out of a limo, his implant glowing violet on the side of his skull. He'd wait till it was busy, make a fuss as he entered the most exclusive clubs: Firago's ... Suxspenders. People would see the door swishing open for him, they'd see the pleasure bots rush out to greet him and guide him in. They would know, everyone would know. He fought back the years of hurt that welled up in his eyes. Yeah, he sniffled, they'd friggin well know!

He panted and rubbed his finger on the side of his jeans. Holding it steady, concentrating. The finger hovered above the confirmation area. "A bit wet!" he said. He rubbed the sensor with the corner of his T-shirt, then, blinking, moistening his lips, he reached out, his finger wavered, he was having difficulty. A few millimetres of air separated the Vince he knew, the Vince whose life had been a fight, a fight for the right to exist, the desperation to be noticed and to be treated with respect, and this other Vince, this Vince for whom money would lubricate everything, for whom the future would run smooth and frictionless upon a bed of little round zeros.

Hannah was finding it difficult to hold back.

"Is there a problem!" she blurted.

"Nah!" said Vince, breaking of from foraging for wax in his ear. "Here goes," he said, pressing down his thumb then each finger on his right hand and holding the scanner up to his eye. The machine blipped in recognition.

Vince handed it across to Ludd who looked at it, then looked at Vince.

"You think there's any point?"

"Sure there's a point," said Vince, screwing up his nose. "There's over a billion points."

Ludd looked at him warily then, with big stubby prods of his fingers, he registered and passed the gadget to Foster, who began, with deft taps, to log himself on as a witness.

"Excellent," said Hannah, exhaling. "You might want to tidy up your records at the shop. We wouldn't want anyone finding anything untoward when the accountants wind you down."

"You trying to say we don't keep ..." Vince began, but he faltered, something was beginning to register. He stared at Foster intently working on the logger and at Ludd glowering from beneath the canopy of trees. Hannah didn't wait but was already negotiating the puddle and fading into the mist. Foster hurriedly finished off witness confirmation, pocketed the logger, and, brolly at the ready, made a dash to catch up.

"That's a problem, innit?" said Vince as he disappeared.

Ludd, tall, a colossus, took a couple of steps, straddled the path, and surveyed the marshy land encircled by its shroud of mist. He opened his mouth as if to speak then closed it, his eyelids, pink and moist, lightly covering his eyes.

"We've already cleared up," said Vince. "We torched last month's data. There are no friggin records. Ludd ... LUDD!! Do you hear me! The contract is null. We ... we ... Shiiiiiit!"

Ludd batted his eyelids slowly as the misty rain moistened his face, the only noise the steady exhale and inhale through his nostrils and the distant murmur of traffic.

Chapter 17 Three Months Later

Art Deco. He gazed up to the frosted glass frieze above the big coffee shop window—metal lines, ovals, geometric, clean, without meaning or passion. A daily ritual, a touch stone. Two leather chairs faced out to the street; his only decision was which one to slump into. This—the plate-glass window, the grey slabs, the sandstone buildings—this was his world.

He waited, uncomplaining and expressionless, for the first coffee of the day, looked on as a barista appeared, a figure with a black T-shirt and an apron who moved in and out of his vision without registering—there and then not there, a temporal entity. Then the coffee, real, too real on the low table before him. There was no hurry, no reason to pick it up and no reason to leave it be. It would be too hot to hold, he had to let feeling come back into his fingers. So he just looked at it for a while, eyes gazing unthinking at the cup and the white porcelain and the layer of froth sprinkled with cocoa. Then he turned his gaze to the window to the street and the buildings opposite and the junction where cars shiny and silent, floated by, slowing and lurching and turning, their indicators flashing, their wheels bouncing upon the cobbles like a procession of toys.

For no reason, no reason he could discern, his arm reached out for the drink. Cupping the hot mug in his hands, he felt the warmth and took slow, tentative, body-warming sips. He placed the cup back on the table; it was heavy, unnervingly heavy, too heavy to hold on to. His arms, his head and his shoulders, were like lead, their weight unbearable. He slumped back into the seat, his breath shallow, imperceptible, the leather curve of the chair his support, the caffeine in his stomach his sustenance.

She was gone; the system had won. Erased, forgotten, not a trace left behind. Now, it was merely a matter of waiting … waiting, a formless limbo of waiting … waiting to be led away, waiting for them to pierce his forehead, waiting for the darkness and the descent and the disintegration of his mind. They would come, come when they wanted to come. And it didn't matter, none of it mattered.

He waited and he watched, watched as vehicles traversed the polished grey cobbles, watched as pedestrians ambled back and forth over the cracked pavement. He saw it all in great detail, the age in their faces, the sense of worth in their stature, the bespoke tailoring, the broken zip, the nylon top stretched across the junk-food belly; he noticed the pressures, the hopes, the determination, he saw each life, each being with unfiltered clarity. But he registered nothing. No sense of why or who or what these people were. They were as postage stamps in a catalogue or telephone numbers in a directory. They were merely there, moving, static, things that happened, events without reason played out within his field of view. Sometimes a connection would register, a van, the same van as the day before, pulled up on the pavement, its hazard warning lights on, making its daily delivery; or a person might appear more than once, striding up the street, a few minutes later coming back down, or pausing on the edge of the pavement, crossing at the junction, trying to get someone on their phone. But, though they were recognized, they were nothing more than duplicates, repeats, with no more meaning than the recurring pattern on a tiled floor.

Time passed without heed, hours merged into days and days followed one upon one. When the café shut for the night, and the staff apologized and told him he'd have to go, he meandered, haphazard, directionless, along back alleys, down side streets to a park bench or a doorway. Someone with a battered hat would guide him into an old building with rows of beds, and when he left in the morning and traversed the lino of the cavernous hallway, he was wearing different clothes—he didn't know why. But always, wherever he slept, he would wander back to his seat at the window to sit behind the glass, to stare out at the street. Continuous, endless, without beginning or end. Each day, the same winter skies, the same huddled people, the same procession of vehicles, the same cobbled street. It never occurred to him that the men never came or that, as he sat there, that the Earth, the whole mass of the planet, was tilting on its axis and that the seasons were moving.

"Excuse me," said a voice, soft, barely audible. Andy blinked and kept staring. "Someone to see you." He had no inner voice to tell him what to do, to respond, inside he was silent. Something, some instinct, told him to ignore this, to keep his eyes fixed on the street, but the barista placed her tray on the table and squatted between him and he window, faced him, took centre place in his field of vision. He'd seen her before, seen her many times. She was in her 30s with puffy skin round her eyes and loose, strawberry-blonde curls piled high on her head. She reached out to him with her soft grey eyes and carefully watched for his reaction. "You don't mind, do you. It's good to talk isn't it? ... This lady knows you. She knows your name. Andy, isn't it? ... Andy, why don't you let someone help." Andy looked flatly at her, watched her, saw her look up to her left to someone outside his field of his vision. She nodded to the other person and the soft skin of her eyes crinkled as she came back to him; then she stood and whispered something to the person, and moved gently away.

"Andy, it's me—Victoria." Calm, measured, she took the seat next his and faced out of the window.

She wasn't sure what to say. She'd come looking, but hadn't expected a stranger. On entering the café, while waiting at the counter, she hadn't recognized him. She could see now that it was him. But it hadn't been the gaunt cheeks or the facial hair or the unkempt appearance that had fooled her, but his stature, his lack of spirit. She'd been looking for Andy, a languid, limbs askew, sliding-off-the-seat Andy. The person next to her was like a carcass, propped up, frail, fingers clasping at the arms of the chair.

"Andy, what happened—are you all right?" He continued to stare, muscles frozen, expressionless, body set in position. She forced herself not to react and resisted asking more questions. She would try to be patient, natural, act as if everything was normal.

"Your door was broken—we got someone to fix it. Stan— Stan and I. It's all right now." Her nerves were showing. "I phoned, Stan kept an eye on them when they came. We weren't sure what to do about the lock. The man said it was twisted but it might do for a while. We got him to put it back on. It seemed best; we couldn't find you, there was no way to give you a new set of keys."

The barista approached and, keeping discreetly to the side, served her an Americano, a side jug of cold milk and a toasted cheese sandwich. She exchanged glances with Victoria and returned to the counter.

"Andy, something to eat." She held the plate up. He looked right through it. "Perhaps you'd rather have something else. I can call the waitress. What about soup? Or a toasted Panini?" She laid the plate down, and stared silently for a while, acutely aware of him being right next to her yet not able to reach out. She considered phoning someone, but she couldn't think who, then, wary of leaving him, made up her mind to call over the barista. It was then that she saw his arm extend, slow, wavering, as if the act of moving had become unfamiliar, saw him reach out, saw him take up one half of the sandwich.

She made no comment but sat silent, wary of distracting him. Relaxing a little, she poured a white swirl of milk into her coffee and watched the black liquid diffuse and lighten. She drank in slow measured sips, waited till she was down to the last third before resuming conversation. It was casual, everyday chatter. She had to concentrate, suppress the tremor in her voice, resist the urge to bombard him with questions, and she took heart as, in seemingly random fits and starts, his bony hand reached out for the food. She talked about the forecast and how they were saying the worst of it was over and tried to recall things she'd heard about the cricket and the furore about the increased prices on the tube.

Growing bolder, she mentioned Techdomestic, talked about how reluctant they were to respond to her enquiries and that they wouldn't even confirm whether he was on holiday, or working from home, or away on a project. Andy said nothing.

She wondered if she should go through events chronologically, recount the weeks after he went missing. But tell him what? How Diana, their Techdomestic insider, couldn't find out anything except that he'd completed his last assignment. That Daisy, his aunt, had tried contacts, old school mates, the band, but got nowhere. That one of her salon staff put missing persons notices on the net and only got one tentative lead—a young woman cramming for an exam on her bus commute noticed a young man fitting his description and with a Techdomestic tie—but that was the Saturday before he went missing. Tell him that the whole block was hit with a rash of cyber-security scans—checking for latent roach colonies. Grey suited personnel with warrants and scanners and questions sifting through everyone's stuff. She wasn't going to dump any of that on him now.

When he'd cleared the plate, she asked: "Do you want another?" He shook his head and she smiled at the small victory—the first response, negative, but it was communication.

It was getting to mid-morning, she checked her phone—she was already late for her rehearsal. Looking across again, the questions surged though her mind. Where had he been? Had he been away? Had he been back to the flat? What about Dorothea? Patience, patience ... in the fullness of time.

She caught the attention of the barista and, without trying to get a response from Andy, ordered two soups with wholemeal bread. Andy seemed not to notice their arrival, but, after a time, he took up a spoon. As they ate, she relaxed a little and told him about what had been happening at work, prattled on, filling the space with everyday news and situations, telling him about their new conductor and about the rehearsals and the pressure of performing Beethoven by night after rehearsing Britten by day.

"I don't know about his conducting, but his arrogance is world class," she said, stabbing with her spoon. "He senses the underlying nuances of the music—we wouldn't see anything like that. We're just a bunch of hacks ripping notes of the sheet. It works though. Not just because he inspires us, and he does, but because he makes us struggle, dig deeper, fight for something better—whatever that means! But, it is just so harrowing at times ... If we don't achieve his vision, we don't stop, we work late. An aversion to dragging my cello through rush-hour traffic is driving my creative endeavour. How sad is that!"

Victoria paused and looked as she talked, taking note of his body language, finding great pleasure in seeing him butter his bread and wiping his mouth with a napkin, ordinary movements and actions that normally would mean nothing but signified a gradual resumption of life. She detected something else, in his eyes, in his expressions: uncertainty, flickerings of recognition and feeling. Bit by bit the shroud was falling away and she knew, in his silence, through an inner mist, he was, little by little, picking his way through the wreckage.

The temptation to be forthright, to voice all that she wanted to say, surged up from within, but was tempered by caution: she couldn't take the risk, she might expose him to some unbearable hurt. It was as she struggled with how far to go, that Andy spared her the decision.

"She's gone," he said, a simple fact, like laying down a bowl. He looked into her eyes, revealing the incomprehension within, then turned back to the window.

"I know ..." she said.

But she hadn't known for long. After those first weeks, she'd resigned herself to the idea that he and Dorothea had simply run off together, vanished. And that they'd both be alright. A recent delivery to his flat had sunk that particular theory, and set her back on his trail.

"Andy, she sent you a bouquet of flowers. And a card

She sensed a slight movement. It had triggered a reaction.

"It came on the fourteenth. Last Monday. I nearly missed the delivery. The courier was pressing all the security buttons when I arrived back."

Andy paused, blinking, lips moving silently as if trying to recite forgotten lines. "Dorothea?" he said faintly.

"I don't think she's in London at the moment, Andy," cautioned Victoria, realising what he might be thinking. "She ordered it up some time ago. I went to the florist yesterday. I thought they might have her contact details." Victoria lifted her bag again and checked through the compartments. "The lady remembered Dorothea, and she remembered you. She gave me a note of the order. Here—here it is." She held the slip up to the light. "Monday—Monday the 7th November, 9.47am.

That's the Monday—the Monday of the weekend she was here, isn't it?"

Andy didn't say anything but the glimmer of recognition in his eyes and the lack of denial were enough.

"The flowers are still there for you, back at the flat ..."

She left it for a while, allowed him time to absorb.

"Andy, I have something to give you. This was in with the bouquet, it's addressed to you." She exhaled, then passed over a small cream-coloured envelope. He took it carefully, opened it, lifted out the thin white rectangle that lay within. "Andy ... I know it's a digi-wafer ... but I just want you to know that ... well ... that it doesn't have a message or video on it, not as far as I can tell. Maybe she didn't have enough time, maybe something went wrong ... I don't know. There could be all sorts of reasons. But she cares for you. That's what matters."

Victoria paused for breath and noted the uncertain look in his eyes; she dearly wished for a more definite response. If only he would fly off the handle or break down, give her something to work with. Steadying herself, resolving to progress regardless of how long it would take, she resumed in a warm, explanatory tone: "The reason I know there's no message, Andy, is because I checked. Now I know I shouldn't have; it's an invasion of privacy, but, Andy, I tried to report you missing to the police. They said it wasn't at all clear that you were actually missing. I don't know if you remember, but I'd already called them out about that accident with the beer glass on the Saturday night ... They were reluctant to get involved a second time.

"Anyhow, all I had to go on at that stage was the wafer. I loaded it up in the hope of finding a forwarding address or a contact, or maybe some kind of explanation. But ... well ... I put it into seven different readers—nothing. Then I got an IT company to check it out. They said a file was using up all the storage, but it wasn't anything they could open. They said all they could do was reformat it so that the wafer could take data.

Anyhow, less of the tech-talk, did you see the inscription on the envelope? Isn't it beautiful?"

Andy picked up the envelope and, turning it slowly, rotated it till the writing was the right way up.

His name was written in the top corner. Across the middle, embossed in a gold, ornate, scrolling typeface ran a two line inscription. He brought it close, read it, without saying a word.

There remains faith and hope and love.
But the greatest of these is love.
Corinthians 1 13:13 '

Victoria waited till he'd stopped studying the envelope, gauged that the time was right.

"We should probably get back before the rush hour," she said, brightly. "Check out the flowers Dorothea sent you. You can have a hot shower, get into some fresh clothes and I'll fix us a hot meal. Ok?" He didn't confirm but she knew he was capable of saying no. "Good! Your hand should be fine for playing the guitar. Oh! ... and I'd really, really appreciate it if you'd stay around for a couple of days. You're the only person I know whose normal status is 'missing'."

Her voice was acting upon him, smoothing the scars, like the surge of the sea, the rhythmic healing rush of the waves. He looked up, up through the plate glass window, up at the wakening street life and the chill, lemon-sharp sunshine with new recognition. He'd seen every detail, every aspect, every line and shade and fibre, but had not understood. Winter was giving way to spring. A wash of cleansing light was flooding the top half of the buildings opposite; the sun had risen over the rooftops, and its rays were lightening the damp, winter-drenched stone.

He watched for quite some time, watched as the occasional person hurried by, going to work, catching a bus, meeting someone to talk and exchange ideas. Individuals. He saw them hunched up against the cold, realized that they'd struggled up in the dark winter morning, washed and dressed and brushed their teeth and that now they were out there, braving the cold, facing the capricious, fickle existence called life. He felt a simple, honest, workmanlike admiration for each of them, he felt like going out into the street and congratulating them, shaking them by the hand for their courage. Life was uncertain—no guarantees—none, just their belief in what they were doing and where they were going. The only certainty was that there'd come a fateful day when they'd set out one last time and not make it to the end. But earth, ever faithful, the mother that had nurtured them, that had bathed them and held them close to her in the warm light of the sun, would carry them even then, but gently, for they would lie still, asleep and untroubled, in her perpetual embrace.

But for now they had faith, they were out there, striving and laughing and helping each other on their way, giving of themselves. He watched them for a while, eyes fixing on and following each person as they came into his vision.

When enough time had passed and she sensed the tension in Andy's body had waned, she dared to resume.

"You're not disappointed about the wafer," she said, "because one day, I don't know when, but one day we'll arrange something and Dorothea will tell you in person".

Andy had been holding the wafer in the palm of his hand. Now he opened his fingers and gazed at it, then put it carefully into the envelope, and slid the envelope into his shirt pocket. He clasped her hand.

"Did they?" he said.

"Did they what? Her tone was calm, restrained, her gaze was fixed on the street

"Format it?"

"Did I let them reformat the wafer?" She continued to look straight ahead, a quiet smile, a light squeeze of his hand.

"That wouldn't have been very clever, would it," she said.

THE END

What Next - Sequel - Feedback

We hope you enjoyed this book, thank you for taking the time to read it. **Feedback, reviews, ratings, no matter how brief, would be greatly appreciated**. Responses are important for writers, it is incredibly difficult, if not impossible, for an author to see a book from the viewpoint of someone encountering it for the first time. Please choose one or two of the following outlets and spare a moment to make your views known.

Your views or ratings can be made through or to:

1 Review facilities at the sales outlet from which you purchased the book.
2 Goodreads or other book discussion sites
3 Facebook: Archie Gerard
4 Twitter @AZTIX1
5 the publisher's list of social media at www.aztix.com
6 Other social media, blogs, magazines, publishing and cultural media

Social Media and Contact

The publisher, AZTIX, can be contacted at www.aztix.com

Lists of social media related to Innocence and Ice, and to the author will be posted there. Forums, surveys, online chat sessions or involvement with other blogs or events may develop at fairly short notice. To be kept informed or find out the latest news, please sign up for the AZTIX email-newsletter via the web site.

Please note that writing a novel requires long, unbroken periods of concentration, often for many months at a time. During these stages the author is unlikely to be able to respond or participate directly in social media. Lack of response is not in any way a criticism or value judgement on content posted on social media. Some social media links to this book and updated news on ways of keeping in touch are listed at www.aztix.com

Other Books by the Author

A second Science Fiction novel, the Planet Club, has already been drafted and is planned for release in 2016. See the publisher's website and sign up to the newsletter of follow in social media. Further details at www.aztix.com

A sequel to this novel is under consideration. If you'd be interested in reading a sequel then feel free to inform AZTIX, the publisher

The Soundtrack

When writing this novel, I met up with crime writer, Alison Bruce, in Cambridge. Alison includes soundtracks with her novels. As someone who tends to see the plot unfold as if watching a movie (then has to find the words to describe it) I felt that this was an excellent idea.

Where specific pieces of music were running in my head at the time of writing or simply clicked with certain scenes at a later date, I am listing these online. I am also open to suggestions to specific tracks that others feel match up and I may attempt to set up an online Innocence-and-Ice-Custom-Soundtrack option that would allow readers to post their suggested soundtrack or songs to tie in with scenes or people or places. See www.aztix.com and navigate to publishing or I and I to see how this is progressing

Other Art and Cultural Tie-Ins

Different media and forms of expression (see The Soundtrack above) such as the visual arts, poetry, writing, dance, theatre, design, installations etc. connect the concepts, emotions and values that matter to us and add to our experience. Forms of expression that either relate to Innocence and Ice or are appreciated because they add something new, or valuable, or that provide an alternative viewpoint, will feature. at www.aztix.com or on social media linked to from that site.

GLOSSARY

Some of the terms listed here may already exist but may be unfamiliar or used in a different context in the 2070s setting of the novel; others have been created specifically for this novel. This is not a comprehensive list of every novel-specific term but hopefully will be of use to some readers.

bio-D - - - - - - - - - - - biometric identification system

Bostyle - - - - - - - - - - muscle freezing process (limits facial expression, reduces wrinkles)

cam - - - - - - - - - - - (abbreviation) video camera

comber - - - - - - - - - - - person or automated system that gleans data for selling or exploitation

corpcrud- - - - - - - - -misleading corporation PR

data sweep- - - - - - - - spectrum of data shown on a screen or viewer

domestoid- - - - - - - - -android designated to carry out domestic duties

digicard - - - - - - - - - a card-shaped control unit

digi-wafer- - - - - - - - - a thin memory card

domestoid - - - - - - - - domestic robot in human form

droid- - - - - - - - - - - - - suffix indicating robot in human form,eg, taxidroid, spydroid

frack - - - - - - - - - - - - to completely mess up, as in severely damage by fracking. Also used as general expletive.

frag- - - - - - - - - - - - to fragment, distort or falsify personal data to avoid identity recognition

implant- - - - - - - - - -electrodes connecting brain directly to internet or devices

LoveFlux- - - - - - - - - -treatment that regularizes and smooths skin

Luxbounce- - - - - - - - hair treatment that makes hair springy

mobile- - - - - - - - - - - -mobile pc with links to internet and vizars (see below)

real(s) - - - - - - - - - - - -person/people aware of the world immediately around them (unlike virt)

search snare - - - - - - - -data transmission filter that seeks for data in transit

snoop snare- - - - - - - - -type of trap that lures data searchers down dummy data-harvesting paths and into hazardous parts of the internet

specs- - - - - - - - - - - - - abbreviation for 'specifications'

vacant- - - - - - - - - - - - abandoned body, the brain connected to an alternative reality

vid or vidcam- - - - - -—video camera

vidphone- - - - - - - - -—video and phone in one unit

virt- - - - - - - - - - - - - - person logged into virtual reality world

vizars- - - - - - - - - - - - visual augmented reality spectacles (shades with head-up display)

Don't miss out!

Click the button below and you can sign up to receive emails whenever Archie Gerard publishes a new book. There's no charge and no obligation.

Sign Me Up!

http://books2read.com/r/B-A-XJFC-CDHH

BOOKS 2 READ

Connecting independent readers to independent writers.

About the Author

Archie Gerard is a physicist, writer, occasional activist and sporadic designer/inventor. Based in Scotland with his wife, hyperactive Jack Russel, Schrodinger the cat, and two fox-defying hens, he enjoys whisky, quantum mechanics and chaos theory, not necessarily in that order. Favourite culture and social activities include modern art, Dilbert, Led Zeppelin, requiem masses, cycling (the Camino). Favourite SF: novel-Day of the Triffids, movie-Dark Star, TV-Red Dwarf.

When not involved in writing, the author uses social media for ideas and research. His Twitter name is @ArchieGerard For other social media, see his profile and contact page on the www.aztix.com website..

Read more at www.aztix.com/sf-author-archie-gerard.html.

Printed in Great Britain
by Amazon.co.uk, Ltd.,
Marston Gate.